'Absolutely origi... and unfailingly amusing…Readers will take to this series like a thirsty man to strong drink and bang the bar for another round.' *Publishers Weekly* (US)

'Temple has captured something quintessentially Australian here, the essence of the place, the way we are, and how we conduct our relationships. He has it nailed. Read Peter Temple for his plots. Read him for his characters and atmospherics. But most importantly, just read him. You'll be hooked.' *Limelight*

'Entertaining, exciting, and convincing as most politicians only wish they were, *Bad Debts* is a good read and it's great to see it back in print.' *West Australian*

'Temple can be as tough as nails, but also displays a wickedly droll sense of humour which…frequently has the reader holding his sides with laughter even while immersed in some particularly unpleasant scenario…With *Bad Debts* Temple has created a world-class novel.' *Sydney Morning Herald*

'Wonderful, quintessentially Australian stuff, full of authentic, diehard types, old culture cops, backstreet humour and inner-city dialogue you can overhear in the bars of certain hotels, the ones with framed pictures of horses on the walls. It is the genuine article and an absolute pearler of a read.' *Australian Book Review*

'Temple writes with the urgency of someone who wants to disrupt an official investigation, and his story is kept up like taut wire. Brothers and sisters in crime, worship at the Temple.' Graeme Blundell, *Australian*

'WOW!' *Age*

'An engrossing thriller told with uncluttered clarity and a nice leavening of wry and rapid humour.' *Adelaide Advertiser*

'The prose is tight, the pace breathless, the dialogue inspired, and

Temple's take on the Victorians' football mania hilarious.'
Sun-Herald

'Arguably Australia's best modern crime drama…the story
literally explodes off the pages.' *Geelong Advertiser*

'If you like your crime fiction hard and fast
then this is the ticket.' *Pulp*

Praise for *Black Tide*

'*Bad Debts* and *Black Tide*…make for an excellent introduction
to Temple's clever, irresistibly entertaining thrillers.'
Time Out New York

'Peter Temple wields his words like a blunt instrument, sometimes
belting you with a short, hard, arse-kick of a sentence, then
relaxing enough to work up a longer, more contemplative swing
at the subject…The story is gutsy, pacey and multi-stranded.'
Australian's Review of Books

'Rips, snorts and crackles with a delicious pace.' *Age*

'Temple writes with sophistication and wit.' *Washington Post*

'Confirms Temple's rep as the top hard-boiled crime writer on the
local scene.' *Courier Mail*

'A highly complex and magnificently crafted thriller from a top-
drawer practitioner…deft, dry, sharp-eyed, inventive…Temple is
the business.' *Australian Book Review*

'Puts Temple at the forefront of contemporary Australian crime
fiction.' *Sydney Morning Herald*

'A fast, funny, fabulous thriller…a stunning and welcome return.'
Adelaide Advertiser

Praise for *The Broken Shore*

Longlisted for the Miles Franklin Literary Award 2006
Australian General Fiction Book of the Year 2006
(Australian Book Industry Awards)
Ned Kelly Award for best crime novel 2006
Colin Roderick Prize for Australian writing 2006

'A towering achievement that brings alive a ferocious landscape and a motley assortment of clashing characters. The sense of place is stifling in its intensity, and seldom has a waltz of the damned proven so hypnotic. Indispensable.' *Guardian*

'A stone classic. Hard as nails and horrible, but read page one and I challenge you not to finish it.' *Independent*

'Peter Temple is Australia's leading crimewriter, and *The Broken Shore* makes it clear why. The writing is lean and muscular, but like the best mystery fiction is not afraid to tackle important issues… the British public will finally have a chance to discover one of the world's finest crimewriters.' Mark Billingham, *The Times*

'The first of Peter Temple's books to be published in the UK and at last we can see why he is acclaimed as one of Australia's leading crime writers…This is a very fine book. Characterisation, dialogue and the quality of the prose are all top-class.' *Telegraph* (UK)

'The greatest joy is Temple's use of language. Every word in *The Broken Shore* contains meaning. It's all killer, no filler.' *Courier-Mail*

'Although *The Broken Shore* might have been written with the intention of crossing the restrictive boundaries of genre, it might well be the best crime novel published in this country.' Graeme Blundell, *Australian*

'If you only read one crime novel this year, read *The Broken Shore*. It's not just a good yarn—there are plenty of those—what Peter Temple achieves here is much, much more, capturing a specifically Australian perspective in prose as spare as it is precise. This book is the best yet from a writer who has already won a well-deserved reputation as one of our finest crime writers...Most of all it's about the writing, and in that regard *The Broken Shore* might just be a great Australian novel, irrespective of genre. Read it for what Temple does with words.' Sue Turnbull, *Age*

'What elevates this in Temple's already impressive canon is the always present cause of Cashin's damage and how he deals with it. Great use of language and characters.' *Herald Sun*

'It's hard to know where to start praising this book. Plot, style, setting and characters are all startlingly good, and even lovers of crime fiction will recognise that Temple has taken his writing beyond the usual boundaries of that admirable genre...One of those watershed books that makes you rethink your ideas about reading.' Kerryn Goldsworthy, *Sydney Morning Herald*

'A powerful novel told in Temple's typically sparse style that keeps the tension taut and the reader on edge...*The Broken Shore* is a compelling novel about place and provides a fascinating portrait of a decaying community...Highly recommended.' *Canberra Times*

'Serious, unflinching, relentless—and often hilarious.' *Australian Bookseller & Publisher*

'Temple renders the demotic of provincial Australia with diamond-hard lyricism. This is less a crime thriller (although it is that in spades) than the dismantling of that romantic furphy beloved of sea changers: the rural idyll.' *Australian Financial Review*

'Peter Temple has been described as one of Australia's best crime novelists, but he's far better than that. He's one of our best novelists full stop...Great plot, believable, fallible characters and some terrific dialogue.' *Sun-Herald*

'Temple has to be writing the best Australian crime fiction right now...Powerfully economical writing, an ear for dialogue, eye for observation, and a chilling sense of the way things are.' *Bulletin with Newsweek*

PETER TEMPLE

THE JACK IRISH QUINELLA

BAD DEBTS + BLACK TIDE

Text Publishing Melbourne Australia

The paper used in this book is manufactured only from wood grown in
sustainable regrowth forests.

The Text Publishing Company
Swann House
22 William Street
Melbourne Victoria 3000
Australia
www.textpublishing.com.au

Bad Debts
Copyright © Peter Temple 1996
First published in Australia by HarperCollins 1996
First published by the Text Publishing Company 2003

Black Tide
Copyright © Peter Temple 1999
First published in Australia by Bantam 1999
First published by the Text Publishing Company 2004

This edition published by the Text Publishing Company 2007
Reprinted 2008

Design by Chong Weng-ho
Printed and bound by Griffin Press

National Library of Australia
Cataloguing-in-Publication data:

Temple, Peter, 1946– .

The Jack Irish Quinella

ISBN 978-1-921145-70-4

1. Crime - Australia - Fiction. I. Temple, Peter. Bad Debts . II.
Temple, Peter. Black Tide . III. Title.

A823.3

BAD DEBTS

For Anita and Nicholas: true believers

I found Edward Dollery, age forty-seven, defrocked accountant, big spender and dishonest person, living in a house rented in the name of Carol Pick. It was in a new brick-veneer suburb built on cow pasture east of the city, one of those strangely silent developments where the average age is twelve and you can feel the pressure of the mortgages on your skin.

Eddie Dollery's skin wasn't looking good. He'd cut himself several times shaving and each nick was wearing a little red-centred rosette of toilet paper. The rest of Eddie, short, bloated, was wearing yesterday's superfine cotton business shirt, striped, and scarlet pyjama pants, silk. The overall effect was not fetching.

'Yes?' he said in the clipped tone of a man interrupted while on the line to Tokyo or Zurich or Milan. He had both hands behind his back, apparently holding up his pants.

'Marinara, right?' I said, pointing to a small piece of hardened food attached to the pocket of his shirt.

Eddie Dollery looked at my finger, and he looked in my eyes, and he knew. A small greyish probe of tongue came out to inspect his upper lip, disapproved and withdrew.

'Come in,' he said in a less commanding tone. He took a step backwards. His right hand came around from behind his back and pointed a small pistol at my fly. 'Come in or I'll shoot your balls off.'

I looked at the pistol with concern. It had a distinctly Albanian cast to it. These things go off for motives of their own.

'Mr Sabbatini,' I said. 'You're Mr Michael Sabbatini? I'm only here about your credit card payment.'

'Inside,' he said, wagging the firearm.

He backed in, I followed. We went through a barren hallway into a sitting room containing pastel-coloured leather furniture of the kind that appears to have been squashed.

Eddie stopped in the middle of the room. I stopped. We looked at each other.

I said, 'Mr Sabbatini, it's only money. You're pointing a gun at a debt collector. From an agency. You can go to jail for that. If it's not convenient to discuss new arrangements for repayments now, I'm happy to tell my agency that.'

Eddie shook his head slowly. 'How'd you find me?' he said.

I blinked at him. 'Find you? We've got your address, Mr Sabbatini. We send your accounts here. The company sends your accounts here.'

Eddie moved aside a big piece of hair to scratch his scalp, revealing a small plantation of transplanted hairs. 'I've got to lock you up,' he said. 'Put your hands on your head.'

I complied. Eddie got around behind me and said, 'Straight ahead. March.'

He kept his distance. He was a good metre and a half behind me when I went through the doorway into the kitchen. There were about a dozen empty champagne bottles on various surfaces around the room—Perrier Jouet, Moet et Chandon, Pol Roger, Krug. No brand loyalty here, no concern for the country's balance of payments. The one on the counter to my right was Piper.

'Turn right,' Eddie said.

I turned right very smartly. When Eddie came into the doorway, the Piper bottle, swung backhand, caught him on the jawbone. The Albanian time-bomb in his hand went off, no more than a door slam, the slug going Christ knows where. Eddie dropped the gun to nurse his face. I pulled him into the room by his shirt, spun him around and kicked him in the back of the right knee with an instep while wrenching him backwards by his hair. He hit the ground hard. I was about to give him a kick when a semblance of calm descended upon me. I spared him the grace note.

Eddie was moaning a great deal but he wasn't going to die from the impact of the Piper. I dragged him off by the heels and locked him in the lavatory along the passage.

'Mate,' he said in a thick voice from behind the door, 'mate, what's your name?'

I said, 'Mr Dollery, that was a very silly thing to do. Where's the money?'

'Mate, mate, just hold it, just one second…'

The freezer had been stocked for a two- or three-week stay, but all the recent catering had been by Colonel Sanders, McDonald's and Dial-a-Dino. Dessert was from Colombia. There were dirty shirts and underpants all over the main bedroom and its bathroom. The mirror-fronted wall of cupboards held three suits, two tweedy sports jackets and several pairs of trousers on one side. On the other hung a nurse's uniform, a Salvation Army Sally's uniform, a meter maid's uniform, and what appeared to be the parade dress of a female officer in the Waffen SS. With these went black underwear, some of it leather, and red suspender belts. My respect for Mrs Pick, florist and signatory to the house's lease, deepened. By all accounts, she had a way with flowers too.

I was passing the lavatory on my way back from looking over the laundry when Eddie Dollery said, 'Listen, mate, you want to be rich?'

He had excellent hearing. I stopped. 'Mr Dollery,' I said, 'meeting people like you is riches enough for me.'

'Cut that smart shit. Are you going to do it?'

'Do what?'

'Knock me.'

His was not a proper vocabulary for someone who had been an accountant. 'Don't be paranoid,' I said. 'It's that marching powder you're putting up your nose.'

'Oh, Jesus,' said Eddie. 'Give me a chance, will you?'

I went into the sitting room and telephoned Belvedere Investments, my temporary employer. Mr Wootton would return my call, said Mrs Davenport. She'd had twenty years as the receptionist for a specialist in sexually transmitted diseases before joining Wootton. J. Edgar Hoover knew fewer secrets.

I looked around some more while I waited. Then I sat down next to the phone and studied what I could see of Mabberley Court. Nothing moved except a curtain in the house opposite, a building so sterile and with surroundings so perfectly tended that it could have been the Tomb of the Unknown Suburbanites.

The phone rang.

'Jack, my boy. Good news, I hope. Speak freely, old sausage.' Wootton was in a pub.

I said, 'Dollery thinks I'm here to kill him.'

'Got him, have you? Bloody spot on.'

'I expect to be warned about the armed and desperate, Cyril. There'll be an extra five per cent deduction to cover my shock and horror at having a firearm pointed at me.'

Wootton laughed his snorting laugh. 'Listen, Jack, Eddie's a disloyal little bugger with lots of bad habits but he wouldn't actually harm anyone. People like that think the worst about everything. It's the guilt. And eating icing sugar with their noses. What's on the premises?'

'Ladies' uniforms,' I said.

Wootton laughed again. 'That's one of the habits. He's got the stuff on him, hasn't he?'

It was starting to rain on Mabberley Court. Across the road, an impossibly white cat had appeared on the porch of the Tomb.

On my way out, I stopped to speak to Eddie. You can't help admiring a man who can get the local florist to dress up in Ilse Koch's old uniform over crotchless leather panties.

'Mr Dollery,' I said outside the lavatory, 'you're going to have to be more cooperative with people whose money you have stolen. Pointing a firearm at their representatives is not the way.'

Eddie said, 'Listen, listen. Don't go. Give me the gun back and I'll tell you where to find ten grand. Go round the back and put the gun through the window. Ten grand. Notes. Old notes.'

'I know where to find ten grand,' I said. 'Everybody keeps ten grand in the dishwasher. And everybody keeps seventy grand in the airconditioner. Wootton reckons you're short twenty. I'm pushing a receipt for eighty grand and a pen under the door. I want you to sign it.'

There was a moment's silence.

'Mate,' Eddie said, 'every cent. Tell him every cent.'

'You tell him. Just sign,' I said.

The receipt came back, signed.

'The pen, please.'

The pen appeared. 'Thank you. Goodbye, Mr Dollery.'

Eddie was shouting something when I closed the front door, but he'd stopped by the time I reached the car. Across the road, the white cat was watching. I drove out of Mabberley Court. Two hours later, I was at Pakenham racecourse watching a horse called New Ninevah run seventh in a maiden.

The next day, I went to Sydney to talk to a possible witness to a near-fatal dispute in the carpark of the Melton shopping centre. It was supposed to be a six-hour quickie. It took two days, and a man hit me on the upper left arm with a full swing of a baseball bat. It was an aluminium baseball bat made in Japan. This would never have happened in the old days. He would have hit me with a Stewart Surridge cricket bat with black insulation tape around the middle. Except in the old days I didn't do this kind of work.

It was 5.30 p.m. on Saturday before I got back. I listened to a summary of the football on the radio on the way from the airport. 'Fitzroy started in a blaze of glory...' said the announcer. I felt like switching off. The only question left was: By how much? By 114 to 78 was the answer.

I turned off at Royal Park and drove around the university and through Carlton to the Prince of Prussia. It was one of the few pubs left in Fitzroy that still made a living out of selling beer. Most of the proud names had been turned into Thai–Italian bistros with art prints in their lavatories.

I parked a block away, two wheels on the kerb in a one-way street, and made a run for the Prince. I could have found it by smell: a hundred-odd years of spilt beer. My grandfather used to drink there. So did my father. His dark, intense face is in the faded photographs of the Fitzroy

Football Club sides of the late 1940s on the wall near the door marked GENTS.

There are only a few dozen Fitzroy supporters left who remember my father; to them I represent a genetic melt-down. Three of these veterans were sitting at the bar nursing glasses of beer and old grievances. As I stood brushing rain off my sleeves, they looked at me as if I were personally responsible for Fitzroy's 36-point loss to despised Carlton on Saturday.

'Three in a row, Jack,' said Eric Tanner, the one nearest the door. 'Played like girls. Where the hell were you?'

'Sorry, men,' I said. 'Business.'

Three sets of eyes with a combined age of around 220 examined me. They all held the same look. It was the one the boy in the gang gets when he is the first to put talking to a girl ahead of kicking the football in the street.

'I had to go to Sydney,' I said. 'Work.' I might as well have said I had to go to Perigord for truffles for all the excul-patory power this statement carried.

'Should've taken the team with you,' said Wilbur Ong.

'What kind of work does a man have in Sydney on Satdee arvo?' said Norm O'Neill in a tone of amazement. These men would no more consider being away from Melbourne on a Saturday in the football season than they would consider enrolling in personal development courses.

I caught the eye of Stan the publican. He was talking in undertones to his wife, Liz, at the serving hatch to the kitchen. Only half of her face was visible, her mouth a perfect Ctesiphon curve of disgust. Stan said a last word and floated over, a big man, thinning head of pubic hair, small nose like an afterthought pinched out by the divine sculptor. His eighty-six-year-old father, Morris, owned the pub and wouldn't sell it. To Liz's disgust, he also wouldn't die.

'The boys missed you today,' he said.

'They told me how much,' I said. 'Cleaned these pipes yet?' The beer had been tasting funny for weeks.

Stan looked at me pityingly. 'Jack, you could give a baby milk through these pipes. I had the bloke in. Nothing come out 'cept clean steam. Clean steam in, clean steam out. Chucking my dough away, he reckons.'

He put the first full glass on the counter. 'Your Mr Pommy Wootton's been ringing. The old bat said to give him a tinkle when you came in, quick smart.'

'He's about as pommy as you are,' I said. 'His old man taught welding at Preston Tech.'

'Wish my old man'd taught welding at Preston Tech,' Stan said with controlled venom. 'Then I wouldn't be standin here till all hours listenin to old buggers fartin on about footie games sixty years ago.'

I rang Wootton from what Stan called his office, a midden of old bills, junk mail, newspapers, telephone directories. Under the telephone was a Carlton & United Breweries page-a-day diary. The year was 1954.

'Mr Wootton has made a number of attempts to contact you,' said Mrs Davenport. 'Please wait while I see whether he's free.'

'Free, free, like a bird in a tree,' I said. I don't know why.

'I beg your pardon?' said Mrs Davenport, not startled.

'It's a line from an American poet, E. A. Presley.'

There was a silence of precise duration. It told me my

flippancy had been noted. Then Wootton came on the line, querulous.

'What's the point of having an answering machine if you don't plan to respond to messages? I even resorted to ringing that filthy hole you drink in.'

'Even as we speak I am in that hole.'

'Well, see if you can get out of it by Monday to do a small task for me.'

'Cyril,' I said, 'do I detect a hint of the master-servant relationship creeping in here? Let's start with a nice thank you for the parcel I dropped off on Thursday. And then we can talk about the possibility of future dealings.'

'Thank you,' he said ungratefully. 'I notice that you remunerated yourself rather lavishly in excess of the agreed fee.'

'The agreed fee didn't cover uniform fetishists armed with dodgy guns. I explained that on the phone.'

'Perfectly harmless little turd.'

'There's no such thing as an armed harmless little turd.'

We went on like this for a while. Then I went back to the bar, drank a beer with the lads, ate a toasted cheese sandwich crafted out of recycled sawdust and polyvinyl by the reluctant hands of Liz. I was at the door when Stan said, 'Another bloke looking for you. Thursday, I think it was. Said he'd been round your office.'

'Name?'

'Didn't say. Didn't ask. Said he'd come back.'

'What'd he look like?'

Stan thought for a while, squinting slightly. 'Short,' he said. 'Dangerous.'

'That's half the people I know.'

I went home. The flat smelled of musty books. It took me back to the start of my legal career, searching through document boxes stacked like tin coffins in a crypt. I put my bag in the bedroom and opened the sitting room windows. The cold came in like a presence. At the end of the lane cars flicked by. The rain held in the streetlight's cone seemed to rise from the sharkskin pavement.

I made a drink of whisky, ice and tap water and slumped on the sofa beside the telephone. In the gloom, the little red light on the answering machine blinked nervously. I went to push the button and thought, bugger it. Tomorrow.

I finished the whisky, made some Milo and took it to bed, feeling tired and lonely. It took six pages of a Bolivian novelist to put me away.

On Sunday I fiddled around, doing nothing, restless, vaguely sorry for myself. I spent an hour writing a letter to my daughter in Queensland. Claire was cooking on a fishing boat out of Port Douglas. In my mind, I saw her, a beautiful stick with wrists the size of some men's knuckle-bones. She was circled by large males, blond men with permanent sunburn and the eyes of dead sharks. I thought about the first time I saw Claire's mother, on Bells Beach. She had been surrounded by testosterone-crazed surfers, all lying belly down to hide their erections.

I reread Claire's most recent letter. It made too many mentions of the boat's skipper, a man called Eric. I ended my letter with some delicately phrased warnings about the distorting effects of propinquity on judgment. Still, at least Eric had a job.

I walked to the corner to post the letter. The sky was low, the colour of misery, wind whipping the naked trees. There was no-one in the park except a man and a small boy sitting at a table near the playground. The boy was eating something out of a styrofoam box, his eyes on the table. The man was smoking a cigarette. He put out a helpless hand and touched the boy's hair.

I went home and the winking light on the answering machine caught my eye as I came in the door. I pressed the button and slumped on the couch.

Jack, Andrew. Thought you'd be back by now. Listen, I've pushed a little lease thing your way. Bloke called Andropolous. I just got his cousin off a couple of obtaining-by-deceptions. Andy's all right. Cash in hand. Pause. *By the way, Helen's fucked off. Give me a ring when you get back. Cheers. Oh, my secretary says a guy called McKillop was around here today looking for you. Ex-client, I gather. See you.*

The machine's deep voice said: *Thursday, July 23, 6.20 p.m.* Andrew Greer, former law partner.

Jack. Mate, it's Danny McKillop. Pause. *Danny, y'know, the hit-and-run? In '84? I'm out. You said ring you, like if there was something? I'm in a bit of strife, mate. You reckon you can give me a ring? It's 9419 8432. Tonight if you can. Cheers.*

The machine said: *Thursday, July 23, 7.47 p.m.*

I stopped the machine. Danny McKillop. *Y'know, the hit-and-run?* It meant nothing. A former client? A client who went to jail. Plenty of those around. I pressed the button again.

Jack, Laurie Baranek. Look, this agreement needs a bit extra, know what I mean? Can we stick in a coupla other penalties? I just want it so he understands he don't deliver, he's in big shit. Get my meaning? Ring me. Not at work, I'm on the mobile.

Friday, July 24, 2.28 p.m. Laurence Baranek, vegetable merchant and property speculator.

Jack, it's Danny. McKillop. Get my message? Listen, ring any time, doesn't matter what time. Pause. *Jack, I'm in deep shit. Can you meet me in the carpark of the Hero of Trafalgar in Brunswick? It's off Sydney Road. Seven o'clock tonight? I wouldn't ask only I'm shitting myself, okay? Cheers.*

The man said it was Saturday, 25 July, 3.46 p.m.

There were no more messages, just a lot of silences and disconnections. Danny McKillop? The name still meant nothing. I rang the number. No answer. I put on Mahler, made a beef stew, opened a bottle of wine, rang my sister and listened for half an hour. The day passed.

On Monday, Cameron Delray, the small man's enigmatic footsoldier, picked me up at Taub's Cabinetmaking in Fitzroy. It's in Carrigan's Lane, a grubby one-way that runs down to Smith Street, Collingwood. Cam blocked the street with his Kingswood. I was at the back of the shop making myself useful, ripping some ash for a bureau carcass. I switched off the machine with my knee and took off my helmet.

Cam gave me a nod and walked over to where Charlie Taub was fine-tuning some clamps on a George III writing table.

'G'day, boss,' Cam said. 'How's the apprentice coming on?'

'Not bad,' said Charlie, taking the long-dead cheroot out of his mouth and looking at it. 'Five, six years, he'll make a joint that fits. Then I'll sell him the business and retire.'

I was taking off my leather apron. 'Retire at ninety?' I said. 'Premature, that's what they'll say. Best work still ahead of him.'

Cam said, 'Get along without the boy for a bit?'

'I'll try,' Charlie said. 'Fifty years on my own, if I'm ready yet I don't know.' He gave me his appraising look from under the exploding grey eyebrows. 'I blame myself,' he said. 'Introducing you to Harry Strang.'

I said, 'Don't torture yourself, Charlie. People have introduced me to a lot worse than Harry Strang. By a factor of about three thousand.'

'Horse business,' Charlie said. 'Never met a man it didn't ruin.'

'I should be so lucky to be ruined like Harry Strang,' I said. 'I'm scared Harry'll die before he ruins me.'

'Material possessions,' Charlie said. He lit the cheroot with a kitchen match and coughed for a while, waving the smoke away with a hand the size of a tennis racquet. 'Material possessions he's got. Otherwise, a ruined man. Ruined.'

Cam's Kingswood smelt faintly of expensive perfume. The radio was on. An ABC voice, rich with authority, was saying:

The Premier, Dr Marcia Saunders, today defended the six hundred million dollar Yarra Cove project.

Approving the project, which will transform a large section of the west bank of the Yarra, was one of the new government's first acts.

Dr Saunders said she and her party had for years in opposition called for a number of large Melbourne developments to be given the go ahead.

The Premier's voice, hoarse, slightly too loud, the voice of someone you interrupt at your peril, followed.

The previous government was so obsessed by its hatred of anyone who made a profit and created jobs that it allowed this State to stagnate.

Well, the people of Victoria have had enough of social engineering. This government is trying to get this State moving again. We're unashamedly pro-development and so are the people who voted us into office.

The announcer came back.

Opposition leader David Kerr said the Yarra Cove project had no merit whatsoever.

David Kerr's gravelly voice said, *This government would like to hand the whole State over to their pals the developers. Yarra Cove is bad enough, but it's just the beginning...*

'Yarra Cove?' said Cam. 'What the hell is Yarra Cove?'

'Sounds tropical,' I said. 'Topless girls in grass skirts swaying by the banks of the Yarra, that sort of thing.'

'In this climate,' Cam said, 'they start topless, they'll end titless.'

We were on Johnston Street. I closed my eyes as Cam aimed the Kingswood at a gap between two vehicles that had to grow about two metres before he reached it. It obviously grew. I opened my eyes. Cam punched over to 3MP Easy Music. They were playing 'The Way We Were', probably for the fifth time since breakfast. He screamed and punched over to a man talking about public transport.

Harry Strang lived in Parkville, in a huge Victorian house behind high red-brick walls. Cam spoke into the voicebox in the studded street door and the door unlocked itself. The house was fifty metres away, at the end of a stone path that wound through a two-gardener garden.

Lyn Strang let us in. Harry's wife was in her forties, sexy in a bush-hospital nurse way: short hair, snub nose, legs-apart stance. She had a generous mouth, big knowing hands and broad calf muscles. Lyn had been married to a small-time country trainer called Ronnie Braudel. Ronnie lucked on to a horse called Fiery Continent, a little thing with no more breeding than the average can of dog food. But the horse was more than the sum of his parents. He was an equine freak, a once-in-a-lifetime horse.

Ronnie Braudel was just smart enough to keep his mouth shut and look for help with the horse. His old man knew Harry Strang, and Harry knew what to do with Fiery Continent.

It took just under twelve months to set it up, but it was the mother of all paydays for Ronnie. He transferred his operations to Queensland, taking with him a new friend, eighteen-year-old Valma, a highly qualified nail technician from Wangaratta. Harry extended his sympathies to the deserted wife and Lyn Braudel ended up the fourth Mrs Harry Strang. She gave Harry about thirty years' start and he conceded two hands in height but there was an electricity between them.

Harry was waiting in the study. The room was the idea of a study that is stored up in heaven. It had a full wall of mahogany bookshelves, probably five metres high and ten metres wide, opposite the windows. The upper shelves were reached by four teak and brass ladders that moved on rails. On the shelves was what seemed to be every book ever written on horse racing. The other walls displayed a collection of racing paintings and prints. Between the windows hung a set of photographs in walnut frames of Harry Strang winning English and French races in the late 1940s and early 1950s: the English and Irish Derbies, the King Edward VII Stakes, the Queen Alexandra Stakes, the Prix de l'Arc de

Triomphe, the Grand Prix de Deauville, the Prix de Diane, the Grand Prix de Saint Cloud.

Harry could ride at about the same weight now as when he was in the photographs. He was tall by jockey standards and looked taller because of his shoulders-back, chin-up carriage. He had a full head of short hair, dark with some unscented oil, a small-featured face barely lined. Today he was wearing a Donegal tweed suit, dark-green silk tie on a creamy shirt, russet brogues. I could never help staring at his feet. You can't buy handmade brogues to fit ten-year-olds in the shops, so Lobb's in London made Harry's shoes: $400 a shoe.

'Jack, Cam,' he said. 'Sit.'

Harry liked to get on with it.

We sat down in leather club armchairs. Harry went behind the desk, a classic piece in the style of Eugene Harvill made by Charlie Taub. Almost everything in the apartment was made or restored by Charlie.

Harry put his hands on the desk. They were the hands of someone half his age and twice his size: square-tipped, tanned, strong-looking. There was nothing wrong with his eyes, either.

'Crook arm, Jack?' he said.

I hadn't been aware of touching it. 'Just a strain,' I said.

Harry cocked his head. 'Give it the balsam three times a day. Now. Business. A bloke I've done some transactin with across the years, he reckons he's got somethin for us.'

The years spent in Europe had done nothing to take small-town Victoria out of Harry's voice.

There was a knock at the door and ancient Mrs Aldridge, Harry's housekeeper for thirty-odd years, came in, followed by Lyn Strang carrying a tray of coffee things. At the table, Mrs Aldridge took command, shooing Lyn out of the room. When we had each been served a cup of hell-dark brew from the silver pot, plus a chocolate biscuit, business resumed.

'This fella's name is Tie. Rex Tie,' Harry said. 'Trains a few cattle out in the bush.'

Cam said, 'Time Urgent.'

'That's the one,' Harry said.

'You do that Time Urgent thing?' Cam asked.

'What's past is past,' Harry said. 'I want to have a little look, see if Rex Tie's brain's still workin. We'll have to get on the Drizas, motor out to the bush next week. Suit, Jack?'

I nodded.

'Good. Cam, let's step over and look at the movin pictures.'

We went across the passage into Harry's wood-panelled cinema and sank into the plush armchair seats. Cam plugged in the video cassette I'd given him, pressed some buttons on a remote control, and moist Pakenham appeared on the wraparound screen. Harry had been at Pakenham. I'd seen him up near the back of the stand, on his own as always, grey felt hat, undistinguished raincoat, eyes stuck to the X15 binoculars. You never went near Harry on a race-track, that was the rule. You didn't talk to Cam either if you saw him. My job had been to video New Ninevah's run with about twenty thousand dollars' worth of small video camera. For this and a bit of legal work, I got paid a retainer.

'Take the start in slow, Cam,' said Harry.

We watched in silence.

'Again,' Harry said. And so it went on. It took nearly ten minutes to watch a race that was over in 1 minute 24.20 seconds. When Cam put the lights on, Harry looked at me and said, 'Did he or didn't he?'

I shrugged. 'Looked like he was trying to to me. Didn't miss the start this time.'

'No,' Harry said. 'No, he came out fightin. Cam?'

'Clean, I'd say,' Cam said. He was putting a label on the video cassette. 'Reckon he just don't like the wet.'

Harry got out of his chair. 'Course we could be pissin on the wrong campfire again.' He walked over and looked out the window, hands in his jacket pockets. 'Doubt it though.' He sighed. 'Well, that's it for today, gentlemen. Ballarat on Wednesday. Freeze our arses off as usual. Come round nine for a bit of sustenance. Suit? Jack, Cam'll drop you back. Then he's got some computin to do. That and clean the gutterin and prune the roses.'

'After that I'm going to put on my burglar suit and give the dogs savaging practice,' said Cam.

'I forgot,' Harry said. 'They're getting rusty.'

Cam dropped me at my office, which is down the lane from Taub's Cabinetmaking. The sign outside said 'John Irish, Barrister & Solicitor' but I didn't do much that resembled law from the place. Apart from the odd lease or conveyance for Harry Strang, most of my income came from collecting serious debts or finding witnesses. It was something I'd drifted into doing when I stopped being a criminal lawyer.

The office was just one large room on the street, with a small room and a toilet behind it. It had once housed a tailor, and I used the large table he'd left behind as my desk. The man at the corner shop told me the tailor used to sit cross-legged on the table to do his handstitching. I sat down and switched on my Mac, got out my notebook and started work on the statement I'd got from the witness in Sydney.

When I'd finished, I got a salad sandwich from the corner shop and ate it at my table. Then I drove around to the offices of Andrew Greer—my old offices—at the city end of Drummond Street, Carlton. You could walk to the magistrate's courts from there, that was why we'd bought the old terrace house and spent months fixing it up ourselves.

Andrew's filthy old Saab was outside.

There was no sign of his secretary. I was walking down the passage when he appeared at his door.

'Nice bit of cloth,' I said. Drew was wearing a navy-blue suit.

He looked down at himself. 'Bought it with the tip Mrs De Lillo gave me,' he said. 'From Buck's. Nine hundred dollars.' He pointed at a lapel. 'There's a puke stain here you can barely see.'

'Nearly invisible,' I said. 'From about a hundred metres in bad light. I got Mrs Brierley.'

'You beauty. What does she say?'

'She puts your bloke about five metres from the deceased at the vital moment. She says she knows him by sight. Used to buy fish and chips at the shop.'

A smile grew on the long face. He shook his head. 'Lord,' he said, 'thou art merciful, even unto him who hath sinned. Let's have a drink on this.'

'It's 3 p.m., Andrew.'

'Pre-dinner drink. We in the law eat early.'

'Her boyfriend hit me with a baseball bat.'

'What? Didn't break anything? No?'

I shook my head.

'Good, good. Your suffering won't be in vain. I'll get you something for pain and suffering. This bloke's loaded. Dudded plenty of insurance companies.'

I followed him down the passage into the kitchen at the back of the building. We sat at the formica-topped table. Drew opened two bottles of Coghills Creek lager. I had a sip, put the bottle down and put my hands in my pockets. Reformed binge drinkers know how things start.

'What's this about Helen?'

Andy drank about a third of his bottle, held it up to the light and gave a little laugh. 'Gone, mate. Gone to live in Eltham with a painter. Left me with the kids.'

'House?'

'She doesn't get the house. Not if I can help it.'

'The painter. Does he paint houses?'

'Oh. No fucking way. This is a romance. With a serious artist. Though no-one's ever heard of the cunt. Bruce Seal. You ever heard of Bruce Seal?'

'I hate to say this, but yes.'

'You're not supposed to say that. You're supposed to say never heard of the cunt.' He drank more beer and wiped his moustache. 'What have you heard about him, anyway?'

'Just your normal Eltham bloke. Hugely talented artist. Speaks five languages. Plays classical piano. Two-handicap golfer. Fourteenth dan in karate. Twelve-inch dick. Why?'

'Forget it. I don't think I'm going to get the sympathy I'm looking for.' He drained his beer and opened another one.

'How's Lorna?'

Drew looked at me suspiciously. Lorna was a public prosecutor he'd been having a desultory affair with for a long time. 'Lorna's fine. This has got nothing to do with Lorna. Helen doesn't know about Lorna.'

'What do the kids think?'

He held up his hands, palms outward. 'I don't know what Michael thinks. Only five billion people on the Internet know what Michael thinks. Vicky thinks it's cool. She was probably the only girl in her class living with both her parents.'

I had a small sip. 'What's Helen say?'

Drew looked at the ceiling. 'She says she's fallen in love with a wonderful man and it wouldn't have happened if I'd found a little more time for her over the last twenty years. Does she think I've enjoyed working my arse off?'

I said, 'She might. Everyone else does.'

'You prick. This is what I get in my hour of need.'

'Sounds like that's what Helen got in hers. If it's a con-solation, it probably won't last. They say Bruce is more of a hunter than a farmer.'

'They say that, do they? Your artistic friends.'

'You've got to broaden your social horizons, mate,' I said. 'There are people out there who aren't lawyers, cops or crims. Listen, what did you do with my old files?' I had a final swig of beer, got up and poured what was left into the sink.

It took me about twenty minutes to find Daniel Patrick McKillop's file. He'd pleaded guilty in the County Court on 22 November 1984 to a charge of culpable driving. The victim was a twenty-year-old woman called Anne Elspeth Jeppeson, knocked down in Ardenne Street, Richmond, at 11.40 p.m. on 18 June 1984. She died instantly. The Crown called a witness who saw McKillop driving the car minutes after the collision and later picked him out of a line-up. McKillop was found asleep at the wheel of the vehicle about an hour after the collision. He had a blood alcohol count of 0.1. Blood and clothing fragments on the vehicle matched those of Anne Jeppeson.

The headline on a clipping dated 23 November 1984 said: WITNESS SAW JEPPESON DEATH CAR.

The story read:

The car that knocked down and fatally injured public housing campaigner Anne Jeppeson was seen swerving almost out of control three blocks from the scene, a court was told yesterday. The driver, Daniel Patrick McKillop, had a blood alcohol reading of 0.1 more than two hours later, according to evidence.

Mr McKillop, 24, of Zinsser Street, Richmond, pleaded guilty in the County Court to a charge of culpable driving on 18 June.

Anne Elspeth Jeppeson, 27, of Ardenne Street, Richmond, was killed instantly when she was struck by a vehicle outside her home on 18 June.

Mr Ronald Bishop said he was driving along Freeman Street, Richmond, at 11.40 p.m. on 18 June when a yellow car came weaving towards him.

'It almost hit the parked cars on my side of the street then it swerved across in front of me over to the other side and almost crashed into the cars there. The driver had to brake to avoid hitting them. It was almost out of control.'

Mr Bishop said he saw the driver's face clearly. He noted part of the car's registration number and telephoned the police when he got home.

Senior Constable Ivor Wilkins said Mr McKillop was found asleep behind the wheel of a yellow Ford Falcon belonging to him in the garage of his home. Mr Bishop later identified Mr McKillop as the driver of the vehicle he saw in Freeman Street.

Senior Constable Lauro Martines, of the traffic alcohol section, said Mr McKillop's blood-alcohol content was 0.1 per cent more than two hours after the accident.

Dr Alfred Hone, of the police forensic laboratories, said blood and fragments of cloth found on Mr McKillop's vehicle matched those of Miss Jeppeson.

Mr McKillop was remanded for sentencing until 4 December.

I found the clipping on 5 December under the headline: JEPPESON DEATH: DRIVER GETS TEN YEARS.

The story said that Daniel McKillop had a previous conviction for driving under the influence and had just emerged from his licence suspension at the time of the accident. He had been drinking in two hotels earlier that evening and had no recollection of the accident. The judge said some harsh things about drunken drivers, expressed regret at the loss of a 'courageous young woman with her life ahead of her' and complimented Mr Ronald Bishop on his public-spirited behaviour. McKillop got ten years in spite of his lawyer's plea that he was as much a victim as Anne Jeppeson: 'an unloved boy who has drifted into multiple addictions'.

I looked for his previous convictions. They took up half a page, mostly juvenile stuff. He had two convictions for drunken driving and was on a two-year suspension at the time of the accident. Somehow he'd never been to jail. The judge made up for that: McKillop got a non-parole period of eight years.

All of this was complete news to me. I looked at the date again: November 1984. It was at the beginning of the forgotten zone, the year or so I spent drunk and semi-drunk after my wife's death.

I looked through the other files for 1984 and early '85. There were only five or six after McKillop. I didn't remember any of them either.

I went back to Drew's office. He was reading something, beer on the desk.

'When I went off the rails back then,' I said, 'after Isabel's death…Did you try to keep me out of court?'

He took off his glasses and rubbed his eyes. 'I think you could say that,' he said. 'If it's worrying you, I hijacked all the defended matters between that day and the day you quit. I don't think you did any damage. Except to yourself.'

'And the firm,' I said. I felt a rush of gratitude towards this gangling, unemotional man.

He put his glasses back on and reached for the beer. 'Nothing permanent,' he said. 'We had a fair bit of goodwill to live off.'

'This McKillop who was looking for me. Remember him?' I offered him the file.

He took a minute to look it over. 'No, not him. The woman was a bit of a name on the left. Used to drink at

28

the Standard with the free housing push.' He handed the file back. 'Danny got what was coming to him, Jack. Probably just in the shit again.'

At the front door, Drew said, 'I think I might take up seriously with Lorna.'

I put my hand on his shoulder. 'Mate, first look up "holiday" in the dictionary. It's an experience you might want to try. Want to come to the football on Saturday?'

He screwed up his face. 'We haven't been to the football for a bit, have we?'

'No,' I said. 'A lot of the same names still around though. Only it's the sons.'

'Fuck off. We'll go. Have a steak afterwards. At Vlado's.' He paused. 'Or Vlado's son's.'

Why did Danny McKillop want to see me so badly? I'd again put off ringing the number he'd left on the machine until I had him placed. The phone rang for a long time before a woman answered. I asked for Danny. There was a long silence. I could hear heavy traffic.

'Danny's not here.' The phone went down. I dialled the number again. The woman picked it up straight away.

I spoke quickly. 'Danny rang me. Left this number. Can you give him a message?'

Again, I listened to the traffic for a while before she spoke. 'Danny's dead,' she said. 'There's no point in ringing here.' Click.

I went to the window and watched the women from the pressing sweatshop across the lane on their smoko.

They leant against the wall, laughing a lot, taking deep drags on their cigarettes. Then I looked up McKillop in the phonebook. There was a D. P. McKillop in Windermere Street, Northcote. I put my hand out to dial several times and withdrew it. Danny McKillop comes out of a black hole in my past, looks for me everywhere, and a few days later is dead. I opened the file I'd brought from Drew's. Danny would have been in his late thirties. Died of what?

When I finally dialled the number, a child answered, a girl, four or five perhaps.

'This is Kirsty McKillop speaking,' she said in precise tones. 'Mum's hanging up the washing.'

'Could I speak to her please, Kirsty,' I said.

'Hold on. I'll call her.'

I heard her shouting, 'Mum, a man's on the phone, a man's on the phone...'

When she came on, the woman was out of breath. 'Hello, Sue McKillop.'

I said, 'Mrs McKillop, sorry to bother you. Is that the home of Daniel Patrick McKillop?'

I could hear her breathing. 'Danny died, was killed on Friday night.' Her voice was flat, slightly hoarse.

'I'm terribly sorry,' I said. 'My name's Jack Irish. I was his lawyer once. He was trying to get hold of me last week, but I was away...'

'Yes, well, thank you for ringing, Mr Irish.'

'Forgive me asking, but how...'

She didn't let me finish. 'A policeman shot him. Murdered him.' She was making a statement of fact.

'Where did it happen?' I asked the question without thinking, and as I did a chill came over me.

'In a pub carpark. In Brunswick.'

'What pub was—'

'The Hero of Trafalgar.'

I never blamed myself for my wife's death. Not then or now. A client of mine, Wayne Waylon Milovich, shot and killed Isabel in a parking garage in La Trobe Street. When he'd done that, he taped a letter addressed to me to her forehead and went back to his car, a 1974 Ford Falcon with one hundred and thirteen unpaid parking tickets against its number. He then detonated two or three sticks of gelignite on his lap. The letter went: 'Mr Judas Lawyer Did You Now My Wife Run Away And Took My Kids While I Rotted In Jail Were You Sent Me Because You Wood Not Listen To What I Was Telling You As Your Clynt You Bastard.'

Deranged clients. It's a risk you run. Isabel knew that. She practised family law, where practically all the clients are deranged to some degree. I didn't blame myself. I just raged against fate. I couldn't get that through to people. They kept telling me to stop torturing myself. They *wanted* me to blame myself. I wasn't walking around drunk, crying in pubs, getting into fights with strangers because I was blaming myself. I was in a state of incoherent rage. I had lost someone who had cast a glow into every corner of my life. I was entitled to my feelings. Loss. Hate. Hopelessness. Worthlessness. Only the return of Isabel would have been enough.

Isabel and I were very different. Her childhood was the opposite of mine: she grew up in a fierce tribe of children, all lovingly neglected by their parents, a musician and a painter. She had emerged from the chaos clever, funny, diligent, dreamy, sensuous, and with an affection and concern for other people that descended indiscriminately like warm summer rain. She came into my habitual gloom and dispelled it, dissolved it, with one endless, helpless laugh.

After her death, I lost control for months. I would have put Wayne together again fragment by fragment just to tear him apart with my hands and teeth. I could not be still. I could hardly bear to sit down. I could not listen to music, read, exchange more than a few words with anyone. I slept only when hopelessly drunk; I woke within minutes, slick with cold sweat. All food tasted like dry oats and I did not eat for days on end. After I walked out on Andrew Greer, I drifted for months, driving without aim, drinking all day in sour little country pubs, lapsing into unconsciousness in the car or in some paper-walled motel room. I got arrested eventually in a sodden town in Queensland called Everton. Someone went through my wallet and got word to Andrew Greer. He pulled strings with a relative, a Cabinet Minister in the Queensland government, to get me off a variety of charges without a conviction. My car had vanished. We flew home together. I'd been in the cells for six days, hadn't had a drink, was over the worst. I stayed at home for weeks, going out only to buy food, and then I began slowly to resume some sort of normal life.

Sitting in my office, elbows on the tailor's table, thinking about Danny McKillop brought the darkness of those times back to me. I wasn't over Isabel. I would never be over Isabel. She had made things complete, and they would never be complete again without her. I felt the pang of her absence every day, and at those moments I sometimes uttered an involuntary groan and shook my head like a dog.

Danny McKillop had been shot dead outside the pub where he was hoping I would come to meet him. I couldn't just leave the matter there. I knew I *should* leave it there, but I couldn't. At the worst time in his life, Danny had needed a sober lawyer. He had got me. Years later, he had turned to me again. And I didn't show up. I must have got home around 6.45 p.m. Would I have gone to the Hero of Trafalgar if I'd listened to the messages on the answering machine instead of going to bed? Probably. I'd have cursed a lot, but I'd have got there by 7 p.m. Sydney Road was only minutes away at that time on a Saturday night.

The phone rang. It was Drew.

'Seen the *Herald*?'

'No.'

'Daniel McKillop's on page three.'

I got the paper at the corner shop. A small item on page three said:

Police have identified the man shot dead by police in the carpark of the Hero of Trafalgar hotel in Brunswick on Saturday night as Daniel Patrick McKillop, 34, of Northcote.

Assistant commissioner Martin Doyle said the fatal shots were fired after Mr McKillop pointed a pistol at policemen who saw him behaving suspiciously in the hotel carpark shortly after 7 p.m.

'A full inquiry into the circumstances of Mr McKillop's death is in progress, but we have no reason to believe that the officers acted improperly, Assistant Commissioner Doyle said. 'They feared for their safety.'

Mr McKillop was released from prison several years ago after serving eight years for killing a woman in a hit-and-run accident.

There wasn't anything to do except see Danny's widow.

Sue McKillop was on the plump side, with short dark hair and an open face made to smile. Her eyes were red. She was wearing a green tracksuit.

'You mind coming in the kitchen?' she said. 'I'm in the middle of Kirsty's tea.'

We went down the passage into a large, warm room that had a kitchen on one side and lounge chairs and a television on the other. The girl was in pyjamas with small roses on them in front of the television, watching a game show.

'Kirsty, this is Mr Irish. Say how do you do.'

Kirsty said it.

I sat at a pine kitchen table and watched Sue McKillop cut toast into squares and pile on scrambled eggs from a pan.

She found a small fork in a drawer.

'You can eat in front of the TV tonight, darling,' she said, taking the plate over to the girl and kissing her quickly on the forehead.

When she came back, she sat down opposite me. 'My dad's coming from Queensland tonight,' she said. 'He's nearly eighty. I told him not to. We'll be all right.'

I said, 'What about Danny's family?'

She smiled, a wan lip movement. 'We're it. He was brought up by his nanna. She died while he was inside. There's just a cousin.'

'Danny left a message for me to meet him at the Trafalgar on Saturday night,' I said. 'I didn't get it until Sunday. Why did he want to see me?'

She moistened her lips. 'He was scared. They waited for him outside here on Thursday night, but he parked around the corner and when he was walking towards the house he saw them.'

'Who?'

'I don't know. Men. It's from the accident. Something, I don't know.'

'The accident Danny went to jail for?'

'Yes. He didn't do that.'

'Why do you say that?'

She shrugged. 'Someone told him he was fitted up. Someone who knew.'

'Do you know who the person was?'

'No. It was a woman. Danny said something about her husband dying.'

'When was that?'

'About a month ago. He changed all of a sudden. Got upset easily. Why do you want to know?'

I hesitated. 'I may be able to do something.'

She hugged herself. 'You can't do anything. You can't bring Danny back.'

'You said the police murdered him.'

'Danny never had a gun. And if he'd had one, why would he threaten the police?'

'Perhaps he didn't know they were police.'

She ran a hand through her short hair. 'The policeman who came here said the men identified themselves to Danny as police.'

'Danny been okay since he came out?'

She looked me in the eyes. 'Danny wasn't a crim. He finished school in jail. He worked with a friend of mine at Marston's. That's how I met him. It's a car part company in Essendon.'

'He used to be on smack.'

She shook her head. 'In another life. He wouldn't even drink more than two stubbies.'

I believed her. One thing practising law gives you is a feeling for some kinds of truth.

'When he saw the people waiting for him outside,' I said, 'what did he do?'

'He went to a callbox and rang Col Mullens next door and Col came over and called me to the phone.'

'Why didn't he ring here?'

'I don't know.'

'What did he say?'

'He said he couldn't come home because the house was being watched and he'd stay somewhere else for the night and sort it out on Friday. He was scared. I could hear it.'

'Why didn't he go to the police?'

She shook her head and took a tissue out of her sleeve. 'Danny reckoned the cops were in on it.' She blew her nose. 'Had to be the cops fixed him up for the accident, didn't it? Did you know they gave him pills and stuff to take every day before the trial? Danny said he didn't hardly know where he was.'

'No, I didn't know that. So the men outside could have been cops?'

'Suppose so.'

'He didn't say they were cops?'

'No.'

'Have you told all this to the cops?'

'Yes. Friday night when they come around here.'

The girl came over with her plate. 'Cream, please,' she said, eyes fixed on me. Sue got up, took a tub of ice cream out of the fridge, put two scoops in a bowl and handed it to her daughter.

'Would you like some?' the girl said, showing me the bowl.

'No thanks, Kirsty,' I said. 'I haven't had my tea yet.'

She nodded and went back to the television.

Sue said, 'I'm sorry. I haven't offered you anything…'

I shook my head. 'That's fine. What did Danny do after this woman phoned him about being fixed up for the hit and run?'

'He said he was going to get the case opened again. The person who told him said there was evidence.'

'And did he find any?'

'I don't think so. I don't know. He wasn't a big talker, Danny. He'd sort of plan things in his head for weeks, just sit thinking, and then one day he'd just start doing something and he wouldn't stop until it was finished.' She looked around in pride and wonder. 'Like this room. Danny built the whole thing in two weeks in his holidays. I didn't even know he could knock a nail in.'

'Great piece of work,' I said. 'Does this phone number mean anything to you?' I read out the number Danny had left on the answering machine.

'No. I don't know that number.'

I had other questions but suddenly I wanted to be out of the snug room that Danny McKillop had built for his little family and out in the cold, streaming evening. I gave Sue my card and left. The child came to the front door and waved at me.

'I should've taken the fucken package, Jack,' Senior Sergeant Barry Tregear said.

We were sitting in my car in the carpark of the Kensington McDonald's, eating Big Macs. Barry Tregear also had two large French fries and a large Coke. He was a big man with a pear-shaped head, its summit and three upper slopes thinly covered in greying blond stubble. He always looked two slabs of beer away from fat, even when I'd first met him in Vietnam, but nothing moved when he walked.

'You could've gone back to Hay,' I said.

Barry grew up somewhere out on the endless plains around a town called Hay in New South Wales. His father hadn't come back from World War II, along with half of the other fathers of the kids in his school.

'Fuck Hay,' said Barry. 'Bloke offered me half a motel

outside Lismore. Was in Licensing with me. Turned it down like a stupid prick. He sells out a couple of months ago, doubles his money. And I'm still driving around in the fucken rain, member of an elite group. Number eight on the new Commissioner's Top Ten shit list. Is that judgment or fucken what?'

He took a savage bite of his Big Mac.

A lot of work had drifted my way in the old days because of Barry. He'd been in Consorting and then Major Crimes, squads closed down now but once home for hard men all but indistinguishable from the criminals they spent most of their time with. I'd had plenty of clients who'd come in and said variations on 'Barry Tregear reckons y'might get me a fair shake'.

I said, 'You've got an ex-cop for a Police Minister now. He'll see you old blokes right, won't he?'

Barry took in about eight chips and chewed thoughtfully. 'Garth Bruce is a cunt. And he's got selective amnesia. You hear him sprouting all that shit about getting rid of the old culture in the force? Mate, I'm part of the old culture and fucking proud of it,' he said around the potato.

'What exactly is the old culture?'

'The dinosaurs left over from when it didn't count if you took an extra ten bucks for the drinks when you put in for sweet for your dogs. When you had to load some cockroach to get it off the street. Public fucken service. We're the ancient pricks think it's okay to punch out slime who dob in a bloke who's walked out on the wire for them to fucking Internal Affairs. That's us. That's the old culture.'

I said, 'They got all of you on armed robbery now?'

Barry finished the chips, drained the Coke, put everything away neatly in the recyclable brown paper bag, opened his window and threw the bag out into the carpark. 'The ones they're hoping will take a bullet,' he said. 'We're out there doing the in-progresses. When I done this line of work years ago, only the mad dogs fired on you. Now it's all fucken mad dogs. They all fire on you. Chemical war's going on inside their heads. The stuff come in the nose is fighting with the stuff come up the arm. Cause for concern, I can tell you.'

He looked at his watch. 'Shit. I've gotta get moving. What's your interest in this McKillop?'

'Ex-client of mine. Wife reckons he thought someone wanted to kill him.'

Barry sighed. It triggered off a burp. 'Jesus,' he said, 'I'm all wind. Listen, short story is this Quinn, drug squad, he got a call just before seven Saturday night, there's a handover set for the yard of the Trafalgar, 7 p.m. There was a bit of stuffing around, they didn't get there till quarter past.'

He burped again and patted his pockets. 'Never got a bloody Quikeze when you need one. Anyway, they hang around for a bit, no-one in sight, reckon they've missed the boat. Then they take a stroll through the cars, one from each end, and this cunt pops up with a .38 pointing at Martin, Quinn's offsider. So Quinn, who's behind this guy, puts four in him. Dead on arrival. There's about five hundred bucks' worth of smack in his car. End of story.'

'And McKillop?'

'Form.'

'Not since.'

'Well shit's shit.'

'Wife can't believe it. Kid, job. Says he's been absolutely straight.'

Barry gave a snort. 'That's what Mrs Eichmann said.' He rubbed his stomach.

'What if Quinn went out, knocked him and planted the gun and the shit?' I said.

Barry gave me a long look, shaking his head. His eyes were light green, with little dark flecks. 'Jack,' he said. 'Jack, he's an officer with sixteen years' service. You take my meaning?'

'No.'

He got out of the car and leaned in. 'He'd have knocked him somewhere less public. Mate, I got to go. I'm further up shit creek if I don't get to town in about five minutes.'

'I'll be in touch. Buy you a drink,' I said.

Barry put his head back in the window. 'Drinks, mate, drinks. You're dealing with the old culture here.'

'Danny's dead,' the old woman said through the small opening. 'Who're you?'

I was standing on the leaking porch of a weatherboard house in Richmond. I'd got the address from a prison officer I knew from the days when I visited clients in Pentridge. The prison records had Mrs Mary McKillop, aunt, as Danny McKillop's next of kin. I looked her up in the phone book: it was the number Danny had left on the machine. Sue McKillop hadn't known the aunt was alive and had no idea how to find the cousin she'd mentioned.

'Mrs Mary McKillop?' I said.

'He's dead,' she repeated. 'Whad'ya want?'

'I'm a lawyer. I'd like to talk about Danny.'

'Danny's dead. Bugger off.'

The two-inch opening closed with a crack. I stared at the door's peeling green paint for a while, thinking about trying again. I could still smell the ancient fumes of boiled cabbage and cat piss and decaying ceilings that had leaked out when the door opened. That decided the issue. But as I turned the door opened a sliver.

'Try next door.'

The door closed again.

I tried the house to the right. A thin woman in her forties with lank, dead hair answered my knock. She blinked at me as if unaccustomed to light.

'I'm making inquiries about Danny McKillop,' I said.

She looked at me for a long time, then she put her hands in the pockets of her pink housecoat. 'He's dead. Was in the paper.' Her voice was toneless.

'It's his cousin I'd like to talk to.'

She looked at me in silence.

'It's about the accident Danny went to jail for. It's possible he didn't do it.'

She waited.

'There might be some compensation.'

She cleared her throat. 'You'd better talk to Vin. He's Danny's cousin. He's not here.'

'Is he Vin McKillop?' I said.

She nodded.

'Do you know where I could find him?'

She thought for a while, then said, 'Suppose he's working. Only time he gets up before twelve. Dennis Shanahan in Edge Street'll know.'

I found Dennis Shanahan in the phone book. A woman said he was demolishing a building in Abbotsford, Joseph Street.

There were three middle-aged men, a teenage boy and a lean brindle dog with a studded collar on the site. I could see them all from across the road. One man was sitting in the cab of a truck behind the shell of the single-storey building, the second was prising out a window with a crowbar, the third was feeding a fire of old timbers in the back corner. The teenager was cleaning bricks with a hammer and chisel. The dog was watching him. A portable radio somewhere in the ruin was putting out 'Bridge over Troubled Water' at full volume.

I crossed the road and walked along a plank bridging the exposed floor beams to the first doorway in the passage. A smell of poor lives hung over the place: cooking fat, yellow feet, burnt ironing boards and blocked drains.

'I'm looking for Vin,' I shouted to the window remover. He made a gesture with his thumb without looking around.

I guessed the man in the truck would be the boss, so I tried the man at the fire. I couldn't get close: the heat was intense. It didn't seem to bother the man feeding it. He was short, heavyset, with dark curly hair and sideburns, probably in place since Elvis. The same could be said for his jeans and the grime on his hands and under his nails. His nose was flattened and slightly askew and a big piece of right eyebrow was gone.

'Vin McKillop?' I said.

He had a length of two-by-four hardwood in his right hand, poking the fire. He looked up at me without expression. Boxer's eyes. 'Who wants him?'

'I'm a lawyer,' I said. 'It's about Danny McKillop. I know he's dead but I need to talk to someone who knew him.'

The man threw his two-by-four into the flames.

'What about him?' he said.

'It's about the accident. The woman's death.'

He picked up another splintered piece of wood. 'He done the time,' he said flatly.

'I'm trying to find out if he done the crime.'

The man spat into the flames. 'What's it to you if he done it or not done it?'

'It's complicated,' I said. 'Can you spare me a bit of time? There's an interview fee.'

'I'm on the job.'

'Take half an hour unpaid. I'll pay you for that too.'

Vin McKillop positioned the wood carefully on the fire and rubbed under his nose with a forefinger. 'There's a pub around the corner,' he said. 'Cost you twenty bucks.'

The pub was empty except for two old men sitting at a formica table in a corner looking at nothing. The place smelt of stale beer and carbolic. I got two beers and sat at a table near the door. Vin came in and went straight through the door marked GENTS. When he came back, he stood at the bar. He was making some kind of point. I picked up the beers and went over to him.

'Cheers,' I said.

Vin didn't say anything. He just picked up the glass and

drank three-quarters of the beer. 'So,' he said, 'what's the fee?'

I had a fifty-dollar note ready. I put it on the bar. Then I put a twenty on top of it.

Vin put the money in his top pocket. He took a cigarette out of the same pocket without revealing the pack and lit it with a plastic lighter. He took a deep drag and let the smoke run out his nostrils. I felt like asking him for one. 'You a Jack?' he said.

'No.' I took out a card and held it up for him to read. He looked at it.

'Need glasses,' he said. 'What's it say?'

'It says I'm a lawyer.' Vin couldn't read.

'Danny don't need a lawyer now.'

'There's his wife and child,' I said. 'Had you seen him recently?'

'Seen him when he come out. Didn't know him. Lost about a hundred pounds.'

'What kind of work did he do before he went in?'

'Nothin.' Vin drained his beer and signalled the barman with a big, dirty finger.

'Surprise you when he hit the woman that night?'

Vin flicked his cigarette stub into the trough at our feet. It lay there smoking. He lit another one. 'Yeah, surprised me.' He held his cigarette hand just above the counter and drummed with his thumb.

'Why's that?'

'What's it matter? Cunt's wormfood now.'

Vin's beer arrived. I paid.

'It matters. Why were you surprised?'

He drank half the beer and wiped his mouth on his cuff. 'Hadn't been near the car for months. He was on a year suspended for pissed driving. Fat prick was shit-scared of doing time.'

'But he could've forgotten all that, he was so pissed.'

Vin scratched an armpit. 'Yeah, well, that could be right if you can work out how a bloke that's so legless he's passed out in Punt Road about quarter past eleven can get sober enough to go home and get his car and drive about thirty blocks to cream some bitch at twenty to twelve.'

'Danny didn't mention that before the trial.'

'Fucking right.'

'How do you know where he was at quarter past eleven?'

'Mate of mine saw him.'

'You didn't tell the cops?'

'Didn't hear about it till after Danny was inside.'

'Why didn't your mate tell the cops at the time?'

Vin blew two flat streams of smoke out of his nostrils. 'Cause he was hoping Danny'd get about fifty years. Danny was a dog. There's lots of people hoped they'd throw the fucking key away.'

'Dog for who?'

'Drug squad. He'd dob anyone, every little twat he heard big-noting himself in a pub. Jacks'd pay him off with a couple've hits.'

'He was on smack?'

'On anything.'

Two men in donkey jackets and woollen caps came in from the street. Vin looked them over carefully while draining his glass.

I signalled for two more beers.

'One of his Jack mates was talking to him near the pub that night,' Vin said.

'How do you know that?'

'Same way. My mate. Saw Danny with this cunt Scullin in a car down the road. Danny come in, full of dough, drinking Jim Beam, in and out of the pisshouse, gets off his face. They kicked him out round eleven. Then my mate sees him lying behind a bench, he's drunk another half of JB.'

'That was a quarter past eleven?

'Thereabouts.'

'You reckon your mate would talk to me? For a fee?'

'No.'

'Why's that?'

'Dead. OD'd on smack.'

'The cop's name's Scullin?'

'I forget.'

'Where did Danny keep his car?'

'Garage behind his nanna's house.'

'That's in Collett Street?'

'Yeah.'

'Fair way from Clifton Hill.'

'Fucking A.' He finished his beer. 'Got to go.'

I said, 'Thanks for your help.'

'You got nothing from me, mate. Is that right?'

'It's right.'

Vin McKillop looked back at me before he went out the door. There was still nothing showing in those boxer's eyes but he wasn't going to forget my face.

We went to Ballarat in the big BMW, Harry driving through Royal Park and on to the Tullamarine Freeway like the late James Hunt on cocaine. The day was fine, thin cloud running west. In ten minutes we were passing through Keilor, the beginning of a huge sprawl of brick veneers nominally divided into suburbs with names like Manna Gum Heights and Bellevue Hill. These were the places where teenage dreams came to die.

'Heights,' said Harry in wonder. 'Flat as the paper under the lino.'

I was in the back, reading the *Age*. Cam was in front, fiddling with the laptop.

'Wootton tells me you put the squirrel grip on one of his commissioners, Jack,' Harry said.

'Not without difficulty,' I said. Harry knew Wootton well. He used him for big jobs.

'More buggers doin a runner these days, seems to me. Probably time for another Happy Henry.' Harry turned to look at me while accelerating passed a tradesman's ute with two cattle dogs on the back, barking into the wind. I paled.

'You know about Happy Henry, Jack?'

'No.'

'Hidden history of the turf,' Harry said. 'Commissioner called Happy Henry Carmody. Happy shot through on a big punter, Baby Martinez, came from Manila, Hawaii, somewhere like that, got into a few duels with the books. Silly bugger, really. Happy did a bit of work for him, came highly recommended too. Then one Satdee Happy had a kitbag of notes owed to Baby, thought bugger it, Baby's just some dago'll cop it sweet, go home and weep under the palm trees.'

Harry looked around again.

'Baby's friends come on Happy up in Brisbane. The dickhead, it took so long to get there in his Falcon, he thinks he must be in a foreign country. He's tossin Baby's dough around, whores, cards, buyin drinks for the cops and politicians and the like.'

There was a pause while Harry groped for the Smarties box. In the interests of self-preservation, Cam found it for him.

'Anyway, next thing Happy's up in the little hills they got there, nailed to a blue gum. Five feet off the ground, they say. Six-inch nails. Like Jesus Christ.'

'Fuck,' said Cam.

'Not again either,' Harry said. 'Cut it off, put it in his shirt pocket like a little cigar. Was a while before any of your commissioners' minds went wanderin again, can tell ya.'

51

Harry chuckled to himself for a while. Then he said, 'Give us a rundown on the field in this Topspin bugger's race, Cam.'

While Cam talked, consulting the laptop, Harry kept a steady thirty kilometres over the speed limit and we covered the 110 kilometres in sixty-five minutes. It wasn't raining in Ballarat and the locals were standing out on the pavements, looking at the sky in amazement. Many of them had the pale, staring look of people newly pushed out of institutions. Someone once said that nobody went to live in Ballarat; you had to be committed by a magistrate.

Dowling Forest is on the other side of town, at the foot of a round, bald hill. By the time we got there, thin and steady rain was falling.

'That's more like it,' said Harry. He'd said nothing since the Happy Henry story, listening to Cam in silence. He parked well back from the gate and took over my newspaper.

Cam locked the laptop into its housing under the dashboard.

'Well?' he asked, big hands on his thighs.

Harry reached into his Donegal tweed jacket with his right hand and came out with an envelope about a centimetre thick. 'I'll give you the nod,' he said. 'Yokels lined up, I take it.'

'Better be,' Cam said. He put the envelope in the inside pocket of his trenchcoat and set off briskly.

I got the Sakura Pro FS100 out of the boot, loaded it, hung it around my neck, put on my Drizabone and followed. Harry was on the car phone.

We were in Ballarat for two reasons. The first was a

three-year-old filly called Topspin Winder running in the third. She had started five times and her best run was a seventh place at her first outing. After four runs, she'd been given an eight-week rest. When she'd reappeared at Pakenham the week before, she'd run eighth.

I bought a race card and wandered into the huge barn of a betting ring. Most of the city bookmakers were fielding, trying to keep afloat until the Spring Carnival could rescue them. It was five minutes before the second race and there was a fair amount of action by country standards. I went out onto the grandstand. Over to the right, the members were snug behind glass. Out here it was all streaming eyes and snuffling noses.

The second looked a mediocre affair on paper and it proved to be one of those races where it's a pity something has to win. Or come second. Or third.

'Not much pace in that,' said the caller.

'Putting it bloody mildly,' said the man next to me. 'First time I've seen the whole field trying to throw a race.'

I went back through the betting ring to the mounting yard.

Cam was near the hot dog vendor, eating something wrapped in paper. As I looked around, Harry rounded the corner of the stalls. The small man stopped and patted his raincoat pockets, looking down.

When he looked up, he nodded briskly to himself, as if he'd found what he was looking for. Then he set off in the direction of the carpark.

Cam crumpled up the greaseproof paper and shot the ball into a bin a good three metres away. He set off for the betting ring. As he entered the large opening, he patted a thickset man in a greasy anorak on the arm.

I didn't waste any time checking the odds. Topspin Winder was showing 40-1 with the book nearest the entrance and I took it. I invested a modest $50, not enough to scare anybody. By the time I'd finished my circuit, Cam's team of punters had struck terror into the numbers men: Topspin was down to 15-1.

Then the second wave hit the bookies—a panic rush of Topspin's connections, caught napping by Cam's troops and now jostling with the dumb money that was always on the alert for a plunge. The market went into freefall, ending up on 6-1.

On my way to have a look at the beast concerned, I passed Cam, leaning against the mounting yard fence. He was smoking a little cigar and reading the card. Nothing in that Aboriginal/Scottish/Italian face suggested anything other than mild boredom.

Topspin was equally impassive. I'd seen her at her previous three appearances and had grown rather fond of her. She was small, calm, unprepossessing. Her form to date had not prepossessed the racing press either; in the *Age* that morning, Ron Pevsner assessed her odds at 50-1 and Bart Grantley gave her a rating of two out of ten.

Topspin Winder had come to Harry's attention in her first outing, over 1600 metres in pouring rain at Moe. The small horse missed the start completely, then appeared to stumble about ten metres out. By the time the jockey got things organised, the closest horse was twelve lengths away, vanishing into the mist. Cam was out on the fence and for some reason he put the watch on Topspin at the 200-metre mark. About 500 metres out, there was a bad fall, two horses going down in the mud. Topspin was too far back to be affected and ran seventh out of the remaining thirteen, about eight lengths behind the winner. What interested Harry was Cam's estimate that she took under 60 seconds to cover the 1000 metres to the 1200 mark. And that in the excitement over the fall, no-one said anything about it.

We hadn't seen that speed again. In her next three races, all 1600s, Topspin was ridden by another jockey, a leather-faced veteran of the inland circuit called Marty Bacquie. The horse seemed to be trying but she kept getting caught in the middle of the herd, boxed in half a dozen lengths off the pace, and flagging badly over the last two hundred or so. At her last appearance, at Pakenham, I filmed Bacquie talking to the trainer after the race and Harry brought in his trusted lip-reader to look at the video. The trainer was saying nice things to Marty. And that was why we were in Ballarat.

There were twelve horses in race three, 1200 metres. The best performed, Quigley's Pride, had one win and nine places from nineteen starts. Second best was Extension Date with one win from five. After that it was winter. There were no more than a hundred people on the grandstand. I took my usual place out on the eastern edge. Harry was down in the front row, undistinguished in his elderly raincoat and hat. No sign of Cam.

They came out of the gate in a good line. Topspin had a new jockey today, Lance Wallace, a New Zealander in his second season in the big time, rider of several upsets in the past year.

A horse called Denaderise took the front and opened up a two-length lead. I knew Denaderise. This was her role in life. She had about 500 metres in her.

At the 600, Quigley's Pride, specialist placegetter, was a length off Denaderise. There was no pace in it. Topspin was lying well back, perhaps eighth or ninth, nothing outside her.

At the 700, Wallace moved the horse further out, almost to the centre of the track. Denaderise was gone, slipping backwards. Extension Date took over the lead, on the rails, moving well. Quigley's tucked in behind, losing a little ground as they approached the 800. Outside them a horse called Under the Gun, a 15-1 shot, came into contention.

With 200 metres to go, Under the Gun's jockey used the whip and the animal surged past Extension Date, seeming to draw Quigley's Pride along. At the 150, Under the Gun was the winner, stride lengthening, towing Quigley's Pride away from Extension Date.

The race caller was saying, 'It's Under the Gun now coming away, Quigley's Pride hasn't got the finish to stay with him, Extension Date being left…'

Something had gone badly wrong in our calculations. And, presumably, in the connections' calculations, too.

And then, very smoothly, no whip, hands and heels, Lance Wallace and Topspin Winder began their run down the outside. The little horse gave no great impression of speed; the other horses seemed to slow down.

The caller went into overdrive, 'Down the outside Topspin Winder, she's mowed down Extension Date, fifty metres to go she goes up to Quigley's Pride, no resistance there for the plunge horse. It's Under the Gun and Topspin Winder, Under the Gun Topspin Winder, metres to go it's Topspin Winder pulling away, Topspin Winder by three-quarters of a length…'

I looked across at Harry. He was having a little swig of Glenmorangie from the flat silver flask he took to the races on cold days.

I filmed the fourth race, a Class 1 handicap over 1600 metres. This was the second reason we were in Ballarat. My attention was on Red Line Value, a new object of Harry's attention. It went well early, weakened and finished in the middle of the field, making a little ground in the closing stages.

Cam and Harry were in the BMW when I got there. Harry gave me a small smile. 'I think we might have a look at the Dom when we get home,' he said.

We parked a block away from the Peter Lalor Hotel in the middle of Ballarat. Cam went off. He had a date with the commission agent who had organised the team of punters.

'Collectin' can be the hardest part,' Harry said. 'Still, the boy's got a look about him keeps the buggers honest. They know a bare-knuckle man when they see one. What'd ya make of that Red Line?'

Cam was back inside fifteen minutes. On Harry's orders, we stopped at McDonald's on the way out. Harry ordered two Big Macs.

'Take over the helm,' he said to Cam. 'Got to get outside these snacks. Man gets weak up here in the glaciers.'

The second hamburger didn't make it to the city limits. 'Now that's what I call food,' Harry said. 'Not a word to the wife. She reckons you eat the stuff, you end up needin one of them coronary overpasses or whatever.'

He found a Willie Nelson tape and pushed it into the system. 'Give us the sums, Cam,' he said, tilting his seat back. 'Moonlight in Vermont' flooded the car.

'Well,' Cam said, 'we unloaded it, but it's no great average. Round 10-1. Some of these books see a go coming if you put down fifty bucks. It's getting hard to find someone in the bush'll take a decent-size whack.'

'Tens are fine,' Harry said. 'Thing didn't require millions. You don't want to nuke the bastards. We want 'em there next time.'

I had no idea how much money they were talking about. I'd been part of five betting plunges with Harry and Cam and I had no idea of the sums involved. I was happy that way too.

Harry's head peeped around the side of his seat. 'Get that fifty on at something decent, Jack?' He set the figure for personal bets.

'At the top,' I said.

'Goodonya.'

In Parkville, joined by Lyn Strang in a black dress, not small but rippable, we drank two bottles of Dom Perignon. Harry excused himself for a while early on and when he came back said, 'Fair bit of satisfaction in the combinations.' This meant he had done well in the coupling of Topspin Winder with other horses in other races.

Cam and I left at 7.45 p.m. At the door, Harry shook

hands with both of us and slid an envelope into my jacket pocket. I opened it at home: $6000 in fifties. I went downstairs in search of company. Dom Perignon excites the blood.

The next day wasn't productive. I did a lease for a landlord who had come in off the street and put a couple of extra penalty clauses in Laurie Baranek's agreement. At home, I slumped on the old leather sofa in the everything room with the Danny McKillop file and a bottle of Huon Falls Lager. I lived in half of the top of a small converted boot factory near Edinburgh Gardens. I'd owned the whole building in the good times and had managed to hold on to a quarter. No, to be accurate, a suburban lawyer, the fittingly named Prudence Webb, of Moloney, Hassan & Webb, had held on to a quarter for me when I was bent on liquidating all my assets, including myself, after Isabel's death.

The answering machine played two clicks from callers who didn't want to speak, a message from a lawyer about a witness, and my sister, Rosa, twice. She is the only woman named for a communist heroine ever to live in the old-money belt of Toorak. Impregnating my mother with her was one of the last things my father did on earth. What Bill Irish, stonemason, footballer, socialist, would make of Rosa is hard to say. She grew up in total privilege in my mother's parents' mansion in Toorak, doted on by four adults, one of them my mother's nanny, recalled to service at sixty-five.

I read the whole file again. What was clear was that the evidence against Danny at his trial was overwhelming. A witness put him about three blocks from the scene within minutes of the collision. He was found asleep behind the wheel of the car that killed Anne Jeppeson: there were blood and clothing fragments on it belonging to Anne Jeppeson. The witness had taken the registration and the police had identified it as belonging to Danny and gone to his house. The witness had later picked Danny out of a line-up.

In his statement to the police, Danny said he had started drinking at around 3 p.m. on the day. He remembered nothing after about 10 p.m., when he was still in the Glengarry Arms in Punt Road. He had no idea how the evidence of the collision came to be on his car. He said the same in his interview with me at Pentridge.

I put the file down and stared at the shadows on the ceiling. From my notes, it appeared that I'd had no hesitation in advising Danny to plead guilty. I'd certainly made no effort to establish whether there was any other possible explanation for the circumstances. Why should I have? Danny didn't offer any alternative account, his record was terrible and the police case was a prosecutor's dream.

I was fetching another beer when the phone rang. It was my sister.

'Aren't you ever at home?' Rosa said. 'Doesn't that machine of yours work? I need your advice. Phillip wants to marry me.'

'Who?'

'Phillip. Phillip? How many men do you think I'm seeing?'

'It's not a question of number,' I said, 'it's a question of sequence. Which one is Phillip?'

She sighed. 'Jack, you met him at dinner. The investor. With the sexy mouth. You brought that Sydney tart.'

'She speaks warmly of you too. What sort of advice were you after?'

There was a pause. 'Do you think I should?'

'Marry him?'

'Yes. Marry him.'

'No.'

'Why on earth not?'

'I think you should hold out for a less than one hundred per cent shit. What happened to Kevin? He seemed to have a lot of decent Catholic guilt. For a currency speculator, that is.'

She sighed again. 'Jack, Jack, Kevin is a two hundred per cent shit. He's got a little computer thing, you can see what's happening to the dollar and the yen and the fucking zloty. He goes to the toilet in restaurants and looks at it. Can you believe that? I know it for a fact. The rest of them are in there snorting and admiring each other's cocks and Kevin's drooling over his little money meter. His wife left him for a nightclub bouncer, all of twenty-two, I believe. Can you blame her?'

'I can't find it in my heart to, no,' I said.

'The men I meet,' she said, 'if they're not married and on the prowl, they're gay or they're going to a group to come to terms with their female side or they can't shut up about their inner child. I suppose that's why Phillip looks like such a find.'

I said, 'It's Phillip's inner shark that worries me.'

I gave her some more excellent advice and we arranged to meet for lunch. Then I made some grilled ham and tomato sandwiches and got back on the couch. I clicked on the box and caught the end of the last segment on 'This Day'. An ABC-type person with fair hair, spots and little round glasses was standing in front of a high diamond-mesh fence with a suave-looking man in a dark suit. Behind them you could see what looked like the beginnings of a vast gravel pit and beyond that an expanse of greasy water and the city skyline.

'Mr Pitman,' the spotty man said, 'as the Minister responsible for seeing the Yarra Cove development through the Cabinet, how do you react to some people's unease over a six hundred million dollar development being approved without public consultation?'

The Minister smiled. He had a thin, sly face with high cheekbones. Something about it said cosmetic surgery. His full head of dark hair was the kind that doesn't move in the wind. 'Well, Andrew,' he said, 'I don't know who these people are you're referring to. Perhaps your colleagues at the ABC. Or at the *Age*. There are always some people who want to knock anything the government does. But they're not the people who elected us to government.'

'But—' said Andrew.

'The people who elected the Saunders government to power,' Pitman went on, 'want this State to come back to life. They lived in the Gulag created by the previous government quite long enough. It's projects like this they want to see come to pass. Projects like this that inject huge amounts of capital and energy into this State.'

Andrew made a few other feeble attempts to put Pitman on the defensive. Pitman ignored them and kept to his line about what the people wanted.

Finally, Andrew gave up and said, 'Within twelve months, this,' he pointed at the gravel pit, 'will be Yarra Cove, a huge six hundred million dollar marina, waterfront shopping and entertainment precinct and, arguably, Melbourne's smartest new address. But will the Saunders government's lack of concern for public consultation over projects that change the face of the city set a precedent for future developments? Andrew Leonard for "This Day".'

After that I had a choice between television entertainment on the themes of a) child abuse, b) parent abuse, and c) tree abuse. Failing these, there was a documentary on the drinking problem in Lapland. I failed all of these, killed the telly and fell asleep over chapter three of Eugene Marasco's *In the Absence of War*.

Some time in the small hours, startled by something in a dream, I awoke and staggered to the bed proper. But sleep had fled. I lay and thought about Danny, one-time police informer, addict, convicted hit-and-run killer, born-again model employee, husband and father. If his cousin's mate, dead of smack, had told the truth, a policeman could have given him an alibi. And therefore the star witness was lying. The witness's name was Ronald Bishop.

I put on the light, got the file from the lounge, and read Ronald Bishop's statement again. It was a model of its kind: Ronnie Bishop didn't have any doubts about what he saw. I put off the light and fell asleep with the strange career of Danny McKillop turning in my mind.

In the morning, I rang Barry Tregear at home to catch him before he left for work. A woman said he'd left but she would pass on a message. I gave her my name. About ten minutes later, he rang. From the noise, he was on a mobile phone.

'Ronald Bishop?' he said. 'Morton Street, Clifton Hill. I'll see what I can do.'

I had breakfast at Meaker's on Brunswick Street, a street which boasted trams and, at each end, a church spire. Sometimes, when a freak wind lifted the pollution, you could see the one from the other. Brunswick Street had been a grand thoroughfare once and a long passage between rundown buildings and hopeless shops for a long time after that. In the eighties, the street changed again. Youth culture happened to it. The old businesses— clothes-pressing sweatshops, drycleaners, printeries, cheap shoe shops, the gunsmith, dim central European coffee and snooker cafes—closed down. In their place, restaurants, coffee shops, delicatessens, galleries and bookshops opened. Suddenly it was a smart place to be.

Meaker's had been in Brunswick Street since before it was smart. It had changed hands several times and moved once but nothing had really changed. Well, nothing except the appearance of the customers. And the staff. There was a new waitress today. She was probably in her late twenties, tall and raw-boned with scraped back hair and an amused, intelligent look.

'I'm Sharon,' she said when she put down the tray holding the Cholesterol Supercharge: eggs, bacon, sausages, fried tomato. 'The cook says you're Jack.'

'So what do you do?' I asked her when she brought the coffee. It was assumed in Brunswick Street that waiting on table was not one's vocation.

'I'm an actor,' she said. 'In the theatre. Don't you recognise me?'

'No,' I said, 'but I don't get to the theatre much these days.'

'What about you?' she said, wiping the table.

'I'm a bishop.'

'Right,' she said. 'Is that a crook you've got in your pocket or are you just pleased to see me?'

I could see she was going to be an asset to the place. Not as religious as one would have liked, but an asset.

I didn't have anything in the legal line to do, so I put in five hours at Taub's. Charlie was making the boardroom furniture for a Perth mining company's new Melbourne office. It was what the business pages call an 'emerging miner'. Usually, your emerging miner wants a table shaped like Australia minus Tasmania, chairs like breaking waves. This outfit hired a decorator who convinced them that big business in Melbourne favoured a more traditional look.

A Charlie Taub look, in fact. The decorator was married to Charlie's grandson: the extended family has its uses.

I spent the early part of the day trying to get Charlie to tell me what I was doing. He'd got out of the habit of doing drawings. 'What for do I need drawings?' he said. 'I don't make anything I haven't made before.'

'Charlie,' I said, 'I haven't made this table before. All I've got is some measurements on this piece of paper torn off the side of the *Age*. I'd like to have some idea of how what I'm doing fits into the plan you've got in your head. That's a lot to ask?'

He went off grumbling to the office and came back in ten minutes with several school exercise book pages. On them were detailed working drawings of an armoire designed to contain bottles, glasses and television and video equipment, a boardroom table, very severe, and a chair, equally spare.

'You want drawings, I give you drawings,' he said.

I went around the corner to Flash Advanced Tele-communications, prop. G. Bertoli, former telephone-repair person, and made two copies.

Barry Tregear rang at noon while I was reading the *Age* and eating the corned beef and gherkin on rye sandwich I'd brought from home. He couldn't find any trace of a Ronald Bishop.

I knocked off at 1.30 p.m. and drove around to the address in Clifton Hill, no more than a few kilometres away. Morton Street was close enough to Collingwood Football Ground to hear the sobbing when Carlton beat them. Fitzroy used to beat them once upon a time but it would take divine intervention these days.

The bourgeoisie had long since occupied most of this once deeply working class area pinched between two main roads and a freeway. Morton Street, however, had the unloved look of a trench fallen to the rentiers.

Ronald Bishop had once lived at number 17. But not even the house still lived at number 17. It had been extracted like a tooth, its earthly remains some blackened broken bricks where a fireplace had stood and a mound of damp ashes that had saved the demolishers the trips to the tip. I knocked at number 19. No-one was home or admitting to it. I trudged off to number 15.

The bell didn't work. I tried tapping and then gave the door a couple of thumps. The door was wrenched open and a large red-faced man in his sixties glowered at me. He was wearing a dirty blue nylon anorak zipped up to the neck and black tracksuit pants with a stripe, possibly white once, up the side.

'Don't fucken hammer my door,' he said. 'Whaddafuck d'ya want?'

I apologised and gave him my card.

'So?' he said, not noticeably impressed.

'I'm trying to find out about someone who used to live next door,' I said. 'About twelve years ago. Were you living here then?'

'Depends,' he said. He ran both hands through his long, greasy grey hair.

'We have a standard fee of twenty dollars for useful information,' I said.

'Who's the someone?'

'Ronald Bishop.'

'Come inside,' he said.

I followed him down a passage dark as a mineshaft into a kitchen that smelled of sour milk and burnt fat. All surfaces were covered in dirty plates, open tins, takeaway containers, empty cigarette packets. The gas stove had a baked and blistered topping of spilt food.

'Garn!' the man shouted at a huge tabby cat walking on tiptoe across the littered table. It floated its flabby body across to an impossibly small perch on the sink.

'Wanna beer?' he asked.

'That'd be good.' There was no knowing how he would take a refusal.

He took two cans of Melbourne Bitter out of an old fat-bodied fridge. The light inside wasn't working. We sat down at the table. I couldn't find anywhere to put my can down so I held it on my lap.

'So what, he's inherited some dough?' he said. He gave the can the suck of a man who measures out his days in tinnies.

'Not that I know of,' I said. 'His family's trying to get in touch with him. Did you know him when he lived next door?'

'Fucking poof,' he said. 'Bloody lucky he got outta here alive. We was just about to give him a hammerdrill up the arse when he pissed off.' He wiped spit from his lower lip with his thumb and took a packet of Long Beach Lites out of the anorak. 'Smoke?'

'No thanks. What made you like him so much?'

He gave me a suspicious look over the flame of the plastic lighter. 'Bloody house was fulla kids. Sleepin all over the place. He used to come back here in the bloody middle the night, half a dozen kids in the car. Street kids they call 'em now. Bloody drug addicts. Should lock 'em away. You wouldn't believe the bloody racket they made.'

'So Ronald was trying to help them, was he?'

He looked at me with utter scorn. 'Where the hell've you been? He was tryin to root 'em. Tryin and bloody succeedin. Half of them's so off their faces they wouldn't know if a gorilla rooted 'em.'

He took another measure of beer, dragged on the cigarette and tapped ash into a catfood can.

'And how long was he here?'

'Would've been about a year. Been a bloody lot shorter if I hadn't been…' He scratched his neck. 'I only come back a coupla weeks before he pissed off. Bloody Moira put up with him, Christ only knows women. Used to talk to the little cunt over the fence.'

'He just left, did he?'

'Showed up one day in a white Triumph sports. Y'know the kind? They don't make 'em any more. TR something. Just packed his case, buggered off. Left the old Renault standin out there. Coupla them kids took off in it. Never come back, neither.'

'He didn't leave because of you?'

He shook his head. 'I hadn't got round to him yet. He just pissed off. Reckon the cops were on him.'

'Why's that?'

'Two come round there a couple times.'

'What, uniform cops?'

'No. Plain clothes.'

'You sure?'

He had another suck on the can. 'I know the one,' he said.

'You know his name?' I had a big swig of my beer.

'Scullin. His name's Scullin. He grew up round Abbotsford.'

'So the cops came around twice and then he left?'

He nodded. 'More than twice. Coupla times. Told Moira before he pissed off some bullshit about he'd won some money, something like that. I reckon it was drugs.'

'Anyone else around here know him?'

He thought about it, smoke seeping out of his nostrils. 'No,' he said. 'Bloke on the other side's dead.'

I drained the can. 'This is helpful,' I said, getting up. 'Much obliged.' I took out my wallet, found a twenty and offered it. He took it and put it under the catfood can.

At the front door, I said, 'Well, thanks again.' He gave me a little wave.

I was at the gate when he said, 'I'm just thinkin. Remember the bloke on the other side, Greek he was, tellin me one day he read where Ronnie dobbed in some hit-and-run bloke.'

I paused. 'When was that?'

He spat on to the path. 'Dunno.'

'Was it while he was living here?'

'Must've been. Bloke said he remembered Ronnie gettin in a car all smartened up. Then he read where he dobbed this other fella. That's what the Greek said. Don't get time to read the paper myself.'

'That's useful,' I said. 'Thanks.'

I went back to my office, made some black tea and sat in the client's chair. Where was Ronnie Bishop now? Last seen tooling off in his Triumph, fresh from doing his civic duty in the matter of *R. v. McKillop*. And where was a policeman called Scullin, whose circle included the accused and the star witness?

Barry Tregear didn't need to think about the name Scullin.

'Martin Scullin. I know Scull,' he said. 'What's the problem?'

'No problem. He might be able to help me with something.'

'You still farting around with that McKillop business?'

'On and off.'

'You've missed Scull today. By about six years. He took the package. Gone fishing.'

'What about a number or an address?'

'Big ask. I'll have to talk to the man. What do you want to see him about?'

I thought for a moment. 'Tell him it's about an old dog of his, Danny McKillop.'

'Where'd you get that?' Tregear asked.

'Widely known at the time.'

'I'll get back to you. Where are you?'

I gave him the number.

I gave the R. Bishops in the phone book a quick run-through. There were only two Ronalds and neither of them had ever lived in Morton Street. I rang an estate agent called Millie Vincent I'd had dealings with and asked her to check the Landlords' database for Ronald Bishop. She rang back in twenty minutes.

'They'll drum me out of the trade for doing this,' she said. 'A Ronald Arthur Bishop rented a house in Prahran in 1984–85. Then a Perth agent ran a check on him for a property in Fremantle in late '85.'

She gave me the name of the agent.

I got through to a man called Michael Brooke. He got the impression I was a fellow real estate agent and told me a Ronald Bishop had been the tenant of a house in Walpole Street, Fremantle. 'Then he bought it at auction in, oh, '86 or '87. Paid a bit over the odds then but it's turned out to be a smart buy. By the way, he calls himself Ronnie Burdett-Bishop now. Moved upmarket.'

R. A. Burdett-Bishop was in the Perth phonebook.

No-one answered at the first two attempts. The phone rang for a long time before a low-voiced male answered on the third try.

'Could I speak to Ronnie, please,' I said.

'Who is that?'

'An old acquaintance suggested I call him.'

There was a pause. 'Ronnie's in Melbourne.'

'That's where I'm calling from. Is there some way I can get in touch with him here?'

There was another pause. 'Who did you say you were?'

'My name's Jack Irish,' I said. 'I'm a lawyer. You'll find me in the Melbourne phone book.' For some reason, this statement sometimes had a reassuring effect on people.

'Well, I'd like to help you,' the man said. 'My name's Charles Lee. I'm a friend of Ronnie's. I'm keeping an eye on his house. No-one seems to know where Ronnie is at the moment…'

'You don't have a Melbourne address for him?'

'Um, you could try his mother. Would you like her number?'

I wrote it down, said thanks and goodbye, then dialled it. No-one at home.

It's nice that there's a special occupation for the anal retentive. It's called librarianship. The thin man with the silly little cornsilk moustache gave me a smile of pure dislike and went away. I was sitting at a table in the *Age* library on the fourth floor of the paper's hideous building on Spencer Street. A message from Steve Phillips, the assistant editor, had preceded me but that had only made me more unwelcome. I went back some distance with Phillips. In the early '80s I'd got his teenage son off a drugs charge. I'd been recommended by a reporter called Gavin Legge for whom I'd obtained extremely lucky verdicts on a bunch of charges arising from his birthday party at a fashionable restaurant called Melitta's.

Mr Silly Moustache took all of ten minutes to produce the file. I slid the fiche onto the platen, switched on and, as always, found that it was upside down. When I'd corrected this, I zoomed across to the end and worked backwards.

The last clipping was a short item from 1986 about the setting up by her parents of the Anne Jeppeson Memorial Scholarship at Monash University. It was to go to a student studying politics. Before that came the court reports I'd already seen in my file on Danny, then the report on Anne's death. It was a page three story, with a picture of the scene and an inset photograph of her. She had short hair and a snub nose and she looked smart and formidable. A quick look at the headlines on the rest of the clippings suggested that this was the case. I wrote down the bylines on those stories that had them.

Anne Jeppeson had been a campaigner for public housing and public housing tenants. At the time she was killed she was involved in trying to prevent the closing down of a public housing estate called Hoagland in Yarrabank.

I leaned back in the upright chair and closed my eyes. Ronnie Bishop had helped send to jail the man accused of killing a woman campaigning against the closing of a public housing estate. Why would he lie to do that? Public-spiritedness? It didn't sound like Ronnie Bishop.

I asked SM whether I could get the Jeppeson file photo-copied. He looked at me as if I'd asked for a colonic irrigation.

'Would it help if I went through Steve Phillips?' I said sweetly.

'It'll take half an hour,' he said. 'There isn't anyone to do it now.'

I said I'd come back and went looking for a caffeine jolt.

I came upon the drinks machine without warning, which made it impossible to avoid my former client Gavin Legge. He looked up from stirring his styrofoam cup. The smile of a professional greeter appeared on his face.

'Jack Irish,' he said. He put down the cup and stuck out a small hand. 'Great to see you. Who's in the shit this time?'

Legge was in his early forties, with greying curly hair and small features being overwhelmed by pudge. Behind thick-lensed designer glasses his eyes were slitty. All his stories in the paper seemed to involve free travel and free eating and drinking. He also dropped a lot of names. At the time I was defending him, one of his mercifully unneeded character witnesses said of him, 'For a free sausage roll and a couple of glasses of plonk, Gavin Legge will get six mentions of anything you're selling into the paper.'

'Using the library,' I said. 'Maybe you can help.'

'My pleasure.' He was eager to please. As well he might be, given that it had taken me a year to get any money out of him.

I put the coins in the machine and pressed for white coffee. I got out my notebook and found the three bylines on the Jeppeson stories. 'These people still around? Sally Chan? Matthew Lunt?'

'Jeez, you're going back a bit. Chan went to Sydney about ten years ago and Lunt's dead.'

'Linda Hillier?'

'Return of the starfucker. Came back to Melbourne a few months ago. She works for PRN, Pacific Rim News, it's a financial news outfit. Just around the corner. Want to meet her?'

'Wouldn't mind. I saw your byline on a story about Yarra Cove.'

Legge whistled. 'Now those boys know how to treat the media,' he said. 'Nothing but the French at the launch. Non-vintage but the French. Like the good old days. It's been local pissfizz at these things for years.'

'Only the fittest have come through,' I said. The machine started spitting out my drink.

Legge took a sip of his coffee and pulled a face. 'This stuff tastes like piss too. Bloody machines. Christ knows why we put up with it. Fucking useless union. Follow me.'

We left the building and walked up two blocks towards the city centre. Pacific Rim News had the fourth floor of a small office block. A security man gave us labels and we went into a huge room full of formica desks and computer terminals.

Legge said, 'I still owe you that lunch. What about tomorrow? It's on the paper. I'm reviewing a new restaurant. They fall over themselves.'

'Don't you do these things incognito?'

'Certainly do. But I gave them an anonymous tip-off.' He laughed, an unpleasant gurgling sound.

'Thanks,' I said, 'but I'm out of town tomorrow. Some other time would be nice.'

Linda Hillier was in a corner of the room where several desks seemed to have formed a huddle. She had been alerted and watched us coming, a pencil crosswise in her mouth between toothpaste-commercial teeth. When we got to her, Legge said, 'Linda Hillier, I want you to meet Jack Irish, the lawyer who kept me out of jail for punching that food bitch.'

Linda Hillier removed the pencil from her mouth. She was in her mid-thirties, shiny brown hair, a full mouth, dark eyes and a scattering of faded freckles. She wasn't good-looking but she was handsome.

'Hello,' she said. 'Next time tell us what you'll take to throw the case.'

'Jack's interested in something you covered when you were a young groupie,' Legge said.

'That far back?' Linda said. 'When you were still married to that nice plump girl from Accounts? The one who was sweet enough to blow all the *Age* copyboys at the Christmas party?'

'Touché,' said Legge. 'I can't stand around all day talking about old times. Jack, I'll ring you about lunch.'

We watched Legge walk off. I noticed that all the men in the room were frozen into poses suggesting deep concentration while all the women seemed to be typing. Could it be that the men were transmitting thoughts to the women, who were typing them up? I suggested this to Linda Hillier. She looked at me speculatively.

'Thoughts?' she said. 'Most of these guys couldn't transmit herpes. What's your interest in history?'

'I'm interested in the Anne Jeppeson hit-and-run,' I said. 'Remember her?'

She nodded.

'I saw your byline on some stories in her file.'

She said, 'Is this a legal matter?'

'No. I don't practise much anymore.'

'What do you do?'

'Live off my wits,' I said. 'Gamble. Drink.'

She smiled, an attractive downturning. 'Then you'll be keeping much the same company as before. Well, what can I tell you about Anne Jeppeson?'

'Did it cross anyone's mind at the time that she might have been deliberately run down?'

'By that drunk? Was he capable of forming an intention?'

'What I mean is, did anyone think he might have been used to kill Anne Jeppeson?'

She shrugged. 'I've never heard anyone suggest that.' She paused and looked at me intently. 'Hang on a minute. It's just come back to me. Didn't you appear for the driver?'

I nodded. 'Not with any distinction. He came out of jail a few years ago. New person, good job, wife and kid. Then a cop shot him dead in Brunswick last Friday.'

'Jesus,' she said. 'I read that the bloke'd done time for hit-and-run. I didn't make the connection.'

The phone on her desk rang. She talked to someone in monosyllables for a while, then put the phone down. 'Look,' she said, 'I'm under the gun here for a while. I've got to file a story for Hong Kong in about eight minutes.'

I took a chance. 'Can we talk outside hours?'

She gave me a questioning look. 'You mean tonight?'

I hadn't had a date in two years. 'If you're free,' I said.

There was a pause. We looked at each other in a new way.

She said, 'Ring me here at seven. We can fix something.'

It was raining outside. I didn't mind much.

Linda Hillier said she'd be finished by eight. We agreed to meet at Donelli's in Smith Street, Collingwood. It was owned by Patrick Donelly, an Irishman who wanted to be an Italian and who owed me money.

Linda was wearing a tailored navy jacket. I watched her hanging up her raincoat. She was taller than I remembered. Then I remembered I'd never seen her standing up. She felt my eyes on her and turned her head to look straight at me across the crowded room. For some reason, I felt embarrassed, as if I'd been caught looking down her dress. She came across and I stood up and pulled out a chair.

'Thanks,' she said. 'This is a nice way to end a real pain of a day.'

I poured her some of the house white, the menus came and we inspected them for a while. When we'd ordered the same things, she said, 'Gavin Legge rang up and told me about your wife. I'm sorry.'

'Thank you,' I said.

'Well,' she said, 'what else can I tell you about Anne Jeppeson? I've been thinking about her since you left. I talked to her the morning before she was killed. She was like a happy attack dog. "I'm going to get the bastards," she kept saying.'

'You weren't one of her admirers?'

She thought for a moment. 'There were things about her I admired. But, no, I wasn't one of her admirers. She had this deep contempt for the media and this equally deep need to be the subject of its attention.'

'You had dealings with her before the Hoagland business?'

'Long before. She cultivated me when she was trying to market herself as a barefoot paralegal in Footscray. It wasn't enough for justice to be done. Anne Jeppeson had to be seen to be doing it.' Linda drank half her glass. 'Hoagland was her chance for real fame.'

I said, 'My memory's pretty vague about that period. I read the clippings today. It's not clear how she got into the limelight.'

'She was a natural for the part from the moment it leaked out that the government was going to knock down the Hoagland Housing Commission flats. Do you know Yarra-bank?'

'Vaguely. I had a client from there once. Stabbed someone in a park. His best friend, I think it was.'

'That's what Yarrabank friends are for,' said Linda. 'It's

shitsville. Maybe it's going to be Venice when the Premier's mates are finished with it, but it was darkest shitsville then.'

I suddenly connected. Yarra Cove—the new development I'd seen the sly-faced Planning Minister, Lance Pitman, and the spotty ABC reporter going on about on TV—was on the site of the old Hoagland housing estate. There was a freeway on one side and once there'd been collapsing warehouses on the riverbank, filthy docks all around. There was a munitions factory there in the forties, a battery factory burnt down there in the early sixties. Christ knows what the soil pollution level was.

'How did a Housing Commission block ever get there?' I asked.

'One of the great mysteries of our time. They've shredded the files and composted the bits. People say the land was bought from a mate of the then Housing Minister for about ten times its value and the buildings were put up by another mate for about five times the going rate. The story goes the three of them bought half of Merimbula with the proceeds.'

'How did they get anybody to live there?'

'No choice for some people,' she said. 'That or under a bridge. And the Commission shunted in their problem cases from all over. Move to Hoagland and we'll forget about the three years' rent owing and the fire and the explosion and the missing hot water system. That sort of thing. It was a hellhole. The cops called it the Leper Colony, LC for short.'

'Small, though?'

'Couple of hundred inmates. Small by Housing Commission standards, fifty flats, three three-storey walk-ups.

When it leaked out that the government planned to close it, the Ministry said the place was so wrecked it was cheaper to build new flats than to fix it. But Yarrabank was not the place to build them. The place to build them was on land the Commission had bought on the outskirts of Sunshine.'

'Not from the same mate?' I said.

'One day we'll know.'

'What did the residents think?'

'Well, you'd have thought that even Sunshine would look like Surfers Paradise from Hoagland. But we don't actually know what the residents thought because Anne Jeppeson came on the scene like Batwoman and after that all we knew was what the Fight for Hoagland action committee thought. Well, what Anne Jeppeson said the committee thought. All the media attention was on her. It was the Anne Jeppeson Show.'

'What was her background?'

'Strictly middle class. Deep suburbia. Volvo in every drive. Private school. Did politics at Monash. Worked for the Footscray Legal Service for a while. Tried to organise piece-workers in the rag trade, then she got together a bunch of leftier-than-thou people and founded Right to a Roof. She organised a lot of squats in empty mansions in Toorak, that sort of thing. Great TV pictures.'

Linda finished her drink. I poured some more. 'Anyway, when Hoagland turned up, she stitched together a big coalition of left groups. Christ knows how. They were people who hated one another. She got about five thousand people out for a demonstration, got the Building Workers' Alliance to black-ban the Sunshine site, talked the public service unions into running stop-works. She was all over the papers, TV. The camera liked her. Joan of Arc come back in tight jeans and boots.'

'And then she got killed.'

Linda nodded. 'Without her, the whole Hoagland protest fell apart. Fight for Hoagland didn't actually exist without her. No-one really gave a shit about Hoagland, least of all the tenants. They came out and said: "Please God, can we move somewhere else?" Suddenly the Housing Commission discovered it had empty flats all over the place. Hoagland got flattened inside a month.'

I said, 'So it wouldn't be likely that she was killed to stop her obstructing Hoagland's closure?'

Her eyes flicked around the room and came back to me. A little smile. 'Bit of an extreme step for the Housing Commission to take, don't you think?'

I told her how the witness against Danny had abandoned his old Renault and taken off in a sports car for a new life in Perth after the trial.

She listened with her chin on her hand. 'What does that suggest to you?'

'I don't know. I'm told Danny was unconscious near a pub miles from his car about half an hour before the car hit Anne Jeppeson. I'm groping around.'

'Why would anyone pay Ronnie Bishop to tell the lies that sent McKillop to jail?'

'Well, maybe it was the only way they could get the verdict,' I said.

'Are we talking about the cops?'

I poured some more wine. You don't get much waiter-pouring at Donelli's. 'It's possible. A drug squad cop called Scullin knew both Danny McKillop and Ronnie Bishop.'

Linda said, 'Let me get this straight. Someone wants a conviction for Anne Jeppeson's death. They use Bishop to frame McKillop. Is that right?'

'That's my extremely vague line of thought.'

'Let's move over to the "How". As I recall, Ronnie gave the cops the car rego that night and they ran the number and went to McKillop's place and found him asleep in the car. Blood all over the front.'

'That's right.'

'And then Ronnie identified McKillop in a line-up.'

'Yes.'

'So if McKillop is innocent, someone else drove the car? And planted him in it later?'

Our first course arrived: honey-cured salmon with a mild peppercorn sauce. This was very fast for the establishment. People had eaten their shoe-leather while waiting for their first courses at Donelli's. Donelly was obviously feeling some remorse about his outstanding debt and had given our order priority.

We talked about other things as we ate. Television, newspapers, the law. Linda had a sharp eye for a target and a spare, funny delivery, but she didn't give away much about herself.

There was no pause between dishes. Donelly himself, head like a sculpture in Virginia ham draped with seaweed, white jacket tight as a bandage on his fat torso, came out of the kitchen with the main course.

'If I may say so, Irish, it's impeccable taste you're showing dining with this lady, and she with you,' he said, eyes never leaving Linda. 'Not to mention your choice of establishment.'

'It chooses itself, Patrick,' I said. 'For many reasons.'

'All of them sound,' he replied. 'And you'll do me the honour of accepting a little libation I'll be sending over with the young fella.'

It was an old-fashioned Italian dish, chicken and veal risotto, the kind of thing you might cook yourself on a Sunday if you had someone to eat it with. Donelly's libation arrived, a bottle of Barolo by Giuseppe Contratio, ten years old.

Linda tasted it. 'Wow,' she said. 'They know you here.'

'Carnal knowledge,' I said. 'In a manner of speaking.'

We got back to Ronnie Bishop over coffee. Linda came back from the women's room, slid into her seat and said, 'Listen, Jack, let's say that the driver, let's say that McKillop was the target. Someone wanted him in jail and they framed him. So Anne was just unlucky.'

'Chosen at random, you mean?' I said.

'Yes. They had to knock someone down at a certain time of night, in a certain area. And she was there. Could've been anybody.'

'It's hard to see why anyone would go to that trouble to put Danny inside. Easier to knock him off.'

She nodded. Tips of hair slipped around and touched the corner of her mouth. She was faintly flushed from the wine. I found her very attractive and she knew it. 'Maybe the Hoagland tenants saw their chances of escaping from the ghastly place slipping away and put out a contract on Anne Jeppeson,' she said. 'And whoever did the job decided to give Danny the credit.'

We laughed. I poured the last of the wine. 'Can we do this again?' I said. 'Are you free to do this kind of thing?'

She looked at me with a half-smile still on her face. 'You mean eat and drink?'

'That or whatever else takes your fancy.'

'You're asking me if I'm involved with someone else?'

'In my awkward and out-of-practice way.'

'I'm free to do this kind of thing but I don't think I've been much use to you,' she said. 'Can I ask you something?'

'Sure.'

'Why are you going over all this ancient stuff?'

It was the question I'd been putting off thinking about. 'I'm not sure,' I said after a pause. 'Part of it's guilt. I'm not sure that I gave Danny a fair shake when I represented him. I was either drunk or monumentally hungover for all that time. It was just after my wife's death. That's not an excuse. That's just the way it was. I didn't ask any questions about the evidence against Danny. The cops got the bloke to trial in an amazingly short time, jumped all the queues. His wife tells me he told her they fed him pills from his arrest onwards. I didn't know that. But I wouldn't have noticed at the time.'

I stopped talking. I could have gone on for a bit but I was just thinking aloud.

Linda smiled at me. 'Sounds like a good enough reason,' she said. 'I've got to go. I've got a running engagement at 6 a.m. Call me next week. I'll think about Anne Jeppeson.'

'Noise? I'm in Hoddle Street. In the mother of all fucken jams, that's the noise. What's the name of that fucken street you're in?'

I told Senior Sergeant Tregear.

'Be there in, I don't fucken know. I'll hoot for you. Gimme a word outside.'

Ten minutes later, he hooted. I went outside. He was in a blue Falcon fifty metres down the street, half on the kerb. When I got close I saw his eyes in the rear-view mirror. He raised his left arm and pointed to the passenger side. I got in. The car was warm and smelt of cigarette smoke and Chinese food.

'Jack,' Barry Tregear said. He was wearing a blue suit, a green shirt and a violet tie, all tired looking. 'What's with the fucken overalls? Joined the working class now?'

'Helping out,' I said. I didn't feel like explaining.

Barry took a packet of Newport off the dash and extracted a cigarette with his teeth. He lit it with a throw-away lighter.

'I got two minutes,' he said. 'Jack, listen, this McKillop business. Can I give you a word of advice?'

'Everyone else does.'

He took a deep draw, puckered his lips and blew a thin jet of smoke up past his nose. 'I'd give it a miss if I were you.'

'Why's that?'

'I don't think it's something you want to get mixed up in now. Sensitive business these days, cops shooting people. Wait for the inquest.'

'That doesn't answer the question,' I said.

'Trust me, mate. I've got your interests at heart.'

'I'll think about it. Did you get hold of Scullin?'

Barry nodded. 'Not easy. He's a busy man.'

'I thought you said he'd gone fishing.'

'Just a manner of speaking. He's a smart fella. Runs some kind of security business now. Makes big bucks.'

'What did he say about McKillop?'

'He says he never talks about police business.' Barry wound down his window and flicked the cigarette stub out. It landed on the bonnet of a car on the other side of the street.

'That's all?'

'That's all.'

'You drove around here to tell me that?'

'No. I wanted to tell you something else.'

'What's that?'

'Jack,' he said, 'don't ask me any more questions about McKillop. Okay?'

Ronnie Bishop's mother lived deep in working-class Brunswick. But even here the first seeker after capital gains had appeared. Right next door. The humble weatherboard dwelling had been given a picket fence, brick paving, two silver birches, a paint job and a brass ship's bell. Mrs Bishop's cottage appeared to be trying to lean on the newly straightened frame of its facelifted neighbour.

Mrs Bishop looked at me long and hard from behind a security gate after I introduced myself. Behind her the house was dark. She was probably in her seventies, small, sharp-featured, well-preserved and dressed like someone going out.

'I rang about Ronnie,' I said.

She held up a hand. 'Sorry to stare. You look like my sister's late boyfriend. Now there was a devil. Come in.'

We went down a dark passage, two doors on each side. She opened a door at the end and light flooded in. Beyond was a large new section, the width of the house, with full-length windows looking on to a paved terrace crammed with greenery.

'This is nice,' I said, looking at the glossy sealed floor-boards, the newish upholstered chairs and sofa. Next door wasn't the only place on the street that had been smartened up.

'Ronnie paid for it,' she said. 'Sent me to Noosa for two weeks, rained all the time, never mind that. Came back,

I nearly fell over, I can tell you. Opened the door and there it was, new furniture, everything. Like a dream, really. Sit down. I've just made some tea.'

There were biscuits too, bought biscuits but nice, on an EPNS server in the shape of a giant leaf.

'Nice and warm, isn't it,' Mrs Bishop said. We were both sitting on the sofa. 'Ronnie put in the central heating. Before that I used to sit on a hot water bottle with my feet on another one some days. Cold as a mother-in-law's kiss, my late husband used to say.'

'You said on the phone that Ronnie was depressed…'

Mrs Bishop looked away and when she answered all the cheerfulness had gone out of her voice. 'Ronnie has AIDS, Mr Irish.' Tears began to run down her powdery cheek, turning pink in the clear light from outside. I felt deeply helpless. I cleared my throat.

'Do you think that had something to do with his disappearance?'

She turned back to me, shaking her head. 'I don't know. When I went to the police, they didn't seem interested after I told them Ronnie was…was sick.'

'How long was he going to stay in Melbourne, Mrs Bishop?'

'Only a few days. Then he said he had to see someone and he'd be back soon. And he didn't come back. And I've heard nothing. He wouldn't do that.'

'Why did he come to Melbourne?'

'To see someone. And to see his mum, of course. He's a lovely boy, Mr Irish. There's no harm in him.'

'Yes, I'm sure. Did he see the person?'

Mrs Bishop tidied her hair. 'I don't know, Mr Irish. But he said something to me a few days before he disappeared.'

I nodded helpfully.

'He said, "Mum, if anything happens to me I'm insured for two hundred thousand dollars and most of it goes to you." And then he said something else.'

She put both hands on my sleeve. 'He said, my blood went cold, Mr Irish, he said, "Mum, if I turn up dead somewhere don't ever believe it was my own fault." That's what he said. He was standing over there by the window. He'd been walking around the house for hours. Just smoking cigarettes and walking around.'

'You told the police this?'

'Of course. I told the lady policeman, Miss Ryan. She wrote it all down.'

'Mrs Bishop, do you know any reason why anyone would want to harm Ronnie?'

She looked out of the window again. 'No.'

'And you don't know who the person was he came to see?'

'No, I don't. Ronnie never talked about himself, Mr Irish. Doug always said Ronnie would make a good spy.'

'Did he take anything with him that day?'

'No. Nothing. Everything he brought is here. I even found a CD he'd brought for me. Didn't say a word, just slipped it into my rack. Just like him. He gave me a kiss and said he was going out for a while and he didn't come back. I wanted to put a bandaid on the scratch on his cheek but he didn't want me to.'

'He had a scratch on his cheek?'

She nodded. 'He said he scratched it on a hedge on his way to the corner shop to buy cigarettes.' She looked at me as if something had just occurred to her. 'You're not a policeman yourself are you, Mr Irish? Two policemen came and had a really good look around. I'm not sure what they were looking for.'

'No, Mrs Bishop. I'm a lawyer. I was involved in a trial years ago where Ronnie was a witness. There's been some new developments lately and I thought Ronnie might be able to help with some information.'

'I'm sure he'd be delighted to help,' she said. 'Did you know he was a social worker once? Helping the poor homeless children on the streets. Of course, what he really wanted to do was make films. Ronnie loved films. He saved up to buy a movie camera. He was always filming things.'

'Was he a trained social worker, Mrs Bishop?'

'Well, not really. He was a clever boy and he started at Melbourne University but he didn't really settle down. Doug and I were living in Queensland then, for Doug's health. Not that it improved. He missed the football so much, you know, I think it lowered his resistance.'

'So Ronnie was a paid social worker, was he?'

'Oh yes. He worked for the Safe Hands Foundation. They help the homeless.'

I'd never heard of the foundation but that didn't mean anything. 'Why did Ronnie move to Perth, Mrs Bishop?'

She pondered this for a moment. 'I don't know, really. Just wanted to go somewhere else, I suppose. Young people are like that, today, aren't they?'

Ronnie was always going to be a young person to his

mum. 'He bought a new car before he left. That must have been expensive.'

She smiled. 'He won some money on the Lotto. He took me to Georges to buy a winter coat. I've still got it. Beautiful. He's such a generous boy.'

It was time to go. Mrs Bishop came to the front gate with me. In front of the house next door, a man in a dark double-breasted suit was leaning against a BMW, talking into a mobile phone. He gave Mrs Bishop a wave: five stiff fingers moved from side to side. He'd be making her an offer for the house any day now. I said I was sure Ronnie would be in touch soon, gave her my card, shook her small hand, and left.

I went back to my office and brooded for a while. Ronnie Bishop came to Melbourne a worried man. Perhaps his friend Charles Lee, the man who'd answered his telephone, could tell me why. He certainly wasn't going to tell me on the phone. That meant going to Perth. I didn't want to go to Perth. Did I owe it to Danny? What did I owe Danny, anyway? Bloody something. I phoned Veneto Travel.

'Perth?' said Shane DiSanto. He had recently inherited the business from his uncle Carlo. It was a big change from panel beating.

'Put Denise on, Shane,' I said.

'Jack, Jack, Jack, I'm the boss here now. You're talking to the owner. I can handle this. What you want to go to Perth for? You don't go to Perth in winter. I can do you Hamilton

Island. You can't live at home and eat McDonald's for what I can do it. Dirt, Jack, dirt. Are you listening?'

Shane eventually agreed to let me go to Perth and made the booking. I rang Linda Hillier and left a message on her machine. Then I considered ringing Charles Lee and decided against it.

When I went to pick up the ticket at the airport, they'd never heard of me. I rang Veneto and got Denise.

'You're lucky it's only Perth,' she said. 'He made all the bookings for Frank La Bianca's daughter's honeymoon. High season in Florence. Lucky couple had to have sanctified root numero uno in the back seat of the Hertz car.'

I hired a Corolla in midair from a steward called David. He thought a person like me would be happier with a BMW. So did I.

It takes hours to get to Perth, flying over the huge shark-infested dent in the continent called the Great Australian Bight. And when you get there, you're two hours in the past. I didn't know Perth; it was just an airport on the way to Europe. They tell me the locals have secessionist tendencies. I can understand that. Judging by the accents, they'll probably have a fight over whether to rename the State Manchester or Birmingham.

It was a sunny day in Perth, insignificant wisps of cloud decorating a sky the colour of old blue jeans. I studied the map book for about ten minutes and set off for Fremantle. On paper, getting there was a matter of keeping to the high-roads. On land, however, the Corolla had a tendency to wander off the beaten track. On my second sighting of the same pub I stopped for lunch and directions. I sat out in the beer garden with a bottle of Swan Lager and a big piece of charred West Australian steer. Around me the locals, mostly Britons with flaking skins wearing towelling hats, were being enthusiastic about the chances of the West Coast Eagles against Carlton. I thought it would be nice if they both lost but this wasn't the place to say it.

After lunch, I took some counsel from one of the Poms and went off driving again. By the time I found Fremantle I had a fair idea of Perth. It was a huge suburb built on sand dunes around a shallow estuary. The upmarket bits had more dark-green vegetation and more trees. I went through the city centre with its standard collection of glass towers and roughly followed the course of the Swan River to its mouth, which is the port of Fremantle.

Fremantle looked like an English Channel port transported to the Mediterranean; handsome Victorian stone buildings looking slightly uneasy in the hard light. There were plenty of signs of the tourist trappings that had made the place so dangerous during the America's Cup challenge, but it also felt like a working harbour.

I had a good cup of coffee in a place full of voluble Italians and people with time to read a book in the middle of the day, walked around the fishing harbour, visited the maritime museum, browsed in a bookshop, had another cup of coffee.

Ronnie Bishop's house was two or three blocks back from the waterfront, a sandstone dwelling in a street of smart revamped houses. It had two young palms in front, high walls blocking off the neighbours and a severe wrought-iron fence with spear tops. Morton Street, Clifton Hill, this was not.

The front door was a nice piece of woodwork, a rich, dark jarrah frame with panels of pine oiled to a dark honey colour. I pressed a brass button in a brass plate and heard the chime. No-one came. I took a walk up the street. The house next door bore a brass plate saying Souter & Whale, Architects. I was back in the car reading a novel I'd bought called *The Means of Grace* when a white Honda Civic drew up outside Ronnie's address and a man in jeans and white golf shirt got out. He checked Ronnie's mailbox, unlocked the front door and went inside, leaving it open. He was out again in minutes and set about watering the garden.

I got out of the Corolla and went over to the fence. He caught sight of me approaching.

'You must be Charles,' I said.

He was a tall man, early forties, light tan, thin and fit-looking. What remained of his hair was close-cropped. He looked like the mature outdoor male in an advertisement.

'Yes,' he said, warily. He held the hose as if ready to water me.

'I'm Jack Irish, the lawyer from Melbourne. I rang you about Ronnie.'

His face relaxed.

'You've come a long way,' he said. 'Let's go inside.'

I followed him though a small hallway with a highly polished floor into a sitting room furnished in a dark masculine style. He opened the curtains and we sat down in Morris chairs.

'Well,' he said, 'I'm very worried. I didn't know anything until I rang his mum about the break-in.'

'The break-in?'

'Last Wednesday. We've cleaned up, but my God, the mess.'

'What did they get?'

'My dear, they walked off with the weirdest stuff. And they took housekeeping money as far as I can tell. Ronnie told me he'd left it in the usual place, which is under the breakfast cereals. Not a lot. I think it's a hundred dollars. Mrs G says it's not there.'

'They gave the place a going over, did they?'

'Certainly did, my God! The study you would not believe. A shambles. All Ronnie's business papers on the floor, all the books off the shelves, all the drawers out of the desk.'

I said, 'Charles, why would Ronnie disappear?'

He shook his head. 'Jack—may I call you Jack?—I can't think of any reason why. He's been very, very depressed, of course, but…' He looked away into the middle distance.

'Why was that?'

'Well, business has been terrible, for one thing.'

'What business is that?'

'Ronnie's in video. It's suffered with the rest of the economy. And he put a lot of capital into some compact disc venture. CD-ROM. Very high tech. A mystery to me.' He put his right hand to his mouth. 'I haven't even offered you a drinky. I generally have a G and T around this time.'

I accepted a gin and tonic. It came large, with a smudge of bitters. Charles folded a leg under him as he sat down.

'Ronnie's mother says he has AIDS, Charles.'

He sighed. 'The dear old girl. That's simply not true.

Ronnie is HIV-positive. There's a big difference, you know. He'll probably outlive us all.'

'Did he think that way?'

He eyed me like a dog show judge. After a while, he said, 'I'm not sure that I understand what's going on.'

'Going on?'

'Going on. Something's going on and I'm the poor bunny in the middle of it.'

'Well, as I said on the phone, I'm interested in talking to Ronnie about evidence he gave in a trial in Melbourne years ago.'

'You must be very interested to come to Perth to ask me questions.'

I shrugged. 'I'm feeling a bit driven. And Ronnie's the only person who can help me. If I knew a bit more about him, I might be able to find him.'

Charles looked at his nails. Clean, pink, blunt nails. 'Well,' he said, 'ask away.'

'Why did he go to Melbourne?'

'He said he had to see someone.'

'Do you know what about?'

'I'd only be guessing.'

'Even a guess might help.'

'There were phone calls from Melbourne.'

I waited. Charles sipped his drink. There was a beautiful sunset going on outside. I could see a coral glow on the wall of the neighbour's house. You don't see sunsets in Melbourne in winter. It isn't even clear to me that the sun rises in Melbourne in winter.

'A man rang twice.'

'Was that unusual?'

'Yes. To ring here, that was unusual. I stop in on my way from work every day and give the garden a sprinkle, that sort of thing. It'd die if it was left to Ronnie. He doesn't come home until all hours, so I listen to the answering machine and I ring him at the shop if it's anything he needs to know about. The only person who calls from Melbourne is his mum and she generally rings on Sunday mornings.'

'What did the man say?'

'He said he needed to speak to Ronnie urgently. I rang Ronnie and gave him the message. Twice.'

'Did he say anything?'

Charles was silent again for a while. He was still at war with himself about answering my questions.

'The first time he said something like, "Oh, Christ, no". Something like that.'

'The man gave a name and a number to ring?'

'Yes.'

'Can you remember the name?'

'I'm afraid not. I'm hopeless about names. It'd be on the tape.'

I felt a small flush of excitement. 'You've got the answering machine tape?'

'No. The burglars took all the tapes. They took all the CDs too, but you can understand that. Ronnie didn't wipe any answering machine tapes. He just put in a new tape. Some of them have got messages that go on for half an hour or more, my dear. He's got these weird girlfriends. They don't seem to want to talk to him. They just pour out all this drivel about men and shopping and films to the machine.'

'But all the tapes were here?'

'Yes. They were all in the phone table drawer. The burglars dumped the drawer on the floor, my dear. Gave it a kick too, by the look of things. Pens and stuff everywhere. They took the tape out of the machine, too.'

I tried the name Danny McKillop on him.

'I can't say yes and I can't say no,' he said. 'I think it *was* an Irish sort of name. But I can't be sure.'

'Did Ronnie ever talk about his past?'

'Never. The man was like the Sphinx. Could've been born yesterday.'

What had Ronnie's mother said? *Doug always said he would make a good spy.*

'He never mentioned any names?'

Charles picked up his glass and stuck the tip of his tongue into the liquid. He looked at me over the rim. 'Not ever. I've been over all this before. I told the detectives that. They asked these questions. I told them the same thing. Ronnie simply did not talk about himself except in the vaguest way.'

'These were the detectives about the break-in?'

'Oh, absolutely not. That was PC Plod from the local station. These were men in plain clothes. Rather grubby plain clothes in the case of one of them.' He laughed, a light laugh, verging on the nervous.

'And they identified themselves as policemen?'

He didn't answer for a few seconds, turning a gold band with a single red stone in it on the little finger of his right hand. 'No,' he said. 'They didn't. They came to the door at home. It's just around the corner. My unit. About nine at night. Smelling, reeking of drink, if you don't mind. One expects more.'

'You assumed they were detectives?'

'Yes. I did. They were, I think. They had that manner. The smaller one took out some sort of notebook. He wasn't small, mind you. The opposite. Just small*er*. He said something like: "It's in connection with the disappearance of someone you know. Ronald Bishop. We'd like to ask you some questions."'

I savoured the last of my drink. 'Can I get the timing sorted out?' I said. 'This visit was after the break-in?'

'Two days after. Mrs G and I had spent hours cleaning up and then I came home, utterly drained I can tell you, and I'd had a shower and slipped into a gown and there they were pounding on the door.'

'What did they want to know?'

'Refill time,' Charles said. His drink was hardly touched but he took both glasses away. I took out my notebook, full of horse observations, and made a few entries. When he came back, Charles sat on the edge of his chair, glass held in both hands.

'All they were interested in, Jack, was what Ronnie had told me about going to Melbourne,' he said. 'Names. They wanted to know any names he'd mentioned. And they wanted to know what he'd told me about his life in Melbourne before he came to Perth.' He leaned towards me. 'They were very crude, Jack. It upset me. I'm not used to that sort of thing. Not at all. I'd have complained if I'd thought it would do any good.'

'Crude in what way?'

Charles made sure we had strong eye contact. 'The smaller one said: "You poofs tell each other everything, don't you? What did your boyfriend tell you about Melbourne?" Those were his words, Jack. Chock full of hatred, I can tell you. Almost spitting. And that is not the nature of our relationship at all. It is not physical.'

I nodded. 'How did you respond?'

He shrugged. 'I said Ronnie was a good friend and that he told me nothing about his early life and never mentioned names. And I said I'd like to have my lawyer present.'

'And then?'

'He became quite chummy in a nauseating sort of way and said they didn't have any more questions. Then he asked if Ronnie had given me anything to look after for him. I said I didn't want to answer any more questions and he said: "Answer me, cockbreath." Those were his words. I felt scared. I said no he had not and would they please leave. And they did. Just walked out without another word.'

'They never said anything about a court case long ago, in Melbourne?'

'No. Nothing like that.'

'Did Ronnie ever speak of giving evidence against someone?'

Charles was looking into his drink. 'No. You don't think they were policemen, do you, Jack?'

'It's hard to tell, Charles. If they come around again, don't let them in. Say you have to get dressed, something's on the stove, anything, and phone the police emergency number and say you're being attacked. Then phone your lawyer.'

'I don't really have a lawyer,' he said.

'Get one.'

I finished my drink, gave him my telephone numbers, and he gave me his.

At the front gate, I asked, 'Charles, would you call Ronnie a trustworthy person?'

He clicked the gate closed behind me. Another sigh, this one much deeper. He put his hands in his pockets and looked at the gatepost.

'No,' he said sadly. 'He didn't tell you much, but what he did was almost all lies. Even when it didn't matter a fig. Variety. That's all he wanted. New bodies, new sensations. Boys. Girls. Didn't matter to him. He got beaten up quite often. Once in this house by some little thug he was tying up. Face swollen like a pumpkin. Kicked in the head, all the money in the house taken, VCR, CDs. I had to take him to casualty. I thought that was what had happened when his mum rang me. That he was probably lying in some public toilet.'

'Did he need money?'

'I think so. He'd borrowed nearly five thousand dollars from me. They refused his American Express card at Latino's the day before he went. I paid for the meal with my card. And there's trouble about this house. It's going to be sold by the bank.'

'How did he get that way?'

Charles shook his head. He looked much older now, less firm of face. 'I honestly don't know, Jack,' he said. 'He didn't tell me and I wouldn't have dreamed of asking.'

We shook hands. I liked him. He clearly deserved better than Ronnie Bishop. Burdett-Bishop.

'Why did he stick the Burdett on his name?' I asked.

Charles sighed and looked heavenwards. 'He was thinking of going into real estate and he thought it sounded impressive.'

I went in search of lodgings, thankful that I'd bought a book.

A weak sun was shining on Melbourne, but to compensate a marrow-chilling wind was blowing. I rang the security parking garage and they sent their little bus to collect me.

'Jetsetting again,' the driver said. 'You joined that Mile High Club yet?'

He was an ex-cop called Col Boon, pensioned off the force for extreme hypertension after shooting another cop during a raid on an indoor dope plantation in Coburg. A tragic mistake, the coroner said. I suppose in some ways it's always a tragic mistake to shoot the man who's rooting your wife every time you're on nightshift and he's not.

'The club reckons I couldn't stand the excitement of high-altitude copulation,' I said.

Col made an animal noise. 'Tell 'em you'll do it sitting down. You growing a beard?'

I felt my two-day growth. 'Stewies like a bit of hair,' I said.

He shook his head. 'Bit? Seen less hair on pussies.' He took a corner with a squeal of balding tyres. 'Talking pussies, you want to pick your stewie. Mate of mine put his hand in the golden triangle, found a big cock. Qantas I think it was.'

I pondered the significance of this story. My maternal grandmother apparently addressed stewardesses as 'waitress'. She would not have taken well to the idea that some of them were, in fact, waiters.

At the parking garage, Col said, 'There's a bit of a problem with your car. That grease monkey rang. Says he took your motor to pieces and he can't put it together again till he can find parts. Two weeks, minimum.'

I groaned. This was what happened when you left your ancient Lark for a service with a backyard mechanic who was a Studebaker fanatic.

'Now you tell me. What am I supposed to do?' I said. 'Walk?'

'He says he's got an old Chevy you can use.'

'I hate old Chevies.'

'Well,' Col said, 'we've got a special on unclaimed vehicles this week. Nice Celica. Say two weeks, hundred and fifty.'

'You work this out together?'

He looked hurt.

I said, 'Throw in a full tank.'

'Give us a break. There's a good bit in it.' He gave me an appraising look. 'Had a call if your car was here.'

I waited.

'Your office. A girl.'

I shook my head.

'No. Well, this isn't the lost and found either. Told her you hadn't parked here for a while.'

'You give a complete service here, Col,' I said.

He handed me the keys. 'I'd say look after it like your own,' he said, 'but that's the last thing we want.'

I thought about Ronnie all the way to Fitzroy. I'd got the addresses from Charles and visited Ronnie's two video rental shops in the Perth suburbs. One was closed. The other was in a small shopping mall and it didn't look healthy. From behind a partition of grey tin shelves came the sobbing breaths, grunts, yells and urgings of a porno-graphic video and the jeers and cheers of a teenage audience. After a while, a sallow youth with a pigtail emerged and said, 'Yep?' It turned out he didn't know Ronnie but was standing in for his friend's friend, who sometimes worked in the shop.

At the workshop, Charlie was finishing up for the day, pottering around endlessly as usual—a dab of oil here, a wipe of a surface there, here a gentle opening and closing of a cabinet door, there a pull–push of a drawer. I gradu-ally worked him through the front doors like a sheepdog with a particularly difficult sheep. We drove around to the Prince of Prussia. Usually we walked, but Charlie's hip was hurting. I parked the Celica around the corner in a loading zone.

'No respect for the law,' Charlie said. 'That's where it all begins. *Und du bist rechtsgelehrt.*'

'Have a heart,' I said. 'It's only a little municipal regulation, shouldn't apply after 5 p.m.' When we were alone, Charlie often expressed his doubts and disappointments about me in German, language of my great-grandfather.

Wilbur Ong and Norm O'Neill were in position, beers, pies, *Herald Sun* form guides on the counter. They gave us the briefest acknowledgment.

'My feelin is we're lookin at a rerun of Kyneton twenty months ago,' said Norm. The peak of his flat cap rested on his spectacles, which rested on a nose of heroic size.

'Well, I've always loved yer feeling, darlin,' said Wilbur, 'but there's a lotta wishful here. He's bin five, seven, five first-up since then.'

''Course he has,' said Norm. 'That's why we're lookin at bloody forties here. Know it in my bones.'

'Relied on your bones,' Wilbur said, 'we'd be round the Salvos eatin rabbit stew.'

'Given these pies, that's not a frightenin thought,' said Norm. He turned to me. 'Jack, prepared to divulge yer thoughts on the gallops at Geelong?'

'People in the know treat my tips as scratchings,' I said. 'However, since it's you lot.'

Charlie Taub gave a snort and went off to talk football to a retired tram driver called Wally Pollard. Wally's only son, Bantam Pollard, ruined a promising career with Collingwood through bad timing. On a Friday night in 1975, the club president took six guests into the committee box to show them the ground's new floodlights. They came on, casting a cold white light on the playing field and on Bantam Pollard's spotty bottom. It was dead centre of the field, bracketed by the fleshy thighs of the president's sixteen-year-old daughter.

We were on race four when a man came in the street door. He was about fifty, bald, of below medium height, with a heavy body. RayBans sat on a darkly tanned bull-terrier face. He'd spent about three grand on his gear, most of it on gold chains and a golden brown leather jacket that fitted him like a condom. The style said Sydney or the Gold Coast; the walk, as if he were rolling a tennis ball between his upper thighs, said cop, probably vice squad.

Stan the barman was at the far end of the counter. He exchanged a few words with Mr Gold Coast and then came down to our end of the bar.

'Bloke's asking for Jack,' he said, looking at Wilbur. 'What'll I tell him?'

'Tell him I'll be along in a minute,' I said. I lingered for a minute or two and then walked down the bar.

Stan had served Mr Gold Coast something with tonic. At my approach, he smiled at me, a lip lift to show lavatory-white capped teeth. It conveyed no more sentiment than a facial tic. He put out a hand.

'Jack. Tony Baker.' The hand exerted no pressure; a hand that felt to be made of one-inch brass plumbing fittings didn't need to do anything other than Be.

'What can I do for you?' I said.

'Have a drink with me.'

'I've got one waiting.'

'You do work among the elderly. That's nice.' He swallowed the contents of his glass and rapped it on the counter several times. Stan responded to the summons by leaving the room.

Tony Baker edged closer to me. The top of his head came up to my chin. This gave me all the physical confidence the giraffe feels when it meets the rhino. He showed me his teeth again.

'Clubby here, am I right? No risk of anyone wanting to join though, mate. Well, this isn't a social occasion. I'm here to straighten a coupla things out.'

'Such as?'

'Such as your getting in the way of an official investigation.'

'Of what?'

'Of a number of matters, one of which touches Mr Ronald Bishop.'

'What do you mean, touches?'

Tony Baker put his hand to his muscular sausage of a neck and turned his head a few centimetres to each side. 'Jack,' he said, speaking softly, 'you don't want to know, right? If you get in the way of this investigation you'll get squashed so fucken flat they'll post you.'

'Who'll squash me?' I asked.

His eyes went hard. I noticed a small gold fleck in the right iris. 'You're not listening, Jack. I'm telling you to back off, drop it. This matter is at a very high level, a national level. I've said too much now.'

'Have you got some identification?' I realised I should have asked earlier.

Tony Baker closed his eyes and sighed. 'Can I get this across to you without a map? You don't want to know anything about me. Take it as gospel: you are obstructing an

113

official operation. Pull your head in, forget about Mr Bishop, or you'll wish it was you that cunt blew up in the carpark. Just fucken butt out.'

He left. I went back to the form but couldn't concentrate. At six-thirty, Charlie's granddaughter, the lovely Augustine, hooted outside. I went out with him. It was intensely cold after the warmth of the pub and the air had the burnt petrol smell of winter cities everywhere.

Charlie got into the car and wound down the window. 'Eat some proper food,' he said. 'You need someone to look after you.'

I put my hand on his shoulder. 'Maybe you can talk your driver here into marrying me. It's all indoor work.'

'Let's talk pay and conditions,' Gus said. She was a trade union official.

Charlie snorted. 'Go,' he said to Gus. 'Some men you don't want in your family.'

I stood in the street and considered whether to go back into the pub and settle down or to go home. I decided to go home. I've learned to take the hard decisions.

The apartment was cold, the bulb in the bathroom had fused and the fridge smelled of five-day-old fish. Cam, Wootton and my daughter were on the answering machine. Claire said: *Listen, Jack, I'm just ringing to say I miss you and I'll be down for a visit soon. I might bring Eric to set your mind at rest. Your letter sounds glum. Don't be. Love you. Bye.*

I made a stiff Jameson's and soda and rang Linda Hillier. She wasn't in the office.

Hardhills was a shop, a garage and a weatherboard pub at a churned-up crossroads. The nearest town of any size was thirty kilometres away. In between, it was all low sky, wet sheep and ponds in every hollow.

There were three utes outside the pub. Harry Strang eased the BMW to a stop beside the shop and switched off. He looked at his watch.

We sat in silence for five minutes. I was thinking about Ronnie Bishop. Cam was reading the *Sporting Globe*. Harry had his eyes closed, head back on the rest. Then he said, 'Now this fella Rex Tie, supposed to meet us out here twelve sharp, he's sittin in the pub over there with this other fella we've come to see. Talkin horses. Couple of the yokels no doubt waterin the tonsils. Publican's hangin about. Rex's takin the view that we'll come in, have a few gargles first.'

'Sounds reasonable,' I said.

'Not in this line of work,' Harry said. 'Thought I'd schooled Rex the last time. Easier to train a horse.'

At 12.15, two men came out of the pub. One of them, a gangling figure in a battered half-length Drizabone, came over to the car. At his approach, Harry pressed the button and his window slid down. The man bent down to look in. He had a long, sad, middle-aged face, much of it nose.

'Sorry, Harry,' he said. 'Thought you might come in for a quick one.'

Harry looked at him. 'Rex, you've forgotten.'

Rex straightened up and then he came down again. 'Jeez, Harry, have a heart. This is bloody Hardhills. There's only about four people.'

'That's four too many, Rex. Drive. We'll follow.'

Rex and the other man got into their utes and drove off, the other man in front. We followed at a distance.

'Harry, why do you need a lawyer for driving around the Western District?' I asked. The question had been on my mind for some time.

He gave me a quick look. 'The yokels've got a lot of respect for lawyers, Jack. Doesn't hurt to show them one. That bloke up front, he's got a horse called Dakota Dreaming, five years old, hasn't run for two years. Not that it ran much before that either. What's the 'rithmetic, Cam?'

'Seven, one, one,' said Cam. He was studying the landscape out of the side window.

'Five-year-old. Seven races. Now that's what I call lightly raced,' Harry said. 'And the reason is, Jack, the animal's got a horrible record, truly horrible. Lucky he's not in the pet's mince or got a big copper's bum on him. The fella up there, he's owner number four, and number three made him a gift of the horse. Gratis and for nothing. He's put two years into patchin up the beast and he reckons it's got one or two big runs in it. Tell Jack the history, Cam.'

Cam looked around. 'He's bred for staying. Third highest price for a yearling in New Zealand in his year. Won his first race by seven lengths. Then Edgar Charlton bought him for a fair bit for a dentists' syndicate. First time out he ran seventh against a good field, pulled up lame. Out for seventeen weeks. Came back at Sandown in December, second in a bunch of spring leftovers. Tendon trouble, twenty weeks off. March at Caulfield. Ninth out of thirteen. Ballarat three weeks later. Stone last. Bleeding. Took the compulsory count. The dentists spit the dummy, sold him. Turned out twice for the third owner for one sixth and one last.'

'Fella trains over near Colac,' Harry said. 'John Nisbet. Gave our friend up ahead the horse with a bowed tendon on his near side and bone chips in both front legs. A dead loss.'

'With respect, this outing doesn't look like an investment to me,' I said.

'Shake,' said Cam.

'Won't hurt to have a look,' Harry said. 'Old Rex's no Rhodes Scholar but he's not Curly Joe.'

The front vehicle turned right. A rutted track ran around the gentle eastern slope of a round-topped hill. At the foot of the northern slope were a farmhouse, stables, assorted sheds, a round yard. Horses in rugs were standing around looking bored in half a dozen paddocks. About a hundred metres from the buildings, the front driver pulled half off the track, got out and opened a gate. He waved us through.

Rex parked next to a shed and Harry pulled up beside him. We all got out and put on our coats. The north wind had ice in it.

'Christ, Harry,' said Cam, 'can't we do this in the summer? Bloody nun's nipple.'

The lead driver parked next to the farmhouse. All the buildings except the stables were old but the place was kept up; fresh paint, taut wire, raked gravel. As we got out of the ute, a boy of about fourteen appeared at the front door of the house.

Harry introduced us to Rex and when the other man came over, Rex said, 'Tony Ericson, this is Harry Strang, Cam Delray, and Harry's lawyer, Jack Irish.'

We shook hands. Tony was jockey size but too heavy, lined face, thick dark hair cut short, big ears.

'Never thought I'd meet you,' he said to Harry. 'Me dad used to say, "Think you're Harry Strang?" when we tried some flash riding.'

'How's your dad?' asked Harry.

Tony Ericson cocked his head. 'You remember me dad? He always said he knew you.'

'Ray Ericson,' Harry said. 'Still goin?'

Tony Ericson shook his head.

Harry patted his arm briskly. 'Sorry to hear it. Ray could get a camel to jump. Now what's the story?'

Tony Ericson looked at Rex Tie. 'You want to, Rex...'

'You go,' Rex Tie said.

'Let's get down the stables,' Tony said. 'I brung the horse in. Lives outside normal. Bugger's had enough soft in his life.'

We went down a gravel path, through a gate and round the corner of a long cinderblock stable building. There were eight stalls but only one horse. It was waiting for us, brown head turned our way, nostrils steaming.

Tony said, 'Rex tell you his name's Dakota Dreamin? We call him Slim.'

The horse snickered as we approached. Tony stroked his nose and fed him something.

'They say he was a deadset mongrel, kickin, bitin, but we never seen it. Like a lamb. Me girl looks after him, ten-year-old.' He looked behind us and said, 'Tom, shake hands with the gentlemen. This is me boy Tom, waggin school. He'll give the horse a little hit out.'

The boy from the front door came up and shook hands awkwardly. Someone other than a barber had given him a recent haircut. He was going to be too big for a jockey.

We walked down a road between paddocks and over a small rise. Below us, invisible from the stables, was a training track. You could smell the watermelon scent of new-mown grass before you saw it.

'Two thousand four hundred metres,' said Tony Ericson. 'Got a twelve hundred metre chute over there.' He pointed to the left. 'Starting gate. Same grass as Flemington. Bloke done it in the sixties. Went bang here. Used to have rails and all. Had sheep on it for twenty years but we mowed it and rolled it and it come up good.'

I looked at Harry. He had his hands in the jacket pockets of his leather-trimmed loden jacket and a faraway expression on his face.

He took a hand out and rubbed his chin. 'Very nice,' he said. 'Pride of the district, I imagine.'

'Don't follow,' said Tony.

'Other people use this?'

Tony shook his head. 'No trainers around here. We only cleaned it up bout a year ago. Whole thing, that is.'

We all turned at the sound of hoofs. The boy, Tom, walked Dakota Dreaming up to us. The horse shone like glass, groomed to a standard only achievable by ten-year-old girls. It had pristine bandages on all legs. I knew enough about condition to know this creature was well advanced in his preparation to race.

Tony held the horse's head. 'Remember what I said. Take him out to the seven furlong. I'll give you a bang. Don't push him. If he's feelin strong at the three hundred, let him go.'

The boy nodded and took the horse off. On the track, they went into an easy canter.

We walked along to where a big tin lollipop painted red marked the finish. Cam lit a cigarette, held it in the corner of his mouth while he fiddled with his stopwatch. Harry took out a small pair of binoculars and hung them around his neck. Tony Ericson put a blank into a starting pistol.

'Don't he mind the gun?' asked Rex Tie.

'Can't hardly hear it over there,' said Tony. 'He's ready. Light's flashin.' He raised the pistol above his head, waved it. The boy's right arm went up and down. Tony fired, a flat smack.

Tom set a nice pace, about what you'd expect for a front-runner over 1400 or 1600 metres on a country track. The straight was about 350 metres. When they came around the turn, you could see that the going was soft and that the horse was not entirely happy.

But the going wasn't going to stop Slim putting on a show. At the 300-metre mark, you could see Tom urge the horse with hands and heels. It didn't require much. With every appearance of enjoyment, the horse opened its stride, lowered its head and accelerated home. They went past the post flat out.

We stood in silence watching the boy, standing upright in the stirrups, slow the horse down.

Harry took off his hat and scratched his head. Cam was looking for a cigarette. Their eyes locked for a good three seconds.

'What's it say?' asked Harry.

Cam found a cigarette and lit it with his Zippo.

'For a stayer,' he said, 'smokin.'

Drew poured some red wine into our glasses, leant back and put his stockinged feet on the coffee table. 'You want my advice?'

Harry and Cam had dropped me off at home but I didn't go in. I'd been brooding all the way back from Hardhills and I felt the urge to talk to Drew. Once upon a time we'd talked to each other about all our problems.

I found him eating takeaway pizza over a pile of files in front of the fire in his house in Kew. The children were nowhere to be seen.

I said, 'Well. Yes.'

'Drop it. Forget Danny ever left the message. Take the gorilla's advice about this Bishop too. You've touched a nerve somewhere.'

'If I hadn't been three-quarters pissed years ago I'd have

tried to find out more about Danny's movements the night of the hit-and-run,' I said. 'I might have kept him out of jail.'

Drew chewed for a while, studying the flames. Finally he said, 'Bullshit, mate. Even if you'd been stone-cold sober and at the top of your form, it would never have occurred to you. You'd have pleaded him. You had to plead him. Since when do lawyers go looking for other explanations when the Crown's got a case like that? Don't kid yourself. There was no negligence there. There's nothing owing on your part.'

We sat in silence for a while, looking at the flames. A wind had come up and every now and again it made a hollow sound in the chimney.

'Remember that week fishing on the Delatite?' Drew asked. 'I reckon that was the best holiday of my adult life.'

'You've never said that before,' I said. 'We caught about three fish.'

'Didn't matter a bugger. It was great. It's all the kids seem to remember of their entire childhoods. Apart from the times I'm supposed to have been awful.'

I never thought about that trip. I'd curtained it off. It was the last holiday with Isabel.

'It was good,' I said. 'Like being a kid again.'

'Can't get enough of that.' Drew shifted in his chair. 'Listen, Jack, Danny was probably knocked for some drug scam. This other bloke, from what you say, was a candidate for doing something unpleasant. If there are feral cops involved, the next thing is that *you* have an accident.'

I nodded. I knew he was right. It was too late to do the right thing by Danny McKillop. The guilt that had taken me to Perth was pointless. With a sense of relief, I held out my wine glass.

'We'll just finish this drop in here,' said Drew, 'and then I want to show you a little 1978 shiraz off vines that were ninety years old then. Client gave me a case.'

I ended up sleeping in the spare room.

I put in the next day at Taub's, cutting a taper on and hand-morticing the legs of the boardroom table. It was soothing work for someone not feeling all that flash. Charlie didn't make tables any more unless he had to. Having me around meant he didn't have to. 'A table is pretty much a table,' he said. 'When you can't make a complete ruin.'

My cabinetmaking began as a kind of therapy on my way back from self-destruction. I can see that now. At the time it just seemed to happen. I noticed Charlie's workshop while looking at the old tailor's shop that is now my office. I went in on impulse. Sunlight was slanting in through the high windows, the air smelled of wood shavings and linseed oil and Charlie was at his workbench whistling while carving the back of a reproduction George III mahogany chair he was making to fill a gap in what the antique trade calls a long set. In that moment I fell in love with the idea of being a cabinetmaker. No such thought had ever entered my mind before. I knew absolutely nothing about woodwork. I went up to Charlie and said, 'I'll pay you to teach me something about making furniture.'

Charlie had given me his interested look and said, 'Three

things let me tell you. Number one, see a doctor. Number two, I'm too old to have an apprentice. Number three, you haven't got enough money.'

After I moved into my office, I began to hang around Taub's, making myself useful where I could. Charlie seemed to like the company. And he couldn't stop himself showing me how to do things.

Just before 4 p.m., the phone rang. It was switched through from my office. It was Mrs Bishop, Ronnie's mother.

'Mr Irish,' she said, 'I'm sorry to bother you but I'm so dreadfully worried about Ronnie. I've been going over everything in my mind and I remembered him making a phone call. Well, I went to the phone, it's in the passage, and looked at the little pad I keep there and there's two numbers written down. By Ronnie.'

I said, 'Good work, Mrs Bishop. Numbers mean anything to you?'

'No. I don't know them. I was going to ring them, but then I thought I'd ask you first. Should I tell the police? Would they be interested?'

'Let me ring them first,' I said. 'The police often take some time to get around to things.'

I took down the numbers and went around to my office. I had a feeling about the first number. My scratchpad was beside the phone and on it a number was circled.

The first number was Danny McKillop's.

I sat down and dialled the second number. The phone rang two or three times and then a voice said, 'Father Gorman's residence.'

It was another sour day, full of wind and rain. It took a long time to get across the city to the address Father Rafael Gorman had given me. The urban planners wrecked the traffic flow when they turned Swanston Street, once Melbourne's spine, into some kind of half-baked pedestrian mall. Urban planners are people who know best. They should make them all marry social workers.

I sat in the jams and listened to Claude Haynes, the afternoon man on the ABC, interview the Premier. Like most men on the ABC, Claude had started out to be a clergyman but tossed in the frock after going a couple of rounds with God in the seminary. I don't know whether the experience of the religious life left these people sadder but it certainly left them believing they were wiser than anyone else.

'Premier,' Claude said, making it sound like an assumed name, 'the Opposition leader says you and your Planning Minister, Mr Pitman, are turning the State into a paradise for carpetbaggers and quick-buck artists. How do you respond to that?'

'With a smile,' said Dr Marcia Saunders, no trace of amusement in her voice. 'Mr Kerr has no commercial experience and no commercial sense. He wouldn't know a carpetbagger from the chairman of the Reserve Bank.'

Claude said, 'Mr Kerr gave AM a list of what he called "Projects for the Pals" this morning—Yarra Cove, the Footscray Sportsdome, the new privately run remand centre and several others. He says they are all being developed by government pals. Are the developers your pals?'

'Mr Kerr should know about pals,' Dr Saunders replied.

'He's got where he is because of pals. If he'd had to rely on brains or ability, he'd still be teaching geography in primary school.'

With the delighted air of someone who thinks he's trapped Wittgenstein in a logical error, Claude said, 'That doesn't answer my question: Are these developers your pals?'

There was a long silence. Then Marcia said, voice laden with menace, 'Mr Haynes, you shouldn't act as a frontman for these has-beens. If Mr Kerr has any evidence of favouritism, he should produce it. Let me assure the people of this State that this government doesn't do favours. It assesses projects and people purely on merit. It follows all processes and procedures to the letter. The developments you've named are both sound commercial propositions and job creators for this State. The people behind them are highly experienced and astute operators who can be relied upon to do a good job. Are you suggesting anything to the contrary?'

Claude cleared his throat. 'But are some of the developers supporters of your party?'

You could hear Marcia's sigh. It combined disbelief with contempt. 'Are you and Mr Kerr proposing that supporters of a governing party should be excluded from commercial life?' she said. Each word was coated with scorn.

Claude's tone went sugary. 'I think you're shooting the messenger here, Dr Saunders,' he said. 'I'm merely—'

'Don't try to hide behind the messenger argument,' snapped Marcia. 'You media leftovers from the sixties are seldom *merely* doing anything. But you might try to make your agenda a little less obvious.'

It went on like this. Claude kept trying to wrap himself in the rags of his dignity and Marcia kept tearing them off. I enjoyed Claude's discomfort but there was something chilling about Dr Marcia Saunders, PhD in physical education from the University of Kansas and former stockbroker. She wasn't the same person who'd smiled down from the election billboards.

After half an hour of traffic snarl, I'd had enough. I did a savage left turn in the face of traffic into a one-way street. One crime led to another, I had a few altercations and near-misses but I got to Father Gorman's address near Albert Park Lake with all the paint on.

I parked in a no-parking zone. Col Boon could knock a fellow cop and get the pension, he could beat parking tickets on this Celica.

Father Gorman's address was an oddly tapering new building. The tenants weren't short of space: there were eight floors and only six brass plates on the plinth outside. The one for the sixth floor said: Safe Hands Foundation.

The name meant something to me. I remembered as I reached the glass doors: Ronnie Bishop had once worked for the Safe Hands Foundation. Helping homeless children, his mother had said. *Trying to root them* had been the view of his former neighbour in Morton Street.

The tenants were fussy about who came to visit them. A security man with a snub nose, pale eyes and skin the colour of dirty underclothing kept me captive between two sets of glass doors while he wrote down my particulars on a clipboard. A tattoo peeped out from under his wristwatch. He wasn't too flash at writing.

Then he wanted my driver's licence.

'I'm not trying to cash a cheque here, sonny,' I said. 'Just phone the man.'

Tight little smile. 'The body corporate lays down the security procedures.' Flat Queensland voice. Pause. 'Sir.'

'This isn't Pentridge,' I said. 'Didn't they retrain you for this job? Just phone.'

He held my gaze briefly, but I'd got him in one. 'I'll check,' he said.

He made his call, came back, let me in, escorted me to the lift, up to the sixth floor, rang the bell on one of the two doors in the foyer, waited until a handsome dark youth opened the door. Through all this, he said nothing and exuded hatred.

'Come this way,' the youth said. His hair was drawn back tightly in a ponytail and he had the superior and slightly miffed manner of the waiters in most Melbourne restaurants.

I followed him through a large, elegant room and down a passage lined with framed architectural drawings to a teak six-panel door. The youth pushed open the door.

The voice from within was rich, warm and full of authority. 'Thank you, Francis. Do remember to knock next time. Mr Irish, come in. Oh, Francis, bring us a pot of coffee, there's a good boy.'

Father Gorman was coming round from behind a rosewood table with a column and platform base. On it were three or four files, a desk blotter and a fountain pen. He was a large man, probably in his sixties, big shoulders, crisp grey hair with just a hint of a wave brushed back, even features tanned the colour of milk fudge. He was wearing a navy-blue, double-breasted suit over a brilliantly white shirt. His tie had what looked like tiny camels on it.

He held out a hand. It was a surprisingly hard hand for a man of the cloth.

'Pleasure to meet you, Jack,' he said. 'Let's sit down.'

He led the way down the long panelled room to a setting of club armchairs and two sofas around a low military chest. A butler's table with bottles and decanters stood against the inside wall, which was covered with paintings, mostly landscapes. French doors in one exterior wall gave on to a terrace. Deep windows in the other provided a view to the Westgate Bridge and beyond. The beyond was dark with rain.

'Beautiful, isn't it?' he said, gesturing with both hands at the room, the view. 'I thank the Lord for it every day. And I thank Joseph Kwitny, the foundation's benefactor whose generosity allows an instrument of the Lord's will to live and work in such splendour.'

I got the feeling he had said this piece before but he said it very well. I sat down first and he took a chair beside me, close enough to lean out and touch.

'Well,' he said, 'and what part of Ireland do the Irish come from?'

'Not a well-known part,' I said. 'The Jewish quarter of Hamburg. My great-grandfather's name was Isadore Reich. He ran away to sea and jumped ship in Melbourne. When he wrote his name down as I. Reich for his first employer, the man pronounced it as I. Rish. That's what he became. Irish. I'm thinking of changing it back.'

130

Father Gorman laughed, a sound of deep enjoyment that washed over you, made you want to laugh with him, made you happy that you'd amused him. And while he was laughing, crinkles of pleasure around his eyes, he leaned over and touched my arm.

'Don't you ever do that,' he said. 'You wouldn't be able to tell that wonderful story any more. And you'd be hurting the whole line of dear departed Irishes.' He leaned back and put his hands in his pockets. 'Well now, Jack Irish, what can I tell you about Ronnie Bishop?'

I had told him on the phone that Ronnie was missing. 'Why did he ring you?' I asked.

'Why, he wanted to come around and see me. I hadn't seen him for years. I've known the lad a long time, you know.'

'I gather he once worked for the foundation.'

'Briefly. He wasn't really suited to the work. Not that I say that in any detrimental sense, mind. It's special work, dealing with the young in distress. Not everyone has the gifts needed.'

'And did he come around to see you?'

'Of course. We talked for an hour and then I had to go to a meeting. That was…' He raised his eyes to the ceiling. 'That was last Friday.'

'How was he?'

'Well, Jack, what do you know of the man's situation?' He fixed me with a look of inquiry that said 'Let's trust each other.'

'I gather he's HIV-positive.'

Father Gorman took his hands out of his pockets, sat forward, put his fingertips together. The nails were manicured. He had a slim gold watch on his wrist. Dark hairs fought to get out from under it. He looked out at the view. 'Yes,' he said. 'He told me that and I felt his pain and anger. And his fear.'

He turned his head to look at me, a clear, steady gaze.

'I'm interested in why he came to Melbourne. Did he say anything about that to you?' I asked.

'I assumed he had come to see his family. He said he was staying with his mother.'

There was a sound at the doorway and the youth came in carrying a tray with a tall silver coffee pot. The small cups chattered as he dropped the tray on the table from a height of at least two inches.

'Ah, Francis,' said Father Gorman. 'We may have to send you to waiter school. Perhaps in your home country.' He was smiling broadly, but there was an edge to his tone, a hint of autumn on a warm wind.

The youth gave him a glance of pure malice, tossed his ponytail and left. Father Gorman's eyes followed him. 'Rescued from a life of abuse and poverty,' he said. 'But still uncertain of what the Lord wants for him.'

I thought the Lord probably wanted a good swift kick up the arse for him, but I held my tongue. Father Gorman poured coffee. We both had ours black and sugarless. It was very bad coffee. I went back to Ronnie. 'He was working for the foundation when he testified against a hit-and-run driver,' I said.

Father Gorman took a sip of coffee. 'I recall that well, yes. A tragedy. Lovely young woman.'

'Did Ronnie ever say anything about his testimony?'

'I beg your pardon?'

'Did Ronnie ever talk about what happened that night?'

Father Gorman put his cup down and inspected me. 'I suppose we talked about it at the time. It would have been odd not to. Is there some reason why I should recall such a conversation?'

'Not if you don't. Did Ronnie mention when you saw him that the hit-and-run driver was out of jail and had been in touch with him?'

Father Gorman shot his left cuff to look at his watch. 'Jack, my heavens,' he said. 'I've a speech to deliver. I'm going to have to be dreadfully rude and cut short our talk. No, I can't say that he did mention anything like that. Would the man want to harm him?'

'I don't think so. I think he wanted something else.'

He frowned. 'And what could that be?'

'It's not clear. Have you any idea who Ronnie might turn to if he wanted to hide, Father?'

Father Gorman was already on his feet. 'Hide? That's a strange thing to suggest, isn't it? Why would he want to hide?'

I got up. 'It seems Ronnie was worried about his safety before he disappeared.'

He furrowed his brow, a look of deep concern. 'His safety? I thought you said the man posed no threat to him? My impression was that he was deeply troubled about his health, Jack. He certainly didn't suggest that he wanted to hide. Are you sure about this?'

He was walking me along, holding my arm. I felt like a parishioner in need of comfort. 'Let me see you out. Don't hesitate to give me a call if there's anything else I can do for you. I'm sorry our talk was so short. My work's an endless round of functions and speeches. I try to find an individual message for each group, but it's a battle. You'd know that. Lawyers understand. Every client's a new client, isn't that so? I toyed with the idea of the law, you know, but someone else had other ideas.'

At the front door, something made me ask a final question. 'When did you last speak to Ronnie, Father? I mean, before he rang you about coming to see you?'

Father Gorman stroked his chin. It was shaven to perfection. 'It would have been as much as seven or eight years ago, Jack. I got quite a surprise when I heard his voice, but I placed it straight away. I don't forget voices for some reason. The Lord's compensation for forgetting everything else, I suppose.'

He saw me to the lift. In the lobby downstairs, the ex-screw made a big show of logging me out.

'Well, old sausage,' said Wootton. 'It'd be another matter if this was an inquiry you were pursuing on my behalf.'

I'd tracked Wootton to the street bar of the Windsor Hotel, a Victorian pile near Parliament, after ringing his office on the way back from Father Gorman's. He stopped off there every day on his way home. It was Wootton's sort of place: wood panelling, photographs of cricket teams.

We were sitting at a window looking out on Spring Street. It was just after 5.30 p.m. and the place was filling up with pudgy young men in expensive suits and club ties. Wootton was wearing a dark pinstripe suit with waistcoat, shirt with narrow stripes and a tie with little crests on it. His thinning hair was brushed back on his perfectly round skull and his moustache, dyed jet black, was bristly but trim. He looked like an old-style Collins Street banker and that was the way he wanted to look.

I'd known Wootton in Vietnam. He'd been a sergeant in stores, thankless work in the service of country. In lieu of thanks, he'd taken money from about twenty bars and brothels for supplying them with everything from Fosters beer to Vegemite. Wootton would have gone home very rich if two military policemen hadn't seized his stash of US dollars two days before he was due to fly out. He never faced trial. The MPs thought the loss would be enough of a lesson to him. He never said another word about his money. And nor did they.

'Cyril, I think I've got more than enough credit in my account to cover this little favour. But if it's too much trouble—'

'Steady on, Jack,' said Wootton. 'No need to get shirty.' He took a sip of his whisky and water and rolled it around in his mouth, lips pursed. When he'd swallowed, he sighed and said, 'I'll have to go and do this from a bloody public phone, you know. Give me the number and the dates.'

I sipped my beer and read the *Herald Sun* Wootton had left behind while I waited. The lead story was another police shooting. A policewoman had shot dead a man who came at her with a knife when she attended a domestic dispute in Reservoir. The new Police Minister, Garth Bruce, was quoted as saying: 'As a former policeman, I know the demands and dangers of the job. I am not, of course, passing any opinion on what took place in this incident. The coroner will decide that. But I'm determined that the police force will move away from the culture of the gun that's become entrenched over the last ten years or so.' There was a photograph of the Minister: a big serious man with short hair and rimless glasses.

Wootton was away about fifteen minutes. He came in brushing rain off his suit. 'Can you believe it?' he said. 'Supposed to be a bloody five-star hotel. Had to go outside in the rain to find a phone that worked.'

A black Mercedes pulled up outside and two Japanese men in soaked golf outfits got out of the back. They stood close together in the drizzle, cap peaks almost touching, watching the driver unload two massive golf bags and wheelchair-size chrome golf buggies from the boot.

'Sons of Nippon,' said Wootton, flicking moisture off his moustache. 'Don't know if I'd go swanning around Tokyo if I'd worked thousands of Japs to death in World War II.'

'Those two look a bit young to have worked anyone to death in World War II,' I said.

'Don't be facetious. I need something to eat.' He went over to the counter. A barmaid served him immediately. They knew the man here. He came back opening a bag of salt and vinegar chips. 'Want some?'

I shook my head. He crammed a handful in under the moustache. Pieces stuck to it. 'Well,' he said, 'it'll take about ten minutes for the reverse directory.'

Until Wootton went back to his phone, we continued our argument about how much I'd added to my fee for getting a gun pointed at me by Eddie Dollery.

When he came back, Wootton took an old envelope out of his inside jacket pocket and handed it over. On the back were about a dozen telephone numbers, all the calls to different numbers made on Mrs Bishop's telephone in the three days Ronnie was there. Against each one, in Wootton's neat hand, was a name and address.

'Well,' he said, 'I hope I've contributed to you finding your catamite.'

'Sodomite,' I said. 'He presumably had catamites. I only asked you to do it for me because I'm sworn to uphold the law.'

Wootton stuffed some more chips in his mouth. Through them, he said, 'Hah bloody hah. Joined the Boy Scouts, have we? Dib, Dib, Dib. Dob, Dob, Dob.'

'That's the Cubs, Cyril,' I said. 'But how would you know?'

I went home and tried Linda Hillier at Pacific Rim News. She was in Sydney, a man said. Back tomorrow. I poured a glass of white wine from an opened bottle in the fridge and studied the phone calls from Mrs Bishop's number. The calls to Danny McKillop and Father Gorman jumped out at me. That left nine calls. I rang Mrs Bishop. We went through the other calls from the beginning of the list. She had made all the calls except the last one. It was to a P. Gilbert, Long Gully Road, Daylesford. Made at 4.07 p.m. on the day Ronnie vanished.

'That must be Paul Gilbert,' she said thoughtfully. 'I haven't thought of him in years. Dr Paul Gilbert, he was. He went to school with Ronnie. Lovely boy, very clever. He had a surgery in St Georges Road.'

'The address is in Daylesford,' I said.

'Well, he's not a doctor anymore,' Mrs Bishop said. 'There was some trouble over drugs. It was in the papers. He started uni at the same time as Ronnie. I used to see Paul's mum sometimes. She was so proud of her boy before it happened.'

I rang the number twice before I went to bed. No answer. I fell asleep thinking about Linda Hillier. She probably had a good laugh at being come on to by the likes of me. Why had Gavin Legge called her a starfucker and a groupie? What star? What group? I hoped she wasn't avoiding me.

The bare limbs of Wombat Hill's English trees still smoked mist as I drove into Daylesford just after 9 a.m. The commuters were all gone and the small town's locals were easing themselves into the day. I parked in the main street and asked at the butcher's for directions to Long Gully Road. Butchers are the most friendly shopkeepers. It must have something to do with working with dead animals.

'Jeez,' said the butcher, 'Long Gully Road. Be out there in the forest, I reckon.' He shouted, 'Les! Where's Long Gully Road?'

A tall youth with red hair came in wiping his hands on butcher's paper. 'G'day,' he said. 'Where's a pen? Have to draw youse a map. It's out to buggery in the badlands.'

I'd tried P. Gilbert's number twice more that morning.

No answer. I was eating my microwaved porridge when I decided to take a drive out to Daylesford. I didn't give much thought then to the pointlessness of driving for an hour to a house where no-one was answering the telephone. On the way I did, and almost turned back.

Twenty minutes after leaving the butcher's I was lost. The bush around Daylesford was veined with twisting, rutted roads going nowhere. Les's map wasn't much use after the first wrong turn. I was about to do a U-turn and try to retrace my route when I saw a man in overalls putting in a fence strainer post. Back in the trees a timber shack leant against a woodpile. He must have heard my approach but he didn't look up until I was out of the Celica.

'G'day,' I said. 'Looking for Long Gully Road.'

He looked at me for a while, big beard, eyes slit, jaws chewing cud. 'Back to the T-junction. Left. Third road on the left.'

I found the turnoff. The sign said NO THROUGH ROAD. Just off the ground, a square wooden board with an arrow had Koolanja Healing Centre, Spa, Massage in peeling white paint on a green background. There were old bullet holes in it. I drove about a kilometre through the scrubby regrowth forest before a duplicate of the first sign pointed down a narrow track.

The buildings were behind a fence in a big clearing at the end of the road: a long, low weatherboard with a verandah along the front, a square cinderblock building with narrow windows and, behind them and to the left, a steel-frame shed without walls. The gate was closed and on it a sign saying CLOSED hung at an angle.

A car was parked in front of the cinderblock building: a BMW, not new. I suddenly realised that I'd never asked what sort of car Ronnie was driving. In the shed, I could see two other vehicles, a four-wheel-drive and an old Holden.

I parked outside the gate and let myself in. No dogs. Dogs appear quickly or not at all. Ahead of me a driveway ran for about thirty metres, ending in a gravelled area in front of the buildings. On either side of the drive, a formal garden had been attempted and long ago given up on. Only the winter rain was keeping the surviving plants going.

I walked down the drive. It had been planted with poplars but they'd never got beyond infancy. Near the house, I could hear the sound of piano music, something classical. The front door was open. The music was coming from inside. I knocked loudly and said, 'Anybody home?' Nothing happened. I tried again. Only the music. Then it stopped and a voice said, 'One of Chopin's loveliest. And now for a complete contrast in composing style...'

The front door led into a long sitting room, furnished with stripped pine country-look pieces. The room was cold and unkempt, as if people had been dossing in it. In a stone fireplace, ashes were a foot deep. There were newspapers everywhere and all the surfaces held empty beer and soft drink cans and dirty plates.

I said my 'Anybody home?' again and went through into a big kitchen. The radio was on a shelf above the work-bench, which was covered with the remains of meals long past.

I didn't look at the rest of the house. I went out the way

I had come and walked over to the cinderblock building. Nothing happened when I knocked and called out.

I opened the door. A wave of warmth hit me. The air was moist and smelled of chlorine. Chlorine and something else. It was dark inside, the venetian blinds at the slit windows closed. I found a light switch. Two fluorescent tubes flickered, then lit up a sort of reception area, with canvas director's chairs and a glass coffee table holding stacked magazines.

I called out again. Nothing. I crossed the room to a half-open door. Beyond was darkness. I groped around and found another light switch just inside the door. I was looking down a corridor with two doors on either side and one at the end, all closed. The smell was stronger here. The air was also steamier.

My shoes made no sound on the grey felt-like carpet as I walked down the passage. I opened the first door on my left.

It was empty except for a pine upright chair and a large, deep coffin-like object against the end wall. There were pegs on the wall to hold clothes. The smell in here was salty. I guessed the giant coffin was a flotation tank, a bath filled with salt water for experiencing weightlessness.

The hatch on top was closed. Without thinking, I walked across and slid it back. It was empty. I felt foolish.

The room on the right held another tank. I didn't look inside. The next door down on the right opened to reveal a room set up for massage: table, shelves with small bottles. There were posters of Nordic scenes on the walls. Pine forests, snow, frozen lakes.

143

I didn't enter the room. As I turned to the door across the way, my eye caught a ghost of steam coming out from under the door at the end of the passage.

I went down the passage and put my hand on the door handle. Then something made me knock. No reply. I waited, knocked again.

Then I turned the handle and pushed the door open.

The smell came out on a great cloud of steam, the smell of stock made with chlorinated water, a pungent, medicinal smell that filled my sinuses and made my eyes water.

I retreated down the passage to the entrance and watched the steam billow out of the room. Just turn around and go home, my inner voice said. Just walk out of this building, down the drive and find your way back to the man putting in the pole. Stop and tell him thanks for giving you shitty directions, you couldn't find Long Gully Road, so bugger it you were giving up. Go back to Daylesford and buy some bullboar sausages from the butcher. Tell Les you couldn't follow his map and it wasn't important. Drive home and have a shower. Forget about Danny and Ronnie and anybody else whose name ended in a diminutive.

But I didn't listen to my inner voice. When the steam thinned, I went back down the corridor.

I'd left the door only half-open.

I pushed it fully open.

The room was still dense with steam but I could see that it was like a large bathroom, tiled floor to ceiling. In the corner to my right, I could dimly make out a large spa bath, above the ground.

I took a step inside the room.

A man was in a sitting position on the floor in the corner to my right. He was wearing a loose pink garment. His left arm was at his side. His right was on his lap with a revolver in his hand. Something long-barrelled.

At first I thought he was wearing something on his head, a kind of big mask. Then I realised his head was twice its normal size, a bloated, suppurating mess.

I felt vomit rise in my throat, but I took another step into the room.

There was something in the spa bath. I couldn't see what. Steam was rising from the surface. The water was much hotter than any bath should be.

I wiped my eyes. Something insubstantial was bobbing gently on the hot bubbles. It was clothing, I thought.

I took another step. And as I did, trapped bubbles turned the clothing around and I saw the skull of a body cooked down to its bones.

The whole spa bath was stock made from a human being. I was going to be sick. I held off until I got outside and then the cold air took the smell out of my nostrils and the urge went away. I stood out in the weak sunlight for a while, thinking. Finally, I took a deep breath and went looking for something to wipe off fingerprints.

You should report crimes to the police. I didn't want to be the one to report this crime. Instead, I drove back to the man putting in the pole. He was tamping with a big metal post. This time I didn't get out of the car. I wound down the window. He looked up.

'You said turn right at the T-junction, didn't you?'

He looked at me with contempt. 'Left,' he said.

I shook my head. 'Well, fuck that for a joke, I've wasted enough time on this bloody call. I've got better things to do than fuck around in this wilderness.'

I took off with the wheels spinning. About two kilometres down the road, I found a signpost to Daylesford. This time Les was in the front of the butcher's shop. Going into a place filled with meat now was an act of sheer will.

'Thanks for the map,' I said, 'but I got lost and I had a flat.'

Les looked mortified. 'Map was okay,' he said.

'Not your fault. I reckon I missed the second turning and took the third.'

Les thought about this, eyes roofward. Then he nodded. 'That'd be right. Then you'd turn into Kittelty's Lane and then you'd be stuffed.'

'Stuffed,' I agreed. 'Anyway, I don't think I want to sell a copier to anyone lives out there. I'd rather do service calls to King Island.'

I bought some bullboar sausages and set off for the city. In Bacchus Marsh, I went to the post office and found the number for the Daylesford RSPCA. A woman came on. There were some animals in shocking condition at the health place in Long Gully Road, I told her. 'You'd better send someone today or they'll be dead.'

'Long Gully Road,' she repeated. 'What's the health place?'

'You'll see the sign,' I said. 'Look in the cinderblock building.'

I was reasonably sure they didn't record calls to the RSPCA. Almost everywhere else seemed to.

On the way back, I thought about Vietnam. In my time there I'd seen a fair number of dead and dying people. It puts another layer of skin on you. I should have been in shock at finding the bodies. Instead, I was feeling mildly elated. My instinct to pursue the trail of Ronnie had been right. Unless this matter was even more complicated than it appeared, one of the bodies was almost certainly his. The other man could be his old pal ex-doctor Paul Gilbert. I thought about the revolver in the man's hand. Had he shot himself? Had he shot the person in the spa first? I tried to remember the colour of the water in the spa. I hadn't registered it as any particular colour. Would it have been dark if the person had been shot in the bath? But the person might have been shot dead earlier and put in the bath.

But even if I had found Ronnie, that didn't advance things much. All I knew now was that the man accused of running down Anne Jeppeson ten years before had died violently, followed shortly by his accuser. I knew that Danny had believed he was innocent of the crime and that his wife said he had been told this by a woman conveying a message from her dying husband. I also knew that Danny McKillop had left messages for Ronnie Bishop. Then Ronnie had come to Melbourne and telephoned Danny.

The only obvious thing about all this was that it went back to Anne Jeppeson's death. That was what linked the dead men. Another obvious thing was that this was a good time to take a holiday in Queensland. I could simply run away from all this. I had run away from the private school my grandfather sent me to. I had run away from my mother's expectations and joined the army. I had run away from my wife's death and from my partner and from my duty to a client. Why not run away? Why change a lifetime's response now?

It's never too late to change. When I got to my office, I rang a man called Mike Drake in the Attorney-General's department. I'd been at law school with him and he had almost gone into partnership with Drew and me.

He sounded tired. 'You want me to ask the NCA if they know someone called Tony Baker? Are you aware that you don't ask the NCA questions? They ask you questions.'

He rang back inside fifteen minutes. The National Crimes Authority denied all knowledge of Tony Baker. 'That might be true,' he said. 'Or it might not.'

'Covers the possibilities,' I said. 'Thanks, mate.' It struck me that a description of Tony Baker might have helped the NCA identify him: five foot six, two hundred pounds, appearance of a .45 slug wearing a leather jacket.

I rang Linda Hillier.

'I've been ringing you,' she said. 'What happened to the answering machine?'

'Forgot to put it on.'

'Listen, that stuff we were talking about. I've been scratching round a bit. Can you meet me in Smith Street?'

Gerry Schuster was fat, and that's putting it politely. She was on a backless ergonomic kneeling contraption in an alcove created out of two computer workstations. I assumed that was what she was on. No part of what supported her was visible beneath a garishly coloured tent big enough to house four small Bedouin.

Linda said, 'Gerry, this is Jack Irish. He's got an interest in this stuff too.'

From beneath a greasy fringe that touched her eyebrows, Gerry gave me the look chefs reserve for three-day-old fish. 'Meechou,' she said. You couldn't have posted a five cent coin through her lips when she spoke.

We were in a large room on the third floor of an old building off Smith Street, Collingwood, not too far from Taub's Cabinetmaking. On the door, a plastic sign said:

UrbanData. The room was divided into three by low hessian-covered partitions. Gerry had the biggest one. Gerry had the biggest everything, as far as I could see. There were five women working at computers. In a corner, a bearded man of indeterminate age, about two weight divisions below Gerry, was staring at a monitor showing a bar graph in at least ten colours.

'UrbanData collect and sell data on anything to do with the city,' Linda had said on the way. 'Cat deaths, bicycle accidents, condom sales, anything. They can make the data talk, too.'

Gerry Schuster shifted, wobbled and said, 'I've got inner-city Melbourne property transfers 1976 to 1980 loaded. What you want to know?'

Her fingers lay on the keyboard like tired sausages, each one wearing a ring.

'Transfers in Yarrabank,' said Linda.

Gerry tapped a few keys. An outline map of greater Melbourne appeared, overlaid by a numbered grid. 'Zone 14,' she said and tapped in the number.

The outline disappeared, replaced by a map of an area of the city, also overlaid by a numbered grid.

Topaz-ring sausage touched the screen. 'This is the sub-zone here,' she said. 'Twelve.'

She tapped in 12.

Up came a gridded map showing Yarrabank, the river and part of the area on the opposite bank.

'It's this area here,' Linda said, pointing at the screen.

'Twelve stroke six,' Gerry said. She hit 12/6.

Now there was a detailed map of part of Yarrabank. At its centre was the Hoagland estate.

'Let's look at the picture.' Gerry pulled down a menu from the top of the screen. On it she blipped a command called Aerial. We waited for a second and then the map turned into an aerial photograph of the part of Yarrabank we'd been looking at.

'This is smart,' I said.

Gerry gave me a look of contempt. The sausages flashed through another set of keystrokes and the aerial photograph changed into a jigsaw puzzle of different-coloured pieces.

'Property boundaries in 14/12/6,' she said. 'Each piece is a separate title.'

She pulled down a menu and blipped a command called Breakdown. A box appeared with about ten options. She chose Number. The figure 27 appeared.

'Number of titles in the sub-sub-zone,' said Gerry.

'Let's say I want to find the owner of that bit,' Linda said. She pointed to a small triangular piece on the bank of the river.

Gerry put the pointer on it and double-clicked it. From a menu called Data, she clicked the Titleholders command. The screen went blank and then a list of names, addresses, dates and numbers appeared.

The most recent was Tilsit Holdings. The date of transfer was 14 February 1984.

'If you've got a name, you can do a search,' Gerry said, looking at Linda.

She pulled down a menu called Search, clicked Name and a box appeared.

She typed in Tilsit Holdings. A list of about eight properties appeared. She typed a command, went back to the jigsaw map and blipped a command called Site. Eight pieces of the mosaic went red. They were dotted along the river frontage in front of the Hoagland estate.

'All owned by Tilsit,' said Gerry.

Linda took a notebook out of her bag, flipped it open and ran a finger down the page. 'Can you try Muscanda Developments?' she said and spelt it.

I looked at her.

'Later,' she said.

The sausages were a blur. About half a dozen pieces of the puzzle in front of and beside Hoagland turned red. Some were tiny, two were quite large.

'Bingo,' Linda said.

I looked at her. Her eyes were shining.

'I've got more names,' she said. 'Can we get the maps and the data printed out?'

'What do you think?' Gerry said. 'This is a business.'

The rest of it took about fifteen minutes. Then we took the folder of printouts around to Meaker's and ordered long blacks. We sat opposite each other, my back against the wall. Linda was wearing a white turtleneck and a leather bomber jacket. Very fetching.

'What's going on?' I asked.

She drank some coffee. 'Well, I was thinking about Anne Jeppeson after our dinner and I mentioned it the next day to a guy at work who was a State political reporter on the *Herald* in those days. Before the drink got to him. He said he remembered there was a huge fight in Cabinet about selling the Hoagland site. The Planning Minister was Kevin Pixley. Remember him?'

I nodded.

'Lance Pitman was the Housing Minister who closed Hoagland. He wanted to sell the site without calling for tenders. Pixley wouldn't have a bar of it and he had a lot of support in Cabinet. Then Harker, the Premier, reshuffled the Cabinet and suddenly Pixley was Transport Minister and Lance Pitman was Planning. And then Pitman approved the sale of the site.'

'Who would have wanted to buy it ten years ago?'

'That's what I asked myself. And why didn't Pitman want to go to tender? The site was bought by a company called Hexiod Holdings, a shelf company with an accountant called Norman Jovanovich and two other people as directors. Hexiod held on to the property until three months ago, when it was sold to Charis Corporation, the Yarra Cove developers. It was sold the day after Pitman and company got back into government.'

'What about the waterfront land, the properties we've been looking at?'

She put out her slim hand and touched my arm. 'Jack, there's something like seventy properties involved. If I read this UrbanData stuff right, at least seven companies started buying or taking options on the riverbank sites about eighteen months before the government announced it was closing Hoagland. At some point, I don't know when yet, another outfit, called Niemen PL, emerged as owner of all the properties. Six years ago, Niemen consolidated all the waterfront properties into one and applied for rezoning of the area as residential.'

Linda paused while what appeared to be members of a female bike gang came in, talking at the top of their voices.

Across the street, a white Holden with tinted windows was parked outside a furniture shop. A tall, balding man in a grey windcheater came walking along from the city side and got in the passenger door.

'Anyway,' said Linda, 'the government knocked them back. They went to the Planning Appeals Board and won. Then the Planning Minister overruled the board.'

'Why was that?'

The driver of the white Holden was getting out of the car. He crossed the road to our side and disappeared from view.

'Said rezoning wasn't in keeping with the government's long-term plans for the area.'

I saw a match flare behind the Holden's tinted driver's side window. The man who had got in the passenger side was now in the driver's seat. He opened the window a couple of inches to flick out his match.

Linda looked at her watch and drained her coffee. 'I've got to go,' she said. 'The last act in this saga is that six weeks ago Niemen sold the consolidated waterfront land to Charis.'

'So Charis now owns the whole site?'

'That's right. There's a road between the waterfront properties and the Hoagland land. The government sold the road to Charis a few days after the waterfront deal. And soon after that Charis announced the Yarra Cove development.'

'Tell us thinkers slowed by age and drink what all this means,' I said.

Linda gave me her slow smile. 'I think it means that closing Hoagland was part of a plan to put together a thirty-acre waterfront site. That's a developer's wet dream. The only reason Yarra Cove didn't get started a long time ago is that the Harker government got thrown out at the '84 election. That meant a ten-year wait till Pitman and company got back in.'

I thought about this for a while. 'And if Hoagland hadn't been closed in '84?'

She leaned across the table. 'Then someone was stuck with a whole lot of falling-down old warehouses and polluted factory sites backed by the toughest Housing Commission flats in the city.'

The driver of the Holden was lighting up again. I said, 'Are we both concluding that Anne Jeppeson's death suited some people?'

'I've got to find out more about the companies involved. But the answer is Yes. I think we should talk to Kevin Pixley.'

'What became of him?'

'Retired. Lives in Brighton. The bloke at work is an old drinking mate of his. I'll see if he can get Pixley to talk to us.'

I said, 'Can we have dinner? I've got to tell you something about Ronnie.'

She gave me an interested look. 'Ring me before eight-thirty. I'm working till then.'

I took my time finishing the coffee. Then I took a stroll down Brunswick Street, marvelling at the dress sense of the young, crossed over to the other side at Johnson Street, walked back to my car.

The white Holden was gone.

I went back to my office and rang the last number Cam had left. He didn't seem to leave the same number twice running. A woman with a French accent invited me to leave a message. My eye fell on the mobile phone in its little plastic case next to the Mac. I'd bought it in a fit of technological anxiety and used it about four times. I left the number with the French lady and walked over to Charlie's.

'So,' he said. 'Had the breakfast. Ready for the day's work.' He was preparing a length of wood for steam-bending, using a block plane to chamfer the edges that would be in tension. This was to stop the wood fibres breaking loose. In the corner, the low potbelly stove was fired up, and Charlie's ancient steam kettle was starting to vibrate.

'I've been out since dawn,' I said. 'Looking for people.'

He shook his head sadly. 'A man with a profession. What

does he do? He goes to the races and he looks for people who should stay missing.'

The mobile phone went off in my pocket, a nasty, insistent electronic noise. It was Cam. 'The big man wants to have breakfast tomorrow,' he said. 'You on?'

I said yes.

'Pick you up quarter to eight.'

I felt Charlie's eyes on me as I closed the flap and put the phone in my pocket.

'So,' he said. 'Mr Big Business Man. Mr Executive. So busy he can't go to the telephone anymore, has to take it with him. Next it's no time even to go for a shit. Take a little shithouse around with you, do it in the motor car.'

'You need to keep up with things in my line of work,' I said.

'Yes,' he said, disbelief in his tone. 'When you going to finish that table, Mr Walking Telephone?'

'Friday. Well, Sunday.'

'Got a big job yesterday,' he said. 'Man wants me to make him a library in Toorak. Panelled. Carved. Don't know if I'm up to it anymore.'

'No,' I said, 'you're not up to it. Play bowls instead. Give the work to somebody who can do it.'

'I just might,' Charlie said. 'Or maybe I'll get an apprentice, hey? Smart girl. Strong. Not afraid of work. Reliable even.'

'Good idea,' I said, heading for my bits of table. 'Anyone would want to spend five years making mortice and tenon joints and finding out about the finer points of lawn bowls.'

Charlie finished his planing and took the boards over to the steam box. It was a length of glazed sewerage pipe, eight feet long, sixteen inches in diameter, plugged at both ends. The steam went in at one end and escaped through a hole at the other. He gave it an appreciative smack with a huge hand. 'You want to know something?' he said. 'You can give a schmuck a walking telephone. But what you got then is a schmuck with a walking telephone.'

'Gee, you can learn a lot around here,' I said, 'just by listening.'

The workshop was warm from the steam box and the rest of the afternoon slipped by. At quarter to six, we called it a day and went around to the Prince. What Charlie called the Fitzroy Youth Club was in position at the bar.

'Jack, my boy,' said Wilbur Ong. 'Did I tell you I tipped eight out of eight three weeks in a row now? In me granddaughter's tipping pool, round this place she works. Hundreds in it. I give her me tips Thursday nights when she comes for tea. Me daughter's girl.'

Norm O'Neill's huge nose came around slowly, like the forward cannon on the USS *Missouri* swivelling to speak to Vietnam. 'You can only get eight out of eight, Wilbur,' he said slowly and with menace, 'if you tip against the Lions.'

Wilbur gave him a pitying look. 'Norm,' he said, 'if you was forty years younger I'd take you outside for jumpin to that conclusion. 'Course I don't tip against the Lions. It's the girl. She takes all me other tips and changes that one. She reckons tippin against the Lions is the only sure thing left in the footie.'

'I don't think you brought your daughter up right,' Eric Tanner said.

Stan came out from behind the bar and switched on the television set on the wall in the corner. It was news time. When the set was first put in, Stan tried to keep it on all the time but the Youth Club kept switching it off. Now it went on for the news and football.

The news opened with a helicopter view of Dr Paul Gilbert's health centre with at least ten vehicles parked outside the front gate.

'Two men have been found shot dead at an isolated property bordering on the Wombat State Forest outside Daylesford,' the woman newsreader said. 'One of the bodies was in a hot spa bath. Police said the men might have been dead for as long as a week.'

The helicopter went in for a closer look. I could see two men in plain clothes standing outside the house. They looked up at the helicopter and the one on the left's lips said, 'Fuck off.'

'Police said the bodies had been identified. Their names are expected to be released later this evening. The property is owned by Dr Paul Gilbert, a Melbourne general practitioner who was permanently barred from practice in 1987 after being found guilty of a variety of drug offences. He served two and a half years of a six-year sentence. Dr Gilbert lived on the property. He has not been seen in Daylesford for more than a week.'

The news went on to other things. I finished my beer and drove home. The streets seemed to be full of white Holdens. Had a white Holden followed me to Daylesford? My neck hair prickled.

When I got home, I rang Linda Hillier. She wasn't at her desk, said a man. He took a message. I was looking sadly into the near-empty fridge when the phone rang.

'We need to talk,' Linda Hillier said.

'Endlessly,' I answered. Then I went for it. 'Can you come around here? No. *Will* you come around here?'

'What's the address?'

I walked around the corner to Papa's Original Greek Taverna and bought some bread, olives, dolmades and an unidentified fish stuffed with thyme and basil from Mrs Papa. Menu price less fifteen per cent, that was our deal.

I was just out of the shower when the bell rang. I pulled on underpants, denims and a shirt.

'Well, hello,' she said. There was rain on her hair.

'You're wet,' I said.

'So are you. At least I've got shoes on.'

She had changed since this morning. She was wearing a trenchcoat over grey flannels, a cream shirt and a tweed jacket. I caught her scent as I took the coat and jacket. It was, in a word, throaty.

'This is nice,' she said, looking around.

We stood awkwardly for a moment, something trembling in the air between us. I looked around at the books in piles on every surface, the CDs and tapes everywhere, the unhung pictures, seeing the place for the first time in years.

'It's sort of gentlemen's club mates with undergraduate student digs,' she said.

I cleared my throat. 'Come into the kitchen and I'll give you a drink. What would you like?' The kitchen was respectable. I'd cleaned it recently.

'Whisky and water if you've got it.'

She had a good inspection of the contents of the open shelves while I got the drinks, watching her out of the corner of my eye and telling her about my visit to Father Gorman. I poured myself a glass of Coldstream Hills pinot noir from a bottle I'd started on the day before.

'Cheers,' I said.

'Cheers. I've met Gorman a couple of times. He's a walker for high-society hags. Something slimy about him.'

'A walker?'

'Takes them to the theatre, to parties. When their husbands are too busy fucking the secretary.'

'You're very knowledgeable,' I said. 'I've got a fish. If you're hungry.'

'A fish,' she said thoughtfully. Our eyes were locked. I couldn't look away. I didn't want to look away.

'It doesn't have to be fish.'

She bit her lower lip. 'What else have you got?'

I wanted very much to bite her lower lip. 'There's some steak,' I said. 'Sirloin. Frozen.'

We had somehow got closer. I couldn't remember moving. She put out her left hand and touched the hollow in my throat with one finger.

'Sirloin,' she said. She put her glass down on the counter and slowly folded her arms under her breasts. It was somehow a hugely erotic gesture. 'Anything else?'

'Dolmades?'

We looked at each other in silence. I wanted to move my erection to a more comfortable position but I was paralysed. She looked down at it.

'Have you got a condom?' she said.

I swallowed some wine with difficulty. 'I suppose you'll think I'm predatory if I say yes?'

She nodded. 'Possibly.'

I put my glass on the counter. She put a fingertip against my lips. I kissed it. As her mouth came nearer I could smell the malt whisky. I put my hands on her buttocks and pulled her close. I could feel the elastic of her panties under my thumbs.

Our lips came together. Her right hand moved between us and cupped me. I thought I'd swoon.

'I'm going to swoon.'

'Perhaps,' she said, 'you should lie down.'

I took her hand and led her into the bedroom. We undressed with the urgency of people shedding burning clothes.

'Bugger buttons,' she said thickly, pulling her shirt over her head. She shrugged out of her bra and, for a moment, stood there naked to the waist, big breasts over prominent ribs. Then she stripped off her grey flannels, pantyhose and white bikini pants. She was built for movement: long bones and long muscles that showed under the skin.

The sheets were like ice. But only for seconds.

Around midnight, we ate sirloin steak sandwiches and drank the rest of the Coldstream Hills. It was too late for fish.

'Did you live here with your wife?' Linda said in a neutral tone.

'Yes. But we didn't sleep in that bedroom. That was the spare room. I couldn't bear to go into the bedroom for a long time.'

She said, 'You knew what I was thinking. Do all the girls ask that?'

'One hundred per cent of them.'

She looked at the ceiling, nodding.

'One girl, one question. That's a hundred per cent, isn't it?'

She smiled. 'I knew this would happen,' she said. 'When I saw you coming down the newsroom with that twerp Legge.'

We were on the sofa, backs against the arms, legs entwined, chewing. Linda was wearing a sort of kimono thing my daughter had left behind. She was about a foot taller than Claire, all of it leg. I was in my old towelling dressing gown.

'I know what went through your mind,' I said. 'Here comes six foot two of solid erotic pleasure.'

'No,' she said. 'I thought, here comes exactly the kind of rumpled, predatory, middle-aged sleazebag I always end up fucking.'

'I thought you said you wouldn't think I was predatory.'

'I said I possibly would. Anyway, that was tonight,' she said. 'You didn't have to be predatory tonight. All you had to do was lie back.'

'I liked the lying back bit,' I said. 'You're born to the saddle.'

'All it takes is a good pommel,' she said and rubbed her instep down my right calf. 'What's that funny shaped scar on your stomach?'

'I was hoping you'd ask. A man shot me.'

'Why?'

'Trespass,' I said.

'Trespass where?'

'In Vietnam. How come you've got such strong legs?'

She put her head back and looked down her nose at me, eyes narrowed. 'Is that a flattering question? Don't answer. Think. Think about the proximity of my heel to your groin.'

I said, 'Higher. A little higher. Gently.'

She moved her foot up my leg. 'I was an athlete,' she said. 'From about ten to eighteen. Then I went to uni. One joint, one paper cup of cheap wine, one night in the sack. Ex-athlete.'

'Ex-track athlete,' I said. 'There are other places to display athleticism.'

Linda put her plate on the floor and slid down the sofa.

The kimono rode up above her pubic hair. She lifted one long, strong leg and rested it on my shoulder. 'That is so,' she said. 'What do you know about the leather sofa half mile?'

'It'll leave a wet spot,' I said.

'Wet spot? It'll float the sofa into the fucking kitchen.'

Later I told her about my trip to Paul Gilbert's health spa.

'Jesus Christ, Jack,' she said. 'How the fuck can you be so calm? You should have gone to the cops.'

'No,' I said. 'Too messy.' But I was starting to have doubts about my decision.

Harry met Cam and me at the front door. He was wearing a hacking jacket in soft grey checks, grey flannels, a pale yellow brushed-cotton shirt, and a silk tie in shades of grey and lavender. We went through into the breakfast room. Rain misted the french doors on to the terrace but concealed lighting made the square room's lemon walls glow and the whole house was warm enough for shirtsleeves.

We helped ourselves to muesli or porridge from the buffet. Harry and I had oatmeal porridge soaked with raisins overnight. Cam had a teaspoon of muesli. Then Mrs Aldridge brought in poached eggs, grilled ham, pencil-thin beef sausages, and grilled tomatoes. Harry once told us she had cooked for an English trainer. He said the man didn't give him a ride for two years after he stole Mrs Aldridge by offering her five pounds a week more than she was getting. 'Ate like a prince after that,' he said. 'Didn't eat often but when I did, by Jesus.'

In the study after the first sip of Mrs Aldridge's coffee, dark and viscous as mapping ink, Harry said, 'Jack, this Dakota Dreamin. We're thinkin of goin for a ride.'

'From what we saw?' I said.

Harry scratched inside an ear. 'Tony Ericson won't run the bugger in a proper trial. Don't blame him. Too risky, history like that.' He sniffed his cup. 'He's happy to see him take it easy on his first outin, though. But we know, there's only a couple of nags runnin around in the mud now could show him a bum.'

I said, 'If form's a guide, this thing may never run like that again, never mind improve.'

'Chance of that.' Harry sipped his coffee. 'Still, Ericson reckons he'll take a race or two. Cam here likes him.'

I looked at Cam. He'd gone off with the boy, Tom, and the horse after the gallop.

'The boy reckons he's taken the horse around that 2400 in just on two-thirty,' said Cam. 'Didn't tell his dad. Tony would have paddled his arse.'

I'd come to realise that Cam's judgment was vital to Harry's operations. Harry watched jockeys. Cam looked at horses. 'Fella's got the Eye,' Harry said to me after my second photography mission. 'Not one in a thousand around horses got it. Can't learn it. Mystery.'

Harry held up the silver coffee pot inquiringly. 'Two-thirty on that sheep paddock is hot stuff. Add a few seconds, it's still smokin.' He poured for Cam. 'Still. Spring would've been best. But we can't hold this thing together that long.'

'Who's inside so far?' Cam said.

'Ericson says it's just Rex Tie,' Harry said. 'Might well be true. Told Rex, he says one word, in his sleep even, he'll train polar bears in Siberia for a livin.' He swivelled his chair, looked out into the dripping garden for a few seconds, completed the circuit. 'I reckon we've got a better than usual chance to keep this thing tight. Not your whole stable and the connections in the know here. Just a few yokels.' He looked thoughtful. 'Fair few things to think about concernin this horse, though. Number one is: do we want to go first up?'

We sat in silence for a while. I wasn't sure that I had a sensible opinion about when to mount a betting coup.

'First,' Cam said. He stretched his legs. You could see he was thinking about a cigarette.

'What's the reasonin?' Harry said.

Cam smiled his thin smile. 'There's two points,' he said. 'One, like Jack says, there might not be a second up. Two, the first time this horse turned out twice in a reasonable time, he bled. The second time he came off lame. I say put on the money and pray.'

Harry was doodling with his Mont Blanc on the blotter. 'What do you reckon, Jack?' he asked without looking up.

'How much is involved here?' For once I wanted to know.

Harry shook his head. 'Not yet. Money clouds the judgment. We want the horse to win for us. Question is, do we want to try for first up?'

I said, 'If we don't, the whole world gets a look at him. If he finishes in one piece and he backs up again inside a reasonable time, someone's going to be looking for the party. We'd be, wouldn't we?'

167

Harry pushed his coffee cup and saucer away, opened the brassbound cedar cigar box on the desk and took out the first of his three Havanas of the day.

Cam was out of the gate as Harry's fingers touched the porcelain cup. He was blowing Gitane smoke out of his nose before Harry had the cigar band off.

'Not an easy one,' Harry said. Eyeing the cigar suspiciously, he rolled it between the thumb and fingers of his left hand. Then he picked up a silver spike and violated the rounded end. After several exploratory sucks, he lit the cigar with a kitchen match, leaned back and waved the small baton at me. 'Sure you won't, Jack? Makes it all worthwhile.'

I shook my head sadly. You can get over love affairs but you never get over Havanas.

'Horse's goin racin with us or without us,' Harry said. 'Thing is, if it's not with us, Ericson and Rex Tie'll go looking for the stake money. They might as well go on the wireless with the news.'

We sat in silence again. The smoke from Harry's Havana drifted up towards the lofty ceiling, meeting and mingling with that from Cam's Gitane. Outside, a gust of wind plucked at the last few leaves on the elm.

Harry made a clicking noise. 'Okay,' he said. 'First up it is.' He opened a drawer and took out a yellow legal pad. 'This is a big one, Jack. We have to spread the risk around, that's the way we do it. Done a few quick sums here. I'm assumin we'll start in the fifties, see the price shrink like a prick in a cold shower when we get movin. If you're in, it's twenty-five grand apiece from you fellas.'

He looked at Cam, at me. 'What's your thinkin?'

Cam blew a perfect smoke ring. 'I'm in,' he said.

'Jack?'

Twenty-five thousand dollars. I was broke as usual. Most of the Ballarat payout had been distributed among my creditors. What would Charlie Taub say? I knew what he'd say. He'd say: *Horse business. Never met a man it didn't ruin.* In any event, the creature would probably break down soon after leaving the barrier and be shot behind a screen.

'How long have I got to raise it?' I asked.

Harry took a draw, studied the cigar, reluctantly tipped off an inch of ash. 'Your credit's good. Day before'll do.' He looked at me. 'I'd offer you a loan, Jack,' he said, little smile. 'Only my late dad always said never lend a gambler money. You're sidin with the devil if you do.'

'A wise father,' I said, 'is worth more than a clever child.' We went into the cinema and watched films of all Dakota Dreaming's races. Only the first one gave me any hope.

Kevin Pixley, former MP for Peterslee and Minister for Urban Development, lived in one of a row of mansions with the bay at the end of their gardens. Peterslee this wasn't. Peterslee was little brick veneers with concrete yards cringing in the flightpath from Tullamarine.

Linda had set up the appointment with Pixley. Then she'd been summoned to see the boss at the headquarters in Sydney. 'It's just bullshit,' she said. 'Randy little Pom with a wife in Singapore. The creep's been trying to get into my pants since he arrived.'

I said, 'Inexplicable. Why would he want to do that?'

'I'll deal with you when I get back tonight. I told Pixley you're helping with legal aspects of a story I'm doing on city planning. Try to keep it as general as you can to start with, okay? No cross-examination. Ask him what he thinks of the

Planning Appeals Board, how attractive is Melbourne to developers, that sort of thing. Work him around to 1984. See if the bile surfaces.'

'Can I wear a hat with a little Press card in the band?'

'Only if that's all you wear. They say his second wife liked a bit of rough trade. New one's probably the same.'

I had to announce myself into a microphone behind a grille next to a door set in a two-metre wall. The door clicked open immediately. Beyond was a short brick path flanked by cumquat trees clipped into perfect balls. It led to a two-storey mock-Georgian structure painted to look like a down-at-heel Roman palazzo.

The front door opened when I was a couple of metres away. It was a woman in her late thirties, dark, pretty in a nervous way. She was dressed for dry sailing: boat shoes, white duck trousers, striped top, little kerchief at the throat.

'Good morning,' she said. She had a professional smile, like an air hostess or a car hire receptionist. 'I'm Jackie Pixley. Come in. Kevin's just having a drink before lunch. He's not supposed to. He's had a bypass, you know.'

It was 11.30 a.m.

We went through a hallway into a huge sitting room with french doors leading out to a paved terrace. An immaculate formal garden led the eye to the view of the bay. It was its usual grey, sullen winter self.

There were two sets of leather chairs grouped around massive polished granite pedestals with glass tops. We went around the setting on the left and though a door into another large room. This one was panelled floor to ceiling in dark wood. A snooker table with legs like tree trunks dominated the room. Against the far wall was a bar that could seat about twenty. Behind it, mirrored shelves held at least a hundred bottles and dozens of gleaming glasses. The top shelf appeared to have every malt whisky made.

Seated behind the bar was Kevin Pixley. I remembered his press photographs of a decade before: built like an old-time stevedore, strong square face, dark hair brushed straight back, oddly delicate nose and mouth. The man behind the bar was a shrunken and blurred version of the one in those pictures. He was tanned like his wife but the colouring looked unhealthy on him. In spite of the warmth of the room, he was wearing a bulky cream sweater. He leant over the counter and put out a hand.

'Jack Irish,' he said. 'Spit of your old man. He was one of the hardest bastards ever to pull on a Fitzroy guernsey.'

We shook hands. I used to get a lot of this kind of thing when I was younger. It always embarrassed me.

'Sit,' he said. 'What'll it be?' There was a tic at the corner of his left eye.

I said beer and he slid along to a proper pub beer tap. His stool was on wheels. I caught sight of the back of a wheelchair sticking out from the corner of the bar.

'Something for you, madam?' Pixley asked. I realised his wife was still standing in the doorway.

'Not just yet, thanks,' she said. 'We'll be lunching at twelve-thirty, Kevin. I'm going shopping. Goodbye, Mr Irish.'

'Pretty economically done, eh,' said Pixley, putting down a beer with a head like spun candy. 'I've got my instructions, you've got your marching orders.' He took a swallow of the colourless liquid in his own glass. There was just a hint of a tremble in his hand as he raised it. 'Now,' he said, 'why are you snooping around for Ms Linda Hillier? Didn't I used to see your name in the papers defending criminal slime?'

'This is just a little job Linda thinks a lawyer might be useful for. I'm not quite sure why. Did she tell you what it's about?'

'Something about planning. Sounded like a cock and bull story to me.'

He finished his drink and turned to the serving counter.

He took down a bottle of Gilbey's gin and poured half a glass. Then he added a dash of tonic and stirred the mixture with a big finger.

'Cheers,' he said. 'I'm not supposed to drink. Fuck 'em. What else is there?' He took a sip and licked his lips. 'She thought a lawyer might be useful, hey? Be the first time. Cabinet was full of bloody suburban lawyers. Think they're the bloody chosen race.'

'We're looking at decisions like the one to close the Hoagland estate,' I said. 'It leaked out in May 1984. We're interested in what happened in Cabinet.'

Pixley put his glass on the bar, put his elbows on the counter and looked me in the eyes.

'This is about Yarrabank, right? What's the shithole going to be called now?'

'Yarra Cove,' I said.

'Yarra fucking Cove. That what it's about?'

'Yes.'

'What are you lot trying to do?'

'It's just a general piece of planning.'

He gave me a smile of pure disbelief. 'Planning shit, Jack,' he said. 'I've been dealing with the fucking media for forty years. Ms Hillier thought she'd have a better chance of getting me to tip a bucket if she sent you.' He leant forward until his face was a handspan from mine. 'I've got it, haven't I?'

I sat back on my stool. There wasn't going to be a general discussion about planning. 'Well, I suppose there's a public service element in shafting the shaftworthy.'

Pixley laughed, a throat-clearing sound. 'I can think of a couple of dozen shaftworthies,' he said. 'So ask me a question.'

I took out my notebook. 'Who made the decision to close Hoagland?'

He shook his head in mock admiration. 'You've got good timing, Jack. I was looking at '84 in my diaries the day before yesterday. The answer is Lance Pitman. He convinced the Premier that shutting the hellhole was a good idea. Stop all the publicity about rapes and fires and general mayhem in the place. Thought he had it all stitched up, usual breezy fait a-fucking-ccompli style. Then he got to Cabinet and some people weren't happy.'

'But the Premier overruled them?'

'No. Harker didn't try too hard to get his way. There wasn't a decision taken then. Pitman looked like he'd been bitten in a blow job. He couldn't believe Harker wouldn't push it through.'

Pixley paused to drink. 'Stage two. After the meeting, someone leaked it that Cabinet had *approved* closing the place. Next afternoon, we had the usual rent-a-lefty crowd outside Parliament screaming "Save Hoagland". Bloody unions making threats. And some cop jockey rides his horse over a twat in a wheelchair.'

'So at that point the Premier could simply have said it wasn't going to happen? Hadn't been approved by Cabinet.'

'And that's what he was going to say, mate. That's what I advised him to do. I heard him tell Pitman that was what he was going to do. He was nervous as hell about the protests. Never expected a reaction like that. Walking up and down in his office saying, "That fucking little bitch". We had an election coming up, all the bleeding hearts in the party on the phone to him saying we had to soften our image after the way we chainsawed the bloody power workers. Last thing anyone wanted was all the clergy and the social welfare industry getting on heat. Next thing you find bloody independents coming up in the marginals like pricks at a pyjama party. What Harker was scared of was that the party would lose the election and blame it on him closing bloody Hoagland. He wasn't going to close it in a fit.'

'But he did?'

'Well, everything changed in a flash when the Jeppeson woman got hit by that prick.'

'What happened in Cabinet?'

'The woman was running the whole protest single-handed. We didn't know that. Once she was gone, it just fizzled out. Meantime, Pitman's people are putting it around that the Premier's authority is on the line, battle for control of Cabinet, leadership challenge brewing, all that sort of shit.'

'So what happened?'

'Harker jumped on all the people who'd opposed closing Hoagland. We had a Cabinet meeting and now everybody's crapping on about we can't have mob rule, need a show of support for the Premier, in the public interest to close the dungheap anyway, that sort of shit.'

'So Lance Pitman won.'

'That's right. Touch and go for the bastard, though. That Jeppeson woman came within a rat's foreskin of getting the closure stopped.' Pixley started coughing and only stopped when he took a mouthful of gin and tonic. 'Jesus, if it's not one thing it's another,' he said weakly. 'Can't even take a piss any more without splashing my boots.'

'And when the estate was sold, there was a bit of a barney over that, wasn't there?'

Pixley studied me for a while. 'You could say that. In spades.'

I said, 'Pitman wanted to sell it without calling for tenders.'

'That's right. Stank like last week's roadkill.'

'Why's that?'

'Well, people who knew Pitman didn't swallow all the bullshit about we'll never get an offer this high again if we put it out to tender until doomsday.'

'What did they know about Pitman?'

He studied me some more, the tic going in his eye. Then he knocked back his drink and busied himself fixing another one. He poured me a beer in a clean glass without asking.

When he handed it to me, he said, 'Let me tell you something about my life, Jack. I joined the party with my dad when he came back from the war. I was seventeen. I just missed the war. I wanted to go, lie about my age, be a hero, fight the bloody Japs. Mum wouldn't hear of it. And I couldn't bring myself to go without her blessing.'

He took a sip and studied his glass. 'Four blokes in my class went. Just the one came back. You couldn't recognise him. Just bones. A skeleton. Bobby Morrisey was his name, little fellow. Never well again in his life. Fucking Japs. There were lots of blokes like that around where we lived. Think the local MP would do anything for them? Not on your bloody life. Too busy fighting factional wars to give a bugger about the voters. Well, I ended up taking that seat from the bastard. No-one thought it was possible. There wasn't even a branch of the party there when I joined. When I got into Parliament I did what I could for Bobby Morrisey and the others. Felt I owed it to them. Something personal, like they'd gone instead of me. Nonsense that, but there you are.'

I nodded. I didn't see where this was going and time was running out before Mrs Pixley closed the proceedings.

Pixley did some more coughing. 'What I need is a fucking smoke,' he said. 'Don't have one on you? No. Bloody woman searches the house like the Gestapo. Bugger that. Thing is, Jack, I found it wasn't an unusual thing to do, look after people. Sure, there were a lot of toffee-nosed dickheads on our side. But they weren't in there to feather their own bloody nests, not in those years. That's why I couldn't understand people like Lance Pitman when they came in, when I realised what the cunts wanted out of politics.'

He looked away for a while, down the bar. Then he jerked his head around and said, 'Nice house this, eh Jack? Cost a bit more than my super, you'll say to yourself. That bastard Pitman put it around that it came out of graft. He's still putting it around, every chance he gets. Well, I'll tell you where it came out of. It came out of me mum's will, that's where. And she got it from Uncle Les when he died in Queensland. I'm not saying the old bastard was straight. I'm not saying he got it by the sweat of his brow. There's a lot of stories about him. But it came to me out of the cleanest hands on earth.'

Pixley lapsed back into coughing. His eyes were streaming. The big bar clock said 12.15. I'd have to come back. I gestured and made to stand up. He waved me down.

'Sit. I'm not done. Pitman. I'm talking about Pitman. You want to know about him? That's why you're here, isn't it?'

I nodded.

'This is all off the record, right? That bloody newspaper even suggests I'm a source, you'll find out I've still got friends, understand me?'

I nodded again.

'Yes, well, Lance Pitman. Mr Lucky, we used to call him. No bigger disgrace to the party ever walked. It means nothing to him, dogshit. He was a fucking little real estate agent out there in Allenby when he saw the whole place was changing. All the basketweavers and potmakers and bloody unemployed architects making houses out of mudcakes were moving back to Carlton and the place was filling up with young people with kids, big mortgages. Next thing he's joined the party, he's branch secretary, he's signed on hundreds of these beancounters and computer salesmen. Before you look the cunt's in Parliament. He'd have joined the Nazi Party if he thought it would carry Lance Pitman to glory.'

Behind me, Jackie Pixley said, 'Lunch is served, Kevin.

You'll have to excuse us, Mr Irish.' Her voice was as cold as the wind on Station Pier.

Pixley's eyes narrowed. 'Leave us alone, woman,' he said. 'It'll be closing time for me soon e-bloody-nough. And get me my diary for 1980.'

I heard her turn on her heel on the polished boards. It made a squeak. We sat in silence. Inside a minute she was back, slamming a leatherbound book down on the bar and leaving. Squeak.

'Nice girl,' Pixley said. 'Met her on the plane to Europe after Ellen shot through. My second wife, that was. She couldn't stand being alone. Took to fucking plumbers, electricians, any bloke in overalls with a tool. Now Jackie can't bear that I can't go out much. And the bloody people around here don't want to know us. Christ knows what that'll lead to.'

'I can come back,' I said.

'Bugger that. I'm warmed up. How's your drink? I'll give you another one.'

When he'd poured the drinks, he said, 'Anyway, the bastard went around brown-nosing every living thing in the caucus. We get into office in '76 and Pitman's in Cabinet. Minister for Police. That's a laugh. He should've been the first one arrested. But they liked him there, the cops. He made a lot of cop friends. They know a shonk when they see one. He howled like a dingo when Harker moved him to Housing.'

I didn't have time for a complete history of the Harker government. 'About Yarrabank,' I said.

He ignored the hint. 'What the bastard really wanted was Planning,' he said. 'He'd have put on lipstick and a party frock and sucked off the whole caucus for Planning. But not even Harker was stupid enough to give it to him. Not then, anyway. Later on, they were like bumboys.'

I said, 'Why did he want it so badly?'

Pixley looked at me sadly. 'Come on, Jack. Where've you been? Cause that's where the big graft is. That's where the big boys play.'

'And that was your portfolio.'

'From '80 till '84. Then Harker dumped me for Lucky Lance over the Hoagland sale. Just before the voters dumped the bloody lot of us. I never took a quid, not a bottle of Scotch, in the job. And it was lying around. Made some fucking horrible decisions, mind you. Some places in the city I can't hardly bear to go. Still. Bloody honest cockups. Pure ignorance and led by the nose by certain people in the department. Some of them pals of Lance Pitman. The bastard came to see me in '80. I'll find it here.'

He picked up the diary with 1980 in gold on its cover and riffled through the gilt-edged pages. 'Got it. Listen:

'"Pitman came to see me this morning. Slimy as ever. Said he understands that I'm much more suited to the job than he could ever be. Knows all about Ellen. Said it's a tragedy the way women don't understand the demands of high office, etc etc. Beat around the bush till I asked him what he wanted. Nothing, he says. Just wanted to say he's there if I need anything. Then he asked would I like some company. He's got a young woman friend, lost her husband, understands grief and so on. Told him no thanks. He hung around a bit more, then asked me how I was going on the Baygate project. I said it was going through due process. He said he thought it would be bad for the party's image with business if it got knocked back. Also, the developers were likely to be generous donors at election time. I didn't show any interest. Then he asked me if I'd heard there was a chance ColdRoads could put their new packing plant in my electorate. I said I thought it was going to Orbison. That wasn't settled yet, he said. Raelene came in and said my appointment had arrived. At the door, Pitman turned around and said, as if he'd just remembered it, that, by the way, did I know that the major shareholders in Baygate were also on the board òf ColdRoads. I don't have any doubt about his meaning, but I don't want to go to Harker with something the bastard will say was just an innocent remark." '

He looked up at me. 'You know what happened?'

I shook my head.

'Baygate got built. I couldn't bring myself to throw it out just because Pitman wanted it built. I should have. That was a good enough reason. But I wanted it to be a fair planning decision. And the department was divided about it. So I ended up going along with the senior man, a bloke called Malcolm Bleek, who reckoned it was a good thing. And come the election, some of the directors of the company, in their individual capacities mark you, came over with big contributions to the party.'

'Could be just sound business practice,' I said.

'Bullshit. But listen to this. Peterslee was always a marginal seat. Held it because people trusted me, bugger my party. But it only took about three hundred pricks to cross over and I'm gone. And in this business you don't come back. Ten days before the election, ColdRoads Australia announces it's putting its new plant in my electorate. Jobs in construction, a whole lot of new permanent jobs. Like a marginal MP's wet dream, eh?'

I said, 'You're saying Pitman believed you'd delivered the goods.'

'I don't think he was sure. But he came in to see me again after the election. Before he could open his mouth, I said to him, "You slimy little shit, if you ever mention the name of a project to me again, that project is dead in the water. I don't care what it is, can be the landing strip for the second coming, it is fucking stone dead." He never said a word, just turned and walked.'

Pixley stared into his glass. 'Like I said, Jack, your timing's good. Three months ago, I'd have told you to fuck off. I took the view that I couldn't get Pitman without hurting the party. And I couldn't do that. Party's been my whole life. Been everything to me. Cost me two marriages, kids who don't want to know me, but that was my choice.'

He finished his drink. 'One for the road,' he said and set to work again.

I drained my beer and waited for him in silence. When he'd put the glass in front of me, he said, 'Mortality, that's what changed my mind. I was lying in the Epworth waiting for the knife and I thought about dying and fucking Lance Pitman coming to my funeral. I thought, fuck me, if I come out of this and a chance comes up, I'll shaft the fucker. It'll hurt the party, but in the long run not shafting him will hurt it more.'

'Is there likely to be any kind of evidence against him?'

'You and Ms Hillier are going to have to find that out. Let me tell you the rest of the story.'

Pixley seemed to have gone down a gear. His eyelids were drooping. He shook himself alert. 'About a year after Baygate, the same senior man in my department talked me into chucking out a planning decision against a company called Hexiod Holdings. Big shopping mall in Apsley. Millions involved. I also had the local MP camping in my office and a man called Massey, Dix Massey. Know of him?'

'Owns racehorses.'

'And other things. He's Charis Corp's chief cocksucker and standover man. Well, a couple of months later the same man in my department, Bleek, comes to see me. He's sweating blood. He says there are things he wants to tell me but he wants indemnity first.'

Pixley drank deeply. 'I said, "Tell me what it's about, I'll think about the indemnity." He won't. The bastard wants forgiveness before confession. We went on like this for a while, I told him to go away and think about it, come back tomorrow. He comes back the next day, says he had a brainstorm, he was talking rubbish on medication. Stress. Overwork. He's taking sick leave. Please forget about the matter. Never came back. Early retirement. Never set foot in the building again. He's dead now. Killed himself about six months later.'

'You're saying this was connected with Pitman?'

Pixley shrugged. 'You can make your own connections. You know the name of the company that had the foresight to buy Hoagland?'

'Yes. Hexiod Holdings.'

He nodded. 'That's the company. Sold it to Charis Corporation the other day, I see.'

'Can I get this straight?' I asked. 'You're saying that Pitman closed down Hoagland so that Hexiod could buy the site and turn it over to Charis?'

'Draw your own fucking conclusions.' He leaned forward. 'What do you reckon's the company that ended up building Baygate?'

'Charis?'

'Fast learner. That's right. Came from nothing to be one of the biggest developers in the state in about ten years. Bloody miraculous. And now Pitman's in the Planning chair again, old Joe Kwitny's two boys can get seriously rich. Charles and bloody Andrew really can't miss now. Next thing the Kwitnys are going to want their pederast pal Father fucking Gorman in Parliament.'

Father Gorman's fulsome tribute to Joseph Kwitny came back to me. 'Close to the Father, are they?' I asked.

'Old Joe's the biggest donor to that shonky foundation of his. And I think Dix Massey's one of the directors or whatever they call them.'

Pixley had another coughing fit. When it stopped, he pushed his glass away. He looked utterly worn out. 'I've said enough, Jack. Time for some lettuce and my nap.'

I stood up. 'Just one last thing,' I said. 'The death of Anne Jeppeson.'

'Spot of luck for Mr Lucky Pitman, eh? Or do people make their own luck? See yourself out, Jack. Come again.'

I said thanks again. On the way out, I saw Jackie Pixley looking out at the bay. I said goodbye and she said something without turning.

We were sitting in front of a fire in the house Anne Jeppeson grew up in, drinking tea out of bone china cups with little roses on them. The room was comfortable: good furniture scuffed by life. Outside, it was raining on the big garden, the usual thin Melbourne drizzle that dampened the heart more than anything else.

'I'm sorry to ask you to talk about something so painful,' I said. I meant it. There's a special kind of dread you don't know about until you have children.

Mrs Jeppeson shook her head. 'Nothing can make it any worse than it is,' she said. She was in her sixties, a thin and pretty woman with short hair and a faraway look. She was dressed for outdoor work: trousers, shirt, sleeveless jacket and short boots. 'Sometimes I'm glad to talk to someone about it. My husband can't bring himself to. But

Anne's death lies there all the time.'

'Did you see much of her?'

'Not as much as we wanted to. She was always busy and she had her own friends. But she came for most Sunday lunches, well, perhaps every second Sunday here and at the sea. We have a place at Portsea. She was there with us for a few days that summer. Our son and his family were here too. They were living in Hong Kong then. He's in banking, like his father.'

She looked out of the window. Some bedraggled sparrows were pecking the terrace. 'Do you find the winters depressing?'

'Yes. Except for the football.'

'Anne liked football. Richmond. The Tigers. No-one else in the family has any interest in it. My husband pretends to be interested when we're with people who are. I don't know why. It's a male thing, I suppose. I spend as much time outside as possible in winter. I try to ignore the weather.'

'Does that help?'

'I'm not sure. I'd have to stop to find out. Why is Anne's death of interest now?'

'There's a possibility that the person convicted of knocking her down didn't do it.'

She didn't react. 'More tea? I think I'll have some.'

'Thank you. It's very good.'

She poured. 'Have another biscuit. They're homemade. Not by me. I bought them at the church fete. I can't bring myself to go to church any more so I go to all the fundraising efforts and buy things that never get eaten.'

I took another biscuit. 'Perhaps you can tell me something about the days before…'

'Her death. We hadn't seen her for a fortnight. She phoned on the Sunday to say she couldn't come to lunch. That Housing Commission business was on the go, so we saw her on television all the time. My husband was secretly quite proud of her, I think. Although you'd never have known it from the fights they had over those squats in people's houses she used to organise.'

'So you never had the chance to talk about the Hoagland protests?'

'Just a few words on the phone. Well, more than a few words, I suppose. It was very difficult to limit Anne to a few words. She was always so passionate about everything, even when she was little. When she was thirteen or fourteen she knew everything about every oppressed group in the world. It drove her father up the wall. He even complained to the school about one of the teachers putting ideas into the girls' heads. They couldn't agree on anything political. If she wasn't arguing with her father, she was fighting with her brother. She enjoyed baiting him. He's very like his father. Conservative, I suppose. He used to call her Annie the Anarchist. It's funny how different children grow up to be, isn't it? Do you have children, Mr Irish?'

'Just the one.'

'I wish we'd had ten, spaced over twenty years. A stupid idea, isn't it?'

'No.'

She smiled. 'Of course it is. You're very diplomatic.'

The time had come. I said, 'Do you know of any reason why someone would want to murder Anne?'

She put her cup and saucer down and looked at me steadily. She had the inner stillness of someone who has found meaninglessness in everything. 'Are you saying that Anne's death might have been murder?'

'There's a possibility she was murdered.'

She looked away. 'I don't know what to think about that. Who would do something like that? No-one ever suggested...'

'It's just a possibility,' I said. 'Both the man who went to jail and the witness have been shot dead in the last ten days.'

'Are the police investigating?'

'Not Anne's death, no.'

'So it's *your* idea that Anne might have been murdered?'

'My first concern was my ex-client's death but other things have turned up. Anne's death may be the key to what's happened since.'

She gave me a doubtful look. 'I don't know what I can do to help you, Mr Irish. Don't you think it's a police matter?'

'Not just yet. Is there anyone Anne might have confided in? I mean, if she had any fears for her safety, been threatened, anything like that?'

'I suppose the people in that group of hers. Right to a Roof? We never knew any of them.' She thought for a while. 'About her safety, I can remember her saying, it must have been at our wedding anniversary party, I can remember her saying she could go anywhere in safety because the Special Branch were always lurking somewhere.'

'At the squats she organised?'

'I think she meant generally. She was on about mining

companies cheating Aboriginals, but I'm afraid I wasn't paying much attention. She usually had something she felt strongly about. Her father used to say she was only scored for percussion.'

There didn't seem to be anything left to ask. I thanked her for seeing me. The passage leading to the front door was wide enough for us to walk side by side. One side was hung with Australian paintings from the thirties and forties: outdoor scenes, sunlit interiors. I recognised a Gruner and a Tidmarsh. The other wall was covered with framed family photographs.

At the front door, I looked to my right and saw a photograph of four solemn-faced girls in school uniform, two blonde, two dark-haired. They looked about sixteen. Under the picture, it said, 'Coniston Ladies' College Debating Team, 1976'.

I looked at the names. Anne Jeppeson was on the top right, blonde, with a snub nose and rebelliously tousled hair. The girl next to her was one of the brunettes.

Her name was Sarah Pixley.

'She loved debating at school,' said Mrs Jeppeson. 'My husband never went to hear her.'

I pointed at Sarah Pixley. 'Was she friendly with Anne Jeppeson?'

Mrs Jeppeson touched the photograph. 'Sarah Pixley. They were great friends at school. Two of a kind in many ways. Her father's the politician. Sarah hated him. She took her mother's name when she left school. Life can be cruel to parents, can't it?'

'It can, Mrs Jeppeson,' I said. 'It can.'

I drove away down streets where the naked branches of elms and oaks were woven overhead like basketwork and you could glimpse the pert backsides of BMWs and Saabs in brick-paved driveways. It took a while before I found a place that looked as if it might make a hamburger. I was starving.

The hamburger was of the old school: pressed flat as a powder compact, burnt mince topped with burnt onion and cold-storage tomato. It was made by a new-school Aussie, a Vietnamese with rings in one earlobe and a beanie in the Richmond colours. It wasn't a bad hamburger. A slice of sun came out and fell on my lap as I sat in the car, eating and watching a deal taking place across the street in a small park. Two boys in Melbourne Grammar blazers were scoring something off a tall youth with a ponytail wearing an oversized leather jacket. Answers to that day's maths homework, probably.

When I'd finished, I had a sudden urge to see what was happening to the Hoagland estate. I set off down Malvern Road in the direction of St Kilda Road. At Albert Park, I got on to Kings Way and went up King Street through the drab end of the business district. As I waited to turn into Dudley Street at the Flagstaff Gardens lights, a dero in a mauve polyester suit with a filthy Fitzroy FC scarf wound around his neck knocked on the passenger window. I leaned across and wound it down.

'Help a bloke can't get a job?' he asked. He had a long, narrow face, with deepset eyes and a big nose. He looked like a country boy lost in the city for forty years.

I found a five-dollar note and gave it to him. 'Go the Roys.'

'You're a prince among men,' the man said. 'Go Roys, make a noise.'

The future Yarra Cove was much larger than it had appeared on Gerry Schuster's computer screen. I parked near a wooden observation platform next to one of the three site gates. A burly man in a dark-blue uniform with a red shoulder patch that said AdvanceGuard was talking to the driver of a ute in the gateway.

There must have been twenty earthmoving vehicles, giant yellow insects, attacking the glum expanse of grey mud. At least as many trucks moved around the area on temporary roads, stretches of coarse aggregate sinking into the clay.

Not a trace remained of anything that had been there before. I stood at the rail, ten metres up, and after a while the ripping and pushing of the machines began to make some sense. They were gouging massive trenches, the width of streets, running from the waterfront. All of them led to an oval-shaped area, bigger than a football field, marked out with yellow nylon cord threaded through the eyes of metre-high steel needles stuck in the ground. The site huts, a small village of them, were in the middle of the oval. Eventually, the oval would be a yacht basin, with the trenches becoming canals leading from the riverfront. The Hoagland flats must have stood where a small digger was unearthing pipes in one ploughed-up patch.

For a while, caught up in the sheer scale of the operation, I watched the machines roaring and grinding, scooping and reversing, dumping, wheeling, their grey breaths pumping out and being snatched by the sharp-toothed little wind off the river. The whole scene was one of power: man and machine changing a landscape by sheer force.

This was what it was all about.

Sheer force.

Anne Jeppeson thought she was taking on the power of Heartless Bureaucracy. What hit her was the sheer force of Money.

She died so that someone could make a fortune out of rich people's desire to park their boats outside their front doors.

It came to me with absolute certainty that my little inquiry into the lives and deaths of Danny McKillop and Anne Jeppeson was of no consequence whatsoever. Nothing would change what had happened, no-one would be called to account for it. Anne, Danny, Ronnie Bishop, the doctor, me—we were all just minor nuisances.

I felt like shouting Fuck into the wind but there was someone else on the platform, a thin man with a week's grey stubble and wispy hair sticking out from under a beanie. He was drinking a can of Vic Bitter. Looking at me, he drained the can and threw it over his shoulder. 'Used to live here,' he shouted over the noise. 'Fucking shithole. Should've flattened it years ago.' He took another can out of his anorak and popped it.

The daylight was almost gone when I parked outside my office. I had the key in the lock when I sensed someone behind me.

'Mr Irish.' It was a friendly voice. I turned. Two men, solid-looking, in dark suits. The one who had spoken held up an open badge wallet. 'Detective-Sergeant James,' he said. 'The Commissioner of Police would like a word, if it's convenient.'

'It's not,' I said. 'Tell him to make an appointment.'

'If it's not convenient, I have instructions to arrest you,' he said, voice still friendly.

'On what charge?'

'Several charges. One is conspiring to pervert the course of justice.'

'In what matter?'

'Murders. Two of them.'

A gap appeared in my social calendar. I rode in the back of their grey Ford. No-one said anything. When it was clear that we weren't going to police headquarters, I asked where we were going.

'Collins Street,' said the spokesman.

At the Hyatt on Collins, the driver showed the attendant a card and we drove into the underground carpark. We parked in a reserved bay next to the lift.

'Let's go,' said the spokesman.

The three of us went up to the twelfth floor. When the lift door opened, Detective-Sergeant James's partner went out first.

'After you,' said James. 'Number seven.'

I followed his partner down the hushed pink and grey corridor. As he passed a door, he indicated it with his thumb and kept walking. I knocked at number seven. The partner had turned around about ten metres down the corridor and was looking at me. James, near the lifts, was studying a print on the wall.

The door was opened by a man in shirtsleeves and red braces. His tie was loose and he had a drink in his hand. 'Come in, Mr Irish,' he said.

It was the Minister for Police, Garth Bruce.

The suite was pale grey and pink like the corridor. We went through a small hallway into a large sitting room furnished with French period reproductions. A bottle of Johnnie Walker Black Label, an ice bucket, a water carafe and cut-glass whisky glasses stood on a table against the wall. A briefcase was open on a small writing desk between opulently curtained windows.

'Thanks for coming,' Bruce said. 'Sorry about the escort. Let me give you a drink. Whisky, anything.'

I said no thanks, curtly.

He was at the side table with his glass. He put it down and turned, a big man, bigger in life than on television. He'd boxed. There was scar tissue around his eyes. It hadn't shown up on television. That would take skilful make-up. 'Jack,' he said, 'this is friendly. Let's have a quiet drink together. It's very much in your interests. Okay? What'll you have?'

I asked for whisky and water. He made two drinks and brought mine over. We sat down a metre apart. He took a big drink.

'That's better,' he said, sighing. 'Jesus, what a day. Politics. Win one, lose ten.' He took a cigarette out of a packet and offered the packet to me. I shook my head.

Bruce lit up with a lighter, blew out a long, thin stream of smoke and tapped the cigarette in the direction of an ashtray. Ash drifted to the carpet. He sat back, shoulders loose, and said, 'Jack, I'm told you've been asking around about a lot of old business, things that happened nine, ten years ago. That right?'

'Who tells you?'

He had another big drink. His eyes never left me. There was an appealing sadness about them. 'Let me tell you a story,' he said. 'I haven't got a lot of time. I don't want to dance around with you. When I got this job, I appointed a new Commissioner and a new deputy. The first thing I said to them, I said: "The fucking joke's over."'

He leaned forward. 'I was a cop for nearly twenty years, Jack. I know the system, I know what goes on. Everything. These new blokes knew that I knew what I was talking about. Cops've been bullshitting politicians for years. They can't do that to me. I'm not going to sit in a high chair and be fed shit with a spoon. That's why the Premier wanted me in this job.'

He drew on his cigarette and studied me. The silence and the open gaze were disconcerting. He hadn't been a cop for twenty years for nothing.

'Anyway,' he said, 'the point is, when this Danny McKillop got knocked behind the Trafalgar, I called in the file. I've had it with all this Dirty Harry shit. They see it on television. Twenty years, I fired three shots, all in response to cunts firing at me.'

He sat back, stubbed out his cigarette, put his hands in his pockets. 'I read the wife's statement, reckoned there were some questions about what made McKillop so scared. Told the Commissioner that. He came back with all the background, the Jeppeson trial stuff, and the missing person's report on this Bishop.'

Bruce got up, took out another cigarette, flamed it with the lighter, went to the windows. 'Can't sit for long,' he said. 'Back's buggered. Anyway, Jack, what the Commissioner tells me is that the blokes he's had going over this business find your tracks all over the place. You're giving Vin McKillop money, you're in Perth, you're everywhere.'

He turned his head towards me. 'What's really worrying, Jack,' he said quietly, 'is that you were out there in the bush at Daylesford and it looks liked you wiped clean a whole lot of places. Places that could have had the prints of whoever topped Bishop and the druggie quack.'

He looked out into the night again. 'Now that is very, very serious,' he said. 'You know how serious, Jack.'

I had seen this coming but I still didn't know how to handle it. Bruce turned. There was a sheen on his face and on his scalp showing through the short, thinning hair.

'I never found the doctor's place,' I said. 'Got lost.'

He gave me a slow cop smile. 'That's a porky, Jack. If you were going to tell porkies, you should've changed the tyres on that motor Col Boon loaned you. Your tracks are all over the place.'

He came back to his chair and sat down carefully. 'That was a really stupid thing to do. The Commissioner wants to charge you. But he came to me first. That's why you're sitting here, not in metropolitan remand.'

We sat in silence for a while. The little carriage clock on the mantelpiece chimed the half hour, a silver splinter of sound.

Bruce picked up his glass, looked at it, rolled it like a thimble between his big, hairy hands. 'I knew that prick killed your wife,' he said, not looking at me. 'Wayne Milovich. Knew him for years. He was always a dangerous animal. Only had to look at his eyes.'

I didn't know what to say. There was silence again. Bruce rolled his glass.

'Crim tried to shoot my daughter,' he said. 'She was in the kitchen, looking in the fridge. Went through her hair, through the cupboard, through the wall. Couldn't pin it on him. Bloke called Freely. We knew it was him. His whole fucking family, about fifty of them, said he was watching TV at the time. Couldn't shake them. And by Jesus we shook some of them.'

'I never heard about that,' I said.

'No. We kept it quiet. You don't want to give the other animals ideas.'

He got up, collected my glass and made the drinks. While his back was turned, he said, voice just a little rough, 'She was sixteen, lovely girl. Not the same again. Ever. Lost to me. To all of us. In and out of the funny farms. Cut her wrists, swallowed anything she could find. They found her on the beach just before Christmas. Her birthday was Boxing Day. Twenty-first that year. My fault, I suppose. My wife thought so, anyway. Never forgave me.'

I looked at the big back, the way he was holding himself. 'You can't take the blame for what mad people do,' I said. 'You couldn't know.' My voice seemed too loud.

'You could say I did know,' Bruce said flatly. 'He told me he was going to do it. Outside court. He said, "Watch your family, Bruce, something could happen to them." I told him, "You wouldn't have the guts, you chickenshit little bastard."

I laughed at him. He was a runt, five foot fuckall. You'd never credit that he would do it.'

He brought my drink over. I got up to take it. We stood together awkwardly, not knowing where to look, some kind of bond of loss between us. I knew now why I wasn't in metropolitan remand.

'Cheers,' Bruce said.

'Cheers.'

We drank.

'Never said anything to you? Milovich.'

'Just the normal abuse. I wouldn't have paid any attention if he had. I wouldn't have done anything.'

'Would you have told your wife?'

I shook my head.

Bruce nodded. He drank again, wiped his mouth and said, 'You see Danny McKillop after he got out?'

'No.'

'So what, you heard about the shooting, started poking around?'

'No. I was away for a couple of days. When I came back there were messages on my answering machine from him. I didn't even remember who he was. He was waiting for me at the Trafalgar that night. Only I didn't play the tape till the next day.'

'What did he say?'

'Said he was in trouble. He was scared.'

'You talk to the wife?'

'Yes.'

'She tell you about the phone call, about Danny getting the idea he didn't kill the Jeppeson woman?'

I nodded.

'You reckoned there might be something in it, did you?'

I nodded again.

Bruce shook his head. 'And Vin McKillop? He help you along with the theory?'

I shrugged.

Bruce gave me the look. 'Jack,' he said, 'don't come the lawyer with me. If I don't help you, you're going to have to practise in Somalia, somewhere like that.'

I didn't ponder the matter. 'Vin says someone saw Danny miles away from his car and dead drunk about twenty minutes before Anne Jeppeson was killed. And there was a cop with Danny earlier. Someone called Scullin. Vin says Danny was Scullin's dog.'

Bruce sighed and shook his head. He went over to his briefcase and took out a manila folder. He waved it at me. 'I can't show you this,' he said, 'but I'll tell you what it says. Sit down.'

I sat down.

'Danny wasn't a dog. Vin was a dog. Vin was Scullin's dog in those parts. And Vin thought that being an informer gave him some kind of immunity. The next thing Scullin hears is Vin is dealing speed on a fair scale and he's claiming he's got police protection. Scullin didn't like that. He put him away. Four years. Vin's been trying to get even ever since. He's obsessed with Scullin.'

I said, 'So?'

Bruce tapped the folder. 'It's Vin fed Danny all that stuff about being innocent, about Scullin being around that night. It's all bullshit. There's no question that Danny was the driver. Vin's idea was that Danny might go nuts and nail Scullin for him.'

I thought about this for a while. Bruce sat down again, gingerly, and lit a cigarette.

'There's something else,' he said.

I waited.

'The gun Danny had on him at the Trafalgar.'

'The gun the cop says he had on him. Yes.'

'It's the gun that knocked Ronnie Bishop and his druggie doctor mate out at Daylesford.'

This took a bit of absorbing too.

'You know what that means, Jack?' Bruce was holding the folder against his chin.

I had an idea. 'Tell me.'

'Danny was going to kill you that night. You and Scullin and Ronnie Bishop were the trifecta. Good thing you didn't listen to your messages. Danny wanted to knock you, mate. He reckoned you helped fit him up.'

My mouth was dry. I finished my drink, got up and opened a bottle of soda. The realisation that you've been a blind prick is not an easy one to come to terms with.

'What about the doctor?' I asked. 'Where's he come into this?'

'Wrong place, wrong time. That's what it looks like. You can tell me something else. This Hillier woman. She's scratching around the Yarra Cove history. What's that all about?'

I said, 'There's not a lot you don't know, is there?'

'I'll be open with you. The Yarra Cove history is a sensitive subject for the Premier. For the whole fucking party. What's Hillier looking for?'

'I don't think I can tell you that.'

Bruce got up, big hands holding his back, and walked over to the desk. He began to pack up his briefcase. 'You can go,' he said. 'Those blokes brought you will take you up the road and charge you. Good luck.'

I didn't feel like going anywhere. I didn't want to be charged. I didn't want to tell my pathetically naive story in court. I didn't want never to be able to call myself a lawyer again.

'She thinks closing the Hoagland estate was part of a plan to put together the Yarra Cove site. It looks like Lance Pitman closed down Hoagland so that some mates could buy it. They'd started stitching up the properties around it long before.'

Bruce stood his briefcase upright. 'She work this out all by herself?'

I said, 'I talked to Kevin Pixley. He as good as shafts Pitman.'

Bruce took his hands off the briefcase and looked at them. 'Jack,' he said quietly, 'do you know who the biggest crook ever to hold ministerial office in this State is?'

'Be an open field, wouldn't it?'

'No. There's a clear winner. Kevin fucking Pixley. You are sitting here and telling me that you and this journo woman are taking the word of a man who was in the pocket of every shonky developer in the State. Did you go to his big house? Did he tell you about the place at Portsea? Tell you about that little six-bathroom shack in Port Douglas? Didn't happen to mention his old uncle who left him the money, did he? Or his brother, good old Wal Pixley, the one who always seemed to know where to buy property? The one with the instinct for buying cheap just before the rezoning sent prices through the roof?'

I drank some more soda water.

'Let me tell you about Hoagland,' Bruce said. 'I know all about bloody Hoagland. Closing it was decided on about eighteen months before it came to Cabinet. Only three people knew. The Premier, Pitman and Pixley. Putting together a big waterfront site was Pixley's idea. He told his mates, small fry, little property crooks he'd helped out, and they started to buy up the land around the site. But things went sour. They say he wanted a huge payoff for his tip. One last payday before the South of France. His mates didn't want to come over with a massive sum of money before they could sell the properties. So Pixley turned nasty. Said, I'll fucking show you. And when it came to Cabinet, all of a sudden Pixley doesn't want a bar of closing Hoagland. He organises a little Cabinet revolt. They say he got his daughter to tip off the Jeppeson woman. And he leaked it that Cabinet had approved the bloody thing.'

I said, 'All or nothing? That doesn't sound smart.'

'It was smart,' Bruce said. 'The story is his mates said okay, okay, we'll come over with the money. Just stop opposing it. Unorganise your little Cabinet revolt. And he did. End of opposition in Cabinet. Then of all the fucking luck, Danny McKillop gets off his face and decides to go for a drive. End of opposition outside Cabinet.'

'What about when it came to selling the site? Pixley opposed that too. How does that fit?'

'Well, there's two schools of thought. One says it was just a replay of the first scam. The bastard wanted another bite at the cherry. More money from his mates. Blackmail. The other school says it was just a big sham. He knew he was going to be rolled out of Planning. He'd corrupted the whole bloody department. Him and his offsider Bleek, the department head. The Premier'd had enough, thank God. So Pixley thought, here's a way to go out with dignity. Rolled on a matter of principle.'

There was a knock at the door. Bruce went out and closed the door behind him. I drank more soda water and thought about Pixley.

Bruce came back in, leaving the door open. He said, 'I'm pressed, Jack, I've got to be somewhere. If your friend Ms Hillier goes on with her inquiries, she's going to find out what a crook Pixley was and how a couple of his mates, small-timers, made a few quid out of Yarrabank. None of it's got anything to do with the Yarra Cove developers. Charis is clean. The site was offered to them and they bought it. But the Pixley part's not a bad story, the fucking *Age* will love it, the ABC's little turds will come in their pants. Their panties.'

He looked at me for a while.

'Jack, I want a favour from you,' he said. 'You've made a cunt of yourself over Danny McKillop, right?'

He waited.

I nodded.

Bruce looked away. 'I think you've had enough pain with this Milovich. I'm going to lean on the Commissioner. I'm going to get them to wipe you out of this like you wiped your

Daylesford prints. I'll get the files cleaned up. No charges. No trace of you.'

I felt a surge of gratitude, a great sense of relief.

'What I want from you is that you get Ms Hillier to back off the Yarrabank story. If it was up to me, I'd give her a hand with it. Pixley deserves his name written in shit on every building in town. But the Premier takes the view that it will sink the government. Taint everything we've ever done, everything we do in future. We'll just limp through our term. And then the voters will dump us. All because of Kevin Pixley.'

Bruce came over and stood in front of me. 'What do you say, Jack? It's not a big ask.'

I stood up. 'I'll talk to her,' I said. 'And thanks.' I put out my right hand. He took it in both of his.

'I'll give you a number for me,' he said. 'Got a pen?'

I got out my notebook and wrote down the number.

'If anything comes up,' he said, 'ring it and say…what shall we say? Say John English wants to talk to the Minister.'

At the door, we shook hands again. 'You're doing the right thing, Jack,' he said. 'This is the only way to do it.'

The two men drove me back to my office, silence all the way.

We were eating ravioli and drinking red wine in front of the fire when I asked, 'What did Legge mean about the return of the starfucker?'

Linda looked at me thoughtfully while chewing. A large piece of glossy hair had fallen over one eye. She was wearing an old pair of my pyjamas. It came back to me that there is a brief stage in relationships when women like to wear your clothes.

'In what context was this remark made?' she said.

'The day I met you. Talking about you coming back to Melbourne. Later on, he called you an ex-groupie and you said something nice about his wife.'

'You give good ravioli,' she said. 'The *Age* is full of people like Legge. Done all their growing up there, can't work anywhere else. What do you do around here, generally speaking, after ravioli?'

'Oh, around here we just horse around, generally speaking.'

'Horse around? Can you show me how that's done? I'm a city girl.' She slid off her chair into a sitting position on the carpet. The pyjama pants tucked up into her groin. 'Is there any special equipment needed?'

'Generally speaking, we make do with the bare minimum. Improvise.'

'Is that so?' she said, unbuttoning her top button with her left hand.

Later on, I fetched another log from the pile under the fire escape. The lights were off and the firelight made the room look both mysterious and comforting. We sat side by side on the couch, silent for a while, companionable.

'Starfucking,' I reminded her.

Linda said, 'I went off with a singer in a rock band. I walked out on my husband of three years and my job. It seemed like a good idea at the time.'

'Good band?'

'Not bad. Power and Imagination, it was called. They looked like artists and poets are supposed to, sort of pale and dreamy and wasted. They got that way on a strict diet of smack, speed and Bushmills.'

She swung her legs over mine and leaned back. 'Eric was just chipping in the beginning. "Everything's under control" was his favourite expression. We had a great time. Played all over Europe, did a tour with Fruit Palace, went to a party with Mick Jagger, met Andy Warhol. What a prick.'

'Were you in love?' I said.

'Madly. I was just a kid. Only I didn't know it. I was twenty-three, never really been out of Melbourne, married to a doctor I met at uni. Then one day this utterly strange and exciting creature came into my life. He had a kind of erotic presence, it was overpowering. And he lived in a world that had nothing to do with shopping and dishes and catching trams and alarm clocks and meals at certain times and lunch with your husband's parents every Sunday. He put his hand on me and I was gone.'

I found the red wine and poured some into our glasses.

'So that's starfucking,' Linda said. 'And it all ends in tears, believe me.'

'Everything's got a price.'

She leaned over and kissed me half on the mouth. 'Mine's cheap. Plate of ravioli is the going rate. You've got a bit of an erotic presence yourself, if I may say so. Of the wounded rogue bull-elephant variety.'

'Many a cow has told me that,' I said. 'I want to tell you something.' I'd been putting this off all night.

'So soon? There's another woman already?'

'I got escorted to see the Police Minister this evening. The cops know I was at the doctor's place. They know I wiped my prints.'

Her eyes were wide. 'How did they find out?'

'Somebody must have remembered the Celica's rego. Bloke I asked for directions, I suppose. They seem to have traced it to the guy who lent it to me. And matched its tyre prints with some I left at the scene. He says they matched them, anyway.'

'What now?' There was concern in her voice.

'There's more.' I told her everything Bruce had told me.

'That's quite a session you had,' she said when I'd finished. 'You believe him?'

'Mainly. It makes more sense than the version I half convinced myself was true.'

'So Danny McKillop ends up getting lumbered with everything. Revenge killer. How come he didn't start with this Scullin?'

I shrugged. 'Could be any number of reasons. No-one will ever know.'

Linda lay back and looked at the ceiling. 'What did Pixley tell you?'

'Lots. He hates Pitman. He says Pitman tried to get him to do things for big donors to the party and shut down Hoagland so that he could sell the site to mates. He says Cabinet didn't approve the sale the first time Pitman raised it. But someone leaked that it had been approved.'

Linda pushed back her hair. 'Pixley says this outright?'

'More or less.'

'Paydirt,' she said. She had the shine in her eyes I'd seen when the fat woman played the computer at Urban-Data.

'Not quite. He won't go on the record. I also talked to Anne Jeppeson's mother. Pixley's daughter, Sarah, was in Anne's class at school. They were close friends.'

'Jesus. That's stretching coincidence a bit. Wait a minute. The Cabinet leak about Hoagland…'

'Bruce says Pixley told his daughter, who told Anne. Pixley also suggested that Bleek, the senior officer in the

Planning department, was got to by Pitman. He's dead too. Bruce says Bleek was corrupted by Pixley.'

'Did Pixley mention companies?'

'Hexiod and Charis. He says they're the same thing.'

'This is heavy stuff,' Linda said. 'Pass the wine.'

I poured some more of the red. 'You won't be able to drive after this,' I said hopefully.

Linda looked at the fire through her glass. 'Dear me,' she said, 'I'll just have to stay over and fuck your face off. Listen, I think Bruce is trying to bullshit you. I've searched all the Yarrabank titles. What it looks like is that about eighteen months before Pitman decided to shut Hoagland eight companies began buying up the area.'

'*Eight* companies?'

'That's right. Eight companies with names like Edelweiss Nominees Number 12 and Collarstud Holdings and Rabbitrun. And they in turn are owned by companies registered in places like the Cayman Islands and Vanuatu and Jersey.'

'Dummies.'

'Your normal shelf numbers. I've talked to five of the sellers. At least three real estate firms were involved. The owners were made reasonable offers. There was no hurry for possession, the agents said. They could stay on, no rent, if they wanted to. They would get sixty days' notice to move. And there was a secrecy bonus if the buyer was satisfied that no word of the deal had leaked out for thirty days after the sale.'

'Was it paid?'

'Yes. More than a year before Pitman went to Cabinet with his proposal the whole area around Hoagland was stitched up by the eight companies. Well, all except one bit, a sheetmetal works. That changed hands about six months after the others. The land anyway. The factory burnt down.'

'Someone who wouldn't sell?'

'Could be. I'd have to talk to the owner.'

'What's all this add up to?'

'I'd say somebody had the idea for Yarra Cove and quietly bought up the properties through the nominee companies. The companies warehoused them, waiting for Hoagland to be closed and sold to Hexiod Holdings. But before anything could happen, the government lost the election. The nominee companies then one by one sold their waterfront properties to a company called Niemen PL and Niemen consolidated them into one property, a semicircle around Hoagland. Niemen applied for a rezoning for the consolidated property as residential. But the new government blocked them. So nothing happened for nine years. Then Pitman's mob came back into power and the next day Hexiod sold the Hoagland site to Charis Corporation. Soon after that, Niemen sold the waterfront strip to Charis. Hey presto, the jigsaw's complete. All is in readiness for a six hundred million dollar development.'

I felt tiredness creeping over me. 'So Charis might only have come into the picture at the end?'

Linda put her glass on the floor. 'I'd guess that all parties were in on the deal from the beginning. Hexiod wouldn't have bought Hoagland if it wasn't sure it could buy the rest of the land. The people behind the nominee companies wouldn't have bought up the whole area unless they were part of a deal with Hexiod and Charis.'

'And nobody,' I said, 'would have done anything unless they knew that Hoagland was going to be closed down.'

'And sold to Hexiod.'

'But you're just guessing,' I said. 'It's possible that Pixley was the one who tipped off the first buyers and that Charis is just the innocent last link in the chain.'

'I doubt that.'

'But nothing you know says that the whole thing was more than a little scam involving some small-time friends of Kevin Pixley's.'

'I don't know what you'd call a big scam,' said Linda.

'Leaving Hoagland aside,' I said, 'there's still no real evidence that Anne Jeppeson was murdered. Or that Danny was framed. In fact, I now think it's extremely unlikely that Danny was framed.'

She hugged herself. 'Because Bruce says so? Five minutes with the Minister and you come out in reverse.'

'What he says makes more sense of the evidence than my conclusions. And no-one's going to prove any different. Even if Pitman was somehow involved, you won't nail him. You'd have to demonstrate a connection between him and one of the other parties. A tangible link. A beneficial link.'

Linda took my right hand and put it inside her pyjama top, under her right breast. 'I love it when you sound lawyerly,' she said. 'Cup that. And demonstrate a connection.'

I wanted to cup it. And its twin. And to show a tangible link. But I felt a dread stealing over me and I took my hand away. 'Linda,' I said, 'I think we've got to close the book on this thing. I've given my word to Bruce.'

She leaned back. 'Your word? Your word what?'

I found it hard to say it. 'I've told him that neither of us will take this any further. That includes the Hoagland sale.'

Linda stood up. 'I don't understand. Why? Why would you do that?'

How do you tell people about your fear that you might lose one of the few things that has given your life any meaning? 'Bruce offered me a trade,' I said.

'A trade?'

'Back off or be charged with a whole raft of offences over my Daylesford excursion.'

Linda shook her head in disbelief. 'Bruce didn't offer me a trade. You can't speak for me. This whole thing doesn't belong to you. You can't suddenly take your ball and go home. This is a huge story. It could bring down a Cabinet Minister. Maybe the whole government. You can't just switch it off because you've got cosy with the Police Minister.'

'Listen to me,' I said. 'I'm not cosy with him. I'm scared. I'm under the gun. They'll charge me. I'll get convicted. Even if I don't go to jail, I'll get struck off the roll. I'll never be able to practise again.'

She looked at me for what seemed to be a long time. Then she turned and went into the bedroom. I waited, stomach tense, not knowing what to do, knowing I was losing her. When she came out, she was dressed. She went over to where her jacket was hanging over a chair.

I said, 'Can we calm this down? I'm—'

She cut me off, voice even. 'Jack, as far as I can see four people have died over Hoagland. It's likely that there's been a spectacular piece of corruption. I was under the impression you cared about that. Now you're telling me that the nice Police Minister has explained the whole thing to your satisfaction. And to help convince you, he's threatened you with legal action. So to hell with justice, you've agreed to shut up. And you've agreed to shut me up. Well, I'm not yours to shut up. I don't know what made you think I might be.'

I tried to get angry. 'Hold on. A minute ago you were talking about a huge story. Now you're campaigning for justice. Which one do you want to sacrifice me for? Justice or the huge story?'

There was something approaching contempt in her eyes. I knew about contempt in people's eyes. In my life even outback barmen had looked at me with contempt in their eyes.

Linda took her jacket and walked to the door. When she got there, she turned and said, 'If your new chum the Minister drops you in it because you can't control me, my view is you should've asked me first. That's about my pride. About your pride, I'd have thought you wouldn't have given a fuck about getting struck off the roll if you could find out the truth about what happened to Danny McKillop. And if you think the Minister's going to supply you with the truth, you have been living on some other planet for the last forty years. Goodbye.'

I rang twice before I gave up. She had the answering machine on. Halfway through my second message I felt pathetic and broke off. What was there to say anyhow? I lay down on the sofa and tried to sort out my thoughts.

It hadn't occurred to me that Linda wouldn't go along with what I'd done. I'd kept nagging at the thing because I felt I'd let Danny McKillop down. Twice. I didn't think that anymore. I believed Bruce: Danny had probably intended to confront me over my part in his jailing; he might well have intended to kill me. And if Danny wasn't framed for killing Anne Jeppeson, then she wasn't murdered. That left the matter of finding out the truth about Hoagland. But I wasn't going to give up my attachment to the law in pursuit of the truth about Hoagland. There wasn't going to be any truth about it. No-one was going to go on trial for what would probably be regarded as a smart piece of property dealing. So it wasn't a choice between getting justice for Danny or facing serious criminal charges. It was a choice between achieving nothing and getting struck off.

When I finally went to bed, I slept badly, the dream coming back for the first time in years, and, after it woke me, the unbidden and random memories of childhood. The dreams began when I was about nine, when we went to live in the grand house in Toorak with my grandfather, my mother's father, after my father's death. My screams would wake my mother in her huge room miles down the corridor. I could never explain the dream or why it was so frightening. It is about surfaces and textures: smooth, cold surfaces like great sheets of iced marble that suddenly become hot and buckle and twist; steel bars that become dense forests of hot, slippery entrails; pale surfaces that feel solid before they turn to blood-red ooze, sucking you down like quicksand. The dream comes with no warning, as if a trapdoor opens and I fall from the safe and known world into a world that is nothing but terrifying sensation in which I am utterly alone.

The childhood memories started after Isabel's death. They rise up in the margin between wakefulness and sleep and they lie on the mind like prints floating in fixer. All of them seem to date from the years before my father's death. In one, I see the back of the house of my childhood friend Chris Freeborn. Chris's little sister is outside the back door, stirring something in a zinc tub. Through the open back door I can see down a passage all the way to the street. There are people on the pavement outside, moving in and out of the frame of the front door. From inside the house,

I can hear someone sobbing and saying something I cannot catch over and over again. In another, my mother is standing behind a high fence, her hands above shoulder-height, fingers hooked in the diamond mesh. She is wearing a dress with large spots on it and her hair is pulled back. The expression on her face is one of anxiety: her chin is lifted, her mouth is open slightly as if she is breathing shallowly through it. There are other women on either side of her, but she is not with them. I am looking at her from the other side of the fence and as I get closer I see that her left eye is full of blood.

These two memories and at least a dozen others fill me with unease, but they have no meaning. I have no other memories of Chris Freeborn's house. Indeed, I cannot bring to mind Chris Freeborn's face. Nor do I know anything about the fence behind which my mother stands. Or, in another memory, who the men are in the car full of cigarette smoke. Or, in another, why my mother and I are shivering in a doorway in the dark, hiding from the headlights of cars. There is no-one I can ask about them. My mother is dead, my sister was born after my father's death, the Freeborn family is scattered to the winds.

At 5.40 a.m., exhausted, I declared the night at an end, got up and made a pot of tea. While it was drawing, I found a novel called *Over Ice* I had been meaning to finish. I read until 8 a.m., when I wrenched myself away from the excitement of a pension in postwar Vienna to clean the flat. Some of the flat. One room. Partly. At 8.30, I drove down Brunswick Street to Meaker's. The street was almost empty, just me and a few party animals in leather and dark glasses moving towards the caffeine with the care of blind people in a strange place.

I almost missed the item on page five of the *Age*. 'Former Minister found dead,' the headline said. The story said Kevin Pixley had been found dead in the bathroom of his Brighton home. A heart attack was suspected. Mrs Pixley was in London.

What appetite I'd mustered was gone. In the night, I'd turned over the idea of going back to Pixley and putting Bruce's accusations to him. In the end, I'd concluded that it would be pointless. Kevin Pixley wasn't going to fall in a heap and confess anything to me.

And what did it matter? Guilt over Danny had started me off. Now I had little doubt that Danny had driven the car that killed Anne Jeppeson. I had nothing to feel guilty about.

I drank a short black and went around to Taub's. The wood and oil smell of the workshop had the power to cheer me at even the lowest times. Down at my end of the workshop, Charlie had laid out on trestles the wood for my boardroom tabletop: three perfect walnut boards, fifteen feet long, eighteen inches wide and one-and-a-half inches thick. They came from what Charlie called The Bank, the timber stacked in the rafters. The first time Charlie had given me a job using timber from The Bank, I'd asked: 'What's this?'

'Piece wood,' Charlie said. *'Swietenia mahagoni*. Cuban mahogany. One hundred years old.'

'I don't think I'm quite ready for this,' I said.

Charlie had taken the cheroot out of his mouth and given my statement some thought. 'Jack,' he said, 'till you make something nice out of it, it's just a piece wood.'

I studied the rough walnut boards with reverence. This was one of the classic furniture timbers. Very few makers ever had the chance to work with wood of this quality and size. I turned one of the boards over. Chalked on the other side was the date Charlie had laid the resawn boards down: 10/3/46. This wood's moisture content was so low that not even the ducted central heating in some Collins Street tower was going to cause it to move. Did an emerging mining company deserve a table made from unobtainable timber air-dried for at least fifty years? Wouldn't some lesser, wetter timber do? The miners wouldn't notice. I'd once asked Charlie the same question about a bureau he was making for a hotel owner with drug connections. 'This *arschloch* I'm not making it for,' he said. 'He's just the first owner. I'm making it for all the owners.'

I set aside my feeling of awe, put on my overalls and went to work. I gave the boards a preliminary pass over the pride of Charlie's life, a near-new high-speed 24-inch surface planer bought from a bankrupt furniture factory. I took off a tissue-paper-thin layer, exposing the figure in the wood. I went outside and stood in the drizzle for a few moments so that I could come back in and smell the fragrance of the walnut filling the workshop. After that, I gave the edges two passes each over the long-bed jointer to prepare them for edge-jointing. Then I set the planer and put the boards through again. They came out almost polished. I dipped a finger in a pot of Charlie's own oil, cold-pressed linseed oil prepared on the workshop stove without chemicals. It was like putting a finger in honey. I drew a squiggle on one of the boards and rubbed the oil in. The wood came to life: smooth, fine-textured, glowing.

I had the three boards on the trestles, admiring the fit of my edge joints, when Drew said from the door, 'I never saw you look at a client that way.'

I looked at my watch. Three hours had slipped by. 'I never had a client wanted to be planed, jointed and oiled,' I said.

We picked up Norm O'Neill and Eric Tanner at the Prince. Wilbur Ong was going to the game with his grandson, Derek Ong, society dentist.

'They can't give this bunch a sheilas a beltin, might as well merge with Brighton Bowls Club,' Norm O'Neill said.

'I heard Vanotti's got a groin problem,' said Eric Tanner. 'There's a number of the fellas got things missing in their groins,' Norm said gloomily.

Things were more cheerful on the way back from the Western Oval. Things were riotous on the way back from the Western Oval. We'd beaten St Kilda 84–79. St Kilda was one of the league's most improved sides and we'd come from behind to win. It was coming from four goals down— that was what mattered. That was the sweetness. Fitzroy had played its usual game: players dropping chest-marks and handballing at each other's knees. But then, in the final quarter, Ansell and McCracken kicked two each. Then Grimmer kicked one. We were in front. And we stayed there, fighting off the Saints for ten agonising minutes. At the final siren, in the rain, we embraced one another and drank toasts from Drew's little silver flask of malt whisky. Around us the Fitzroy supporters croaked out the club song with the joy that comes only to those who have kept the faith through the darkest nights.

At the Prince, the atmosphere was like VE Day. Even Stan was smiling. Even Stan's wife cracked a joke. We had a few toasts, a few songs, relived a few great games. Then Drew and I took his car home and got a taxi to Vlado's in Richmond. The warm room was full of Japanese tourists exclaiming at their handbag-sized steaks. We had almost finished ours and a bottle of '88 Bailey's shiraz when Drew said, 'Hear anything more from that bloke who tried to heavy you?'

I told him about finding the two bodies.

He looked at the roof, looked at me. 'Fucking oath, Jack. Have you gone completely out of your brain?'

'Listen,' I said, 'there's more.' I told him about Linda's digging into Hoagland and my discussion with the Minister.

When I'd finished, he cut the last of his rump in two. 'Jack,' he said, 'you won't mind my saying you're a stupid prick, will you?'

'Not really.'

He put a piece of steak in his mouth and chewed thoughtfully, looking around the room. 'Mate, you don't seem to have got a grip on something,' he said.

'What particular thing is that?' I asked.

'You've gatecrashed a party at the big end of town. With McKillop, I thought you were getting mixed up with some drug business and someone was giving you a chance to pull your head in. Now you tell me you've been trying to tie up the Jeppeson death and McKillop's conviction and death and Bishop's and the doctor's, the whole bloody mess, with Yarra Cove.'

He looked around again. 'This is dangerous stuff. We shouldn't even talk about it in public places.'

'Come on, Drew,' I said. 'This is Melbourne.'

Drew drank some wine. He leaned forward. 'Jack, I think you're out of touch. You're still stuck in the days when the Melbourne Club ran this town. All those pompous arseholes who owned factories and insurance companies and played the market. All went to Melbourne Grammar or similar and basically silly buggers who didn't like Jews or Ities or other kinds of wogs. Otherwise reasonably harmless twerps. Their day's gone, Jack. They woke up one day and found the real money was in property development. Residential sub-divisions. Hotels. Shopping centres. Office blocks. And most of the people making the money didn't give a shit about joining the club.'

He dropped his voice. 'I'm talking about people like Joe Kwitny, mate. Came out here with two pounds and holes in his socks. Got a job as a brickie, didn't know a brick from a banjo. Some old bloke in Preston gave him a crash course for ten bob. Next thing Joe's the gun brickie, the union's telling him to slow down or a wall's going to fall on him. So bugger the union, Joe borrows a few quid, goes off concreting over backyards, putting up brick-veneer houses. That was the beginning. The next thing people like Joe were employing hundreds, doing million-dollar deals, putting up buildings overnight, building whole fucking suburbs out there on the fringes. And on the way they found out how to make sure government gave them the decisions they wanted, how to get the unions on side.'

Drew paused and looked at me for a while, the way

teachers look at less-than-quick pupils. 'These people don't think bribery is a crime, Jack,' he said. 'It's just an alternative way to get things done. Blackmail? Well, some people won't co-operate. Rough stuff, murder maybe? Well, accidents happen. Some of the smarter ones even take the long view. They've gone into politics, stacking party branches, getting the right people into Parliament.'

Drew paused, spoke slowly. 'I'm talking about Joe Kwitny, Jack. Charis fucking Corporation.'

He sat back. I didn't know quite what to say. Drew didn't normally deliver lectures. We ate in silence for a while. Then he said, 'Well, that's the lecture. That's the way the world is now, and mate, you have been wandering around in it like some yokel from Terang in town for the day. You think you're doing something good, not so? You see it in terms of right and wrong, justice, that kind of thing. Well, pardon me, you know and I know that the system is not about fairness. It's not about good and bad. It's not about right and wrong. It's about power, Jack. I know that. You should know that.'

'At least I knew when to back off.'

Drew shook his head. 'I don't know if you've backed off in time. One thing's for sure. Bruce is no white knight. He's going to rebury this smelly stuff you've been digging up. You just have to make sure he doesn't put you in the hole too.'

'I could get myself some insurance.'

He cocked his head. 'Don't follow you?'

'Say it gets into the papers.'

Drew didn't reply until he had aligned his cutlery, wiped his mouth with his napkin, folded it, put it under his side plate, signalled the waiter and ordered two brandies.

'Mate,' he said, 'don't let the thought cross your mind. If they can hang this stuff on anybody, it'll be on small fry and people already dead. And you'll keep. These people have got long memories. They'll come back for you.'

At home, I could smell Linda's perfume on the pillows. For a moment, I lay there, drowning in a sense of loss. Then I got up and changed the sheets and pillowcases. I slept better. The first night is always the worst.

Phillip Epstein, art dealer, didn't ask to see the provenance, although I had it.

'You'd expect, what?' he said.

'I need twenty-five thousand as soon as possible,' I said. 'They should cover that.'

He patted my arm. 'Sisley,' he said. 'I think that's a reasonable expectation. Where on earth did you get them?'

'From my wife. Her grandfather once owned the whole notebook.'

He frowned. 'You've got more?'

'No,' I replied. 'They're the only material thing I've got left that's worth anything.'

'I'll be happy to advance the twenty-five thousand. We'd want to take our time selling.'

'It would help,' I said, 'if it was in cash.'

He smiled. 'Let's go in the back and have a drink. We're not talking used notes in small denominations, are we?'

'Large denominations would be better.'

Hardhills was as we'd left it: cold, damp, three utes and a dog outside the pub. On the way, Harry said, 'Fill you in, Jack, next Saturday's the day. Caulfield, race four. Two thousand four hundred. Bit short for the bloke's breeding but it'll do. Next point. We're puttin a girl on him.'

'I thought it was going to be Mick Sayre,' I said.

Harry popped a Smartie. 'Turns out Mickey's a bit of a worry,' he said. 'Cam here was talkin to a clocker, fella who knows a few things. Says Mickey put a whole Greek syndicate on a plunge up in Sydney. On the day the stable got such a fright when they saw the odds go to buggery, they told Mick, bugger this, we're not goin on at four to one, we'll do it another day. Trouble was, Mickey's more frightened of the Greeks than the stable. Wins three lengths clear. Next start, two to one favourite. Greeks love Mick but he doesn't ride for that stable any more.'

'Who's the girl?'

Harry turned and gave me a wink. 'You might've seen her. Nicest little bum on the turf.'

'That's her qualification?'

Harry smiled. 'Nancy Farmer. Rides for her dad. Harold. Two city wins. Mostly she rides the cattle out in the bush. Cam's happy. Wanted a girl from the start.'

'Why's that?'

Cam was driving the big BMW. He took it around a speeding semi with a smooth change-down and a burst of power before he gave me a glance. 'There's two reasons,' he said. 'One, women can keep their mouths shut. They don't get on the phone, go down the pub, do all their mates a favour. Reason two, a little girl's been looking after this bloke fulltime for a year. They're in love. Her and her brother's all that's ridden him. You don't want to put some cocky bastard on him, hard hands, knows it all, thinks he can thrash him home.'

'I'm convinced,' I said. 'What about her bum?'

'Bum?' Cam said. 'Since when do jockeys have bums?'

We parked in the same place as before. Cam got out to have a smoke. Harry put his seat back.

'She'll be along in a minute,' he said.

'The jockey?'

'Staying at Ericson's till the race. I want her to get to know this Dakota Dreamin.'

An old Land Rover pulled up next to us. A woman in her early twenties got out, moleskins, checked shirt, short hair, windburnt face: lean as string. Cam went over. They shook hands, said a few words.

Cam came back and got in, drove off. She followed us around and over the low hills and parked next to us at Ericson's. She was out quickly, waiting, hands in flap pockets.

It was just as cold as the time before. Cam said, 'This is Mr Strang and Mr Irish, Mr Strang's lawyer.' We shook hands. She was good-looking, big mouth, no make-up, a hint of wariness in the eyes.

'You're on time. That's good,' said Harry.

Tony Ericson came up the gravel path from the stables. More handshakes.

'Use your kitchen table, Tony?' Harry said. 'Bit of talkin to do.'

Ericson led us inside the house and down a passage to a big, warm kitchen with an old Aga stove. We sat down at the table. Harry was at the top. Nancy Farmer was opposite me. She put her elbows on the table and laced her fingers. She had big wrists and strong hands like Harry's.

'Nancy,' said Harry. 'Mr Delray told you he wanted you to ride a bit of track on this Dakota Dreamin before Saturday.'

She said, 'That's right.'

Harry said, 'This horse is goin to win.'

She kept looking at him, no expression.

'It's goin to win,' Harry said, 'because it's the best horse in the race. There's nothin else happenin.'

Nancy nodded. A little tension went out of her shoulders. 'Why me?' she asked.

'Like your style, good hands, got a bit extra out of that Home Boy in the spring.'

'Didn't get me any more races in town,' she said.

Harry smiled. 'This'll be the makin of you. Tony, tell Nancy about this bloke.'

Tony Ericson didn't do much public speaking but he got through it. At the end, he said, 'He goes down the beach every day. Me girl rides him in the water, on the sand. Four days he does a bit of track, not too much. Not the way the others do it, but he's rock-hard now. Just right.'

Nancy said, 'You trialled him at the distance?'

Tony shook his head. 'No. He's bred for the two miles but he'll run a strong race at anything over two thou.'

She looked around the table. 'I'll do my best.'

Harry said, 'You'll understand if I say you can't make any phone calls without Mr Ericson's with you? You got a mobile with you?'

She shook her head. 'Is this big?' she asked.

Harry nodded. 'Big enough.'

The tip of her tongue came out and moistened her lower lip. 'I don't have any calls to make,' she said.

'Good,' said Harry. 'There's a thousand for the week's work here. You want to talk about the race fee?'

Nancy looked at him, unsmiling. 'It's laid down.' She paused. 'Excuse me, are you *the* Harry Strang…?'

'Things go right,' Harry said slowly, 'Mr Ericson here is a generous owner.' He patted the table with both hands. 'Well, business over. Let's have a look at the bloke.'

At Dakota's stable, a small girl in overalls was waiting, stroking the horse's nose. She had short red hair and freckles.

'This is me girl Denny,' Ericson said. 'Slim's sort of her horse.'

Nancy shook hands with Denny. 'Pleased to meet you, boss,' she said. 'Now that's what I call grooming. You want to bring him out?'

The girl blushed with pleasure.

Dakota came out calmly, gleaming like a horse in a painting. Denny handled him as if he were a big labrador. He was saddled and bridled inside a minute. We walked behind Nancy, Denny and the horse to the track. Dakota had his head down, his neck extended. He looked as if he were deep in thought, a horse at peace with himself and his surroundings.

'Walks like a stayer,' Harry said. 'You can always tell.'

At the track, Nancy adjusted the stirrups, swung up effortlessly.

'Have a little muck about, get the feel of him,' said Tony Ericson.

We watched for fifteen minutes while she took him up and down the track, trot, canter, short gallop, bit of walking around. When she came back to us, she said, 'Nice horse, likes to run,' rubbing his jaw. She got off and gave the reins to Denny.

'Walk with me,' Harry said. They hung back. When I looked around, they had their heads together, Harry talking with his hands. At the top of the gravel path, they caught up.

'Friday, I'll be back, talk some tactics, look at some movies,' Harry said.

On the way home, Harry said to Cam, 'Girl can ride. Strong, too. You got a feelin?'

Cam flicked a glance at him. 'You know what Oscar Wilde said? Only one thing makes more of a fool of a man than a woman. And that's a horse.'

Harry said, reflectively, 'That so? Didn't know old Oscar rode horses. Knew he rode everythin else.'

The sun came out as we drove over the Westgate Bridge. Off to the left, far off in the distance, I could see the observation platform at Yarra Cove. They had put three flags on it now. Big flags.

I got in another two hours' work at Taub's. The three tabletop boards had to be joined with hide glue. Charlie wouldn't use anything else for this kind of work. Some cabinetmakers use epoxy resin glues. The joints were claimed to be stronger than the woods they joined. When I mentioned this to Charlie, he said, with feigned incomprehension, 'Stronger than the wood? You want joints stronger than wood, welding is the trade.'

I measured out a quantity of hide glue, golden granules, dissolved them in water, added some more granules and heated up the liquid in the glue pot. While it was warming, I put the boards on the gluing stand and dry-clamped them. The fit was good. I unclamped them and, when the glue was hot, I carefully painted it on two interior edges with a hog-bristle brush. Then I put hardwood strips down the outside to protect the outer edges and one-inch dowels outside them to spread the clamp pressure. I tightened the eight bar clamps, the outside pair first, then alternately on each side. At each end and at three intervals along the surface, I used three-by-three hardwood cauls and C-clamps to make sure that the pressure of the bar clamps wasn't distorting the assembly.

It had to be absolutely flat. There were no second chances.

Then I tinkered with the clamps for a good fifteen minutes, trying to ensure that I had enough pressure but didn't force out glue and starve the joints. 'Trust your hands,' Charlie used to say in the early days. 'If you're straining, it's too tight.' I didn't quite understand this: Charlie could tighten the nuts on the Sydney Harbour Bridge with his bare hands without taking any strain.

When I'd cleaned up, I went home. Reluctantly.

Sunday night. I cleaned the kitchen and the bathroom, fed the dishwasher, tried to read the *Sunday Age*, opened a bottle of wine, drank half a glass, stared at the contents of the fridge. Made a cheese and gherkin sandwich. Women come into your life and all the hard-earned self-sufficiency deserts you. Suddenly you're half a person again.

The phone rang. Long-distance beeps.

'Jack Irish?' Ronnie Bishop's friend Charles Lee in Perth.

I said I was sorry about Ronnie's death. I didn't have the heart to tell him I wasn't interested in Ronnie anymore.

'Jack,' he said. 'I should tell the police this now that Ronnie's dead. Remember I told you about the answering machine tape? How it was missing?'

'I remember.'

'Well, I found it. About half an hour ago. Under the drinks cupboard next to the phone. It must have slid under there when the burglar tipped out the phone table drawer. It's got the messages from Melbourne for Ronnie.'

'Have you listened to them again?'

'Yes. They're from different people. The first one left a name and phone number. Danny McKillop. Do you want the number?'

I said, 'No. I've got that number. What about the other one?'

'There's just a message. No name. It's a man.'

'What's the message.'

'I've written it down. He said, "Ronald, listen to me carefully. It's absolutely vital that you bring the evidence. You were stupid to take it and now you've been doubly stupid. I'll have to extricate you." Then he says something that sounds like "sculling's the one in trouble". And then he says, "Ring me when you get here."'

'Can you play that to me over the phone?' I said.

Charles hesitated. 'I can try. I'll put it on the stereo tape deck and hold the phone near the speakers. Hang on.'

I could hear him moving about the room. There were a few false tape starts, then he came back on and said, 'Here goes.'

There was an electronic whine, a pause, a throat-clearing. Then the rich voice of Father Rafael Gorman said, 'Ronald, listen to…'

When the message finished, Charles said, 'Did you get that?'

I said, 'Loud and clear.'

'Do you know who it is?'

'I think so. Well done, Charles.'

'I should tell the police, shouldn't I, Jack? It could be very important.'

I made a decision without a second's conscious thought. 'Charles,' I said, 'this is important but I want you to wait until I call you before you tell the police. It won't be more than forty-eight hours, I promise. Will you do that?'

He didn't hesitate. 'Yes. Yes, I will. Jack, there's something else.'

'Yes?'

I waited.

'This is probably quite meaningless.'

I waited.

'I certainly wasn't going to tell those men, but there *was* something the day Ronnie left for Melbourne.'

'What was that?' I said encouragingly.

'Well, I drove him into the city that morning. I had the day off. He said he had to get something out of his safe deposit box at the bank. I dropped him outside and waited, double parked. He was only about five minutes. Then we drove back to his place. His suitcase was already packed and he opened the zip compartment and he took something out of his jacket pocket and put it in.'

'Any idea what?'

'No. Something flat, that's all.'

'And you think that's what he'd got out of his safe deposit?'

'Yes. Well, I can't be sure. I felt bad about not telling you before.'

'I'm glad you have now. It could be useful. Keep it to yourself. Thanks, Charles. Ring me if you think of anything else. I'll get back to you as soon as I can.' Then a thought occurred to me. 'Maybe you can help with something else. Someone I don't know knows I was in Perth asking about Ronnie. Have you told anyone about me?'

Again, he didn't hesitate. 'No. It'll be that architect bitch next door. When you were in your car I looked around and I could see her shape against the venetian blind upstairs. She thinks you can't see her, but there's light behind her. I've seen her there before. Once when my friend from work came to keep me company while I was tidying up Ronnie's garden she had a good look. And then she came out and took the dog up the street and back. It was because she couldn't see his licence plate from the window, I'm sure.'

'Who would she tell?'

'Those men, I suppose. The ones I told you about.'

I said, 'Thanks again, Charles. I'll be in touch.'

In the kitchen, I poured a glass of wine. There was a little tingle in my body. I found a piece of paper for doodling and sat at the kitchen table.

Father Gorman had said, *Scullin's the one in trouble*. Trouble over what? Danny McKillop's attempt to get his case reopened? Not if Bruce was to be believed. Why then had Ronnie come to Melbourne if not in response to Danny's phone call? How would Scullin be involved? What was the evidence his old employer wanted him to bring? Evidence of what? Had Gorman steered Ronnie out to the doctor's establishment in the bush so that he could be murdered? Did this have any connection with Danny?

The phone rang again. Blinking, I looked at my watch: 11.15. It was Linda. Just when I'd stopped missing her for three minutes at a time.

'You alone?' she said.

'No,' I replied. 'I had three girls home delivered from Dial-a-Doll.'

'I've been burgled. The place is a shambles.'

I sat upright. 'What's gone?'

'My laptop. All my disks. Whole filing cabinet emptied. Not the television or the VCR or the stereo.' There was a pause. 'It's a bit scary.'

'Don't touch anything. Grab some clothes and come over here. We'll get the cops in tomorrow.'

'No,' she said. 'I'm okay. I've already rung the cops. If I don't stay here tonight I'll never come back.'

'I'll come over.'

'No. It's fine. I just wanted to tell you. Hear your voice, really. There's something else.'

'What?'

'Everything I've put into the computer system at work is gone. Wiped.'

'Accident?'

'I don't think so.'

'Don't you have some kind of security?'

'Yes. There's more.'

I waited.

'That creep in Sydney I told you about? The regional director?'

'Yes.'

'He's told my boss here that I'm to drop any story about Yarra Cove or anything to do with Charis Corporation.'

Suddenly the room felt cold. 'What did you say?'

'I said I'd think about it.'

'Sure you don't want to come over here?'

'Yes. I'll call you in the morning.'

'Call me any time. How did they get in?'

'Don't know. The front door was still locked.'

'Have you got a chain?'

'Yes. And two bolts.'

'Lock up tight after the cops leave. And don't let the cops in without showing you their ID. Get them to push it under the door or through the letterbox. Okay?'

'Right, O Masterful One.'

'I think you're back to normal.'

'Getting there. Talk to you tomorrow.'

'Early. Before you go to work. Goodnight.'

There was a moment's silence. Neither of us wanted to be the first to hang up.

'Well,' she said. 'Missed you.'

'Me too,' I said. 'Life's been lacking something.'

I put the bars on the front and back doors and looked down the lane for a while before I went to bed. I tried to sleep but I kept thinking about Drew's description of the rise of the Kwitny empire. He was right. I had been a bit like a yokel from Terang. For a whole decade, I hadn't paid any attention to anything except cabinetmaking and plodding around looking for people who didn't want to be found.

Linda rang at 7.30 a.m. I was up, just out of the shower.

'Let's have breakfast,' she said. 'I haven't got much time.'

We met at Meaker's at eight and ordered orange juice and muesli.

'I'm not sure what to do,' she said. She looked thinner somehow. 'I'm not as brave as I thought I was.'

'It comes to us all.'

'It's not just the burglary,' she said. 'I was being followed yesterday. I tracked down the man whose sheetmetal works across the road from Hoagland burnt down. He didn't want to know me. Then he rang yesterday and said he'd thought about it and he'd talk to me. I went out to his house, out in Swanreach. Lives all alone in this brick-veneer palace. He says he didn't want to sell at first because it suited him to be in Yarrabank. Then he sniffed that the whole place was being bought up, so he held out, thought he'd get twice what they were offering.'

She was silent while our breakfast was served. We both drank some juice.

'He says two men came to see him at home. Just arrived at the front door. They offered him ten per cent more than the agent's offer. When he said no, one man said there wouldn't be any more offers. No threats. After that, a whole series of weird things began to happen. The two family dogs died, poisoned. About ten kilos of broken glass was put in the swimming pool. Undertakers got calls to go to the house. One night, five different pizza deliveries were made. Then his wife's car went in for a service and when she drove it again the brakes failed. She broke her arm and some ribs.'

'Did he go to the cops?'

'Early on. They said there was nothing they could do. Hire a security firm.'

'Did he tell them about the pressure to sell his factory?'

'He says yes. He went to his local MP, too.'

I said, 'Swanreach? Don't tell me.'

She nodded. 'His MP's Lance Pitman.'

'Eat your muesli,' I said, not feeling like mine. We sat there, eating and looking at each other.

'And then?' I asked when we'd almost finished.

'He says business began to fall off even before the men came to see him. He depended on five or six major customers. Two went, and then after the visit his biggest customer, more than half his business, went elsewhere.'

'Reasons?'

'They gave him a story he didn't believe. He says they

couldn't look him in the eye.' She paused and ate a spoonful. 'And then one Friday night the place burnt down. Blew up, actually. Full of gas cylinders.'

'Cause?'

'Made to look like negligence, he says. Insurance wouldn't pay. He thinks one of his workers set it up.'

'So he sold?'

'Yes. He was ruined. He says he could have sold the business for half a million before it all started. After the fire, it was worth nothing. No customers. No premises. The agents came around and offered half of the original offer and he took it.'

'Why did he change his mind about talking to you?' I asked.

Linda was studying the street. 'He says it's been boiling inside him all these years. He's convinced the whole business killed his wife. And his divorced daughter, who lived with him with her kids, she said he'd gone neurotic and went to live somewhere else.'

'Tell me about being followed.'

She smiled, a thin smile. 'Talking about neurotic,' she said. 'All day Saturday I had this feeling someone was watching me. Then yesterday, after I left Swanreach, I stopped for gas and a car, ordinary cream Holden or something with two men in it, pulled up at the air hose. I realised I'd seen it parked way down the road from the house I'd been at.'

She took a deep breath. 'Anyway, I went in to pay and I buggered about, bought a drink, looked at the magazines, studied the engine additives, fanbelts, whatever. The guy at the air hose pumped three tyres and then he stuck on the fourth one, at the back. His head kept bobbing up. Finally, he hung up the hose and they drove off. I went outside quickly and they were pulling up by the side of the road about a hundred metres down. In front of a parked car. I went by them—I didn't have any choice—and they zipped out, forced their way into the traffic and sat about five cars behind me. I pulled in at a liquor place in Alphington and when I came out, they were at the kerb about two hundred metres back. So I changed direction, went back past them.'

'You realised that would tell them for sure they'd been spotted?'

Linda shrugged. 'I hate to say it, but I was completely spooked. I was hoping I was wrong. I hoped they'd go away.'

'But they didn't?'

'They did a U-turn right in the face of traffic. I drove on for a bit, did an illegal U-turn at some lights, saw them on my right, and then I didn't see them again.'

'Where'd you go?'

'Home first. Put the interview notes on the laptop. Then to work. That's when I got the message from this arsehole in Sydney. Via this spineless arsehole in Melbourne. And discovered my computer wipeout.' She smiled another wan smile. 'First I'm followed, then at work I get two quick kidney punches. Go home for the knockout blow. Every square inch of the place searched. I kid you not. My old photo albums, Christ. They took the top off the lavatory cistern. Left it in the bath.'

I thought about Eddie Dollery and the money in the dishwasher. Was that only two weeks ago? Our coffees came. I was trying to think of something to say that wouldn't reveal the jellyback in me when Linda said, voice low, 'Oh, and about your friend Ronnie Bishop.'

'What?'

'I talked to someone I know from when I was on the compassion beat at the *Age*. She's a welfarey, a youth worker, knew Ronnie Bishop from way back. She says she wanted to give a party when she heard he was found dead.'

I waited.

'She says she thinks he got a whole lot of street kids into porn movies. She says she's heard that Father Gorman runs the Safe Hands Foundation as a kind of brothel for sleaze-bags looking for under-age sex. Ronnie was a recruiting agent on the street.'

I remembered something Mrs Bishop had said: *Ronnie loved films. He saved up to buy a movie camera. He was always filming things.*

Linda lowered her voice even further. 'Here's the really interesting bit. My contact says that around the time of the Hoagland business, she was working in a youth refuge, lots of street kids with drug habits. One of them, a girl about fourteen, saw a man on TV one night and said, "That's the bloke who fucked me and my friend." '

'Ronnie?'

She shook her head. 'No. Lance Pitman MP, then Housing Minister.'

I closed my eyes and said, 'Jesus. Did they go to the cops?'

'No. No point. The girl wouldn't talk to the cops. But she fingered Ronnie Bishop as the one who set it up.'

I looked out the window. Ronnie and Father Gorman and Lance Pitman and Scullin the cop. Under-age sex and porn movies. And the Kwitny family, patrons of the Safe Hands Foundation and owners of Charis Corporation. 'What did they do about it?' I asked.

'This woman and another youth worker went to see Father Gorman. He gave them a lot of charm, said he'd look into it. They didn't hear anything more. Ronnie wasn't seen on the streets again.'

'And they left it at that?'

'They're both good Catholics. He's a priest.'

I said, 'What are you going to do now?'

She gave me her unblinking look. 'What the burglars didn't know is that I'd backed up everything at work and on the laptop on disk. And the disk is in my bag. I'm going to try to link Charis Corporation to the companies that bought up Yarrabank. That's the link I need. But if I can't tie them together, I'll write the story of the buy-up and see if the *Age* will run it.' She blinked. 'I'm sorry, Jack, I have to.'

I sighed and put my hand on hers. 'Don't be sorry,' I said. 'Let me tell you about my phone call from Perth.'

There was a piece of cardboard torn off a beer carton slipped under my office door. On it was written: *I rembered somthing else about what you was asking about. See me at my house.* It was signed: *B. Curran, 15 Morton Street, Clifton Hill.*

It didn't mean anything for a moment, and then I

remembered I'd left my card with the man who'd lived next door to Ronnie Bishop in Clifton Hill.

A car hooted outside. It was Cam. We had a meeting organised with Cyril Wootton and his chief commissioner at the pub in Taylor's Lakes. Cam favoured places in the suburban wastelands for meetings like this.

It started to sprinkle with rain as we hit the freeway in Kensington.

We were in the fast lane, doing ten over the limit. On the right-hand bend coming up to the Coburg exit, Cam shifted into the middle lane, giving a furniture truck no more than a second's warning.

Five hundred metres further, he went back into the fast, no warning. A hooter blared at us.

'Having fun?' I asked.

'Two pricks on a bike been with us since Carlton,' Cam said, voice normal. 'Just wanted to see what they'd do.'

'What'd they do?'

'Dropped way back. Put your hand under the seat, will you, mate. There's a little case.'

I found what looked like a small aluminium briefcase under the seat. It was heavy.

'It's loaded. Keep it out of sight,' Cam said.

I unsnapped the lid of the case. Inside, nestled in hard foam, were a long-barrelled revolver, cleaning equipment and about thirty rounds of ammunition.

'Ruger Redhawk,' Cam said.

'That's nice. What the fuck's going on?'

Cam had his eyes on the rear-view mirror. 'Dunno. Could be just two pricks out for a ride. Could be someone thinks we've got the cash for the Commissioner on board.'

'Who knows we're meeting him?'

'It's a her. Just Wootton.'

The Essendon exit was coming up. Cam waited until it was almost too late and then swung off sharply on to it without signalling. 'I'm going first left, round the sports fields,' Cam said. 'Hold your tummy.'

I looked back. Three hundred metres behind us, four cars in between, a motorcycle with two figures in black wearing fullface helmets on it was coming off the freeway.

'Bloke on the back's got a little bag,' I said.

'His playlunch maybe,' Cam said. 'When last you shoot anything?'

I felt fear for the first time. It had seemed a bit of a joke up to then. 'In the Mallee about ten years ago,' I said. 'Shot a few rabbits.'

'Take that thing out of the box.'

I took the Ruger out and looked back again. The motorcycle was accelerating past the cars, closing the gap between us quickly.

The engine screamed and the tyres squealed as Cam changed down and took the left, but the car held its line. 'Nice bus this,' Cam said. 'But it hasn't got the legs for this kind of thing.'

The bike leant over at forty-five degrees as it came around the corner behind us, perhaps two hundred metres away.

We were on a street with houses on our right and sports fields behind a high wire fence on the left. We had to turn right at the corner coming up or go into a parking lot for the sports complex.

'I think we've got to show these boys the iron,' Cam said. 'Can't outrun them. I'm going to broadside in this parking lot. Get out quick, I'm coming out the same door.'

My eyes flicked to the speedo. We were doing a hundred when we went into the parking area. There were three cars in it, all near the gate at the left.

I looked back again. The bikers were close now, perhaps a hundred metres. The sun had come out and their leathers gleamed like otter skins.

Cam swung left towards the cars, slowed, then swung right. As the car came around, he hit the brake.

We went into a broadside skid across the tarmac, the right-hand wheels lifting. We came to a stop side on to a fence a few metres away.

'Out we go,' said Cam calmly.

I opened my door and half fell out. Cam was right behind me in a crawl.

'Keep down,' he said. 'Give me the gun.'

We crouched behind the front of the car. I could feel the heat from the engine on my face. Cam pulled back the Ruger's hammer.

The bike came into the parking lot almost without slowing and went right. As it turned half side-on to us, I got a view of the passenger.

His bag was slung around his neck by the strap now and he was holding something black and blunt.

'Fucking Christ,' said Cam.

It was a sub-machine gun.

The rider slowed and swung left. He was going to make a run parallel to us.

We both ducked. They must have been about twenty metres from us when the passenger opened up, flat, coughing sounds, not loud. Most of the first burst was high, over the top of the car. But the last rounds hit the front windscreen with sharp tapping noises. A large, jagged hole appeared on the passenger side and the rest turned to mosaic.

A second later, the next burst of hard coughing. They went low. Some hit the car, some hit the tarmac underneath, ricocheted and pinged off the chassis.

The bike was past, accelerating into a turn for another run.

'Fuck this for a joke,' Cam said. He straightened up, Ruger in both hands, and leant his long forearms on the bonnet.

I put my head up. The bikers were side-on, just starting the turn towards us. The passenger saw Cam and raised the fat barrel of his weapon.

Cam fired.

He missed.

He fired again.

The bullet hit the back of the gunman's helmet. His left arm went up as the impact lifted him off the bike and spun him on to the tarmac.

The rider, unbalanced, veered sharply towards us, gained control and swung savagely away.

'One down,' Cam said softly, steadying himself for a shot at the rider.

The passenger got to his knees, left hand to his helmet, sub-machine gun still in the other. He was small, no bigger than a fourteen-year-old. He shook his head like a dog, then turned to look at us.

Cam was aiming at the rider.

The small man brought the sub-machine gun up.

'Down!' I shouted, grabbing Cam's coat and pulling him onto me.

The weapon coughed again, bullets whining just over the bonnet where Cam had been.

'Little fucker,' Cam said.

The bike's engine roared.

Cam put his head up. 'Party's over,' he said.

I stood up. They were going out of the parking area exit, sun glinting on their helmets, engine screaming in second gear.

We listened to the sound of the bike going up the road, turning left, getting fainter. Then it was still, just the hum from the freeway and the jungle sounds of small children playing far away. It had taken no more than forty seconds from the time the bikers came into the parking area. Now only the smell of cordite hanging in the cold air spoke of violence and near-death.

I looked around, expecting to see people everywhere. There was no-one. The silenced sub-machine gun had probably gone unheard, Cam's shots taken for a car backfiring.

Cam finished putting his Ruger back into its case and took a packet of Gitanes out of his top pocket. 'You smoking?'

'Just this once,' I said. I cupped my hands around the lighter flame. They weren't shaking. Not yet. The first draw almost made me sit down.

'Well, you can rule out money,' said Cam. 'That ain't the way they go about taking it off people.'

Something was gradually dawning on my adrenalin-soaked brain. 'Where did you say you first saw them?'

'Top of Elgin Street. They couldn't have been behind me long. I'd have seen them on the freeway.'

I took another draw. Another reel. 'Mate,' I said, 'I don't think this is connected with the horses. Something else. Little job I've been doing.'

Cam blew smoke out of his nose, looked around. 'Don't take any big jobs,' he said. 'You want to get the cops over here?'

'No,' I said. 'I'll have to take care of it myself.'

I didn't need to think about it. There wasn't anything the cops could do for you if people wanted to kill you. Not unless there was something you could do for the cops, and then you ended up living in a caravan park in Deniliquin on the witness protection program.

We inspected the car. Apart from the windscreen, there were about half a dozen bullet holes.

Cam took out his mobile. 'It'll probably go,' he said, 'but I don't want to explain these holes to the jacks. I'll get a mate to bring some wheels around, take this away. Wonder where that prick got an Ingram?'

I said, 'Is that what it was?'

'Not your normal scumbag piece of iron.'

Cam got through to someone. 'Henry,' he said. 'I want you to think about how much you owe me…'

Fifteen minutes later, a Ford Granada came into the parking lot, followed by a tow truck. The tow truck driver, a huge man with a beard, stuck masking tape over all the bullet holes. He'd done this sort of thing before. We were on the freeway in the Ford in five minutes.

After a while, Cam gave me a quick look. He was steering with his fingertips, cigarette drooping from his mouth. 'Knew their business,' he said, 'we'd both be looking at the lid.'

'I'm glad they don't know their business,' I said. I put my hands out and looked at them. I was shaking. 'I'm just starting to react.'

Cam said, 'Want somewhere else to stay?'

I was thinking about phone calls. Calls from Charles and Linda last night. All my calls in the past weeks. I really was a yokel.

'I'll need room for two,' I said.

'Two, twenty,' Cam said. 'You can use my current's place. She's gone to Italy.'

'I wish I was in Italy,' I said. 'Italy, Bosnia, anywhere.'

Cam opened the window and flicked his cigarette out. 'Things go right Saturday,' he said, 'we can all go to Italy. First class.'

Wootton was waiting in the parking lot of the pub, a hideous pre-cast concrete affair with flagpoles all over the front. He was in his XK Jaguar, reading a magazine. He put it away when he saw us coming. I went around to his side. The window was down.

'Can you get someone to debug my place?' I said.

He frowned. 'Really, Jack, are you sure you're important enough for people to want…' My expression stopped him. 'When do you want it done?'

'Now,' I said.

'Now?'

'Now. The person can pick up a key from the ground-floor flat. Number one. Say Jack sends his fondest regards and the bloke will hand over the key.'

Wootton took out his mobile phone and got out of the

car. 'What's the address?' he asked. He punched in a number and spoke to someone in cryptic terms, giving the address and the introduction. 'It's urgent,' he said.

The commissioner was waiting for us in the lounge, a pinkish chamber, full of angular chrome and plastic furniture. I didn't know there were people who'd place your bets for a commission who didn't look like Eddie Dollery or like market gardeners in town for the day.

Wootton did the introductions. He introduced me as Ray and Cam as Barry. The Commissioner was called Cynthia. She was in her late thirties or early forties, grey suit, tall and slim, an intelligent face of sharp planes relieved by a lower lip as plump as an oyster. Her shoulder-length dark hair slipped silkily around her head.

She was business-like. Harry would approve.

'How big?' she said.

'As possible,' Cam replied.

'They're gun-shy these days,' she said. 'You'll have to spread it around.'

Cam nodded. 'This is the drill,' he said. 'You wait for the second call. We expect the price to drift. Then we want as many fair-sized hits as we can get without collapsing the price. Then send in the troops, like they've heard the late mail. Take it all the way to the floor.'

She smiled a cautious smile, cocked her head. 'Some organising here. Small army. There's not that many reliables around.'

I thought I caught a hint of working-class Tasmania in her voice, perhaps one of those bone-hard timber towns, full of red-faced men with pale eyes and bad breath, the girls with one pretty summer before the babies and the cigs and the mid-morning start on the wine cask. Cynthia would have got out early, escaped to the mainland.

'We're told you can do it. But if you can't…' said Cam.

She crossed her legs. In my trained observer way, I registered that they were exceptionally long legs. Part of me couldn't believe that I was sitting in this garish place looking at legs and listening to talk about backing horses when people had recently been trying to kill me.

'I can do it,' she said. 'What happens interstate?'

'You get first go,' Cam said. 'We'll take what we can get elsewhere.'

'The TAB?'

'Don't worry about it,' he said.

'When do I know?'

Cam lit a Gitane and blew smoke out sideways. 'Cyril will tell you where to be,' he said. 'You've got to be ready to push the button, go straight off.'

'Not even the race number?'

Cam shook his head. 'No.'

'Makes it hard if it's going to be the eighth.'

'Life's hard,' Cam said. 'Cyril says we don't have to worry about collecting. Is that right? We hate worrying.'

Cynthia gestured with her hands, palms upward. 'You don't have to worry,' she said. 'I'm not going anywhere. I've got three teenagers to look after.'

'I know that,' said Cam. 'Think about them. We'll need a full accounting. Every bit of paper. Anything else I can tell you?'

She shook her head and stood up. 'Nice to do business with you,' she said.

'We hope so,' Cam said. 'We hope so.'

We were waiting at the St George's Road lights when the ambulance came through and did a screeching right turn.

'Just live for speed,' said Cam.

I saw the smoke before we turned into my street, a dark plume against the cigarette-smoke sky. When we turned, we saw the street was blocked by three police cars. People were everywhere. Further down, a fire engine was paralleled to the pavement. Its ladders were up and firemen on them were spraying water into a huge hole in the building's roof.

It was my building.

The huge hole was in my roof.

My home was burning.

Cam pulled up and looked at me. 'Your place, right?' he said.

I could only nod.

'Better wait,' he said, opening his door.

I slumped against the door pillar. I could recognise at least a dozen people standing around. Neighbours. The man from the corner shop.

Can was back inside five minutes. He didn't say anything, did a slow U-turn. We were heading down Brunswick Street when he spoke.

'Cop reckons the bloke turned the key and the whole place went up. He might live. Door could have saved him.'

'It was supposed to be me,' I said. Cam didn't need

253

telling. I needed to say it. I wasn't feeling scared. All I could think about was the flat. It contained everything I valued. My books. My music. The paintings and prints Isabel had bought, always as presents for me. The leather sofa and armchairs we'd bought together at the Old Colonists' Club auction. It was my home, the only place that had ever meant anything to me since leaving my first home at the age of ten. It was my history, my link with Isabel. If Cam could have taken me directly to the person responsible for destroying it, I would have committed murder.

After a while, Cam said, 'Where to?'

My first thought was my office. Then it sunk in. I couldn't go near my office or Taub's. People were trying to kill me. They'd been prepared to kill Cam this morning. They would kill Charlie if he got in their way. They probably intended to kill Linda.

Now I felt fear, a knot in my stomach.

'I've got to make a call,' I said. 'Talk to someone.'

Cam turned into Gertrude Street and parked next to the Housing Commission flats. Three men in overcoats, all bearded, were sitting on a scuffed knoll, passing around the silver bladder of a wine cask.

I took the mobile and got out. In my wallet, I found the number Garth Bruce had given me. I'd transferred it to the back of a business card. About to press the first button, I hesitated. How could I trust Bruce? Linda didn't. Drew didn't. Then I remembered the awkward way we'd stood together, two men struggling to come to terms with their grief, and his words: *I think you've had enough pain with this Milovich.*

I punched the number. It was answered on the second ring. A woman. I said John English wanted to speak to the Minister.

'Please hold on,' she said.

I leaned against the car. The sun had come out, making the day seem colder. One of the bearded men on the knoll was trying to strangle the last drop of wine out of the bladder.

'Yes.' It was Bruce.

'Someone's trying to kill me,' I said. 'Twice today.'

He said nothing for a moment. I could hear him breathing.

'God,' he said. 'You all right?'

I said yes.

Another pause. 'Where are you?'

'In the street.'

'Jack,' he said, 'this is getting out of hand.' His speech was measured. 'I think I've underestimated Pixley's old mates. We'll have to put you somewhere safe till we can shake some sense into them. The Hillier woman too. Can you get in touch with her?'

'Yes. She's being followed.'

'That so? Be the same people. Okay, listen, we've got to do this carefully. Yarra Bend. There's a park up there, near the golf course. Know it?'

'Yes.'

'Get hold of Hillier and get up there, park as far away from those public toilets as possible. What are you driving? What's the rego?'

I walked around the back of the car and read out the number. 'Ford Granada,' I said. 'Blue.'

'Right. Let's make it in an hour's time. The two blokes from last time will pick you up, get you somewhere safe.' He paused. 'Now this is important. Don't talk to anyone except Hillier. And don't say a word about this arrangement to her on the phone. She's probably tapped.'

'Right,' I said. 'An hour from now.' The lead ball of fear in my stomach was dissolving.

'Good,' he said. 'You'll be fine. Just take it easy. We can fix this up in a day or so. I'll see you tonight.'

I rang Linda's number. She answered straight away.

'I want you to make sure you're alone and get a cab to the place where we ate. The first time, remember?'

'Yes,' she said. 'What's wrong?'

'Something very serious. I'll tell you when I see you. Get the cab to park as close to the place as possible. Wait in the cab until you see me.'

'Jack, what's going on?' she said.

'Half an hour from now. Okay?'

'Yes. Okay.'

'See you then. Love.'

'Yes,' she said. 'Love.'

I got back into the Granada. Cam was reading the paper, smoking a Gitane.

'I'll get off your back in an hour's time,' I said. 'I won't take up that offer of yours. Need to disappear for a day or so.

Cam gave me a long look. 'I'll miss the excitement,' he said.

I was looking in my wallet to see how much money I had. There was a piece of cardboard in the note section. I took it out: *I rembered somthing else about what you was asking about. See me at my house. B. Curran, 15 Morton Street, Clifton Hill.*

Clifton Hill was as safe a place as any to pass the half-hour until it was time to pick up Linda.

'Can we take a little drive around to Clifton Hill?' I said.

The man was wearing the same outfit as before: dirty

blue nylon anorak, black tracksuit pants. There was every chance that it hadn't come off since our previous meeting.

'Wondered when you'd come,' he said.

'You remembered something else about Ronnie Bishop,' I said.

He looked at me, said nothing.

I took out my wallet and offered him a twenty.

He took it. 'Had to walk round to your place,' he said. 'Bloody long way. Had to take a cab back. Me legs is bad.'

I found a ten and gave it to him.

'Wait,' he said. He shuffled down the dark passage and came back a minute later, folded newspaper in his hand. ''Member I said cops come around next door couple times?'

I nodded.

He coughed and spat past my right shoulder. 'One's a cunt called Scullin.'

'You told me that.'

He sniffed. 'Didn't know who the other was. Do now.'

'Yes? Who?'

He unfolded the paper. It was the *Herald Sun*. He looked at the front page. 'This bastard,' he said.

He turned the newspaper to face me. There was a large colour photograph of a man sitting in front of microphones. He was flanked by two high-ranking policemen in uniform.

'Which cop?' I said, studying the policemen.

'Not the cops. The cunt in the middle. The fucking Minister. That's him.'

I was about to put the phone down when the woman answered.

'I need to get in touch with Vin McKillop,' I said.

She started coughing, a loose, emphysemic sound. I waited. When she stopped, I said again, 'Vin McKillop, I need—'

'Vin's dead,' she said. 'Overdose.'

I didn't ask her any questions.

I went into the sitting room. Linda was standing in front of the huge fireplace in the centre of Cam's absent girl-friend's place off Crombie Lane in the heart of the city. Her apartment occupied the top floor of an old six-storey ware-house. She was an artist. Paintings were everywhere, mostly landscapes at different stages of completion.

'Vin McKillop's dead,' I said. 'Pixley's dead, Vin's dead. It's like a battlefield.'

'Oh, Jesus,' Linda said. 'Oh, Jesus.'

'Garth Bruce visited Ronnie Bishop with Scullin more than once around the time of Anne Jeppeson's death,' I said. 'If Scullin fixed up Danny for killing her, Garth Bruce must be part of the whole thing. He was setting us up.'

Cam was lying on a sofa, long legs over the arm, head propped up by cushions, drinking Cascade out of the bottle.

'So Bruce's got the motor's number,' he said. He'd had no trouble grasping my explanation of what was going on. It didn't seem to surprise him either.

'I suppose that was dumb,' I said, 'but you don't expect the Minister for Police to try to kill you.

'It's just possible he's not involved,' Linda said. She was dressed for business in a suit, cream silk blouse, black stockings and high heels. Overexcited though I was, the sight aroused a frisson of lust.

'I don't think we should operate on that assumption,' I said. 'What can we do about the car?' It was now in the girlfriend's garage on the ground floor.

Cam swung his legs to the floor. 'It can stay where it is. I'll get my mate to report it stolen, give me another one.' He stood up and walked off down the long room in the direction of the kitchen.

Linda's eyes followed him. 'What does he do for a living?'

'He's a gambler,' I said. 'He shot a midget firing a sub-machine gun off a motorbike this morning. That's how I'm here.'

She nodded. 'I can believe that,' she said. 'What do we do now?'

'Think. Think about evidence. Evidence is the only thing that can help us now.'

'Did you tell me once,' Linda said, chin on her palms. 'Did you tell me that Danny's wife said there was evidence he didn't do it?'

I thought back to the night, in the family room Danny built. Yes. She said a woman phoned Danny. The woman said her husband had died.'

But she didn't give Danny the evidence?'

'No.'

'I don't suppose it follows that if it's evidence that proves Danny didn't do it, it's evidence of who did', Linda said.

'It might be.' I was thinking. 'What kind of person would have the evidence? It would have to be a cop, wouldn't it?'

'Could be someone connected with Charis Corp.'

I sighed. 'That's right. This is a dead-end.'

Linda got up and crossed to a huge steel-framed window. Her high heels went tock on the polished concrete floor. She had to stand on tiptoe to look out. Her calf muscles tensed deliciously. At any other time I would have been seized with an impulse to rush her from the rear.

'Let's say it's a cop. Was a cop,' she said. 'What then?'

'Died some time before Danny was shot. At least a month.'

'How do you know that?'

'I'm assuming the woman got in touch with Danny soon after her husband's death. That's when she rang. About a month before Danny was killed.'

Linda turned around. 'What date was that?'

I told her.

'Where's the phone?' she said.

'Coming up.' Cam was coming back, carrying a cordless phone. 'I'm taking a stroll to pick up some other wheels. I'll come back, see if you need anything.'

Linda took the phone from him. 'Phone book?'

'In the kitchen. On the fridge.' He gave me a wave.

When she came back, Linda took a notebook out of her bag, sat down and punched a number.

'Hello, Police Association? Can I speak to the secretary? Right. Who could I speak to about membership records? Oh, you've got a membership secretary. Denise Walters. I'd like to, yes.'

Linda waited, looking at me. 'Denise, hi,' she said. 'My name's Colleen Farrell. Dr Colleen Farrell. From Monash University Medical School. Denise, I wonder if you can help me. We're doing a study on police mortality in Australia. Do you know about that? No? It's at the early stages, but we think it'll help the police case for a stress loading on salaries.'

Pause. 'Yes. Abnormally high levels, we think, Denise. We've run into a little problem you might be able to help us with. We don't have any data for Victoria for the last two months.'

Pause. 'Yes, that's right. We got the other data directly from the Commissioner's office but the person there has gone on leave and I'd like to get up to date before *I* go on leave.'

Pause. 'That would be terrific, Denise. I'll wait on.'

We sat in silence looking at each other. Linda reached down, took the hem of her skirt and began to work it up, slowly, one thigh at a time, flexing her thigh muscles and moving her bottom from side to side. I could see the dark at the fork of her legs when she said, 'Still here. Right. No serving members so far this year. Good. What about non-serving?'

Pause. 'Two in January. None in Feb. One in March. One in April. Okay. Now, Denise, I'll need the names to check against our register.'

Pause. 'H. J. Mullins. T. R. Conroy. M. E. F. Davis. P. K. Vane. That's V-A-N-E, is it? Terrific. I see we've got them all except Vane. You wouldn't have any biographical data there, would you, Denise?'

Pause. 'Just service dates. Um. '63 to '88. Special Branch 1978 to '84. Look, Denise, you've been a great help. Thanks very much. Much appreciated.'

Linda put the phone down and pulled her skirt back to respectability. 'I can't bear to see a man salivate,' she said.

'The only possibility is P. K. Vane. He was in the Special Branch when Anne was killed, though.'

'I'd say that lets him out. They spent all their time hanging around anarchist meetings. Six people and a collie dog and two Special Branch. Our bloke would probably be in Drugs, one of Scullin's mates.'

There was a sound in the hallway. I felt my shoulders tense. Cam came in.

'All fixed up,' he said. 'Listen, I'm shooting through. You want me, press auto and 8 on the phone. It'll page me.' He opened his jacket and showed the pager on his belt.

'I'm in your debt, mate,' I said.

Cam said, 'Saturday, that's the day we pay off debts. There's plenty of food here.' He eyed Linda appraisingly. 'Try the cupboards in the big bedroom for clothes. You're not far apart in size. Jack, there's men's clothes in the other bedroom. One of her exes. Biggish fella, I gather. Nice line in shirts. Help yourself.'

I went with him to the front door. He was outside when he said, 'That little case of mine, that's in the kitchen now. Under the sink. I wouldn't open this door to anyone if I were you.'

I detoured to the bathroom on my way back, looking for aspirin. Pumping adrenalin leaves you feeling dull and headachey. I was studying the contents of the medicine cabinet when it came to me out of nowhere.

I can remember her saying she could go anywhere in safety because the Special Branch were always lurking somewhere.

Anne Jeppeson's mother. That was what she had said.

263

The Law Department at Melbourne University looks the way universities should. It has courtyards and cloisters and ivy.

I loitered downstairs, near where a girl had set fire to herself during the Vietnam War. Nobody paid any attention to me. The whole campus was full of people in ex-army overcoats wearing beanies. I was just older than most of them. By about thirty years.

My man came out ahead of his students, striding briskly, looking the way lecturers usually look after a lecture: happy and smug. His name was Barry Chilvers and he taught constitutional law. He was also a civil liberties activist and knew more about the Special Branch than most people.

'Barry,' I said when he was level with me.

He jerked his head up at me, eyes startled behind the big glasses.

I took the beanie off.

'Jesus Christ, Jack,' he said, exasperated, 'where'd you get that coat? And the beanie, for Christ sakes. It's a Collingwood beanie. How can you wear a Collingwood beanie?'

'Ensures that I'm not recognised,' I said. 'Got a moment?'

We went upstairs to his office. It was the same mess I remembered: books, papers, journals, student essays, styrofoam cups, newspapers, bits of clothing everywhere. Two computers had been added to the chaos.

I cleared away a briefcase and a pile of files from a chair and sat down. 'You were looking very pleased with yourself,' I said.

He scratched his woolly grey head. 'One of the better days at the pearl–swine interface,' he said. 'Some days I come back and headbutt the door. To what do I owe this visit?'

'Do you remember Anne Jeppeson?'

'Sure. Got run down. She was a spunk. Politically loony but a spunk.'

'Would the Special Branch have watched her?'

He put a thumb behind his top teeth, took it out. 'It's hard to say. Who says so?'

'She said something to her mother.'

'There was a lot of paranoia about the Branch. If you believed all the people who said the Branch was watching them, it wouldn't have been a branch, it would have been the whole bloody tree.'

'But it's possible?'

He shrugged. 'More than most, I suppose. She was into a whole lot of stuff the Branch would have had an interest in—Roxby Downs, Aboriginal rights in Tasmania, East Timor. You name it.'

'East Timor? The Special Branch? I thought it was only interested in local stuff?'

Barry shrugged again. 'The Branch, ASIO, ASIS, you can't separate them. They scratched each other's backs. So it's possible, yes.'

I told him what else I needed to know.

He groaned. 'Where some Branch goon was at a certain time in 1984? Jesus H. Christ, Jack, you don't have modest requests, do you? When in '84?'

I told him.

'Not long before Harker got the boot and the new government closed the Branch down.'

'That's right. There'd be records somewhere, wouldn't there?'

Barry shook his head. 'Shredded. On orders from the highest authority. All records to be destroyed.'

'So there's no record of what they were up to?'

He clapped his hands. 'Shredded,' he said. 'But not before being copied.'

'Shredded? And copied?'

'What do you expect?' said Barry. 'I think it was something the cops and the new Opposition found themselves in agreement on. Think about it. The files represent about five billion hours of coppers standing around in the rain dying to have a piss. You shred them and a couple of years later another government gets elected and wants you to start all over again, spying on the same bunch of harmless sods. They say they went through three copiers. Twenty-four hours a day for days.'

'Who's got the copy?'

'What copy? No-one's ever admitted the files were copied.'

I said, 'Barry, I'm talking life and death.'

He did another big head scratch, rolled his chair back till it hit a pile of books. The pile toppled, slithered to become a ziggurat.

'Okay,' he said. 'I can't promise you anything, though. I'll ask a man who might be able to ask another man, who might know someone.'

I stood up. 'I need to know today. It's that bad.'

Barry stood up. His eyes were level with my middle great-coat button. He looked up at me. 'You serious?'

I nodded.

He nodded back, sadly. 'I'll go after my tutorial. You can't phone him, this bloke. Paranoid. Give me the date and the name, anything that'll help.'

'God loves you, Barry,' I said.

'There is no God and you know it. Ring me at home after five. But I can't promise anything. I don't know if they copied this kind of thing.' He paused. 'I'm only doing this because of your old man's record for Fitzroy, you know. I wouldn't do it for you.'

'I know that,' I said. 'Go Roys, make a noise.'

I found Linda at a laptop computer in a long, narrow room off the kitchen. A bench down one wall held three computers, one with a huge monitor, and two printers. The other wall was covered in corkboard, with dozens of computer-generated colour images stuck up. They seemed to be tryouts of the landscape paintings.

'Cam's woman's a computer freak,' Linda said. She was scrolling text on her screen. 'She's got enough power here to run the tax system.'

'What are you doing?'

'Tell you when I've done it.' She was tapping keys.

I went into the vast sitting room. It was 4.30 p.m. Both the fire in the fireplace and the day outside were dying. I brought in a log from the woodpile in the entrance hall, put it on the steel dogs and scraped all the embers together under it. Then I did an inspection of the premises. Apart from the sitting room, computer room and kitchen, there were two huge bedrooms, two bathrooms, and a studio the size of a pool hall. Next to the steel front door, another steel door opened on to the building's internal staircase.

When I'd done the tour, I sat down in front of the fire, put my hands in my pockets, stared into the flames and tried to work out how we could come out of hiding safely. All I could think of was to have Drew negotiate with the police. Negotiate over what, was the question. The bombing of my flat was certainly proof that I needed protection. Or was it? People had been known to boobytrap their own houses. After all, it wasn't me who was blown up. Maybe I'd set a trap for someone else.

What about the men with the sub-machine gun on the motorcycle? We hadn't reported it. We'd had the car spirited away. By now, the body was probably crushed to the size of a tea chest. Cam's friend who took it away wasn't going to jump up and testify for me.

As for Linda, what exactly was she in hiding from, they would ask? No-one had tried to kill her. She'd been burgled, that's all. Everyday occurrence.

And the Minister? The Minister wouldn't recognise my name.

It was 5.30 p.m. before Linda emerged, carrying a printout.

'Hey, let's get some light here,' she said. 'It's like a set for *Macbeth*.'

I realised with a start that the room was in deep gloom, the firelight playing on the unfinished landscapes around the walls.

Linda found a panel of switches next to the kitchen doorway. 'Fuck. Like a Boeing.' She hit several switches. Concealed lighting came on all over the room.

'That's more like it,' she said. 'Save the firelight for later. I've got something. Remember all the companies in the Yarrabank buy-up turned out to be owned by other off-shore companies?'

'Yes.'

'Well, I've been searching all the finance databases for anything on the offshore companies and one database turned up three of the companies at once. The Jersey companies. They were suspected in 1982 by the Securities Commission in Britain of warehousing shares for an Irish company that was trying to take over a British construction group.'

'I'm lost already,' I said.

'Wait. It becomes clearer. The three companies were all run from Jersey by an accountant. The securities people forced him to disclose where the money had come from to buy the shares in the construction group. It didn't come from the Irish company. It came from the company that owned the Jersey companies. This one was registered in the Cayman Islands. It's called Pericoe Holdings. That's where the story stops. The Securities Commission lost interest in the inquiry.'

She paused.

'But you didn't?' I said.

She nodded. 'I was searching a new South Pacific database at the university in Suva. Just to see what it held. And I turned up a little item from 1981 in a defunct publication called *Pacific Focus*. Just been scanned into the system. They reported that a Cayman-registered company had a shareholding in a company that wanted to set up a bank in the New Groningen Islands. And what was the Cayman company's name?'

'This is a test, isn't it? My answer is: I don't know.'

'Pericoe Holdings.'

'This is it?' I said.

She nodded. 'Pericoe was obliged under local law to disclose its shareholders.' She read from the printout. '"Shareholders: J. Massey of Carnegie Road, Toorak, Melbourne, Australia; M. Jillings of Miller Street, Kew, Melbourne, Australia; and H. McGinty of Carnham Close, Brighton, Melbourne, Australia."'

'Do we know these people?'

Linda came over and stood in front of me. 'J. Massey is Jocelyn Massey, ex-wife of Dix Massey, Charis Corp's fixer-in-chief. M. Jillings is Maxine Jillings, wife of Keith Jillings, a major shareholder in Charis Corp. H. McGinty is Hayden McGinty, who sucks to get on the social pages and is the wife of Martin McGinty, chief executive of Marbild, a wholly-owned subsidiary of Charis Corporation.'

She flicked the printout in the direction of the coffee table and put her hands on her hips. 'This is the jackpot,' she said. 'This is it. This is the connection between Charis and the buying up of Yarrabank. It's going to take an awful lot of explaining away. And it sure as fuck ain't gonna work to say these Charis Corp girls put their spare housekeeping money into real estate.'

'You're pretty smart for a good-looking person,' I said. 'Do people tell you that?'

'Only when they want to fuck me. What about the Special Branch man?'

'I've got to phone Barry Chilvers.'

A child answered at Barry's number. A girl. Barry had obviously started on a second round of procreation, probably with a graduate student. That was the price of academic life. Inexplicably, first wives stopped being turned on by your mind.

When he came on, he said, 'Chilvers.'

I said, 'It's the man in the Collingwood beanie.'

'That's got to be cryptic enough. Hello, phone-tappers. Mate, your conjecture turns out to be correct. The female person was an object of attention.'

'And the male person?'

'Not attending on her, I'm afraid. He was keeping an eye on an East Timor activist in town for a rally. Does that make life easier?'

'Barry,' I said, 'it may make it possible. What does his log record?'

'Nothing. Uneventful. He said the man spent the evening with known friends in Scott Street, Fitzroy, then went back to his hotel. That's it.'

'The man in the Collingwood beanie thanks you very much.'

Barry said, 'Go Roys, make a noise.'

I went back into the sitting room. Linda was at the bank of windows. She turned.

I said, 'I want you to think very carefully. On the night

Anne was killed, P. K. Vane of the Special Branch was keeping track of an East Timor activist visiting Melbourne.'

Linda nodded. 'That'd be Manuel Carvalho,' she said. 'He was here often. I remember now, there was talk of Anne having an affair with him at some stage.'

'Can you remember where Anne was earlier that evening?' I asked.

'With friends. In Fitzroy.'

'Sure it was Fitzroy?'

'Absolutely. Scott Street. I knew the people vaguely.' She lifted her head. I saw the shine in her eyes. 'Wait. You're going to tell me Carvalho was in Scott Street that night, aren't you?'

I gave her a double thumbs-up. I felt like someone who'd tipped a 500-1 shot for the Melbourne Cup. 'That's exactly what I'm going to tell you. I'm betting that Manuel Carvalho went back to Richmond with Anne. And that P. K. Vane, doing his duty, followed them there. And then P. K. saw something. And for some reason he kept quiet about it. He's our man. He's the one. His wife rang Danny. He's the one with the evidence.'

Linda put her head back, closed her eyes, smiled and ran her fingers through her hair.

I slumped on to the sofa, legs outstretched, flooded with elation and relief. There was hope.

Linda walked across the room. When she was standing between my legs, she reached down with both hands and began to pull up her tight black skirt, working it up slowly over her thighs. When her stocking tops and suspenders came into sight, I said, trying to speak normally, 'Since when do you wear a suspender belt?'

She wriggled her skirt up higher. She wasn't wearing panties. My eyes were level with her dense pubic bush. She put her hands on her hips and pushed her pelvis at me

'I always wear a suspender belt,' she said, 'when I want someone to fuck me senseless on the floor in front of a fire.'

She started unbuttoning her blouse. I reached out and put my hands around her waist. She stopped unbuttoning and pulled her skirt up over her hips.

'Now you've seen mine, Irish,' she said. 'Take off your pants and show me yours.'

How can you make love when people are trying to kill you? You can. Does perfect love drive out fear? For a while. I reflected on these matters afterwards as I lay naked, sweat beginning to chill, in front of the fire.

Linda came in wearing blue jeans and a denim shirt. 'This girl's got everything,' she said. 'Maybe I should start painting.'

I got up. I have always felt silly naked the minute the other person puts something on. I kissed her and went off to shower.

I was under the spray in the room-sized shower when Linda said from the door, 'Get a move on. I've found the champagne.'

The ex-lover's clothes did fit me. I borrowed a corduroy shirt. I was passing through the kitchen when Linda said from the computer room, 'Your glass's on the fireplace. I'm just trying the name P. K. Vane on the *Age* news database.'

It was Krug, vintage, utterly delicious, the tiniest prickles on the tongue. I felt my whole body relax.

We were going to get out of this. For the first time, I felt that.

Linda came out of the kitchen.

'There is a God,' I said. 'Where's your glass?'

She said, 'Paul Karl Vane didn't die of natural causes. He was shot dead in the driveway of his home in Beaumaris. Shot six times, four shots from close range, three of them in the head.'

Linda went to bed at 10 p.m., subdued. Finding out about Paul Vane had taken the gloss off linking Charis Corp to the Yarrabank buy-up. I sat in front of the fire, drinking a small amount of malt whisky. My bombing was the second item on the 10.30 Channel 9 news. The helicopter looked right down into my sitting room through the hole in the roof. I looked away.

The newsreader, a woman with the teeth of a much larger person, said, 'Police are tonight looking for the owner of the flat, Jack Irish, a Fitzroy lawyer. He is described as in his forties, tall, heavily built, with dark hair. He may be with another man, Cameron Delray, of no fixed address. Delray is in his thirties, tall, slim, dark hair and sallow skin. The men may be accompanied by a dark-haired woman, also tall, wearing a dark outfit. Police say the men were involved in a shooting incident earlier today and are believed to be armed.

They should not be approached. Please ring the number that follows if you think you have seen these people.'

Jesus.

I felt the panic rising again. I got up and added some whisky to my glass. Now I had to get hold of Drew or we were going to meet the fate of Danny McKillop in the Trafalgar carpark.

First, my sister. She picked it up instantly. 'My God, Jack,' she said, 'what on—'

I spoke quickly. 'Rosa, listen. I'm okay. I want you to ring Claire and tell her I spoke to you and I'm fine. It's all a mis-understanding. Don't worry about the television. I've got to keep down for a bit but it's going to he okay. I'll ring you.'

'Does that mean our lunch is off?'

'Not necessarily. I'll be in touch. Love.'

I put the phone down. Lunch. I shook my head in wonder. Drew. I was putting out my hand to dial when the phone rang.

I picked it up. 'Yes,' I said, tentatively.

'Jack.' It was Cam. 'Listen, mate,' he said conversation-ally, 'time to go. There's blokes coming up for you. With guns. Go into the studio. There's a ladder in there, extension ladder, against the left-hand wall. You'll see a square hole in the roof in the left-hand corner, like an inspection hatch. You with me?'

'Yes,' I said. The phone was trembling in my hand.

'Get up there. You can slide the cover open, get on the roof. Pull the ladder up. First thing, go round that lift housing building up there and bolt the steel door to the stairs. Okay?'

'Okay.'

'There's no other way up there. It'll give you a bit of time. Get moving now. They're on their way up.'

The line went dead.

'What is it?' Linda was in the doorway, pillow marks on one side of her face. She'd fallen asleep fully dressed.

I tried to imitate Cam's calm. 'Put your shoes on. Get the disks. Quickly. We've got to get out of here. Come to the studio.'

The ladder was aluminium, lightweight. I had it up against the wall beneath the hatch in the roof when Linda came in, wide-eyed, carrying a laptop and her bag.

'I'll go first,' I said. 'Get the hatch open.'

It was at least six metres to the roof. The ladder flexed alarmingly, not made for my weight.

I was halfway up when the banging started at the front door.

'Jack Irish,' a voice shouted. 'Police. We know you're home, Jack. Open the door. No-one gets hurt.'

I put one hand up and found a handle on the hatch cover. I tugged it. It didn't move. The hatch cover wouldn't open.

Something hard hit the front door. They were trying to break in.

The ladder was flexing alarmingly. I braced myself and got both hands to the handle.

I tugged. It wouldn't budge.

There was a louder impact from the front door.

I tried again. I moved the handle from side to side, desperately. It shifted.

I tried again. Backwards, forwards. It moved. I'd been forcing it in the wrong direction. I pushed the handle away from me and the hatch slid open. I grabbed the edge of the hole and pulled myself up the last steps and out on to the roof.

By the time I'd turned back to the hole, Linda was half-way up the ladder. When she was near enough, I leant down and took her bag and the laptop. Then I pulled her up.

The ladder came up easily. We stood panting on the concrete roof in the dark, cold night air.

'Close it,' Linda said, pointing at the hatch. As I bent down to slide the door over, there were four sharp sounds from below. Gunshots. They were trying to shoot open the lock on the front door.

I slid the hatch closed and stood up.

What was I supposed to do now?

The roof door to the internal stairs.

I looked around. About ten metres away I could make out a large, square structure. The lift housing.

'Wait here,' I said and ran. The roof was slippery, some kind of moss growing on the concrete. At the corner of the housing, I fell, sliding across the rough surface. I got up, sharp pain in the left knee. The door was a few metres away, open. I got to it, closed it and felt for the bolt.

There wasn't a bolt. The door couldn't be locked.

I opened it slowly, stuck my head in and listened.

Silence. The men weren't at the front door any more. They were in the flat. There was nowhere to hide there. They would very quickly know we had got out.

I closed the door again and looked at it, felt it. Nothing on the surface of the door.

My fingers touched something on the door frame to my left. I felt to the right of the door. The same. Steel brackets.

The door was meant to be barred, not bolted.

Where was the bar? I felt around frantically, seeing better now, eyes getting used to the dark. No bar.

I looked around the roof. Away to my left, there was something moving.

I squinted, trying to see better.

Washing. Someone had hung a line of washing on the roof. Hung the line between what? I limped over. Two lengths of one-inch pipe with welded crossbars held up the washing line.

I went over to one, put both hands around it and pulled with all my force. It came out so easily that I fell over backwards, pipe clutched to my chest. Scrambling to my feet, I wrenched off the washing line and ran for the door, pipe at the port arms.

I was a few metres from the door when someone in the stairwell shouted something. I could only catch the word 'stairs'.

I got to the door. I could hear footsteps thudding metres away.

The door wouldn't close fully.

I stood back and kicked the door so hard I felt the impact in my wrists and at the top of my skull.

The door closed.

I stepped back, winded.

Something hit the door like a sledgehammer. It swung open and a man—short, bald—came through, left shoulder first, right arm coming around with a long-barrelled revolver held shoulder-high.

He was so close I could smell his breath: alcohol and garlic.

I brought the steel pipe I was holding around with all the force I had. It only had to travel about half a metre before it made contact with the side of the man's head.

He went over sideways, hitting the doorframe with his right shoulder and falling back into the stairwell.

I dropped the pipe, slammed the door shut again and rammed the pipe though the brackets.

When I turned, Linda was behind me.

'Jesus Christ,' she said. 'Come on. Cam's on the roof next door.'

For a moment, I was too winded to move. Then I staggered after her. When we got to the parapet wall to the left of the roof hatch, I saw Cam.

He was on the roof of the building across the lane, sitting on the parapet wall, smoking a cigarette. Next to him on the wall were Linda's laptop and bag. She must have thrown them to him.

'G'day,' he said. 'Shove that ladder over.'

I looked over the edge of our wall. Six floors below, light was reflected off wet cobblestones. I looked over at Cam. His building was about four or five metres higher than ours. The gap between us was about the same.

I went over and got the ladder. It seemed terribly flimsy. I got it upright and leaned it over until Cam could catch the top rung. He pulled it up until he could hold the sides standing up.

'Ladies first,' he said.

I looked at Linda. She smiled, a tight little smile. 'We used to do this at Girl Guides,' she said. 'Piece of cake.'

She scrambled across in seconds.

My turn. My knee was aching. I'd grazed my hip. I was having trouble breathing. I felt a hundred years old.

'I was happier doing conveyancing,' I said to no-one in particular.

Then I went across that inadequate bridge like a big monkey.

Cam had a ute this time, a battered Ford with a lashed-down tarpaulin over the tray. It was parked in a narrow blind lane off Little Bourke Street.

'What's the next stop?' he asked.

We were all leaning on parts of the ute, trying to control our breathing.

'Shoreham,' said Linda and caught her breath. 'On the Mornington Peninsula. I know a place there. It'll be empty.'

Cam straightened up. 'Country air,' he said. 'Let's go.' He started loosening the tray cover. When he had the back open, he looked at me and said, 'They're looking for two blokes, mate. Hop in.'

'In the back?'

'There's a mattress. And pillows. Lots of air gets in. You can have a kip.'

I climbed in and lay down. Cam lashed the cover down. It was pitch-black under the cover, dark and claustrophobic and smelling of engine oil. I had to fight the urge to try and break out.

We were reversing over cobblestones. The springs transmitted every bump. I found a pillow, dragged it under my head, closed my eyes and tried to think about sharpening the blade of a number 7 plane. I was trying to learn how to grind a hollow angle and then hone the blade on that angle with a circular motion the way the Japanese did. I was thinking about how to improve my honing action when I fell asleep.

I woke with a start, no idea where I was, tried to sit up, bounced off the taut nylon tray cover, fell back in fright.

Cam's voice said, 'Nice place. They'd have something to drink here, would they?'

I knew where I was. How had I managed to fall asleep? I lay still and listened to my heartbeat while Cam loosened the cover.

'Breathing?' he said. 'Relaxed?'

Inside ten minutes we were drinking whisky in front of a fire in the stone hearth of what seemed to be an enormous mudbrick and timber house. I went outside and stood on the terrace. There was a vineyard running away from the house.

I went back inside. Cam was on his haunches, fiddling with the fire.

'Were they cops?' I asked. I felt wide-awake. I'd slept for more than two hours.

'Moved like cops,' said Cam. 'Very efficient. I gather you decked one.'

'Tony Baker he calls himself,' I said. 'Came to the pub to scare me off. Made out he was a fed of some kind.'

'If he's a dead fed,' Cam said, 'we have other problems.' He stood up and yawned. 'That's enough Monday now. I'll find a bed.'

I looked at Linda. She was asleep, head fallen onto the arm of the sofa, hair fallen over her face. In the end, perfect exhaustion drives out fear.

'I'll just sit here,' I said. 'Reflect on how I got everybody into this shit.'

'That's the past,' Cam said. 'Think about the future. How to get everybody out of this shit.'

After a while, I got up and found a blanket to put over Linda. She didn't wake up when I swung her legs onto the sofa and arranged a pillow under her head.

I kissed her on the cheek, got some whisky, put some more wood on the fire. The future. But we weren't finished with the past yet. What had Paul Vane seen on the night Anne Jeppeson died? What was the evidence he knew about? And what was the evidence Father Gorman had told Ronnie to bring to Melbourne and where was it?

Time passed. I fed the fire, listened to the night sounds. It was after three before I felt tired enough to find a bed. Sleep eventually came.

Sunlight on my face woke me. It was after 9 a.m. My knee was stiff and sore and the skin around my hip was tender. I felt dirty. Looking for a shower, I went into the kitchen.

Cam was sitting at the table, eating toast and jam, clean, hair slicked back.

He pointed with his thumb over his shoulder. I went that way. Linda was sitting at a big desk, looking at her laptop screen. She looked clean too.

'Does that thing work anywhere?' I said.

She looked up and smiled. 'I've written the whole fucking thing. All of it. The whole Yarrabank saga. And I'm plugged in to the world again. Through my trusty modem.'

I said, 'Modem's not a word you can love.'

She tapped the computer screen. 'There's a P. K. Vane in Breamlea,' she said. 'Must have moved from Beaumaris. We can take the car ferry.'

There wasn't a single thing to lose.

'I'll have a shower,' I said. 'See if you can find the departure times.'

The woman was tall and thin and her labrador was old and fat. She was wearing a big yellow sou'wester that ended at her knees. Her legs were bare and she was barefoot.

There was no-one else on the beach. Just Linda and I and the woman and the dog and the gulls. We saw her a long way off, walking on the hard wet sand, hands in pockets, head down, getting her feet wet when the tiny waves ran in. The dog walked up on the dry sand, stiff-legged, stopping every few yards for a hopeful inspection of something delivered by the tide.

When she was about a hundred metres away, I got up and went towards her. The labrador came out to meet me, friendly but watchful. I stopped and offered him my hand. He came over, nosed it, allowed me to rub his head.

When she was close enough to hear me, I said, 'Mrs Vane?'

She nodded. She had strong bones in her face, big streaks of grey in her hair, skin seen too much sun.

'Are you the widow of Paul Karl Vane of the Victoria Police?'

She nodded again, still walking.

'Mrs Vane, I'd like to talk to you about your husband and the deaths of Anne Jeppeson and Danny McKillop.'

She kept looking at me and didn't say anything until she was close, three or four metres away. The dog went to her.

She leant down and rubbed its head, eyes still on me. Her eyes were startlingly blue.

'I was hoping someone would come,' she said. 'I don't think I've had one happy day since they killed that girl.'

She put out a hand and I took it. We walked up the beach.

The shack was up in the hills behind Apollo Bay. We got lost once, retraced our route, found where we'd gone wrong. Cam was driving, the three of us crammed onto the bench seat, Linda in the middle.

On the way from Breamlea, keeping to the back roads, Cam said, 'How come she doesn't know what it is?'

'Paul Vane never told her,' I said. 'He woke her up on the night Anne was killed and told her he'd seen it happen. He was electric, sat drinking all night. The next day, when the television had the news of Danny's arrest, he told her Danny hadn't done it, that it was murder, that he knew who'd done it but couldn't tell anyone.'

'So she kept quiet too,' said Cam.

I moved my cramped arm from behind Linda's head. 'She says it haunted her. When she read about Danny's sentence, she was sick. Paul became morose, drank more, used to say he'd done the wrong thing but it was too late. Eventually he took early retirement. Then he got sick, bowel cancer. He kept telling her he was going to give her the evidence, that he was going to get a lot of money to provide for her after he was gone, that she should tell Danny that he was innocent and give him the evidence.'

'Money?' asked Cam. 'Did he get it?'

I shook my head. 'No. She thinks he tried to blackmail someone over Danny's death and that's why he was murdered. He told her where the evidence was the morning of the day he was shot.'

'And then she rang Danny?'

'Later. After Paul's murder, the house was broken into and searched from top to bottom. Then Paul's boat caught fire at its moorings at Sandringham and blew up. She says she was too scared to fetch the evidence. And then she was watching television and saw the news that Danny'd been shot. After that, there didn't seem to be any point.'

'That must be it up ahead,' Linda said. She'd fallen asleep a few times on the trip, head lolling on to my shoulder.

The shack was old, just a big room and a lean-to, probably a timber-getter's humble home. It was made of timber slabs, weathered to a light grey, but still solid. The whole place was leaning slightly, held up by a huge brick chimney.

We got out, stretching stiff limbs. The air was cold and moist. Far away, we could hear a vehicle changing gear on a hill, then silence. The birds were quiet at this time of day.

The front door was padlocked, no more than a gesture considering the condition of the door and its frame.

I opened the lock with the key Judith Vane had given me.

Inside it was dark, almost no light coming through the dirty panes of the two small windows. To my right was the fireplace, a huge red brick structure, the front blackened almost to the roof by thousands of fires.

You couldn't light a fire in it now. The opening, about the size of two fridges side by side, had been closed in with fibreboard. Some kind of wooden frame had been built in the opening and the fibreboard nailed to it. This work was recent compared to the age of the shack.

'It's in there,' I said, pointing at the chimney.

'There's a crowbar in the ute,' Cam said. He went out to fetch it.

Linda and I looked at each other.

'So, Jack Irish,' she said. 'This is it.'

I nodded.

Cam was in the doorway, a weary little smile on his face. He didn't have the crowbar.

'No crowbar?' I said.

He took a step into the room.

There was a man behind him holding a pump-action shotgun. It was Tony Baker, with a big plaster on the side of his face where I'd hit him with the steel pipe.

'Move along, coon,' he said.

Cam came into the room. Baker came in too, a safe distance behind Cam. He'd done this kind of thing before.

Another man, in an expensive camelhair overcoat, came into the doorway. He was tall, somewhere beyond fifty, that was the only safe guess: full head of close-cropped silver hair, narrow tanned face with a strong jaw and deep lines down from a nose that had seen contact. He had a young man's full, slightly contemptuous mouth. In one hand, he held a short-barrelled .38. In the other, he had the crowbar.

'Jack Irish,' he said. 'I'm Martin Scullin. You're a fucking pain in the arse.' His voice was as flat and his diction as slow as Barry Tregear's. Country boys both, grown old in the city. Or maybe it was the standard issue voice in the old Consorting Squad.

'I've heard a lot about you,' I said. To my surprise, my voice sounded normal.

'Where's the stuff?' Scullin said. He didn't sound particularly interested.

'I don't know. We're just looking.'

Scullin looked at Tony Baker, no expression on his face.

Baker clubbed Cam across the jaw with the shotgun barrel. Cam went down like a suit slipping off a clothes hanger. He fell to his knees, tried to stand up.

Baker stepped over and hit him in the face with the barrel again. Twice.

Blood spurted out of Cam's nose, turning his shirt black.

Baker turned his bull-terrier head and looked at me. Even in that light, I could see the gold fleck in his eye.

'I'm going to kill this coon,' he said. 'Then I'm going to kill that bitch.'

He kicked Cam in the ribs, a short, stabbing movement, full of power. Cam shook his head like a swimmer trying to clear water from his ears.

Baker kicked him again, harder. Cam put his hands on the floor, got into a sitting position, looked up, eyes closed. His mouth was wide open, a cave streaming blood.

Baker hit him under the jaw with an upward movement of the shotgun butt. Cam fell over sideways.

Baker stepped back, readying himself to kick.

'Leave him,' I said. 'It's in the chimney.'

Baker looked at Scullin.

Scullin said to me, 'Get it.'

Baker pointed the shotgun at me. Scullin passed me the crowbar.

I looked at Linda. She was kneeling next to Cam, holding his head, blood all over her arms.

The fireplace cover came off easily, nails squeaking. In the fireplace was an old stove, a Dover, filthy with soot, stovepipe rusted.

'Get up there,' Scullin said.

There wasn't room for me and the stovepipe. I took it in both hands and worked it loose. It came off and fell behind the stove with a crash. I got on the stove awkwardly, kneeling, bent over, and looked up the chimney. Soot fell on my face. Dark. I couldn't see anything.

'Get up there,' Scullin said again.

I pressed my hands against the chimney sides, got on one leg, then the other. I was in the chimney from below my waist up.

I put my hands up and began to feel around.

Nothing. Just flaking soot. I reached higher. A ledge. The chimney had a jink.

My fingertips touched something. Smooth. Cold. I felt sideways, found an edge.

A box. A metal box. Felt up. A projection. The lid. Ran my fingers left and right.

'What the fuck you doing up there?' Scullin said. 'Is it there or what?'

There was something on top of the box.

'It's here,' I said. 'It's here.'

I bent my knees slowly, got the right one on the stove, turned my body to the left, arms above my head.

'Get a fucking move on,' Scullin said.

I ducked down, came out of the chimney, soot falling like a curtain, bringing my right arm down and around my body.

'Here,' Scullin said, 'give it to me.'

He was just a metre away.

I shot him in the chest, high, right under the collarbone. He went over backwards.

Baker was looking at me, a little smile on his face.

I shot him in the stomach. He frowned and looked down at himself.

I got off the stove and shot Scullin again, in the chest.

Baker was bringing up his shotgun, slowly. He was looking at the floor.

'Steady on, Jack,' he said thickly, like a very drunk man.

I shot him again, in the chest. The impact knocked him up against the wall. Then he fell over sideways.

'Stop now,' Cam said. 'I think they understand.'

We were going through Royal Park, Linda driving Scullin's dove-grey Audi, Cam in the back, strapped up and stitched and plastered by the doctor in Geelong. I came out of my reverie. No-one had said anything for eighty kilometres.

Something flat, that's all. Ronnie's friend Charles's words. Ronnie had brought something small and flat to Melbourne.

'Ronnie's evidence,' I said.

Linda glanced at me. 'What?'

'I know where Ronnie's evidence is,' I said.

I gave her directions.

Mrs Bishop took a long time to open her door.

'Mr Irish,' she said. 'How nice to see you.' She inspected me. 'Have you been in mud?'

'Doing a dirty job,' I said. 'Should have changed. Can I come in if I don't touch anything?'

We went down the passage and into the sitting room. I looked around. On a bookshelf between the french doors was a small stereo outfit, no bigger than a stack of three Concise Oxfords. On top was the CD player.

The CDs, a modest collection, perhaps twenty, were on the shelf above in a plastic tray.

'Mrs Bishop,' I said. 'I wanted to come around and say how sorry I am about Ronnie. But I had to go away.'

She nodded, looked away, sniffed. 'Both my men,' she said. 'Both gone.'

I wanted to pat her but my hand was too dirty. I waited a while, then I said, 'You told me Ronnie put a new CD with your others.'

She cheered up. 'That's right. It's Mantovani's greatest hits.'

'Have you played it?' I said, and I held my breath.

She put out a hand and found a cleanish place to touch my arm. 'I haven't been able to bring myself to,' she said. 'It's the last thing Ronnie gave me.'

'Do you think we could put it on for a little listen? It might help me.'

Her look said that she thought all was not well with my thinking processes, but she switched the player on, found the CD in the tray and, holding it like a circle of spiderweb, put it in the drawer.

She pressed Play. The drawer slid in.

We waited.

The silken strings of Mantovani filled the room.

I expelled my breath loudly.

'Thank you, Mrs Bishop,' I said. 'I don't think it's going to help me after all.'

Her eyes were closed and she was moving her head with the music.

I got into the car and slammed the door. 'I don't know where Ronnie's evidence is,' I said. 'Shit.'

Cam started the motor. 'Let's think about a drink,' he said.

Doug always said Ronnie would make a good spy.

'Hang on,' I said. 'One more try.'

This time, Mrs Bishop opened her door in seconds.

'Sorry to be a nuisance,' I said.

'Not at all, Mr Irish.'

'Did you live in this house when Ronnie was a boy?'

She smiled. 'Oh yes. We've always had this house. It was Doug's mother's. Doug grew up here, too. I wanted to sell it when we went to Queensland, but Doug wouldn't have a bar of it. He was a very wise person, wasn't he.'

'Very. Mrs Bishop, did Ronnie have any special place in the house? A secret place?'

'Secret? Well, just the roof cubby. But that wasn't a secret.'

'The roof cubby?'

'Yes. It's a little hidey-hole in the roof. Doug's father made it for him when he was a boy.'

'Ronnie didn't by any chance go up there?'

She frowned. 'To the roof cubby? Why would he do that?'

'He didn't?'

'Well, I don't know. I wasn't here all the time, but—'

'Could I have a look at it?'

She didn't reply for a moment. Her eyes said she was now reasonably certain that I was deranged. Then she said, 'Are you any good at climbing trees, Mr Irish?'

The entrance to the roof cubby was the ventilation louvre in the back gable of the house. It was about six metres from the ground, brushed by the thick, bare branches of an ancient walnut.

I considered calling for Cam. But pride is a terrible thing.

'You wouldn't have a ladder?' I said.

Mrs Bishop shook her head. 'That's how you get up there. The tree.'

I took hold of the lowest branch of the tree. There was moss on it. I groaned.

It took five minutes to get up there. I almost fell out of the tree twice and a branch poked me in the groin before I got close enough to the small door to put out a hand and push it. It resisted. I put out a foot and pushed.

The door opened with a squeak, swinging inwards and pulling in a short length of nylon rope attached to a ringbolt in the bottom of the door. I puzzled over this for a moment before I realised that this was how you closed the door from the outside: you pulled the rope.

I clambered across from my branch, got my head and shoulders and one arm in and pulled myself across.

The floor of the hideaway was below the level of the doorway. I lowered myself tentatively into the gloom. About a metre down, my feet touched the floor. For a while I couldn't see anything, then gradually I made out the corners of the room. Light came from the door, now a window, from gaps between the bargeboards and the roof. It was a little box, perhaps three metres square, with a pitched ceiling, boarded off from the rest of the ceiling of the house. The floor was covered with flower-patterned linoleum.

It was empty.

Not even cobwebs.

Nowhere to hide anything.

There was no sign that anyone had ever used the room, had ever had a secret life up here.

I groaned again. Going down would be even harder than coming up.

I squeezed my upper body through the entrance, reached out and got a grip on a branch above my head. I pulled myself up to it, getting a knee on the sill, then standing up. As I did so, the jagged end of a short dead branch almost took out my left eye.

I pulled my head back.

The tip of the branch was just inches away. It was bone white, except for odd grey marks, almost like fingerprints, on the underside.

I wanted to put a bandaid on the scratch on his cheek but he didn't want me to.

That's what Mrs Bishop had said when we first talked about Ronnie's disappearance.

Ronnie had been here.

Standing just where I was standing. A scratch on his cheek bleeding.

Ronnie had scratched his cheek on the branch. He had put his left hand to his cheek and it had come away with blood on it. In anger, he had grabbed the branch and tried to break it.

But it wouldn't break. And he left his blood on it, dark marks now weathered to grey.

'Are you all right, Mr Irish?'

Mrs Bishop was looking up at me, eyes wide.

'I'm fine,' I said. 'I'll be down in a minute.'

I scrambled back through the small door.

Somewhere in here. Somewhere in this empty room was Ronnie's evidence.

I went around the walls carefully, feeling for a loose board, a door to a hiding place. It took about five minutes.

Nothing.

The floor. Perhaps there was a gap between the floor and the ceiling below. I knelt down and tried to lift the nearest corner of the linoleum.

It wouldn't come up. It was held down by tacks, one every few centimetres.

I went all round the lino edge under the doorway, trying to lift it with my nails. It was tacked down tight. Along the right-hand wall, it was the same.

In the right-hand corner, a small piece came up.

I tugged at it.

It was just one broken tack. The rest held.

Along the back wall, all hope gone, feeling the regular line of tackheads.

The tacks stopped.

I ran my fingertips into the corner, perhaps thirty centimetres away.

No tacks.

I ran them down the left-hand wall.

No tacks for the first thirty centimetres.

I felt in the dark corner. The lino curled back slightly. I pulled at it. A triangular piece peeled back stiffly. I felt beneath it with my right hand.

There was a small trapdoor, perhaps twenty centimetres by fifteen.

I pulled it up with my nails. It came away easily.

I put my hand into the cavity.

There was a box, a long narrow box, shallow, lidded.

I got my hand under it and took it out of the cavity. It was a nice box, pearwood perhaps, the kind that used to hold the accessories for sewing machines.

I got up and went to the entrance, to the light.

The lid had a small catch.

I opened it.

Cam's girlfriend's flat was the way we'd left it, apart from the battered front door. My malt whisky was still standing next to the telephone in the kitchen.

Cam was in the Barcelona chair, holding himself upright, drinking Cascade out of the bottle again. I was on the sofa, drinking nothing, nervous. Linda was at Channel 7.

'They'll run it you reckon?' asked Cam.

'Depends what's on Vane's film.'

We sat in silence in the gloom. After a while, I got up and drank some water. Cam finished his beer, got up painfully to get another one out of the fridge. When he came back, he said, 'That shooting today. Made me think of my German.'

'Your German?'

'Last bloke who shot at me. Before…when was it? Yesterday.' He lit a Gitane. 'Gary Hoffmeister. We were shooting roos out to buggery, out there in the Grey Range. I only met him the day before we went. Off his head. Had a whole trunk of guns. Rifles, handguns, shotguns. Never stopped shooting, shoot anything, trees, stones, anything. He was full of Nazi shit, too. Kept asking me about my name, how come I was this colour. I just said, I'm a tanned Australian, mate. I thought, you'll keep. Wait till we're out of here.'

Cam drank some beer.

'Last night out,' he said, 'Gary was off his face, talking about Anglo-Saxon purity, Hitler was right, the coming Indonesian invasion. I went to take a piss round the back of the cooltruck. Came round the corner, .38 slug hits the truck next to my head. Into reverse, got to the cab to get my rifle, he fires about five shots, trying to hit me right through the driver's door.'

He appeared to lose interest in the story.

'What happened?' I said.

'Got the iron, off into the scrub. Took about half an hour to get a clear shot at the bastard. He was trying to stalk me like Rambo. I put him in with the roos, took him to the cops in Charleville. He was nice and cold. They knew fucking Gary there, handshakes all round, good bloody riddance.'

'They charge you?'

'Had to. Court found I acted in self-defence. Had to come back from WA. Took a little trip back to the scene while I was there. Near there, anyway.'

'What for?'

Cam smiled his rare smile. 'Dig up the ten grand Gary had in his gun crate. And that Ruger. No point in giving that kind of stuff to the cops. Spoils 'em.'

The phone rang. It was 6.25 p.m.

I went into the kitchen and picked it up.

'Put on the TV,' Linda said. 'Seven at six-thirty.'

I went back to the sitting room and switched on the set.

'Something's on,' I said. 'Six-thirty.'

The ads went on forever. We sat in silence.

The current affairs show began with its montage of news footage: bombs, riots, politicians talking.

Then the serious young woman came on, dark top, little scarf, air of barely controlled excitement.

'Tonight,' she said, 'this program deals with allegations about the involvement of a Cabinet Minister, public servants, a clergyman, trade union leaders and others in an under-age sex ring. It also alleges police involvement in the death in 1984 of a social justice activist, and massive corruption surrounding Charis Corporation's six hundred million dollar Yarra Cove development.'

She paused.

'These are serious and dramatic allegations. And we believe they are fully substantiated.'

Another pause.

'First,' she said, 'we show you, exclusively, shocking photographs taken by a Special Branch detective on the night in 1984 when social justice activist Anne Jeppeson met her death.'

First, we saw some old footage of Anne Jeppeson leading

a Save Hoagland march and answering questions at a news conference. A male voice-over gave a quick history of the Hoagland closure.

Then the woman said, 'On the night of 18 June 1984, Anne Jeppeson was leaving her terrace house in Ardenne Street, Richmond, at 11.40 p.m. Unbeknown to her a Special Branch officer, Paul Karl Vane, was watching her house from a vehicle parked across the street. He had a camera and began taking pictures as she left the house.'

I held my breath.

The first photograph came on, startlingly clear. It showed Anne Jeppeson, in a leather jacket and jeans, coming out of the front door of a terrace house. Her head was turned back, as if she was speaking to someone. It must have been Manuel Carvalho.

The next picture showed Anne stepping off the kerb. She was looking to her right, not alarmed.

The next one showed her almost in the middle of the road, still looking right. Now her mouth was open, her right hand was coming up, the whites of her eyes showing.

Then the camera turned its attention to where she was looking. The picture showed a car, a Kingswood, two figures in the front seat, faces just white blurs.

There was another shot, the car closer, the faces clearer.

In the next picture, Anne Jeppeson was lifted off the ground, top half of her body on the bonnet of the Kingswood, the lower half in the air.

Now you could see the faces of the driver and the passenger clearly.

The driver was Garth Bruce, Minister for Police. Younger but unmistakably Garth Bruce.

The passenger was Martin Scullin, now lying dead on the floor in the shack in the Otways.

'We have every reason to believe,' the presenter said, 'that the driver of the vehicle seen colliding with Anne Jeppeson is Garth Bruce, now Minister for Police, and that the passenger is Martin Scullin, then a Drug Squad detective and now owner of a security company, AdvanceGuard Security, the company started by Garth Bruce after leaving the Victoria police.'

Cam made a sound of triumph that could have been heard by low-flying aircraft.

Then they got on to Ronnie Bishop's videos, the ones I had found in the nice sewing machine box under the floor of the roof cubbyhouse. They did their fuzzy pixels to prevent us seeing exactly what was happening but it very clearly involved sexual acts with young people of both sexes who couldn't be said to be willing partners.

They did show us the faces of the adults.

Lance Pitman, Minister for Planning, was there.

Father Rafael Gorman was there.

So was a man the presenter identified as the late Malcolm Bleek, once the highest ranking public servant in the Planning Department.

Then there were two leaders of the trade union movement, a prominent financial entrepreneur now living abroad, and other men the presenter didn't identify. Someone would recognise them. Wives. Children. Colleagues.

There were a lot of close-ups. Ronnie had made sure everyone was identifiable.

'These shocking films,' the presenter said, 'are believed to have been taken by Ronald Bishop, an employee of the Safe Hands Foundation, an organisation founded by Father Rafael Gorman to help homeless young people. It is likely that the films were used to blackmail Mr Lance Pitman and others seen in them. It appears likely that Bishop kept a copy of the films, perhaps as some form of insurance.'

Then Linda came on, poised and professional, and told the full story of Yarrabank and Hoagland. Names, dates, everything. How Anne Jeppeson came close to torpedoing the whole thing and was murdered for it. How Detective-Sergeant Scullin probably provided the helpless Danny McKillop to take the rap and how Father Gorman probably provided Ronnie Bishop to seal Danny's fate.

The whole thing took half an hour. Much of the detail was conjecture, but it made a powerful case. When it was over, Cam got up, flexed his shoulders gingerly, and said, 'Shocking. Could undermine faith in grown-up people. There's some Krug around here. What about you?'

I looked at him and said, 'Give me a beer mug full to start.'

There is ice in the wind at Caulfield on a Saturday in late autumn. Long-legged Cynthia the head Commissioner and Cyril Wootton were both dressed for it: tweedy, scarves.

At 2.50 p.m., I was looking at Nancy Farmer, Tony Ericson, and Dakota Dreaming, aka Slim, in the mounting yard. Nancy was fidgety, patting the horse, tugging at her silks, pushing strands of hair into her cap. Tony was worse. He had the air of a man waiting for the jury to come back. But the horse was calm enough for the three of them. He looked at the ground mostly, like someone who knows about waiting.

Tony's children were at the rail, popeyed with excitement. The girl had been neglecting her grooming. Dakota didn't look as lustrous as when I'd last seen him. It was worth trying, but it wasn't going to fool anyone. The horse was right: rippling, tight behind the saddle, poverty lines on the rump.

The man next to me was looking at Dakota too.

'Nothin wrong with that bugger you can see,' he said, pointing at the horse with his rolled up copy of the *Herald Sun*. 'Shockin history though.'

'Shocking,' I said. Ron Pevsner in the *Age* thought so too. He assessed Dakota's price at 50-1. That was about tops for Ron. His colleague Bart Grantley rated the horse at two out of ten. No-one knew what a horse had to do to get a rating of one. Die in its previous race, perhaps. The form comment was: 'Comeback race. Lightly raced but injury prone and seems fully tested. Hard to have.' All the other form guides said much the same. The Wizard assessed his odds at 100-1 and said: 'Must improve.' It would be hard to argue with this daring judgment.

I'd driven Harry to the track. Cam was in Sydney, handling the plunge on the interstate ring at Randwick.

Harry was in a philosophical mood. 'Jack,' he said, 'pullin off a coup's a bit of a miracle, y'know. I've had a coup horse run last. Stone motherless last. Goodbye seventy grand.' He smiled. 'There's a number of worries. The horse, the weight, the jockey, the barrier draw, the track. Any one can sink you. And then there's another tiny matter. Today, thirteen other bloody cattle. Some of 'em even trying to win.'

Before we parted, he said, 'Lunch money in your pocket?'

I nodded.

He said, 'Jack, somethin extra I want you to do. Occurred to me.'

At 2.45 p.m., I went over to where Wootton was reading his race book. He looked every inch the bank manager at his leisure.

'Well, Cyril,' I said, 'I've been thinking about another one of your commissioners. Eddie Dollery. I hope your Cynthia doesn't have a taste for rooting men wearing uniforms and crotchless underwear.'

I gave him the small white card. He took it with the lack of enthusiasm of a man being offered a business card by an encyclopedia salesman.

He turned it over and read: 'Six nine.' He looked at me for confirmation.

I nodded. 'Six nine.'

Then I gave him Harry's last-minute instruction. Cyril didn't blink, put his race book into a side pocket of his jacket and walked off. Cynthia was talking to a tall man with the hair of the young Elvis Presley and the face of peatbog man. She saw Wootton coming, cocked her head and said something.

Wootton walked straight up to her, gave her the card, said two words.

Cynthia said two words back, looked at Elvis Peatbog, walked off briskly.

Dakota Dreaming opened at 50-1. The favourite, Shining Officer, was at 4-1. The second favourite, Steel Beach, was 6-1.

I approached a bookmaker called Mark Whitecross, a large man, sour, a reputation for staying well ahead of the punters. Harry saw Mark as a challenge.

'I'll have $12,000 to $2000 on number four,' I said.

Number four was Steel Beach.

Whitecross looked at me without interest. It went into the computer.

When I had the ticket, I said, 'I'll have another twelve to two on number four.'

This time, Whitecross pushed out his cheek with his tongue.

I put the ticket in my top pocket and said, 'Twenty-four thousand to four thousand. Please.'

No interest. I got it. Then I said, 'Same again,'

Whitecross's offsider said something in his ear. He leaned forward to look across at another bookie. I looked too. Cyril Wootton was there. The bookie had just shortened Steel Beach to 2-1.

'It's 12 to 6 now,' said Whitecross.

Between us, Cyril and I pulled Steel Beach down to 9-4 before we stopped.

We also pushed Dakota out to 100-1, which was when Cynthia, Elvis Peatbog and the others went into action.

The 100s dropped to 66s. They shrank to 33s. Then the word came through from Randwick. Cam had struck. The price went to 20s, 14s, 7s. When Dakota and Nancy Farmer set out for the starting gate, the price was 9-4 and nobody was taking very much.

Wootton drifted over. 'Mission accomplished,' he said, your World War II RAF squadron leader back from holding off Jerry above the fields of Devon.

'Part one,' I said. 'Part one.'

'Tremendous interest in this race,' the race caller boomed. 'A big plunge on number ten, Dakota Dreaming.

Very big plunge. Interstate too. Hammered in from 100-1 to 9-4. Not often you see that. Lots of excitement. A three-State plunge. Someone must think they know more than the form shows. If this horse gets up, there'll be a lot of bookies stopping off at the teller machines on the way home to get some Sunday collection money. Surprise of the century some would say. Longer than that. Lazarus gets gold in the marathon. This horse hasn't seen the track for two years and didn't exactly go out in a blaze of glory then. Money too for Steel Beach in the early stages and it tightened for a while. Then the Dakota Dreaming avalanche hit the books.'

He went on like this until they were ready to go.

The interval between the time the light on the starting gate began flashing and the instant the horses lunged needed a calendar to measure.

Nancy Farmer missed the start. Badly. They were all on the way before Dakota Dreaming. That wasn't in the plan.

Dakota was coming out of barrier 10, which was not good news at Caulfield. Harry's instructions to Nancy were to get across onto the rails as quickly as possible.

'You don't need a Rhodes Scholar to tell you that,' he'd said to Nancy the night before, after we'd watched videos of all the main contenders racing. And a few Caulfield Cups for good measure. 'There's a heap of good horses never won from a wide gate at Caulfield.'

We'd watched videos of two of Steel Beach's races. 'Not much class,' Harry said, 'but he's the danger. One-pace stayer. Genuine stayer. If he gets the drop on you, out in front, settin the pace, in his stride, I don't know if you can catch him. Even five kilos to the better. Might be too big an ask for this fella Dakota. Too big for this Shining Officer, that's for sure.'

Six hundred metres from the start, Nancy found a gap and got onto the fence. Just in time. The long curve began after the first chute and to be trapped wide then meant covering many more metres than the rails horses.

The caller said, 'At the eighteen hundred, Steel Beach's drawing away from Sir Haliberd, who's weakening, Shining Officer's coming up on the rails.' He rattled off a string of names before he got to Dakota Dreaming.

She was fourth or fifth last. This wasn't good.

I got my glasses on the field and picked out Nancy's black, white and green hoops. She had several horses outside her and a slowing one in front. I could see her looking around. Desperately.

At the 1200, the caller said, 'I don't know what the rest can do here. Bit of a procession. Steel Beach's looking good, Sir Haliberd's gone, Shining Officer's hanging on, third is Celeste's Bazaar, followed by Fear or Favour. Gap to Fashion Victim. Well back is the plunge horse, Dakota Dreaming. Deep sighs of relief from the books at this stage, I suggest.'

I had my glasses on Nancy. She was at least fifty metres behind Steel Beach, in a pocket and looking for a way out. A bad mistake had been made, I thought. I loved the Sisley drawings. Isabel had loved them. I'd hoped to give them to Claire one day. Now I'd lost them and $25,000.

I lowered the glasses and looked around. Harry was two rows back, a dozen metres along, anonymous-looking as usual. He had his glasses up.

The caller said, 'Signs of life from the plunge horse here. Farmer's taken her out wide at the turn. Don't know about that. And it could be too late now. It's eight hundred to go.'

Nancy had come off the rails, gone between two horses and moved Dakota wide, out towards the middle of the track. It was an act of desperation.

There were six horses between her and Steel Beach, strung out. The leader was fully extended, comfortable, ready to run all day. His jockey turned for a look. Nothing to alarm him.

Nancy was on Dakota's neck. They went up to horses number seven and six in what seemed like a dozen strides.

Then it was five's turn to be swept away. Next was Shining Officer. He appeared to lose heart, running out of pedigree, carrying five kilograms more weight than Dakota.

It was Celeste's Bazaar's turn. The horses ran stride for stride.

'Two-fifty to go,' shouted the caller. 'Celeste's Bazaar's gone. It's Steel Beach and Dakota Dreaming. Unbelievable. Come from near-last to challenge. They're at the two hundred. What a race. The plunge horse. Bookie's nightmare. Sayre looks back. Taken the whip to Steel Beach. Hundred to go. Can he hold?'

Nancy and Dakota. She seemed to be whispering in his laid-back right ear, all her weight on the horse's neck. Gradually, the gap closed.

They were at Steel Beach's rump.

Not enough track left for Dakota to win.

Nancy, only hands and heels, every fibre of her body urging Dakota to win.

The horse responded.

Dakota's stride seemed to lengthen by half a metre. They surged, seemed to drag Steel Beach back.

Level.

Metres to go.

Dakota stretched his neck and put his head in front.

'Dakota,' shouted the caller, 'Dakota! It's Dakota Dreaming! Steel Beach second, Celeste's Bazaar a miserable third. What a finish! What a disaster for the bookies!'

Nancy was standing in the stirrups, up above the horse. She raised her whip in triumph. That would cost her a fine. But she didn't care. She'd come from ten goals down at three-quarter time. Life would never be the same again.

We were home.

I looked for Harry. He was unscrewing the top of the little flask of Glenmorangie. He took a swig. I caught his eye. He gave me a nod.

Down below, I could see Tony Ericson and Rex Tie dancing together. The boy, Tom, had his sister on his shoulders.

'Dakota,' said Linda from behind me. 'That's the word you said in your sleep.'

I turned. She was in her leather jacket, windblown, full of life. 'Don't tell Harry Strang I talk in my sleep,' I said. 'Get here in time?'

'Only just. But I didn't know what I was looking for.'

'As long as you found me,' I said. 'That's the important thing.'

She leaned across and kissed me on the mouth. 'Yes. That's the important thing.'

We didn't stay for the rest of the day's racing. On the way back, I put the radio on. Fitzroy was leading Collingwood by two goals with eight minutes to go.

'Got anything on it?' Harry said.

I said, 'Just my whole life.'

'That's too much,' Harry said. 'It's only a game. Not like the horses. You and the lady free for dinner? Cam'll show up, gets out of Sydney alive.'

BLACK TIDE

For Anita, Nicholas, and Louise:
the Charity, the Hope, and the Faith.

In the late autumn, down windy streets raining yellow oak and elm leaves, I went to George Armit's funeral. It was a small affair. Almost everyone George had known was dead. Many of them were dead because George had had them killed.

My occasional employer and I sat in my old Studebaker Lark a little way down from the church. When the first mourners came out, mostly men in raven suits, Cyril Wootton said, 'Most relieved lot I've seen since the plane out of Vietnam. Still, they won't sleep easy till the ground subsides. May I be told why we're here?'

'Your bloke's mate's in deep to the Armits,' I said.

'How'd you find that out?'

'Anyone could find that out. Wade through sewage for a week, that's all it takes. George liked him. He'd be dead otherwise.'

Two big men, sallow, black hair, moustaches, came out, followed by two women.

'The sons, Con and Little George Armit,' I said. 'Con's wife's the thin one.'

'Well,' said Wootton. 'The other one appears to have shoplifted watermelons and put them down the front of her dress.'

Con and Little George and the wives lined up, backs to us, each with wife to the right. Con put his right hand on his thin wife's shoulder. His left hand moved around slowly and squeezed his brother's wife's high right buttock.

'Racked with grief,' I said.

'Reflex action,' Wootton said. 'Armits have been in the fruit business for many years.'

'Here's George.'

The box had a hard black sheen, a perfect match for the Mercedes hearse. It was carried by six young men, tanned, even height, thick necks, could have been a surfboat crew.

'Relying on professionals to the end, I see,' Wootton said.

When George was in place, the mourners made for their cars.

'Well, that wasn't exactly paydirt, old sausage,' Wootton said. 'You've brought me out here in this appalling conveyance, this hot rod, for sweet bugger all.'

'Somewhere Tony's going to pay his respects. In so deep, he's got no choice,' I said. 'Strong on respect, the Armits. If he's not here, the bastard's last chance is to arselick the boys at the cemetery.'

'I'm paying you for your time,' Wootton said. 'Who's paying me for mine?'

'Believe me, if I could do this without your presence, I would.'

The priest came around the corner in a white turbo Saab, its Michelins giving a plump little squeal of pleasure. He looked at us as he passed, a nightclub-owner's pale face, cigarette tilted upward in the mouth, mobile phone at his ear.

I started the Stud and did a U-turn. A block down the street, I looked right and saw the car. A Hertz car. I turned first left, left again and parked behind the church.

'I'm going in to say a little prayer,' I said, opening the door. 'Keep an eye on the back gate.'

'Spoken like an officer,' Wootton said.

'Still rankles, doesn't it, corporal.'

'Sergeant.'

I'd known Wootton since Vietnam. He'd been in stores, stealing more goods than he dispensed.

The church door was open. Inside, the blood of the martyrs fell from the stained-glass windows and lay in pink patches. The air smelled of incense, stale vase water and brass polish.

I didn't see him at first. There was a row of pillars across the church and he was sitting in front of the one nearest the wall to my right: man in his early forties, crew cut blond hair, little folds of tanned fat over his collar.

I walked across and stopped behind him. 'Hello Tony.'

Tony Ulasewicz didn't look at me, didn't say anything.

'Brendan sends his regards,' I said.

Silence.

'Remember Brendan? Brendan O'Grady. From Reservoir? From school? Your best man? Your friend? That Brendan.'

Tony sniffed loudly. 'Whadda you want?' He shot his left cuff and looked at his watch, a big black diver's watch.

'Me? I don't want anything. Brendan, he wants you to tell a lawyer where he was on the night of February 11 at 11.26 p.m.'

Tony looked at me, shrugged. He had a small scar above his left eyebrow, like a worm under the skin. 'Dunno what you're saying.'

'The two hookers, Tony,' I said. 'Sylvia and Carlette? Out there in that fancy hotel in Marysville. You and Brendan and Jim Beam and the hookers. Chatting, reading magazines. Just when some person unknown was shooting Frank Zakia in his driveway in Camberwell. With a .22 pistol. Many times.'

'Know nothing about that,' said Tony, getting up. 'Gotta go.'

I put a hand on his shoulder, a meaty shoulder. He resisted, I leaned, he sat.

'Tony,' I said, 'Brendan's going down big time. Frank's wife ID'd him, not a doubt in her mind. She knows him. He was in the house three days before, arguing with Frank. Now Brendan says he couldn't have been the one topped Frank because at that moment he was off with you, screwing hookers in Marysville. But you're gone, the hookers are gone, hotel doesn't know if it was you and Brendan or the Pope and Elvis in the room. Plus the cops find the .22 in Brendan's office. Plus Brendan's got more form than Phar Lap.'

Tony's chin slowly moved down to meet his collarbone.

'Brendan's going, Tony,' I said. 'And blokes in there are waiting for him. Death penalty, that would be easier. Nicer even.'

Tony's shoulders went weak. He tilted at the waist until his forehead rested on the pew in front.

'Can't,' he said, voice spitty. 'Fucking can't.'

'Why? He's your mate.'

'People want him. He's owed big, three hundred grand, more, three-fifty, I don't know. He put the weight on them, they want him gone.'

'Frank's wife? The ID?'

'Bullshit. Bitch wanted Frank done. In it over her tits.'

'How's that?'

'Fucking. True fucking love fucking. She's rooting a bloke, his brother owes Bren. This way, they top Frank, she gets Frank's money. Then there's about eighty grand belongs to Bren. Frank was hanging on to it. Bitch gets that too. And Bren goes in, close that gate, he's history, everyone's happy.'

'And you?'

Tony looked up at me, sniffed again. 'I live,' he said. 'I fucking live.'

'You know Frank was going to get it?'

He shook his head. 'No fucking way.'

I took my hand off his shoulder. 'Brendan says, "Tell Tony I'm still his mate. I know he's under the gun. He should've told me. Tell him, he does the right thing now, it's forgotten. I'll look after him."'

Tony sighed, a desperate, drawn-out sound. 'Bren's a dangerous bloke,' he said.

Silence. The light in the stained-glass windows was dimming, shadows growing everywhere, the sort of cold only churches can harbour coming up from the flagstone floor.

'He says he knows how the Armits fit. He'll settle them, take the push off.'

Tony tried a laugh, ended up coughing. 'Jesus,' he said when it stopped. 'Fucking smokes. Bren got the fucking vaguest what it costs to get the Armits off my back?'

'One-sixty.'

Tony's head came around, eyebrows up. 'He knows that?'

I nodded.

He sucked his teeth, hissing noise. 'Where'd he hear that?'

'I told him.'

He studied me. 'Well,' he said, 'fucked if I know where you got that. Anyway. Bren walks on the Frank thing, it's not over.'

'Bren knows that. He says he can handle these people. He also says to tell you he's got people who still owe him favours. That is, if you feel you can't tell the truth about where he was.'

5

Tony suddenly found the back of his right hand interesting, freckled back of hand. After a while, he said, 'How'd y'know I'd be here?'

'Not an interesting question,' I said. 'The question you want to ask, Tony, is this: Am I better off square with the Armits and onside with Bren or one-sixty deep and offside with Bren?'

He looked at me, parts of his face moving, fingers moving. 'Fuck,' he said, 'you think about it, I'm a prick. Tell Bren I know I'm a prick. Know him since I was eight. His mum made me playlunch. He's my mate. I'm a prick. Okay. What do you do when you're a prick?'

'The man who's looking out for Bren's interests, he's outside. And we need the hookers.'

Tony stood up and moved his shoulders, rubbed his jaw. We walked down the side aisle towards the door.

'Come down for the night,' he said. 'Gold Coast hookers. Ballet dancer the one. Sylvia. Got too big. You had experience of ballet dancers?'

'Not that I can remember.'

'You'd remember. Your whole life. Looking at the lid you'd still remember.'

Wootton got out of the car when he saw us.

'Tony, this is someone hired by Bren,' I said as Wootton approached.

They shook hands.

'Tony's happy to place Brendan elsewhere on the night,' I said. 'Also to tell you where to find a ballet dancer who got too big and had to take up another mode of self-expression.'

'Too big?' said Wootton. 'For me, ballet dancers can never get too big. Tony, Jack'll go with you, show you where my office is. We can get everything sorted out.'

Tony looked at me. 'Armits,' he said. 'Squared first.'

'It's got to be up front,' I said to Wootton.

'What's the figure?'

'Hundred and sixty,' Tony said.

Wootton whistled. 'Asking. So they'll take what?'

'Hundred and sixty,' Tony said, with certainty.

'That hard?' Wootton frowned.

'That hard.'

Wootton went for a little walk around a tree, nodding his head, preoccupied, air of a man hearing music in his head. When he came back, he pulled a face, held up his pudgy right hand. 'To be clear, Tony, you are into the Armits for this sum. Fully paid, they would have no objection to you making a statement that will clear Brendan?'

Tony nodded, licked his lips. 'George said to me, with Little George there, "Tony," he said, "you can pay me what you owe, I can kill you or you can fucken do what I tell you till I think you've paid me off." '

Wootton was still frowning. 'And you can produce the ladies?'

'Yeah. Well, I reckon.'

'That's yes?'

'Yes.'

Wootton looked at me, tilted his head, oiled hair gleaming in the fading light. 'Armits,' he said.

'Not at the graveyard,' I said. 'I draw the line.'

'After they drop George,' said Wootton. 'A quiet word with Con. A man who squeezes his sister-in-law's buttock at his father's funeral will understand the meaning of urgency. We'll run out the distance but start at eighty grand. Half tomorrow, half after we get the hookers on tape.'

He was waiting outside my office, cracked leather briefcase on the pavement, a thin figure with a long face on which all the lines seemed to run south and a full head of silver hair, combed back. Most of his weight was on an aluminium walking stick with a fat rubber tip. The autumn wind, full of broad and nasty hints of winter, was whipping his grey raincoat around his legs.

'Looking for me?' I asked.

He gave me a looking over with clear blue eyes. 'Jack Irish.' Not a question.

I nodded.

He sniffed. 'Don't ya keep office hours?'

'Called out urgently,' I said. 'Should have put a note on the door.'

He carried on eyeing me, the look of a talent scout. A faintly disappointed talent scout. 'Spit of yer old man,' he said. 'Big as. And the face. Bill was pretty hard though.'

I looked down at myself, gained no pleasure from the experience. 'Well,' I said, 'I'm a bit older than he was.'

The man thought about this. 'Still,' he said. 'Bit soft.'

No immediate way to controvert this statement occurred to me.

He changed hands on the walking stick and put out his right. Big hand, swollen knuckles. 'Des Connors. Saw ya in yer bloody pram. Never knew what happened to Bill's family after. Then I'm thinkin about needin a lawyer, look in the book, see this John Irish.'

We shook hands. Age hadn't entirely withered his grip. I unlocked the door, ushered him in, got him seated. He put the briefcase on his lap, looked around the spartan chamber. 'How are ya?' he asked. 'Mum still sound?'

'Dead.'

Des shook his head. 'Happens,' he said. 'Pity. Looker she was. My oath. Remember when Bill spotted her. We was buildin at the Shop, Melbourne Uni, just after the war, up on the scaffoldin, hot day, first week of the footy season. Can still be bloody hot then. Course it can be bloody cold too. Anyway, bunch of girls, three, four of em, rich girls, very smarty. Not the girls we went dancin with, I can tell ya. They come along, sit down on this bit of grass, just down there where we can see em, us standin up there on the boards with the bloody great bits of rock. Mind you, married man, back from the war, didn't give em a look.'

'No,' I said. 'You wouldn't.'

'Well, you have a look, don't ya? Just a look. Not a lot of harm in that, is there?'

'No harm at all, hardly,' I said.

'No. Tell you, any bloke's a bloke'd have a look at your mum, scuse me sayin that. Fetchin lass, the hair like copper.' He got a faraway look. 'Still a fair bit of copper goin into buildins then. Copper and lead. Lasts fer bloody ever, y'know. Repels the elements. Everythin's rubbish today. Bloody plastic.'

'That's how he met my mother?'

'A character, Bill, a character. Course, finished the school. Smart. Coulda bin anythin. Doctor, anythin. Had a wit, too, you'd fall off the bloody scaffoldin, you'd be laughin that hard.'

'What happened then?' I didn't know any of this. My

9

mother never talked to me about my father. The only people who talked to me about my father were ancient Fitzroy Football Club supporters and they regarded me as an evolutionary cul de sac in the Irish family.

'What happened? Oh. Well, Bill, he looks over and he says, puts on this serious voice, he says, "Now girls, read us rough workin men somethin improvin." And the girl, yer mum that is, she doesn't blink, not a giggle, she opens a book and she reads a poem out loud. Bill, he didn't expect that. Just stood there. Can't remember a word but it sounded lovely.' Des paused, blinked a few times. 'Anyway, that's a long time ago.'

'Go on. She read the poem. What then?'

'Nothin. We give her a clap and the girls got a bit embarrassed and went off. Didn't do for uni girls to fool around with workin blokes in those days. Anyway, we're knockin off that day, all sweaty, full of dust, and yer mum comes along by herself. Bill says to her, brassy bugger, he says, "Comin to the football tomorrow?" She says, "What football?" He says, "Fitzroy wallopin Melbourne, that's what football." "Give me one good reason," she says. Bill thinks a bit, then he says, "Cause I'm playin for Fitzroy." "Not good enough," she says, and off she walks. Well, we thumped em, one of Bill's good days too, and I'm there shoutin as they go in and I see Bill goes off to the side of the gate and who's standin at the fence there?'

'My mother.'

'Right. Six months later they're married. Anyhow, you'd know all this.'

'No,' I said, 'I don't know any of it.'

Des sniffed. 'Well,' he said, 'that's the story. Anyway, come about a will. Lady across the street says I should have a will. You do wills?'

10

'I can do a will.'

'What's it cost, a will?'

'Wills are free.'

'Free? What's free in the world?'

'Wills. The last free thing.'

Des looked uneasy. 'Not lookin for charity,' he said. 'Pay me way.'

'Not offering charity. Plenty of lawyers will do you a will free. They make their money when you die. Winding up your estate.'

'Right,' he said, thoughtful. 'Hang on. How'd they get the money out of dead blokes?'

'Not the dead blokes. The people they leave things to, they get the money out of them.'

He nodded. 'Fair enough. Well, I need a will.'

I took down the particulars. It was straightforward: no existing will, everything to go to someone called Dorothea Joyce Skinner.

'No kids?' I asked.

'There's Gary.'

'Only child?'

Des sat back in his chair, rubbed his jaw. 'First boy died. Brain thing, matter of hours. Nothin anyone could do. Still, think if we'd done somethin sooner, might've bin different. The wife took that to the grave. Anyway, Gary come along, bit of a shock, I can tell you. Past the forty then. Woulda bin fifteen years between the boys. Don't know if that…well, Gary's rubbish. Smart but rubbish. The smart's from the wife's side, bugger all to do with the bloody Connors. Keegans. Schoolies, the two other sisters. The brother was on the ships, officer on the P&O. Didn't take to him myself, little beard. Always doin this.'

Des clawed his chin gently with his right hand. 'Got on the nerves somethin painful.'

'So you don't want to include Gary?'

'No.'

'You'll need an executor,' I said. 'Someone you can trust to make sure it's all done properly when you're gone. I take it Gary wouldn't be the choice.'

'Bloody oath.'

'Someone else you trust.'

He thought. 'All dead,' he said, 'everybody I trusted. What about you? Reckon I can trust Bill's boy?'

'You can but you'll probably outlive me. What are you planning to leave? Own your house?'

'Buggered old place, fetch a bit though. Next door, bloody chimney's all that's holdin it up, but these two girls give a hundred and fifty grand.' He paused, lines between his brows deepening. 'Anyway, wife left the house to Gary. You lawyers collect debts too?'

'Some debts, yes.'

Des looked down for a while, hands on the briefcase, left thumb rubbing the knuckles of the right hand. 'Gary's got sixty thousand dollars belongs to me,' he said. 'Me sister leave it to me. From the sale of her property. Bastard come over, first time for years, come over and talk me into it. Mad, I musta bin mad. Mind you, I had the flu somethin chronic, thought I was dyin, couldn't think straight. Umpteenth time he done me. Well, done the family. He's a bloke gets his mum to lend him the bit she got from his Nanna Keegan. Six grand I think it was. Lot of money to us. Gone.'

'You lent him sixty thousand dollars?'

'Three weeks, he tells me, double the money, guaranteed. Knew I had a bit cause the bugger got twenty grand hisself

12

from the old girl. Must've done that dough pretty smart.'

'What was he going to do with your money?'

'Shares. Goin through the roof. Mate of his had the mail on it.'

'Any contract?'

'What?'

'Lend money, the thing is you should have an agreement written down. Says how much, when it has to be paid back, that kind of thing.'

He shook his head. 'Give him a cheque.'

'Des, how does a man who doesn't have a wonderful opinion of his son's character hand over sixty grand?'

He put fingers through his hair, teenage hair, fingers swollen like leaves of some desert plant. 'Way I felt that day, I'd've given the bugger anything to get him to go away.'

'When was this?'

'Two months ago. Bastard's got the answering machine on.'

'Maybe he's forgotten, gone on holiday.'

Des sniffed. 'Forget he owes me sixty grand? Pig's arse. Bastard's lyin low.'

'Let me be clear on this. Gary owns the house you live in?'

'The wife left it to Gary but I thought I could live there until…y'know. Now this fella from the bank comes around. He says Gary took another mortgage on the house. Eighty thousand bucks. And he hasn't paid anything for more than six months. So they're gonna sell the house. He says Gary told em, "Go for ya life."'

I whistled. 'Des, how did your wife do this in her will? She should have left the house to you for your life-time and arranged things so that it passed on to Gary after you were gone. She didn't do that?'

He shook his head. 'Left it to Gary.'

'Who did your wife's will?'

'Bloke Gary sent. Lawyer he knew. He come to see her in the hospital and told her how to do it.'

I closed my eyes and said, 'Oh shit.' When I opened them, Des was looking at me with concern.

'You all right?' he said.

'What's Gary do?'

'Beats me. He was a copper. That didn't last. Reckons he resigned. I reckon they give him the arse. Then he had a job with some transport bunch. Then I don't know. Got one of them German cars, cost more than a house. Lives in a flat in bloody Toorak, know that, got the address. Got the bloody keys too.'

'How's that?'

'Give em to me that day when he come smoodgin around for the lend. Dad this and Dad that. Dad, d'ya mind hangin on to me spare keys, case I lose mine?'

'This was before the man from the bank came round?'

'Oh, yeah. Don't think I'd've lent the bugger the money if I knew he'd got a mortgage on his mum's house, do ya?'

I didn't say anything. Des looked down at his hands again. He wanted something from me. I wanted to give him something.

'I could write him a letter,' I said. 'Lawyer's letter. Tell him we want the money or else.'

'Or else what?'

'Or else we'll institute proceedings for the recovery of the debt.'

'That any good?'

I scratched my head. It wasn't itchy. Vestigial animal body

language revealing doubt. 'Depends,' I said. 'Works with some.'

'Won't work with Gary,' said Des with absolute certainty. 'Brass balls.'

'Well,' I said, 'not much one can do otherwise.'

Silence. Des had the disappointed look on his face again. Finally, he said, 'Go around to his place and see if the bastard's still livin there. That's what I'd do if I could.'

'We could go around to where he lives,' I said.

'You and me?'

'I could drive you around there.'

'No,' said Des. 'Not your problem. Just came to make me will.' He never took his eyes off me.

'Enjoy a drive,' I said. 'You could tell me a bit more about my old man.'

He brightened. 'Bill Irish,' he said. 'Stories I could tell you.'

'Tuesday. About 10 a.m. Give me your address. I'll pick you up.'

'Jack,' said the voice on the office answering machine. 'Ring me. You never ring me, you shit.'

I didn't ring her. No phone call to my sister, Rosa, lasts less than half an hour and, from the canyons of Fitzroy, the beer was calling. I was still tired, sagging from my two weeks looking for the alibi witnesses who could save Cyril Wootton's client Brendan O'Grady.

But.

My days wandering through the toxic wasteland of Tony Ulasewicz's life would keep Brendan out of jail for a crime of which he was certainly innocent.

Justice for Brendan.

But.

In a world of perfect justice, would Brendan walk free?

Absolutely not. In such a world, the naked Brendan would be dragged from his round waterbed, subjected to ritual humiliation, then thrown face forward into a pit of starving hyenas. Too extreme? What of the ideal of rehabilitation? Certainly Brendan was capable of changing. He could be permanently changed, perhaps into rose fertiliser, a kilo and a bit of blood and bone.

At peace for the moment, I walked the fifty paces to Taub's Cabinetmaking, down the narrow lane that ran to Smith Street, Collingwood.

I opened the battered door, stood for a moment. The smell of the workshop: wood shavings, linseed oil, Charlie's Cuban cheroots, coffee. Charlie was at the back of the large space, opening and closing the raised-panel door of a narrow, elegant rosewood cupboard. Joints, doors, drawers. For Charlie, it was pistonfit or nothing.

Out of the corner of his eye he saw me coming. 'So,' he said without looking at me. 'Man who finds the scum of the earth. Man who breaks his parents' hearts. Horses and criminals. That's his life.'

'It's too late for him to break his parents' hearts,' I said. 'And sometimes the criminals are on the horses. That door fits.'

Charlie closed the cupboard door, opened it a fraction, closed it. 'An old man,' he said, 'should be retired. But no, he goes on, teaches something to this person who won't go away, this nuisance person. What thanks does the old man get?'

I walked around to look at the back of the cupboard. The back of a Charlie Taub piece, destined to be seen only by removalists, was treated the same way as a violinmaker treats the bottom of the violin. 'Let me guess,' I said. 'Bugger all?'

'Those who hear not the voice of the conscience,' Charlie said. 'Those are the truly deaf. Karl Bernsdorf. He said that. A great man.'

I said, 'I quote him all the time. Maybe they could train a conscience dog for handicapped people like me. You even think about not behaving well, the dog nudges your leg.'

Charlie made his snorting noise. 'Nudges? Pisses on it. Eat your leg off, right up to the hip even, won't help.'

I came around to look at the severe pediment. 'I gather you missed me a lot then?'

Another snort. 'What I miss, I miss someone finishes little jobs I give him. Like little tables. Day's work for a man who actually works.'

'Finished tomorrow,' I said. 'Good as done. Now, time for a beer.'

Getting Charlie out the front door took me another ten minutes. He was quite unable to end the working day without going around touching, fiddling with, and testing the work in progress. Left alone, this could amount to half an hour of shuffling, muttering and whistling.

Outside, the coming winter was in the polluted air, the cold sharpening the smell of the hydrocarbons. We walked to the Prince of Prussia, Charlie telling me about his latest bowls triumph.

'Youngsters,' he said. 'We draw to play these *junge*. They think, old buggers, goodbye. I say to Freddie Chan, he thinks we got no chance, "Freddie, I say, what do these pishers know about skill? Nothing, that's what." He doesn't believe. Well. Next thing, the little fat boy and the other one, the chemist. Mr Pills. In the gutter. You follow?'

'Every word.' We were walking past the old chutney factory. A yellow Porsche and a huge four-wheel-drive were parked on the pavement. Two men, one shaven-headed, the other with a ponytail, were talking in the open doorway. You could smell the sweet, vinegary smell of the long-gone chutney barrels.

'The pricks like the industrial look,' the man with the pigtail said to shaven-head as we came abreast. 'Some paint, some plumbing, don't even have to hide the fucking pipes.'

'So where am I lying?' said Charlie. 'So close, a veneer you can't get it in between. That's where I am and that's the end of these smart boys. Freddie, he can't believe it. He says to me, "Charlie, you're a master."'

'Toothless whip ruthless,' I said. 'These pishers, how old are they, more or less?'

18

Charlie shrugged, waved a huge hand. 'Sixty, sixty-five, there around.'

'Pishers,' I said. 'They should have a junior league for them.'

The Prince was its usual vibrant, cutting-edge-of-the-hospitality-industry self. Stan, the publican, was at the far end of the bar reading a paperback called *Desperado: Success Secrets of the New Small-Business Bandidos*. At the counter, the men Charlie called the Fitzroy Youth Club, Wilbur Ong, Norm O'Neill and Eric Tanner—all men who were shaving when Fitzroy won the 1944 Grand Final—were reflecting on past injustices. Next to them, Wally Pollard, retired tram driver, was talking bowls with a man called Alec Leach. Three other men were seated at a table in the corner studying the racing pages of the *Herald Sun*. Under the window, two thirtyish women, serious-looking, short hair, business clothes, were studying what looked like proof copies of the telephone directory.

Charlie veered off to join the bowls talk. I sat down next to Wilbur Ong.

'Bloody disgrace,' said Norm O'Neill, huge nose pointed roofwards under the peak of his flat cap. 'Rot set in, there and then. Bastards never give us a fair go years after that.'

Eric Tanner caught sight of me. 'Jack,' he said. 'You ever hear about that '49 scandal?'

'Not that I can recall,' I said.

'Three goals in front, five minutes to go. Two of these Tiger girls get in front of Bill. He's taken to the air, you understand, big leap. Bill had a big leap, not the biggest but big. Big enough for this lot certainly. Anyway, he's up there, reachin, and these pussycats they're buggerin about and they

19

end up bangin their heads together, altogether accidental. One wobbles around whinin, the other, he's an actor, he falls over, they have to help him off. Crebbin, that's his name. Umpire gives the Tigers a free. Well, a few of our fellas get around him, give him a few words, next thing the kick's bein taken plumb in front.'

'First of three,' said Wilbur Ong.

'Three frees in a row,' Eric said. 'Roy puts a hand on these sheilas, they get a kick. Win by a point.'

'The next week…' said Norm O'Neill.

'I'm tellin this story,' said Eric. 'The next week this actor Crebbin that got the little knock on the head, he gets married. Nice-lookin girl from the picture in the paper. And who d'ya think's standing next to her at the altar, givin her away?'

'Could it be her father?'

'Her bloody father. And who's her bloody father?'

'Surely not?'

'Too bloody true. The bloody ump give the game to the Tigers. How d'ya like that?'

'Not at all,' I said. 'Not at all.'

Stan put down his paperback and came over, scratching the surviving corkscrew hairs on his head. 'You bin scarce,' he said.

'Duty called,' I said. 'Been out there saving a man from a cruel miscarriage of justice.'

'Don't have to go out. Save a man from a cruel bloody miscarriage of justice right here,' said Stan. 'You're the old man's lawyer, talk him into sellin this dump, save me wastin my whole life listenin to old farts goin on about dead footy players.'

Stan's father, Morris, owned the pub and, at 87, showed

no interest in selling it.

'Find a suitable buyer and I'll think about it,' I said and ordered a round.

Stan was at the tap, drawing beers without looking, when he said loudly, 'Speakin of dead footy players, had a bloke in here this mornin, wants to buy the pictures.'

All talk stopped.

'The pictures?' said Wilbur Ong. 'What pictures?'

Stan gestured around the walls with the back of a meaty hand. 'The photos. All this junk.'

'Bloke,' said Norm O'Neill, cold voice. 'What kind of a bloke?'

Stan put down a glass, hitched his pants over his paunch. 'Very nice bloke. Well-dressed. Blazer and grey flannels.'

'What kind of a bloke?' said Norm, voice now icy.

Stan drew the last beer with great concentration, held it up and inspected the head. 'Brisbane Lions bloke,' he said. 'Reckons the photos'd be better off in Brisbane in this Lions clubhouse they got there, big luxury clubhouse. Carpets. Got a Lions Wall of Fame. In the bistro.'

'In the what?' said Eric Tanner.

Stan shook his head in sadness. 'Italian term we in the hospitality industry use, Eric.'

In the silence, you could hear the traffic on Smith Street, hear two women talking as they walked by outside.

I looked around the pub walls. The bits you could see between the photographs were stained the colour of black tea by a hundred years of tobacco smoke. The photographs recorded Fitzroy Football Club sides and players going back to the turn of the century. On my way to the toilet through the door marked GENTS, I often paused to look at my father, big, dark Bill Irish, in the sides of the late 1940s.

My grandfather was on the wall too. He had three seasons in the seniors before breaking an arm in two places against Collingwood. His team's faded photographs were near the dartboard.

'Lions Wall of Fame,' said Eric Tanner, head tilted, eyes slits. 'What Lions would those be?'

'The way he put it,' Stan said. 'Fitzroy Football Club's in Brisbane now, photos should be there too.'

The silence was absolute.

Norm O'Neill's nose seemed to grow larger, now much more than a prominent feature on a facial landscape, now it was the landscape, a nose and glasses with a face attached. He cleared his throat.

'Stanley,' he said, 'Stanley, you're missin somethin.' He was speaking slowly and clearly, leaning forward, knuckles on the bar. 'Fitzroy Football Club's not in Brisbane, Stanley. Fitzroy Football Club can never be in Brisbane. Nobody can take the Lions to Brisbane. Why is that, Stanley? Because Fitzroy Football Club can only be in Fitzroy.'

Norm paused, looked around the room. Then he said, 'Well, bloody Brisbane can put a lion on their jumpers but that doesn't mean the Lions are now in that bloody tropical hellhole. The Lions are here, in this bloody pub. And they're not yours to sell. Grasp that, can you?'

Silence, all eyes on Stan.

Stan picked up a beer glass, held it to the light. 'Be that as it may,' he said. 'Pretty good price offered. Never thought the old photos'd be worth anything.'

'You talk to Morris about this?' asked Wilbur.

'Don't need to talk to anyone,' said Stan. 'I'm the manager. He's sittin in the sun in Queensland with all the other ancient buggers got any brains. This pub, I decide what happens.'

'I remember you when you were two bricks and a pisspot high, your mum made a little Roys jumper for you,' said Wilbur.

'Given it a lot of thought,' said Stan. 'Bloke gets an answer tomorrow.'

Without even glancing at one another, Norm, Wilbur and Eric stood up. Charlie rose from his barstool. Wearily, I got up, put on a menacing look.

'And what, Stanley,' asked Norm, 'and I want you to think hard about this. What is the answer?'

There was a long silence. Stan looked at each of us in turn, little smile on his face, put the glass down, turned and set off back to his paperback. Over his shoulder, he said, 'Given it a lot of thought.'

He picked up the book and looked down the counter at us.

We waited.

'Reckon I'll tell him to piss off,' said Stan.

We all sat down and went back to drinking beer.

At 6.30, a car hooted outside. Three hoots. I said my goodbyes, went out with Charlie. His granddaughter Augustine's car was at the door. She leaned over and opened the passenger door.

'What did trade unions do to deserve this striking woman?' I asked. Gus was a rising star in the union movement. She looked like Lauren Bacall with brains, a sight to soothe any old worker's eye.

'What did Taub's Cabinetmaking do to deserve the most fetching man ever to mate two pieces of wood?' said Gus.

'They are both the undeserving,' I said. 'We are the deserving. Can we be brought together?'

'Listen,' said Charlie, fighting with the seatbelt. 'In Kooyong, the library. You remember.'

'I thought you made that up.'

'People who look for criminals, they make up. Yesterday, this wife rings up. The man, he's gone. But she wants it still. Measure up next week.'

'I've got tables to finish. Little tables. Day's work for a man who actually works. More for someone like me.'

'Next week.'

'Take him away, Gus,' I said. 'He's ruined a spiritual moment.'

'It's a gift,' she said. 'The whole family has it.'

On the way home, sense of achievement gone, I went via a place in St George's Road for some takeaway Chinese comfort food. They know me there. I don't have to order. As I come in, Lester barks, 'How many?' Until recently, the answer was Two. These days, it's One.

Opening the front door at home, I surveyed the scene with distaste. The minimally converted stable where I live was cold and untidy and unclean, battered leather furniture buried under newspapers, books and items of clothing put down, temporarily.

Friday night is the second-worst night for being on your own. Saturday night is the big one. By Sunday night, you think you're getting the hang of it.

The answer lies in action. I switched on lights, checked the answering machine, got the heating going, went outside for firewood, started a blaze.

Looking for red wine in the unpacked boxes, I found the surviving bottle of '89 Maglieri shiraz. It had been in an unopened carton not two metres from the explosive device that almost removed the top floor of my previous dwelling, an old boot factory in North Fitzroy. Eleven bottles fragmented, glass splinters travelling ten metres, a dark purple spray covering everything. The first people on the scene thought it was blood, enough for at least two. But one bottle was mysteriously spared, a small abrasion on the label. A memento of the end of another bit of my life.

Linda's absence on the answering machine signalled the

closing of yet another piece.

This wasn't the moment for the Maglieri. That called for something to celebrate. The start of something new, perhaps. Now I was at the fag-end of something old. At the back of a cupboard, I found a bottle of Penfolds 128. About right. I put on a Charlie Parker CD.

Home. It means something when you have to do economy class time in planes, sit for hours in small hired cars, sleep in cardboard-walled hotel rooms sprayed with chemicals to mask the smell of other chemicals.

I cleared an armchair and sat down to eat in front of the fire, just in time to watch a weather report. It was delivered by a person who wanted to be a witty weatherperson, not a wise ambition for someone without wit. Still, he clearly relished what he did: waved a pointer vaguely while reading off placenames and temperatures from an electronic prompter. An idiot could do it and an idiot was doing it, a rare example of intellectual capacity and occupation dovetailing.

I fully intended to ring my sister but she beat me to it.

'Jack,' she said. 'I'm in contact with the living Jack Irish? This is he? Him? Don't tell me. I'm going to faint.' She paused. 'Don't flesh and blood mean anything to you?'

'A piece of prime sirloin, well hung, it has meaning to me, yes.'

'Well hung,' she said. 'Well hung's just a memory. I'm lucky to meet badly hung. Hung at all is a blessing.'

'The incredible shrinking men. You may be inside some kind of zone of contracting genitals. A beam from space. The aliens are clearing a landing ground in Toorak. First they shrink the dicks of the rich, then…'

'They send in the alien shocktroops, humanoids hung like

Danehill, to be ecstatically welcomed by the rich women. Speaking of rich women, how's Linda?'

It wasn't a question I wanted to be asked. I slid down the sofa, put my right foot out and moved a log closer to the core of the fire. 'That's not a question I wanted to be asked,' I said.

'You've answered it anyway. A friend of mine saw her with Rod Pringle at a television thing.'

Rod Pringle was the hottest thing in commercial television current affairs.

'Just business,' I said.

'He kissed her ear.'

'They're like that in television. Kiss your ear, kiss your arse, kiss any part of you. Means nothing. Like size.' I drank some red wine. It seemed to have gone sour.

'Jack? You there?'

'Yes.'

'Sorry. I shouldn't have told you that.' A pause. 'Here's a number I've been looking for. Madame Corniche.'

'Please God,' I said, 'not seances. Recovered memories before seances.'

'Cranial massage. Did you know the plates in your skull can be moved?'

'Rosa,' I said, 'if the Good Lord wanted us to pay people to move our skull plates, he wouldn't have given us the front bar of the Royal in Footscray. You want to eat one day? Lunch?'

'You're inviting me to eat? Soon you could be introducing me to your friends. Male friends.'

'I don't know any men I'd like to be related to by intercourse,' I replied.

'Don't worry about it. I'd rather be introduced to men by

27

a warder at Pentridge. Or wherever they put the crims now. Lingalonga Social Adjustment Facility Pty Ltd.'

'They'll be the same people I know,' I said. 'Former clients.'

'Funny thing with lawyers,' Rosa said. 'The respectable ones I know don't have *former* clients. They have clients. It's only the ones like you who have former clients. Former because someone shot them dead or because you couldn't keep them out of jail.'

'Respectable?' I said. 'I didn't know you knew respectable lawyers. Name one.'

'I can name one. One of many. I was at the races with one two weeks ago, in fact.'

'Laurie Phelan. I saw you at Flemington with Laurie Phelan.'

'Exactly. A commercial lawyer. Why didn't you show yourself?'

'Trying to avoid guilt by association. Know what they call Laurie? They call him Mr Omo. Why is that?'

'I don't know. I don't want to know.'

'Because he washes whiter than white. He launders money for drug dealers.'

There was a long silence.

'Well,' Rosa said, 'he's got nice hands.'

'Must be using a kind soap powder. Donelli's in Smith Street, Collingwood. Sunday, twelve-thirty. In the courtyard.'

'Courtyard? A courtyard in Collingwood? I don't think you've got a full grasp of the courtyard concept. They don't have courtyards in Collingwood. Courtyards don't have Hills hoists in the middle. With big old underpants and bloomers and bras like jockstraps for elephants hanging on them.'

'Don't bring Laurie Phelan.'

'You bastard.'

I caught the last ten minutes of 'On This Day'. Rod Pringle's dense and shining hair kept sliding over his quizzical right eyebrow as he tried to get the Premier of New South Wales to concede that you could buy planning permission in Sydney's western suburbs.

The Premier was confident, serious and convincing. Then an overhead camera zoomed in on his sweating scalp, showing the transplanted hair plugs, like an enhanced CIA satellite picture of a failing crop in Afghanistan. After that, he didn't seem quite so convincing.

After a commercial, Linda came on, fetching in dark blue, standing in front of a flashy Sydney building. She pointed over her shoulder.

This building, called Cumulus, is Sydney's newest and most dramatic. It belongs to a private company owned by one of the most private millionaires in Australia, Steven Levesque. We hear little about him from year to year. Yesterday, he came into the spotlight as the buyer of a forty per cent shareholding in Sanctum Corporation, the country's fastest-growing property development company. But Mr Levesque is more than a businessman. He is also said to speak directly into ears at the highest levels of politics.

The camera cut to a vast minimalist office, dwelt for a moment upon a large Storrier canvas, then went to a man sitting behind a glowing slab of 300-year-old jarrah, a handsome man in his forties, perfect navy suit, blue shirt, red tie, lean and tanned face, squared-off chin.

Linda opened with a fast inswinger.

Mr Levesque, people say that you have far too much influence over both the Prime Minister and the Premier of Victoria. Why is that?

Levesque smiled, put his head to one side in a puzzled way. His straight fair hair was naughtily unwilling to stay in place and he disciplined it with long fingers.

Why is what?

Why is this impression current?

Is it? I can't imagine why. The Prime Minister probably wouldn't recognise me, the Premier of Victoria I've known for a long time but I don't see much of. It's usually on public occasions. We commiserate about golf for a minute or so. Also, he once asked me about a horse I had an interest in.

Whether it would win?

No. He liked its name. Momus. He wanted to know what it meant.

The camera went to Linda.

And could you tell him?

Levesque: *Could you have?*

Linda: *Odd to name a horse for the god of ridicule, isn't it?*

Tough point won. She smiled, showing her nice teeth. My lips knew those nice butted-up teeth. You could see why she was a big hit, why the *Sydney Morning Herald* TV guide called her the best interviewer on television, why the *Sun-Herald* said she was a thirty-something spunk who paralysed the channel-surfing finger. Belatedly, Linda was having the career success she deserved.

I understood that the only place she could have that success was in Sydney. Melbourne hated success. It didn't match the weather. Melbourne's weather suited introspective mediocrity and suicidal failure. The only acceptable success had to involve pain, sacrifice and humility. Sydney liked the idea of success, achieved at no cost and accompanied by arrogance.

In this room, I had said those things. And I'd said, 'For Christ's sake, take the job. It's only a couple of hours away. If you don't, you'll spend the rest of your life thinking: What if…?'

Steven Levesque was saying: *I'm an ordinary member of the party and from time to time, people in the party ask my opinion on something and I give it. I imagine they seek opinions from dozens of people. And so they should.*

Last July, the Premier of Victoria took a ten-day holiday in the Caribbean. He stayed at a property on Guadeloupe called the Domaine de Thierry. My information is that you own the property, Linda countered.

Steven Levesque laughed, a real-sounding laugh.

I don't. A company I'm involved with does. It owns three properties in the Caribbean. They're for hire. Anyone can stay there. You can stay there, Ms Hillier. My understanding is that the Premier was the guest of someone who hired the Domaine.

May we know who?

Another laugh. *Even if I knew, Ms Hillier, and I don't, I certainly wouldn't tell you or anyone else.*

I drained my glass. Now I could spend the rest of my life thinking: What if I hadn't encouraged Linda Hillier to take the offer from Channel 6 in Sydney? Would it have been happiness ever after? What kind of idiot encourages a woman he loves to move away in pursuit of media stardom?

It doesn't pay to ponder a question like that. I switched the TV off and went to my cold and lonely bed.

The bed warmed up after a while, the soul stayed cold. Deep in the night, I saw images of people loved. I saw their smiles, heard the sound of voices now stilled, heard our uncontrollable laughter, and felt the touches, the kisses, the hugs, the hand run lovingly over my hair. All gone. Utterly, irretrievably gone.

I awoke before dawn, unrested, got up, made tea, went back to bed and read the last chapter of an English novel in which people were, generally, pretty despondent about the way their lives had turned out. Looking around, noting the terminally unhealthy colour of the sheets that draped me, the soiled socks dotted around the room like the droppings of an exotic animal, the white shirt sleeve hanging from the laundry basket like an inadequate surrender flag, I could sympathise with that view.

I got up, showered, thought about how to pass the day. The days. While I was thinking, they passed. Saturday, shopping, cleaning. Sunday, lunch with my sister.

One sister is a difficult thing. Two would be easy. Three, you'd start confusing their names. Four, you'd be the team mascot. But one sister is your mother, writ smaller and without the uncontested authority, but nevertheless equipped with the means to make you feel guilty.

My sister has a special look. It says many things: you aren't making the most of yourself, you're letting us down, that tie doesn't go with that shirt. The only way to counter the look is through a combination of evasion and attack.

Sunday night, I cooked for the freezer, the first time in a month or more. Beef and bacon in red wine and consommé, chicken pies with olives, onion and sherry.

Early Monday morning, startled awake by something in an unrecoverable dream, I got up. Uneasy, vaguely sick at the stomach, I scoured myself and drove to Taub's in the dark, nothing on the streets but a cab full of drunks.

As always, some peace descended upon me as I stood inside the door of the workshop and looked around. It was the feeling I'd experienced years before when, feeling my way out of the black tunnel of despair and binge drinking I entered after my wife's death, I'd come upon Charlie's business.

Timber, most of it from a time carefree of any concern for the future and unobtainable now, more timber than Charlie could use if he had another lifetime, was stickered side-on against the walls. The most precious was in the rafters under the huge skylight. Charlie called the timber up there The Bank. The workshop had three workbenches, unlike any other benches, built by Charlie: 120-year-old redgum, Emmert 18-inch vices at each end, dog holes lined in 12 mm brass, dogs of *lignum vitae*. Behind them, the planes on their sides in their pigeonholes: thumb planes, block planes, bench planes of every size, planes for curves, planes for angles, moulding planes, multi-planes. Hanging up were the spoke-shaves and drawknives. Next to them, the saws stood upright in their slots beneath two cabinets of chisels and carving tools and a cabinet of measuring and marking tools.

Against the righthand wall were the clamp racks: at the bottom, the monster sash clamps; above them, the lesser sizes; in the next rack, the bar clamps, the infantry of joinery, dozens of them in every size; then the frame clamps, the spring clamps, the G-clamps, the ancient wooden screw clamps that Charlie loved best, and flexible wooden go-bars arranged by length. Finally, an assortment of weird clamps, many of them invented by Charlie to solve particular clamping problems.

At the back of the shop were the machines: a Swiss sliding table saw, an old German table saw, a 24-inch thickness planer, a long-bed jointer, a 28-inch-throat bandsaw, a drill press, and a fifty-year-old English lathe. All Charlie's machines were cast-iron, solid, true, no rock, no play, tinkered with, tuned, kept clean as museum exhibits.

I packed the stove with paper and shavings and little offcuts and a kitchen match set it humming. By 8 a.m., I'd glued up the four small tables made of thirty-year-old American cherry, clamping them with a version of a framing clamp devised by Charlie to ensure squareness. The tables were made to Charlie's design, utterly simple, their elegance lying in the wood, the taper of the long slim legs, and the thin line of black persimmon inlay below the tabletops.

I made tea. Then, without any confidence, I started planing the tabletop edges with the wooden moulding plane Charlie had chosen from his vast collection. Most workshops used routers for this work. Charlie had an irrational hatred of routers. 'Router,' he said once. 'Rubbish. Spinning rubbish. And what can it do a plane can't do?'

'Whatever it does,' I'd said, 'it does it quickly.'

'Mr Hurry,' Charlie had replied. 'Mr Little Phone In My Pocket. You use a machine because the hand way is too hard. Or too slow. Or the machine does it better.'

I'd finished the edges, proud of myself, and was scraping

the last tabletop with a freshly burnished scraper when Charlie arrived. He ran a hand over the perfect surfaces of the other three. 'That's a start,' he said. 'You give up the sleep too now? Don't eat, don't sleep. Next you give up the other thing too maybe.'

He went over to study the tables, giant hands reaching out to test the clamps.

'You don't give up the other thing, it gives you up,' I said. 'Who are these tables for anyway?'

'Politician, some politician.'

'What's the name?'

'I forget. David, some David.'

'David Fitzgerald?'

'Fitz, that's right.'

'He's the Deputy Premier.'

'So?'

'Doesn't the Deputy Premier expect the master himself to make the furniture?'

Pure scorn in the look. 'Buy a Chippendale, you think Mr Chippendale made it with his own hands? Artist's studio this? You notice not? Customer wants four little tables the same, asks nicely, lets me do it my way, he gets them. Now that I think, you tell Rembrandt, that "Night Watch", I'll take four of them, you got them too probably.'

'Seeing myself as being like one of Mr Chippendale's or Mr Rembrandt's helpers, that cheers me up,' I said. 'Do you think they got paid award wages?'

'Only if employed by the business,' said Charlie. 'People walk in off the street, waste Mr Chippendale's time, won't go away like a cat, cost Mr Chippendale money, come and go as they please, those they don't get any award wages. Those they should be grateful for anything they get. Air to breathe.'

'I can see the force of that view,' I said, making a final delicate pass with the scraper. 'I think this one's done.'

'Think?' Charlie said. 'You have to know.'

He took the scraper out of my hand and went over to where the burnisher was lying on a workbench.

'I'm off for breakfast,' I said. 'Then I'll finish up. Cam's picking me up at ten.'

Charlie didn't look at me. 'Gambling,' he said. 'I blame myself.'

'You can do that,' I said, 'or I can blame you.'

'Winter's comin,' said Harry Strang. 'Need a bit of fat to see you over the winter. Fat's bin scarce.'

We were in Harry's study, Harry behind the desk designed and made by Charlie Taub, a piece of furniture that elevated the joining of wood to a breathless height. Behind me, the mahogany bookshelves rose five metres, the walkway for the upper shelves reached by four sliding teak and brass ladders. Behind Harry, I could look through French windows across a brick terrace to a deep garden. A stand of four mature maples was scarlet against a high, dark hedge.

Lyn, the robustly sexy Mrs Strang, came in, escorted by Mrs Aldridge, Harry's housekeeper through thirty years and three marriages. Cameron Delray, Harry's lean and taciturn offsider, and I followed Harry's example and stood up. Lyn had the silver teapot and the bone-china tea-set. Mrs Aldridge had the accompaniments: small, perfect chocolate eclairs, warm shortbread the colour of melted butter.

'One of each for you, Mr Strang,' Mrs Aldridge said. 'And no more than one.'

Lyn made a fist, a fair-sized fist, and touched Harry's cheek with the knuckles. 'Listen to the lady,' she said.

When they had gone, Harry poured tea. He took four eclairs and three shortbreads. 'They mean well,' he said. 'Used to dream about stuff like this when I was ridin.'

I took milk. Harry took lemon. Cam added hot water. We ate and sipped in silence. Then Harry said, 'Now. Business.

Jack, had a talk yesterday. Fellow called McCurdie. Grows somethin or other, dabbles in the cattle out Echuca way. Come via Tony Ericson.'

He bit off half an eclair, looked at the plump layered remains, put them in his mouth. His eyes closed. 'Hmm, lovely. Why does the Lord put bad in with the good? Anyway, this McCurdie. Bit slow but then a lotta the Woops only got one gear forward. Cam's run the ruler over him. Cam?'

Cam was looking out of the french window. 'Well,' he said, 'before this year he had nothing for years and he wasn't ever Bart Cummings. But the strike rate's not bad. Five years ago, run three horses, sixteen starts for three, two, three. Year before, bit better. Four horses, nineteen starts, four, three, four. Much the same the year before.' He drank some black tea. 'A Bob Jane.'

'A what?' Bob Jane was the name of a chain of tyre dealers. Racing always held another mystery.

'Retreads old tyres. Won a race in Albury in '91, nineteen hundred metres, horse called Live Marine.'

'Like that name,' said Harry. He was a connoisseur of horse names, knew thousands, approved of few.

'Nice name,' said Cam. 'Nice age, too. Fourteen. Retired at nine this Marine. Won six out of seventy-five, placed fourteen. Never closer than eighth in the last twelve. Pensioned off, never heard of for five years, presumed dead or carryin kids in some paddock. Come 1991 and aged fourteen, it was like Fred Stolle coming back to win Wimbledon.'

I said, 'I see. Bob Jane.'

'This year McCurdie's got two new little payslips, both won at nineteen hundred.'

'Had other comeback nags before Live Marine,' Harry

said. 'But then the luck run out. Now McCurdie's feelin a twitch in the underwear again.'

I drank some tea. Mrs Aldridge's tea both soothed the stomach and cheered and stimulated the brain cells. What did Mrs Aldridge know about the chemistry of immersing small leaves in boiling water that was unknown to all other tea-makers? Yet another mystery.

Harry held up a video cassette. 'Brought this to show me. Looks like a man with the DTs took it. Bring the cups over.'

On the way across the passage to Harry's elegant twelve-seater cinema, I admired his outfit of the day: Irish houndstooth tweed suit, soft white shirt, silk tie, Lobb's plain toecap shoes the colour of caramelised onion.

Cam pressed the buttons. We watched a three-horse race run on what looked like an abandoned racecourse. The camera operator suffered from both St Vitus's Dance and an uncontrollable urge to play with the zoom. In spite of this, it was clear that a large grey won by about five lengths.

'I see what they mean about country racing being in bad shape,' I said. 'Collapsed grandstand, field of three, crowd of one, jockeys riding in shorts.'

'That's the creature,' Harry said. 'Vision Splendid. Twelve years old. Give Jack the history, Cam.'

'Sir Rocco out of Clancy's Angel. Bred by H. and J. Morrisey, Angaston. Owned by two Adelaide lawyers, sold to Ken Gumble, trains at Mornington, as a three-year-old maiden. Gumble sold half share to a lawyers' syndicate. Lightly raced, forty-four starts, five wins, six seconds, eight thirds, total career winnings $164,500. Not placed in eighteen months, then given to a riding school in Bendigo. That's where McCurdie bought it two years ago. The school's run by a friend of his daughter's.'

'He's run this Vision, has he?' I asked.

'No,' Cam said.

'Man of patience,' Harry said. 'Admire that.'

'Could be patient,' said Cam. 'Could be slow.'

'The beaten nags there,' said Harry, pointing to the screen. 'That's McCurdie's two three-year-olds. Winners the both.'

'Winners in Quambatook and Moulamein,' said Cam, 'where two slabs of Vic Bitter buys off the whole field.'

'So he's looking for another Albury,' I said.

'Not this time,' Harry said. 'Albury he can do himself. No, he's lookin for the jeweller's shop, join those white-shoe boys up in Queensland. Problem is, he's got no capital.'

'Man of ambition,' said Cam. 'Admire that.'

Harry smiled. 'Cheeky. Thought we might go for a little sky-borne inspection. Put a pro on this antique horse. Too bloody far to drive. Jack, you in?'

'Try to keep me on the ground.'

'Good man. Well, let's get out to Kyneton and see what this Burnbank Boy can do for us.'

At the Flemington Road lights, Harry sat tapping his big fingertips on the wheel. 'Mystery's gone out of racin,' he said. 'Blame the cameras. See everythin. Used to be like war out there in the back straight. Life and death. Fellas do anythin. Anythin.'

Cam was reading the *Age*. Neither of us said anything.

Harry opened the ashtray that held the wine gums and chose one. 'Prime example that Wes Gales. Dangerous little bastard. Hard. Cut the teeth over the border, Mindarie, Halidon, places like that. Out to buggery.'

We were in the big navy BMW, tenth in line at an intersection that didn't allow more than seven or eight through at a time. The green arrow came on. Harry revved the machine. The first car was slow off the mark. It wasn't even going to be eight this time. The car ahead of us went through on red. Two lanes of traffic started coming at us.

'Bugger this,' said Harry. He put his foot down, took the BMW into a screaming right-hand turn. We passed across the face of death, alive by a metre or so.

'Sluggish,' Harry said. 'Tuned by these galahs just the other day. Charge like proctologists. Cheaper to keep a horse in trainin. Wes Gales. Wonder what happened to him? Saw him stick his whip up a fella's arse once. On the favourite, Mavourneen's Kiss, good name that, went around on her a few times. We're just at the school at Flemington, Wes pulls the arm back and rams it up him. Hole in one. The fella, Carter, he gives a big squeak, sits down, that's it, runs near last, poor sod. Stable wants his clangers on a plate.'

'Good old days,' said Cam. He didn't look up from the newspaper.

'Hard old days. Inside the door, Carter takes a swing at Wes. Big mistake. Wes slaps him a few, knocks him down, gives him a bit of grace with the slipper.'

'How'd the stewards like that?' I said.

'Not a word said to the stewards. Had to look after yourself back then. I said to Gales, he was lookin pleased, I said, "Wes, you wouldn't put the stick up my arse, would you?" He says, "Only do it to blokes don't enjoy it."'

'Cheeky,' said Cam.

Harry straddled lanes, preparing to take the vehicle between a semi-trailer and a truck carrying huge sheets of glass. 'My word,' he said. 'So I king-hit him. They got the doctor in, the boy's that slow to start answerin questions.

Know yer name, what day's it and suchlike.'

'That would've got the stewards' attention,' said Cam.

'No. Hoops' business. Monkeys fightin, that's the attitude then. Anyway, the little shit wasn't goin to dob. Told em he fell over gettin his boot off, hit his chin on the locker.'

It wasn't hard to think of Harry Strang king-hitting someone, even now. Not when you looked at the set of his shoulders, the big hands on the leather-covered steering wheel. What was hard to accept was that Harry's 20-year riding career had ended at Deauville in 1961 with him winning by three lengths on Lord Conover's Leneave Vale. A few yards beyond the post, the horse pitched forward, folding at the knees, stone dead. Harry went with him, crushing all the ribs on his left side and breaking his left arm in two places. He made a complete recovery, but he left Europe, came home, housekeeper with him, never rode again. It was as if the fall had given him extra time. He was almost unlined, clear eyes, vigour in the walk.

The drive became less nerve-racking when the traffic thinned after the airport turn-off.

'Put on that John Denver,' Harry said. 'Don't mind which.'

'Do I have to?' Cam said. 'Can we vote on it?'

'Yes and no,' said Harry. 'There's a good fella.'

'Rocky Mountain High' came at us from speakers everywhere: roof, seat backs, side panels, window ledges. It was like being embalmed in Rocky Mountain High jelly.

'Went up in one of them little planes, this bloke,' Harry said. 'Can't get a hang of why. Come down like a duck full of shot. Tragedy.'

'There's a silver lining,' said Cam. 'He won't be making any more recordings.'

Harry shook his head. 'No ear, some people.'

In self-defence, I fell asleep soon after the Melton turn-off, put my head against the cushioned door pillar for a moment, closed my eyes, gone. I came to with the car stopping in the Kyneton racecourse carpark.

'TAB gets it when they're heading for the gate,' said Harry. 'Tell the yokels to start dribblin it on at 12.40. Need to get five hundred on above twenty to be comfy.'

He took a fat yellow envelope out of his jacket pocket and handed it to Cam. Over his shoulder, he said to me, 'No personal bets today, Jack, see you don't suffer for it. The missus saw a bloke with a camera in a car down the street from the front gate.'

'What's that mean?'

Harry looked at Cam, shrugged. 'Who knows? Could be there's people think we're pissin on their barbies, want the faces.'

Burnbank Boy looked serene in the mounting yard and came out of gate three like a fire truck. Johnny Chernov got him on the rail, settled nicely, let two no-hopers go up and make the pace. No worries here, textbook stuff. But at the turn, he was suddenly in a crowd, five, six horses bunched. In the viewfinder of the Sakura Pro FS100, I thought I could see defeat on Johnny Chernov's lips. I was right. Boxed to the end, we ran sixth out of eleven.

We met back at the car. We always kept away from one another at the races.

'Funny old game, racin,' Harry said, taking off the old overcoat he wore to the races. 'Coulda sworn we had that one down.'

'Talking about pissing on barbies,' Cam said, looking at Harry. 'You happy with this hoop?'

I had no idea what he meant.

'Pendin,' Harry said. 'Pendin investigation. You drive.'

We drove home in silence. No John Denver. No turf stories.

Gary Connors' apartment was off Toorak Road. There was a look about it that said it had once been an inoffensive three-storey block of units, probably built in the early '50s. Now it was mad-Umbrian-fortress-meets-germ-warfare-laboratory, probably the victim of shaven-headed architects in black T-shirts calling themselves PostUrbana or DeConstructa. It was painted the colour of rust and had narrow gun-embrasures with metal shutters for windows and a huge stainless-steel front door with a brass porthole above it.

'Funny lookin place,' said Des.

'A lot of funny people this side of the river,' I said. 'Rich and funny.'

'That'd be right for bloody Gary.'

We were looking through a narrow steel-barred gate set in a two-metre high roughcast wall. Beside it were six steel letterbox mouths. A parking area was visible to the left of the building. Only one bay was taken: by a white Audi.

'Gary's?' I asked.

Des shook his head. 'Green, Gary's.'

I tried the gate. It opened. We went down a concrete path bisecting a plain of raked gravel, small white stones.

Des stopped to poke the gravel with his walking stick. 'Bit of grass'd be nice,' he said. 'This stuff's for bloody cemeteries.'

'Moved on from grass around here.'

Beside the vault door were buzzers numbered one to six. They'd gone beyond names too, except for number one, which had Manager on a brass plate under it. Each buzzer had a speaker grille.

Des took a full key ring out of his raincoat pocket and looked through the keys. 'Number five,' he said. I pressed the buzzer. No sound, but a yellow light came on beside the buzzer. I looked at the door. We were on camera. I pressed again. Again. Again. We looked at each other. Des offered me the keys.

The deadlock was silk-smooth. The door opened silently to reveal a square hallway with grey slate on all six surfaces. There were doors on either side of the room and a lift door straight ahead, all stainless steel. We took the lift to the third floor. Stainless-steel-lined lift, silent.

'Bugger me, Bill,' said Des, wide-eyed. 'Like a bloody coolroom. Never seen anythin like it.'

On the way over, he'd lapsed into calling me Bill; there didn't seem to be much point in correcting him. In the long run, what's a generation? Besides, I rather liked it. No-one had ever called me by my father's name.

The lift door opened onto a small version of the entrance hall, doors on either side. Number five was to the left. The brass buzzer was high on the door and when I went to push it I looked up into a pinhole security camera.

We waited, tried again, waited.

'Let's get in there,' said Des.

Again, a smooth deadlock. The door opened silently to reveal a small empty entrance hall carpeted in dark grey. I looked for the alarm. It wasn't on. I clicked the light switch beside the door. A spotlight came on over a framed black-and-white photograph of a young female ballet dancer erotically slumped in exhaustion. It was a restful way to enter a dwelling.

To the left of the front door was a small security monitor. Two closed doors led off the room.

'Des, wait here.'

I opened the righthand door. It was a sitting room, carpeted in the same grey and with some good pieces of furniture: modern leather armchairs in the style of Jean-Michel Frank, small writing desk, probably French, elegant side tables. There were more dark-framed ballet photographs, a collection of treen objects on the mantelpiece, an antiqued gilt-framed mirror, table lamps everywhere. Everything about the room said 'decorator'.

The rest of the apartment said the same thing. Gary's bedroom was dark and masculine, the kitchen stark and surgical, the period-style bathroom missing only Winston Churchill smoking a cigar in the giant clawfooted tub. Panelled doors concealed a washing machine and dryer.

The place was clean, too, the feel of a serviced apartment. I came back into the sitting room. Des was standing in the doorway, nodding his head.

'Bloody posh,' he said. 'S'pose this is where me sixty grand went.'

'Des,' I said, 'I'm not mad about this kind of thing but as an anxious parent, would you like me to look around?'

'Look,' he said, no sign of parental concern visible.

Gary hadn't been home for a while. The use-by date on a four-pack of yoghurt in the fridge put the time at a minimum of three weeks. A brass bowl in the kitchen was full of change and half a dozen or so crumpled shopping sales dockets and credit card receipts.

I went around the cupboards. One of them, at eye-height, contained another security system monitor. I switched it on. It came to life instantly, very smart technology, split screen

47

showing the front doorstep downstairs, the empty entrance hall outside the apartment and the fire escape landing beyond the kitchen door. You could see the front door of the apartment across the hall. I switched off and opened more cupboards until I came to the liquor cache. The wine rack held three bottles of Coldstream Hills pinot noir, there was whisky, vodka and gin, and, in a small fridge, four bottles of Carlsberg.

Des followed me into the bedroom. The laundry basket held four dirty business shirts, two golf shirts, three pairs of casual trousers, underpants, all with Henry Buck's labels. The built-in cupboard housed an array of expensive, conservative clothes.

'Boy's got taste,' I said. 'Taste and money.'

'Know where he got the bloody money from,' Des said. 'Taste's the mystery.'

I had a look in the medicine cabinet in the bathroom. Much is revealed in medicine cabinets. Gary's told me only that he had indigestion and a sex life.

Next, the writing desk. Nothing. Just a pad and two pens. Where would his papers be? I looked in all the obvious places, then the less obvious. Nothing.

Des walked around after me, leaning on the aluminium stick. 'Anythin about the money?' he said.

'Nothing.'

There was a phone-fax-answering machine on the desk. I picked up the handset and pressed the redial button.

Nothing. The last number dialled on this phone had been erased.

The answering machine light was blinking. I pressed Play.

Six or seven calls. Not a single message.

'When you rang, did you leave messages?' I asked Des.

He shook his head.

I went back to the kitchen and pocketed the shopping dockets and credit card receipts. On the way out, I had a look in the flat box on the wall under the security monitor. It held a video recorder. Gary could tape his callers. If he got around to putting in a tape.

The front door closed silently behind us. In the lift, I said, 'I'd say he's been away a fair while.'

Des shook his head in disgust. 'Lyin low. Told ya.'

Inside the gate, I offered him the keys. 'You might want to check Gary's mailbox.'

'You do it,' he said. 'Me fingers can't do the fiddly things anymore.'

Box number five was empty.

Outside, Des said, 'Reckon you could run me home?'

'Easily. Anyone been asking about Gary?'

'Ask me about Gary? Might as well ask a bloody sheep where the dog's gone.'

Des lived in deepest Northcote, near the railway line. As we pulled in to the kerb, two young women, both in black, both with cropped bleached hair, comb number one, nose rings, both carrying plastic shopping bags, arrived at the gate next door. One was a full head taller than the other. Des gave them an enthusiastic wave. They waved back, smiling.

'Lovely girls,' he said. 'Strong too. Mow me lawn. Push-mower. Never asked em. The small one, what's her name, forget for the minute, one Satdee she knocks on the door, says she's mowin for exercise, mow anything, free mowin, what about me lawn? I was in that. Thinkin of payin some bloke to do it if I could find the extra. Lots of girls live around here.

Mostly girls, really. Bloody paradise for a young bloke.'

I had my doubts about that, but I didn't mention them.

'Got the phone on?'

'Course.'

'Give me the number. I'll ask around, give you a call.'

Des studied me. 'Dead spit of Bill,' he said with a shake of the head. 'Didn't play any footy, did ya?'

'Not much.'

'Got photos of the old days. Laurie Diggins used to take em. Mad bugger. That day too, day yer mum read us the bit. Hold on. Give ya somethin.'

He got out. I passed him the briefcase. Watched him lurch up the path, struggle to get the key into his front door. Open. No. More struggle. Wait.

I should have gone with him, helped him.

Open. He's in. He was gone no more than a minute, came out with a big black album in his hand. Paused at the gate, rested the album on it, leafed through. Found what he was looking for in seconds, put a finger in the place.

He came over to the car, leant down and looked at me. 'Never took anythin out of this book before,' he said. 'The wife kept it up. Gave her all me old photos, ones me mum took, and she kept it up. The Brownie. Box Brownie. Took good photos.'

I said, 'Des, don't take anything out of the book. I'll come around, you can show me the pictures.'

He pulled a photograph out of its corners, offered it to me.

'The day,' he said. 'That's the day.'

Back at the office, I sat at the tailor's table and studied the small sepia picture for a long time. My mother at nineteen or twenty was striking, a face of planes and hollows, a wryness in the way she tilted her square chin. Something of her was in Claire, my daughter: the sharp cast of face, the emphatic nose, the quizzical eyes.

Women. For men, all I had on the Irish side was my father and his father in old smoke-stained photographs on a pub wall. It was all I wanted. My mother's father, I first feared and then loathed. For the rest, women. My grandmother, my mother, my sister, my transient first wife, my daughter, my wife Isabel, missed every day.

Linda, loved, absent, presumably gone.

I shut down on women, turned my thoughts to the home of Gary Connors. There was no toilet bag in the bathroom. The second largest suitcase of a four-bag set, a three-day suitcase, was missing. Gone on a trip. But the alarm system was off. No tape in the security video recorder. And there wasn't a single personal paper in the place—no letters, bills, statements, nothing.

I had a bad feeling about Gary Connors.

I rang Cyril Wootton.

'Belvedere Investments,' said Mrs Davenport, Wootton's secretary. She was not of the customer-service generation trained to say: 'How may I help you?' Indeed, Mrs Davenport addressed callers in the manner in which a boarding school headmistress might speak to a teenage girl whose underwear drawer has been found to contain a choke-chain, a studded leather bra, two dozen condoms and a photograph of the chaplain, naked and handcuffed to a bicycle.

'Jack Irish,' I said. 'Cyril decent?'

'Mr Irish, this office has spent much of today engaged in an unsuccessful endeavour to contact you,' she said.

'The intelligent office,' I said. 'I've been reading about

that. Very edge of the technology. But, I ask you, Mrs Davenport, will there still be a place in commerce for the old-fashioned warmth radiated by such persons as your good self?'

'Putting you through,' she said. 'Mr Wootton, Mr Irish.'

'Listen,' Wootton said, 'I'm just off to meet the persons expected, sworn statements needed today. Persons wish to catch flight home early tomorrow. Your friend wants to present the other side with the two statements tomorrow afternoon.'

'My friend?'

'The client is now represented by Andrew Greer.'

Andrew was my former partner, a friend from law school.

'What happened to Cataneo?'

'Skiing accident, I gather.'

'Skiing? Where do you find snow this time of the year?'

Wootton coughed. 'Exactly.'

'Encouraging. Why doesn't Drew do the statements?'

'In Sydney until midday tomorrow.'

'Cyril,' I said, 'in this matter, I've swum in the blue-green algae, snorkelled the solid-matter ponds. Get someone else.'

He sighed, the sigh of a man who has just seen the get-out chance in the eighth miss the start by six lengths.

There was a silence. 'I have a professional responsibility to my client to act with the utmost expedience,' said Wootton eventually.

'Right,' I said. 'Professional responsibility to the client. Crass of me. Still rooting that hairdresser client whose hubby did a runner with the Tattslotto win? The man you suggested I needn't hurry to find? Or not find?'

Much longer silence. In the background, men were making playground noises.

'Jack.' He was on the verge of saying Please. I couldn't let that happen.

I sighed. 'When?'

'Flight's due in at 4.30. Say 5.45 tops. Mrs Davenport's staying on.'

'Gee, that's an inducement.' I paused. 'I've got something I want you to do for me.'

He paused. 'My dear fellow, you have only to ask.'

'My,' I said. 'By the way, your responsibility is to be expeditious. Expedience you wouldn't have any trouble with. Second nature.'

I was sitting in Wootton's chair with my feet on his leather-topped desk when the foursome arrived: Tony Ulasewicz, Wootton, the two hookers from the Gold Coast.

'My lawyer, Jack Irish,' Wootton said. 'Jack, meet Sylvia Marlowe and Carlette Foley.'

I stood up and shook hands. Sylvia looked achingly like the late Audrey Hepburn on mild steroids. Close to my height in short heels, clear, direct grey eyes, straight and shiny dark hair, almost no make-up, skin like eggshell. She was wearing a two-button pinstriped short-skirted suit, no blouse and her excessively long legs were bare. I took her to be the ex-ballet dancer. Carlette, on the other hand, looked like a pentathlete: short and wiry, cropped red hair, freckles, wide-legged stance, baggy black pants, tight sleeveless black top showing muscled arms. She radiated health and fitness; all she needed was a number written on her bicep in felt-tipped pen.

'Tony you know,' said Wootton. 'Tony flew down with the girls.'

'With the what?' said Sylvia, looking at Wootton. She was half a metre higher, stronger and much, much prettier.

Wootton smiled, ran the side of his index finger along the underside of his clipped moustache. In the silence, you could hear a small abrasive sound. 'Hah,' he said. 'Excuse the old-fashioned expression. Absolutely no disrespect intended. Absolutely. With Sylvia and Carlette, two—'

'I'm sure everyone understands, Cyril,' I cut in. 'I suggest you leave me with Ms Marlowe and ask Mrs Davenport to come in and record Ms Marlowe's sworn statement.'

'Audio and video,' said Wootton.

'Video?'

Wootton went to the desk, beckoned me over and pointed to two buttons on the second shelf of the bookcase behind his chair. 'When you're ready, press both. Camera's focused on the client's chair. Press both again when you're finished.'

'Video all right with you, Ms Marlowe?' I asked.

She looked doubtful. 'What's it for?'

'Just backup in case the police query your testimony,' said Wootton. 'We won't use it unless we have to. Easier than getting you down here again.'

'Why don't I just give a statement to the cops? Cut out all this.'

'Let's just say,' said Wootton, 'that we're not entirely confident that the officers of the law always have the interests of justice at heart. I'll send Mrs Davenport in.'

Mrs Davenport came in and gave Sylvia her disapproving headmistress look. How the patients must have loved her when she was the receptionist for a specialist in sexually-transmitted diseases.

Sylvia looked her up and down coolly. 'Well,' she said, 'now that matron's here, can we get on with it?'

Both women were smart and articulate and Sylvia took a pleasingly droll view of the world. We had a few laughs in the mere forty-five minutes it took to do the statements. Henceforth it was going to be hard to shake the case that Brendan O'Grady never left the company of Sylvia, Carlette and Tony between 9 p.m. and 8 a.m. on the night Frank Zakia was shot dead in Camberwell. Identity wasn't a problem.

'I think I can be said to know what Brendan O'Grady

looks like,' said Sylvia. 'If necessary, I can supply distinguishing marks and measurements.'

Mrs Davenport's eyebrows twitched.

'I don't think it'll come to that,' I said.

Mrs Davenport took fifteen minutes to produce the documents. She brought them in holding them upright by the edges as if to minimise contact with the paper.

I read the statements to each woman in turn, they read them and signed three copies. Mrs Davenport and I witnessed their signatures and she was out of the front door before the ink was dry.

'I'll be on my way, too,' I said. 'Pleasure to meet you. Have a good trip back.'

Sylvia looked me in the eye. 'What's to do in this dump at night?'

I wasn't tempted. Tempted is a mild state. There is something a step or two up from tempted.

'I'm sure Mr Wootton will see to it that you don't want for anything,' I said.

Wootton was quivering like a retriever waiting for the gunshot. 'Absolutely,' he said. 'Booked you into the Sofitel. Everything you want. I'll come around myself…'

She ignored him, maintaining her disquieting hold on my eyes. 'Can't you take care of that?' she said, wickedness in the tilt of the Hepburn head.

I did the professional smile. 'Love to but I have to take the children to their school concert.'

She smiled too. 'Lying. Still, hookers scare some men.'

'Scare them rigid.'

'I wish,' she said. She put out her right hand, suddenly businesslike. 'Enjoy the concert.'

We shook hands. Our palms made a shell. Then she did

a terrible thing: she scratched my palm with the nail of her longest finger. A gentle, sharp stroke of a scratch. An erotic frisson went through me, I fell through time, years dissolved, my legs felt unworthy of my weight.

My mother had a friend, much younger, Jane Beacham, a tall and slim woman, married to a stockbroker. I was sixteen. I have no idea how old she was. We were standing next to Jane's car, the BMW without door pillars, on the broad driveway of my grandfather's Brighton mansion. Late afternoon. I remember Jane's strong blonde hair, roots dark with sweat after tennis, the gleam that lay on her light-brown skin, that she didn't look at me, that she was looking at my mother, laughing, punching me gently on the upper arm with her left hand, holding my right hand playfully, her palm upward, not letting go.

Then she said, 'Oh God, the time. Off, off. Lucy, darling, lovely afternoon. Jack, you're my mixed partner for Portsea. Knock their socks off. People coming for dinner. Boring brokers. Nothing done, absolutely nothing. Neil will be livid.'

I remember the smell of juniper on her breath.

And I remember something else: her eyes locked with my mother's, she drew a fingernail down the inside of my hand, from the callused flesh at the base of the fingers to the centre of the palm.

And there, in that tender delta, her long nail scratched.

Wanton. Exquisite. Unbearable.

'Changing your mind?' Sylvia said, still holding my hand.

I broke the clasp. 'Another time perhaps,' I said unsteadily. 'Cyril, a word.'

He followed me onto the landing.

I gave him a card with Gary Connors' name on it. 'The favour,' I said. 'Just the most recent spending. Anything with his name on it. Might not be on his plastic. Might have paid cash.'

Wootton didn't look happy. He didn't like to use his expensive network of underpaid credit-card, airline and car-hire clerks when he wasn't making anything out of it. 'I'll ring you after 9 a.m.,' he said. 'Once.'

'Thank you. I leave the witnesses in your capable hands. In a very loose manner of speaking. Mind you don't put it on Bren's bill.'

Outside the bar door of the Prince, hand raised to push, I paused. Raised voices within. I hadn't heard the Fitzroy Youth Club so animated since the night it became clear that the Fitzroy Football Club was going to be given to Brisbane. Given with a bag of money.

I pushed, looked straight across the room into the publican's eyes. Stan was leaning against the service hatch between the bar and what would be called the kitchen if what came out of it could be called food. He gave me a resigned nod.

I sat down on the right flank of the club. No-one paid any attention to me. Norm O'Neill was saying, voice deep and dangerous, hands flat on the bar, heroic nose aimed at the dim, tobacco-dyed, fly-specked ceiling, 'I suppose, Eric, I suppose, it's off with the old and on with the new. Easy as that.'

'Well,' said Eric Tanner, looking a little shrunken, 'can't see the bloody fuss. Always bin me second team.'

'Second team?' Wilbur Ong said. 'Second team? Since when did a man have a second team? Can't recall you tellin us you had a second team. Bit of news. Bit of a shock. Takes a bit of gettin used to, that idea. Second team. Raises a question or two. How does a man get the proper spirit when his first team's playin his second in a final? Got an answer to that? Got an answer, have you?'

'Given the sides,' said Eric, 'that's a bit hyperthetical.'

'Oh it is, is it? Here's an example: 1913.'

'Hang on,' said Eric, 'that's before the first war.'

'Oh right. Thought it was hyperthetical. Depends on bloody when then, does it?'

Eric sighed, made a gesture of dismissal. 'Stuck in the past, you blokes. Can't bring the Roys back, everythin's moved on. Well, it's round five and I'm not sittin around here anymore lookin at your ugly mugs on a Satdee arvo.'

Norm O'Neill took a deep drink, wiped his lips, didn't look at Eric, said at a volume that bounced off the ceiling. 'Yes, well, off ya go. What's a lifetime anyway? Saint Kilda's waitin for you. Club's holdin its breath. Whole stand'll jump up, here's Eric Tanner, boys, welcome Eric, three cheers for Eric Tanner, hip bloody hip, bloody hooray.'

The whole bar had gone quiet. I looked around. Charlie was shaking his head, always a sign that something needed doing. I took a deep breath, cleared my throat. It felt like preparing for my first utterance in court, defending a burglar called Ernie Kyte, a nice man but invasive.

'Time someone raised the matter,' I said. It came out loud. 'Either we go with Brisbane or we go with someone else.'

In the silence, you could hear the screeching complaint of a tram braking on Smith Street, then a match scratched against a box. I was rehearsing back-down strategies when Wilbur Ong let out a long sigh that turned into a low whistle.

'Jack's right,' he said.

Another long silence, Norm stared straight ahead, tugged

at a hairy earlobe. I signalled to Stan for a round. He took his time over it. When the last glass was put down, Norm said, 'Well, bloody Brisbane it's not. Never. Nothin much against the Saints. Few things but not much. Don't mind that little Stanley Alves, gets a bit extra out of the lads. Shoulda won the Brownlow in '75 when they give it to that Footscray bloke.'

'Not averse to the Sainters,' Wilbur said. 'Put me mind to it, I could follow the team. Not the same but I could.'

'Jack?' said Norm. 'Recall your old man used to have a few crafty ales with that Bray bloke, now he was a useful player for the Saints.'

'Pick of the bunch, the Saints,' I said.

There was a moment of indecision, then Norm said, 'Give us the fixtures there, Stan. Let's have a squiz at the order in which we meet the mongrels.'

Stan went off to his office and came back with half a dozen fixture cards. 'Well, well,' he said. 'Saints. Well, well. This mean I can sell the photos?'

All eyes nailed him, slitty eyes, pitbull eyes.

'No? That's no, is it? It's no.'

'So,' said Eric, studying his card. 'It's the handbags from Geelong. That's full marks.'

In the office, the phone rang. Stan went in, came to the door, pointed at me.

With considerable trepidation, I entered the undusted, uncatalogued and unclassified museum to fifty years of pub mismanagement. Only a limited number of people called me here. I wanted it to be Linda and I didn't.

'Jack, it's me.'

Linda. No leap of the heart. Nothing good was coming of this. You always know.

'Listen,' she said, 'the weekend isn't going to happen, everything's in fucking freefall here. I have to be in Queensland tomorrow, this pollie Webb who's resigned, his wife could just possibly be persuaded to go on camera: "My reluctant threesomes with hubby and Brisbane hookers."'

She was speaking at twice her normal speed.

'Wow,' I said. 'Devote yourself to it. Stories like that, it's not an occupation, it's a calling.'

Silence. 'Jack. I don't have any choice about these things.'

'I understand. I'll just say goodbye then. We're pretty much falling freely around here too. Floor looming up.'

I put the receiver down, regretted it instantly, waited for her to call again, waited, waited, dialled the studio, gave the producer's extension. A polite woman answered. Everyone was gone for the day.

Home to the old stable, no prospects but frozen food and uneasy sleep. I sat in an armchair with a glass of leftover red and thought about Linda.

I dialled the silent number. The answering service said: 'Please leave a message. If you wish the number holder to be alerted by pager, please say that the message is urgent.'

I said, 'The message is: The chairs in my parlour seem empty and bare. Jack.'

'Urgent?'

'No.'

In bed, I tried reading a novel called *The Mountain from Afar* brought by Linda on her last visit. Very soon, I could tell a) that it was about men and their fathers, and b) that I was at long odds to finish it.

Men and their fathers.

Had Linda been trying to tell me something by leaving

this book? Was there something I should be aware of? Why was I spending time on Gary Connors? There was nothing at all in it for me. Did I identify Des with my father? Of course I did. His father had seen my father and mother meet, lust across the class barriers.

I didn't see Des as a father-substitute. I saw him as a decent old bloke who was going to be turfed out of his house because, against all the evidence of his experience and in a weak moment, he had trusted his son. Someone had to give him a hand.

Where to start? Wootton's inquiries might take me straight to Gary's door. It was strange how many people of reasonable intelligence kept using their credit cards while going to great lengths to conceal their whereabouts.

But Gary was an ex-cop. Ex-cops wouldn't be that stupid. Still, he was stupid enough to be *forced* to become an ex-cop.

There was hope.

Wootton didn't sound like a man who'd spent the night in a luxurious hotel engaged in a deeply satisfying *pas de deux* with the compelling Sylvia Marlowe and then breakfasted on eggs Romanoff. He sounded like a man who'd spent the night at home in the spare room and then breakfasted on burnt porridge.

'This favour,' he said. 'Person was travelling in Europe. Hotels, etcetera. Came back, paid for airport parking on April 2. Three local things on April 3. Ordinary. That's it.'

'Nothing since then?'

'I said, that's it. Can I be clearer? Is that an ambivalent expression? If that wasn't it, I would have carried on conveying my findings to you. Wouldn't I?'

'Of course, Cyril. Silly reflex question. By the way, look up the word ambiguous. You'll find it somewhere before expedient. And expeditious.'

I rang Des Connors. 'Des, Jack Irish. The day you gave Gary the cheque. When was that?'

'Get me chequebook. Hold on.'

Outside, a high-top truck was beeping as it backed up to the goods entrance of the former sweatshop across the street. I missed the women eating and smoking and laughing on the pavement in their breaks.

'There, Jack? Third of April, that's the day.'

'Right. Des, Gary been married, that sort of thing?'

'Two. He's had two. First one, Judy, she's a nice girl, he

was lucky there. Sends me a card on me birthday, Christmas, never misses.'

'Know where she lives?'

'Dunno. Know where she works. Little milkbar place in town. Down there behind the museum. Makes sandwiches. I used to pop in there before the bloody hips started actin up.'

'Called what? Know the name?'

'Her name. Judy's something.'

'She owns it?'

'Done all right for herself after she got shot of him. You thinkin of goin round there?'

'Might. Have a chat.'

'Won't do much good. Don't reckon she's put an eye on the bugger for years. Hadn't last time I saw her and that's a while. Give her me love anyhow.'

'What about the second one?'

'Wouldn't know her if she wore a number. Never saw her. Don't know her name. Didn't even know he'd done it again till it was over.'

'I'll be in touch.'

I looked up Judy's establishment in the telephone book, walked up to Brunswick Street and caught a tram into the city. As we lumbered into Victoria Parade, the sun came out and people turned their faces towards it like sunflowers.

I had coffee with the ageing beau monde at Pellegrini's, bought a book about duelling at Hill of Content. Duelling was not something I'd given much thought to but I liked the cover. Made me think of dealing with my sister: evasion and attack.

I was also immediately taken with Judy's Pantry. It was on the fringe of the business district, a short and narrow lunch bar strangely untouched by the rushing currents of food fashion. The people who bought lunch here didn't want grilled capsicum, didn't want goat cheese or sun-dried anything. They wanted things like battery chicken, extruded ham, slices of roast beef rich in chemicals, tangy tuna fresh from the can that day, chopped hard-boiled egg. And these things they wanted topped not with Sicilian caper salsa or harissa or Bhutanese sour cucumber relish but with a rip of tunnel-grown iceberg lettuce and two slices of cold-storage tomato recently ripened by the application of gas. And Judy's customers didn't care to have their fillings wrapped in focaccia, ciabatta, bruschetta or Peruvian machaya flatbread. They wanted it slapped on soft, milk-white bread, the bread of their childhood, bread with the texture of Kleenex.

No rush yet. A woman was leaving as I came in, another woman was being served at the counter. The four pine tables down the righthand wall were unoccupied. It was just after 10 a.m. and the bain-marie was loaded, a good sign in a lunchtime food business. Good for the business, not the customers.

Three people were at work behind the glass display counter. A woman in her sixties, long sorrowful Balkan face, was dismantling a greyish cooked chicken. A young man was assembling salad rolls, and a woman, late thirties, early forties, short bleached hair, attractive in a hard-bitten way, was serving the sole customer, putting a sandwich into a paper bag. 'Don't you get tired of eating the same sandwich every day?' she asked.

'Nah,' said the customer. 'Love it. Have it three times a day if I could.'

When he'd gone, I said, 'Is Judy around?'

The woman gave me the pained look that greets salesmen everywhere. 'I'm Judy.'

'Jack Irish. I'm a lawyer acting on behalf of Des Connors.'

The pained look went. 'How is he? He's all right?'

'He's fine. Bit creaky in the hips, otherwise fine. This is about Gary.'

Judy sighed, sagged her shoulders. 'Beats me how a lovely bloke like Des fathered a prick like Gary. What's he done?'

'Got a moment? Could we sit down?'

'Sure. Have a seat at the back table. Things don't get lively till eleven or so.' Peeling off her latex kitchen gloves, she said to the young man, 'Andy, see to customers, will you?'

Judy went into a back room, came out a moment later without her neck-high pink apron. She was wearing jeans and a white T-shirt and wearing them well. 'Nice to have an excuse to sit down,' she said. 'Tell me the sad tale.'

'Des lent Gary money.'

She closed her eyes for a second or two, shaking her head. 'Usually it's the mums won't give up hope,' she said. 'Dream is they'll wake up one day and their little bastard's turned into an angel. Not much money, I hope.'

'Much. Left to Des by his sister.'

'Well,' Judy said, 'that's money past tense.'

'Des asked me to have a word with Gary but he hasn't been at home for a while.'

'Home? Gary? Home? That's a joke. Last place you'd look for Gary. Try whorehouses. Topless bars. Table-dancing clubs. He'll be somewhere near women. Certain kinds of women.'

'Was he still a cop when you met him?'

She nodded. 'Used to come in here. Lots of cops from Russell Street used to come in. Boy, did I think he was a spunk. And the manners. Oh, the manners. The shy way.

The cap under the arm. Did he stand out from the rest of the animals? Like a cathedral choirboy in Pentridge. Mrs Kodja—that's her behind the counter, she owned this place then—she used to say, "That boy, that Gary, take twenty years away from me, I tie him to my bed with a rope." '

A couple came in. Judy heard the door, turned her head, waved at them, watched to see that they were being served, said without looking at me, 'What Mrs K didn't know was that Gary would have jumped at the chance to tie *her* to his bed with a rope. Never mind taking twenty years away. Add twenty, he'd be keen.'

'Did he leave the force while you were married?'

'I came home one day—we were living in Richmond, tiny flat—about six plainclothes cops searching the place. Gary's standing there, in the lounge, holding his cap, winks at me. Anyway, they go, Gary says it's nothing, some scumbag he's booked was out for revenge. Tells the cops Gary took stuff—TV, VCR, things like that—from his house.'

She sniffed. 'I actually believed that garbage. I also believed him, still can't get my head around this, I believed him, it was two days after, he comes around here, and he says, that look on his face, he says, "I've had enough, the force is totally corrupt, won't be a part of it, I've resigned." I thought he was a hero. Serpico. You ever see that film *Serpico*? About the honest cop?'

I nodded.

'The prick is Serpico in reverse.'

'You know that?'

'That's what the other cops say. After I kicked Gary out all these lovely cops from Russell Street pop around the flat, concerned for my welfare, you understand, not trying to get into my pants, just checking that everything's all right. Basically looking for an easy screw. According to these heroes Gary was consorting with some very bad people, should have been busted much earlier, that sort of thing.'

'Don't know the details?'

'Never asked. Didn't care.'

'How long was it from the time he left the force to when you broke up?'

'About a year: 1984.'

'And you didn't hear the stories till then. So you broke up for other reasons.'

She leaned back in her chair, put her chin up. 'You could say. Yes, other reasons. I'd put up with being bashed about. Don't know why. Reason two, he was rooting my little sister. How did I find out? She told me. Why did she do that? Reason three. She was really, really upset. She'd walked in on him rooting my mother.'

I nodded. The practice of the law teaches you that some things require no comment.

'What sort of work did he do after the force?'

'Worked for a transport company. Security. What else can ex-cops do? It's that or deal drugs, armed robbery.'

'Remember the name of the company?'

'TransQuik. They were much smaller then.'

Every time you turned a corner you seemed to be behind a TransQuik truck.

'Know how long that lasted?'

'Still there when I put his case out with the rubbish.'

'Well,' I said, 'that gives me a bit of a feeling for Gary.'

Judy smiled the smile of resignation. 'Wish I'd developed a bit of a feeling for the shit before I married him. As a matter of interest, where does he live now?'

'Toorak. Very smart apartment. Drives an Audi.'

'Jesus,' she said. 'And I'm still in Richmond with a clapped-out Corolla. Hope you find the bastard. Don't suppose there's any chance he could go to jail for this?'

'No. You wouldn't know anything about the second wife, would you?'

Two more customers came in. 'Would indeed. Got to get to work,' said Judy, getting up. 'Friend of mine goes to this hairdresser in Little Collins Street, UpperCut it's called, these two Poms run it, trained by Vidal Sassoon, all that crap. Well, one day the one Pom says Chrissy, his best girl, the bitch, is getting married. To the most divine man, he says. Gary Connors, that's his name. What's he look like? It's Gary.'

I said, 'Chrissy. When would that have been?'

She puffed her cheeks, exhaled. 'About '85. Around there. She's a Housing Commission girl, apparently, Chrissy. Broadmeadows. Not that that matters.'

'You've been a big help, Judy. Thanks.'

She touched my arm. 'Give my love to Des. Tell him to come in any day he feels like lunch. Cab's on me.'

'I'll tell him. Make his day.'

Outside, the sun was gone and a cold, insistent wind was running through the town. I walked to Collins Street, chin tucked in, thinking about Gary. If he could defraud his father, he probably made a habit of taking people's money. The other victims might be less passive than Des. Gary could well be on the run. That probably meant Des's money was history, but there would be no knowing until Gary was found. I didn't fancy my chances.

At the office, I found the shopping dockets I'd taken from

Gary's kitchen. The most recent one was from a bottle shop in Prahran. On April 3, Gary bought a case of beer and six bottles of wine and paid an employee called Rick $368.60.

Customers form relationships with their suppliers. Suppliers very much want to form relationships with customers who pay $368.60 for a slab of beer and six bottles of wine.

A place to start.

Gary Connors' source of liquor was near the Prahran Market and more wine merchant than grog shop. From behind the cash register, a slick young man smiled at me: white shirt, blue tie, long dark-green apron. I showed a card.

'Mr Connors. Got two Connors. One's really old.'

I said, 'He was in here on the third of April, bought six bottles of Petaluma chardonnay and a slab of Heineken.'

'Police?'

'No. I represent his father. Mr Connors junior seems to be missing.'

He took this seriously, frowned. 'Rick reckons a bloke was after Mr Connors that day.'

'Rick?'

'Works here. He's in the back.' He went to the back of the shop, opened a door and shouted the name, came back. A tall youth appeared in the doorway: teenage skin, cropped hair, wearing the green apron over a white T-shirt and jeans.

'Rick, Mr Connors, the one you deliver to in Toorak?'

'Yeah.'

'About the bloke following him.'

The youth took a few paces, stopped, sniffed, wiped his nose with a thumb. He had intelligence in his eyes. 'I was at Ronni's. On the corner. Saw Mr Connors get out of his car in the carpark.'

'Remember the car?'

'Yeah. Green Audi. Carried lots of stuff to it before. Anyway, he crossed the road, walked down this way and came in here. Then a bloke parks, blue Commodore, illegal park, on the lines, that's why I noticed. It's a joke around here—bout a million tickets a year in that spot. He jumps out, then he walks casual, like he's just window-shoppin, round the corner. And he stops across the road.'

Mick pointed to the other side of the street. 'See the bookshop there? He looks in the window, looks over his shoulder. Then he goes inside, I can see him lookin out the window. And he stays there till Mr Connors comes out of the shop with Sticks.'

'Sticks?'

'Other bloke works here. He carried the stuff to the car. When they get down by the corner, the bloke in the bookshop, he comes out and he's up the street, movin quick, not window-shoppin now. Not quick enough, the cop's just puttin the ticket under the wiper. He gets in, doesn't even take the ticket off. When Mr Connors comes out of the carpark, he hangs a U-turn and he's off after him.'

'What'd he look like?'

'Sort of medium. Like a businessman. Suit. Dark hair, not long. Little limp.'

'Limp?'

'Yeah. Not much. Like a sore knee, sort of.'

I found a ten-dollar note. 'Thanks, Rick. I'm being paid, so should you.'

He looked at the boss, took the note, nodded, left.

'Thanks for your help,' I said to the man behind the counter.

'Not a problem.'

'By the way, Mr Connors ever talk to any other customers? You get to know people at your bottle shop, don't you?'

'Sure do. Haven't seen Mr Connors' mate for a while either.'

'What mate's that?'

'Mr Jellicoe. Chat down the back there, where the fine wines are.'

'Regularly?'

'Every now and again, yeah. Two, three weeks. Mr Connors comes in when Mr Jellicoe isn't here. But if Mr Jellicoe comes in, you know Mr Connors will be here soon.'

'You wouldn't have an address for Mr Jellicoe, would you?'

Doubtful look. 'Not supposed to give you that. Shouldn't give out customers' addresses.'

'It's just to ask about Gary,' I said. 'We're very worried about him. His father would appreciate your help. No mention of how we got the address, of course. Absolutely confidential.'

'Well, if you don't mention us. He's on the mailing list, gets the newsletter.'

He went over to the computer, tapped a few keys, gave me an address in East St Kilda.

Mr Jellicoe lived in a narrow single-storey house, fifties infill, behind a high pale-yellow wall. I pressed the buzzer. No answer.

A newish Saab did a smart reverse park outside the house next door and a thin middle-aged woman in denim overalls got out, pulled a briefcase after her.

I buzzed again, longer. Waited, tried the solid wooden gate. Locked. No luck here.

'No-one living there,' the Saab woman said sternly. She

73

was standing at the next-door gate, key in hand.

I smiled at her. No response. Inner-city suspicion.

'I'm looking for a Mr Jellicoe,' I said. 'He lived here until recently.'

'He's dead,' she said. 'Someone bashed and strangled him. Police say he must have surprised a burglar.'

'Wow,' I said. 'Dead for a VCR. When?'

She softened a little, pulled a face. 'Early April. Third or the fourth,' she said. 'We've been done over twice in a year. I came in and found the one. Pathetic creature, really. Hanging out for a hit. It's totally out of hand.'

'Makes you want to move to the country,' I said. 'Country of Lapland. I don't even know what Mr Jellicoe did for a living.'

'Something to do with travel,' she said. 'In the city.'

I drove back to Fitzroy. All the way, at the lights, men in cars and utes and panel vans picked their noses, admired the findings. The greasy-grey day, in its terminal stage, had a ruddy tinge, whole western sky the colour of a feverish child's cheek.

Sitting in the clotted traffic provided lots of time to think about Gary. Gary and his sophisticated switched-off security system, Gary being followed by a man, Gary vanishing, the man Gary regularly met at his liquor store being murdered.

Stuck at a light, I rang Wootton. 'That earlier inquiry,' I said, 'I need more.'

'On a fee-for-service basis, I presume.'

'At the discount rate extended to people who have performed services far, far beyond the call of duty. Yes.'

Wootton sniffed. 'What exactly do you need?'

'The party's source of income.'

Wootton laughed, a flat, false laugh. 'That's quite impossible, I'm afraid. Not a service on offer.'

'Just a thought,' I said. 'Having a drink after?'

'Very likely.'

I parked at the stable and took a tram into the city, only half a dozen people on board. Going the other way, the trams were crammed with the tired and oppressed on their way home.

I got off at the first stop in Collins Street and walked back up the slope to Spring Street. The street had its winter evening feel: light the colour of a ripe peach falling across the pavement from the windows of expensive shops, falling on hurrying people, people in dark clothes, overcoats, scarves, a dark red the colour of drying blood the colour for women's lips this year, background noise of hooting, of clanking trams, and, in the air, the pungent, urgent smell of exhaust fumes. Near the corner, a tall woman, dark-haired, long and intelligent face, severe grey suit, bumped into me, just a touch, a meeting of bodies. But she was wearing Linda's perfume. It overwhelmed me, caught in my nose, my throat, my heart.

Around the corner, in Spring Street, people were disappearing from sight into the underground as if being sucked into quicksand. I looked across at the State Parliament. On the steps, a television crew with lights was filming a fair-haired woman interviewing a man in a dark suit.

Wootton was on his window seat in the Windsor Hotel's street bar, whisky glass on counter, newspaper in hand. At the long bar, the youngish, smartish patrons, not a pierced protuberance or a shaven head to be seen, were braying and whinnying at one another.

I bought a beer and joined him. 'Cheers,' I said.

75

Wootton looked up from the newspaper, took off his horn-rimmed glasses, folded them, put them behind the triangle of red handkerchief in the top pocket of his dark-grey pinstriped suit.

'In the courts this afternoon,' he said.

'Sorry to hear that. Bail obviously wasn't a problem.'

He ignored my flippancy.

'The Crown dropped all charges against Brendan. Free man. As we speak, a free man motoring to his place in the country near Maryborough. There is a just God.'

'A just God,' I said, 'would ensure that as we speak Brendan O'Grady was being crushed by a fully loaded car transporter. As for his country place, it used to belong to a bloke called Cicchini. Bren had him knocked so that he could harvest about four tonnes of weed the guy had ready for market. Plus he wanted to comfort the wife. And the daughter. Possibly the dog.'

I drank some beer.

Wootton coughed. 'Sends you his best regards,' he said. 'Moving on. You're in luck. Tax Office audited that fellow of yours last year.'

'Why?'

'Travel claims, most likely. Probably just picked him up in a computer sweep. Big claims. World traveller.'

'On business?'

Wootton nodded. 'Allowed them, too. Makes a fair living, I can tell you.'

'Source?'

'Variety of sources. Printout's in the bag.' He pointed down at his brown buckle-up suburban bank manager's leather briefcase.

'Occupation?'

'Security consultant. A line of work I often wish I'd pursued. Studying the security needs of large corporations, designing security strategies, advising on equipment…'

'Selling information to the opposition, taking kickbacks. You'd be a natural.'

Wootton sighed, drank. 'Dear me, your discount on this information just shrank to nothing. And the surcharge for gratuitous offensiveness has just cut in. Are you buying the chips? Salt and vinegar, please.'

I bought the chips, then transferred the printout in Wootton's briefcase to a white plastic shopping bag supplied by his formidable woman friend behind the bar. We had another drink and parted. Wootton strolled off to his parking garage. I rattled home on a tram—me, a blind man with a guide dog, four tired-looking Vietnamese women travelling together, and a large, florid drunk who talked and sang to his reflection in the window.

Plastic bag in hand, I hiked along the narrow streets to my stable.

No Linda on the answering machine. Only Andrew Greer, Brendan O'Grady's new lawyer. He didn't identify himself:

Nice little hand of statements there. Pair is good but threes? Other side folded, gave up the game. Bren wants to have your babies. I'm out getting drunk with whores tonight but give me a call tomorrow.

I put on water to boil for pasta, stuck frozen sauce in the microwave to defrost, lit a fire on the ashes of at least ten old fires.

The chairs in my parlour seem empty and bare.

That was a compelling message to leave. Guaranteed to strike a chord in Linda. E. A. Presley's silliest number. Never heard together.

I ate my meal without relish and settled down with the history of duelling. In the course of learning about how painful the consequences of giving offence once could be, I fell asleep, missing the appearance of the thirty-something spunk and the man who kissed her ear. Waking to a dry mouth and audible eyeballs, I made tea and watched an ABC documentary on Ulster. There was clearly something rubefacient in the water or the air of Ireland. More evidence for this came in the person of the presenter of the current affairs program that followed, a man of Irish descent possessing a distinctly russet hue. I went outside to fetch another log and when I got back the host was jousting with a bald man displaying the sad and silken demeanour of an undertaker.

I didn't care about current affairs. I switched off. I wanted to ring Linda, hear her laugh, hear her suggest that loving me and missing me were not out of the question. I wanted to go to sleep in the sound knowledge that impressions to the contrary were paranoid. But the sensible part of my intellect, now only marginally more than vestigial, said No.

I went to bed to confront *The Mountain from Afar*: Men and their fathers. Before I could approach the mountain, however, I had to make the bed, turn down, tuck and tauten the twisted sheets.

It seemed so pointless.

It was so pointless.

I was in Meaker's eating a sandwich of grilled ham with lettuce, tomato and gherkins and reading the *Sportsman* when the floor moved and I lost a lot of my light.

Kelvin McCoy, reformed smack freak, unreformed drunk, gifted poseur in the plastic arts, former client, lowered his bulk into the chair across the table. McCoy had taken over the lease on the sweatshop across the road from my office and was using it as a studio/residence. If people didn't believe he had any talent as an artist, they generally kept it to themselves: McCoy was built like a street-cleaning machine. He had a shaven head, stoved-in nose, small eyes the colour of candlewax, and he kept himself formidably dirty. About fifteen huge canvases a year came out of his studio under such titles as *Patriarchy's Dialectic* and *Rituals of Hegemony*. A man who taught something called cultural studies at Melbourne University provided the names. Inexplicably, rich people rushed to buy McCoy's dark and sinister messes of paint and hair and toenail clippings and unidentifiable but worrying substances. His gallery shark allowed him a small portion of the proceeds, which he made speed to redistribute.

'Good day,' I said. 'You'll find something to read in the basket next to the door. In your case, look at.'

'I see your customer's here,' McCoy said, putting a hand into his armpit to scratch. I'd as soon put my hand into a used-syringe bin.

'What?' I kept my eyes on the paper. You didn't want

to encourage McCoy at this time of day. At most times of the day.

'Miss Clean Living over there.' He flicked his eyes. 'Looking for you. Knocking on your door. Invited her over to look at my work but she wasn't keen.'

'That's showing aesthetic judgment,' I said. 'Which one?'

'Jesus, Irish, take a guess.'

I looked around. McCoy appeared to be suggesting that it would be unusual to call anyone in full bike leathers with three-tone hair and noserings Miss Clean Living. That left the woman in the left-hand corner reading the *Age*. She was in her thirties, dark hair pulled back to show her ears, lightly tanned, tweed sportscoat with a soft leather collar.

'That is probably a serious person in need of the services of a professional,' I said. 'You wouldn't know much about that, McCoy.'

McCoy smiled. It involved his lips moving sideways and three deep creases appearing in his cheek. 'Oh, I don't know,' he said. 'I remember being in need of the services of a professional. And all I got was the service.'

I took a sip of my coffee. 'That's wounding, Kelvin. You do know that whenever two or three lawyers get together, they still talk about the defence I mounted for you.'

'That so?' he said. 'When your old clients get together, in the exercise yard, they still talk about how *they* got mounted.'

I looked at the huge charlatan with respect. Nicotine, dope, hash, barbiturates, speed, acid, smack, Colombian marching powder, ecstasy, alcohol in every form, all had entered the massive frame by some route and in quantities guaranteed to lay waste to the collected brains of three Melbourne universities or eight in Queensland. In theory, a scan of this man's skull should reveal a place as grey and still as Kerguelen Island in winter. Yet from time to time there were clear signs of electrical activity.

'Client loyalty,' I said thoughtfully, studying a hand-written advertisement on the wall for a play called *The Penis Knife*. 'What do you have to do to earn it? Offer to fellate magistrates?'

'Fell eight, fell nine,' McCoy said. 'Whatever it bloody takes. Now here's something more my speed.'

He left me for the company of the large manager of the tapas bar up the street on her coffee break.

The woman in the corner had to pass my table to get to the cash register. 'Simone Bendsten?' I said.

She nodded, wary, bringing a square brown leather brief-case around to protect her pelvis.

'I'm Jack Irish. I gather I missed you at the office. Didn't realise you'd be this quick. I'll be back there in five minutes.'

I'd been in Meaker's earlier, in the cold, dark early day, black rain bouncing off the tarmac outside, sitting in the window reading the Tax Office's report on Gary Connors' income. Stale cornflakes at home and black coffee in the cafe, the place empty except for two young men, not together, both badly on the nod, scratching and snuffling.

In my office, I'd remembered the letter and business card, found them in the righthand drawer: Bendsten Research. At 8.30 a.m., I rang. A woman answered, a person with the calm and rested voice of someone who'd had extensive experience of good, demonless sleep. I told her what I wanted.

'Public companies obviously aren't a problem,' she said. 'Private ones can be difficult. How much detail do you want?' She had a faint accent, hard to place.

'What, where, owners if it's private, that sort of thing.'

'The report will be delivered,' she had said in a formal way.

We left Meaker's together.

'I'll see you there,' she said.

I watched her go. She had long legs for someone so small.

At the office, I'd just sat down when she knocked. There isn't a receptionist, a reception area. You open the door, look left and there I am, behind the table on which the tailor who had worked here for fifty years sat crosslegged to sew his seams.

She sat in the client's chair, briefcase on her lap.

'Any luck?' I said.

She shrugged, opened her briefcase, took out an A4 envelope and put it on the table. 'With two exceptions, as far as I can tell, these are all shells. Three of them share the same address in the Caymans. Following them up gets you nowhere. They're owned by companies who are owned by other companies, and so it goes on. Like Russian dolls, one fits inside the other.'

'The exceptions?'

'One's called Klostermann Gardier. A private bank in Luxembourg. The other's a company called Aviation SF registered in Dublin. I ran all the names through the local databases and only Aviation SF came up. Last year, an Australian company called Fincham Air won a coastal surveillance tender. It listed among its assets 80 per cent of Aviation SF. Fincham itself is partly owned by a company called CrossTrice Holdings. And one of CrossTrice's directors is a man called Lionel Carson.'

Reading my face, she paused. 'Know the name?'

I shook my head.

'Carson used to be a director of Consolidated Freight

Holdings. TransQuik Australia is their biggest company. He's not active in CFH anymore but CrossTrice owns about 25 per cent of it.'

TransQuik. Gary Connors' employer after his departure from the force. And, at a considerable remove, still one of his employers.

Simone looked around the bare office. 'That's it. It's all in the report. You could have done this yourself, you know. The information's all available.'

'No, I couldn't. What do I owe you?'

'The invoice is with the report. An hour's work. Seventy dollars.' Her eyes flicked around the place again. 'Well, say fifty-five.'

'Seventy's fine. Been doing this long?'

'Second month.'

'How's business?'

She looked at the ceiling, at me, quirky smile, shrug of the thin shoulders. 'They're not delivering the money in dump trucks.'

'Yet. Word will spread. Your accent…'

'We came out from Denmark when I was thirteen. Complicated by doing my postgraduate work in Boston.'

'It's nice.'

'Thank you. Well, if you need anything else…'

'I have no doubt that I will.'

I saw her to the door and admired her all the way to the corner. Then I got out the telephone book and found TransQuik's head office.

The pilot of the six-seater Cessna looked to be about sixteen. He was wearing lean purple dark glasses, a huge multi-coloured jumper of the kind teenagers once used to lose within a week of receiving from their grandmothers, and a peaked cap with *Crapdusters Australia* on the front. Facing backwards. In themselves, these things would have occasioned no more than deep unease. What induced the panic was that, waiting for take-off clearance, he appeared to be singing along to rap music in his headphones.

Harry was next to the pilot, looking at him with calm and scholarly interest. Cam and I were seated behind them. Behind us was a long-nosed, melancholy track rider from Caulfield called Mickey Moon. He'd been the leading apprentice in his last two years but he had fat genes.

Cam had his laptop open, studying bar graphs of horses' times. Today, for going to the country, he was dressed like a corporate lawyer: navy suit, white cotton shirt with spread collar, blue and white checkerboard silk tie. In the city, he seemed to favour tight washed-out moleskins, boots and fine-check shirts.

'Cam, shouldn't this, ah, pilot be listening to the control tower?' I said.

Cam looked at me, looked at the pilot's back, went back to the screen. 'Like jockeys,' he said. 'Out of the mountin yard, got your money on em, just pray they know what they're doin.'

Immensely reassured, I closed my eyes and fell to doing

breathing exercises recommended to me by a priest I'd defended on pornography charges.

'Tricky breeze,' said the pilot, his first utterance. 'Bloke flipped a little one here last week, identical conditions. Couldn't handle it. Dork.'

I didn't open my eyes until, after what seemed to me to be a prolonged and vibrating resistance to Wilbur and Orville's idea, the aircraft was on its side and much too close to the roofs of outer Melbourne's brick-veneer sprawl.

To my mind, the pilot was fighting for control of the aircraft.

'Got a CD player?' asked Harry.

'Absolutely,' said the pilot.

'Stick in this,' said Harry.

The pilot took a break from struggling to keep us airborne, let go of the controls and leaned across Harry to put the disc in a slot, punch buttons, adjust volume.

Willie Nelson, singing 'One for My Baby'.

'Hey,' said the pilot, making rhythmic shoulder movements. 'Saw Willie. Saw Waylon. Nashville. Might try that head thing Willie wears.'

'Bandanna,' said Cam without looking up. 'Could be a good fashion look for pilots. Stuff the cop cap. The bandanna. Rebels, outlaws. "Listen, sunshine, the Boein's not goin till I finish this fifth of Jim Beam."'

The frail barque lurched. Would Cam's words be the last thing on the black box?

'Bring anythin to eat?' asked Mickey Moon.

Cam found his briefcase and took out a family-size bag of barbecue chips, tossed it over his shoulder. 'Just tie it on like a feedbag, Mick,' he said.

Mickey ripped the packet open with his teeth, horse teeth.

We gained height, slowly, agonisingly slowly, and the alarming noises became less pronounced. In minutes, the city dissipated. Time went by, my shoulders lost some tension. Beneath us the landscape, seen through floating vapour, was green, dots of trees, Lego houses, small rocky hills, dams glinting, sheep, horses, some cattle. For a while, the Hume Highway was to our right, an unbroken chain of gleaming objects.

'Halfway between Echuca and Mitiamo,' said Cam. 'Draw a bead on Gunbower, you're right over the top of the place.'

The pilot found what looked like a Broadbent's touring map and opened it. 'Gunbower,' he said. 'Now, where is it? Know a bloke landed in a kind of swamp up that way.'

Cam closed the laptop, reached around and found a piece of paper in his suit jacket. 'He says easiest is hit Mitiamo, turn right, road's dead straight, then there's a little elbow left. Round that, then first left, you'll see the old track on your right. Put her down in front of the grandstand. Remains of the grandstand.'

'So this is how modern aviators find their way from place to place,' I said. 'A road map and directions written on a bit of paper.'

'Mate of mine got lost up there near Wanganella,' said the pilot. 'Lookin for this property, it's bloody hopeless. All flat as buggery. Lands on the road, motors in to this petrol station, one pump. Bloke comes out, doesn't blink. Yeah, he says, bugger to find. Come in, have a beer, draw you a map.'

'Be a bit iffy when it gets dark,' Cam said.

'Up there, yeah. Not around here,' said the pilot. 'Worst comes, start lookin for the bloody Hume. Lit up like a Christmas tree at night.'

A snore. Harry was asleep. I closed my eyes and thought about planing a long edge with one of Charlie's pre-war Hupfnagel 24-inch planes. Properly tuned and on a good day, you could take off a near-transparent ribbon the full length of any board. Planing with the right instrument, a rock-solid body holding a precisely aligned heavyweight blade honed like a samurai sword, is the sex of joinery. All the rest is mere companionship, satisfying but not ecstatic.

I woke up with the aircraft sharply tilted.

'Bit of rain here,' said the pilot. 'Had a sorry on a strip like this up in Queensland. Looked good, nice grass. Potholes like bomb thingies under the stuff. Can't see the bastards. Arse over kettle bout seven times. Well, three. Shakes you a bit. Rang the boss, he goes, "How's the kite?" I go, "Bad, comin home on a truck, boss." He goes, "Fine day for travellin, Donny." Didn't know that meant the arse. Liked that job.'

I closed my eyes again, resumed Father O'Halloran's breathing exercises. Take-off had been hard enough. Landing tested every fibre. And found each and every one wanting.

I opened my eyes when we stopped. We were on an old racetrack, derelict grandstand on our right, patched up old rail to the left, all around us flat stubble lands.

'Anythin else to eat?' asked Mickey Moon.

'Here to ride not eat,' said Harry. 'This McCurdie's ready for us. Healthy sign.'

We got out and walked over towards the derelict grandstand where a Toyota four-wheel-drive and a horse truck were parked. Three horses were out, saddled: a big grey being walked by a plump young woman in jeans, two smaller animals in the care of teenage boys.

A man in his forties, greying red hair, came over, hand

outstretched to Harry. They shook hands, an incongruous pair: small Harry, close-shaven, scrubbed, sleek hair, three-piece midweight Irish tweed suit, spotted tie, glowing handmade brogues; large McCurdie, toilet-paper patch on a shaving cut, finger-combed hair, grubby check shirt, stomach overflowing the belt that held up his filthy moleskins, scuffed, down-at-heel workboots.

'Thanks for comin, Mr Strang,' McCurdie said.

'My pleasure,' said Harry. 'Introduce these fellas. Jack Irish, my lawyer, does the things I can't do. Cameron Delray, does the things I won't do. Which is not much. Mick Moon, y'might remember him, rode a few.'

'Do indeed. Jack, Mick.' We shook hands.

McCurdie took us around the horse handlers. The young woman, big, open, freckled country face, was his daughter, Kate. The small and sinewy boys were his nephews, Geoff and Sandy.

Harry and Cam studied Vision Splendid, walking around him. He was a big creature, placid and with the wise look older horses get.

Harry gave him a nose rub. 'Well,' he said, 'best you can say, he's got surprise in his favour.'

'How'd you want to do it?' asked McCurdie.

'This track safe?' said Harry.

'Oh yeah. There's twenty-two hundred rolled and walked every inch. Don't risk me horses. Nor the boys. Grass's a bit long, that's all. There's a startin thing we welded up down there at the eighteen hundred. Ten stalls. Well, they're like stalls. Works pretty good.'

'Ten,' said Harry. 'What'd ya have in mind?'

McCurdie scratched his head. 'At the moment,' he said, 'I can't remember.'

'These three,' Harry said. 'Pretty forward.'

McCurdie nodded. 'Other two racin at Gunbower Thursdee week.'

'They friendly?'

'Oh yeah. The old bloke's the boss.'

Harry nodded. 'Boots on, Mick,' he said. To McCurdie, 'Send em around the eighteen. Put em in four, five and six, the grey in the middle. These boys ride a bit?'

'Ridin since they was little. Ride anythin. Fast work since eleven, twelve. Their dad was a jock, got too big. Tractor fell on him. Me sister's brought em up on her own. We give her a bit of help.'

Harry nodded. 'Mick'll hang around the back. Cam tells me the horse used to like it just off the pace, bit of a kick at the end. Then he lost it.'

'Got it back. He can kick.'

'Tell the young fellas to try to drop him off in the last four, five hundred.'

McCurdie went to give the boys their instructions.

Mickey came back, booted, helmeted, sad as Hamlet. Harry put a hand on his shoulder.

'Mick, few questions. This McCurdie reckons the old retired bugger can still street these youngsters. Now that's good out here in the nothin. Could mean fanny in town. Relyin on you to rate him for us, say in a pretty ordinary eighteen hundred in town? Get the drift?'

Mickey sighed assent.

'Settle in behind, stay out wide, don't care for this rail. See how he handles the pace. He's happy stayin with em, three, four hundred from home, see if he can show em his bum, shut the gate. He does that, it's over. Bugger the post. And don't flog him. He's got the heart or he hasn't.'

89

Mickey screwed up his eyes, looked as if he'd been asked to write a sonnet, a haiku, the preamble to a new constitution.

McCurdie hoisted the riders up, little flick, flick, flick and they went off like a small riding school group. Then he drove off in the Toyota to operate the gate.

'Okay to get on the truck?' Cam asked Kate.

'Oh. Sure. Yes.' She looked at him in a shy and electrified way that said all requests for permission would get serious consideration. At the very least.

Cam stepped onto the front bumper, walked up the horse truck, stood on the cab. From his inside suit pocket, he took binoculars, about the size of a compact disc, thick as a paperback. A thumb-button on the bottom activated a built-in electronic stopwatch with a digital display for the user.

'Stroll down a way,' said Harry.

We walked about a hundred metres and found an intact piece of fence to lean on. 'Largely a waste of time this,' Harry said. 'Not like a race. Nothin's like a race except a race. But you find out a bit about the animal. Mostly whether he wants to be the boss horse. Horse race's just a stampede, y'know, Jack. Some horses always want to be the leader. If they've got the power, jockey's job's the timin. Get em there when it counts. Some want to but there's not enough under the hood. Pick the right races, jockey can do a bit, place em, settle em, hope the others bugger it up. Then there's animals just don't want to. Give up. Happens with the best bred. Bugger all the jock can do. And some want to be boss when they're young and then they say, stuff it. Great horses, they never stop tryin, but the opposition keep gettin younger. This one give it away early.'

Harry lifted his binoculars, an ancient pair, fifteen

magnification, made by Steiner of Bayreuth. 'There they go,' he said.

When they reached the turn, about a thousand metres from us, Mickey Moon was following instructions to the letter, sitting well outside the second horse. The pace was good and the leader picked it up in the turn. In the straight, about six hundred out, the second horse went up to the leader and they came towards us stride for stride. Mickey moved Vision Splendid out a bit further, well away from the horse to his left.

At the four hundred, the second horse's rider went for it, got a head in front, half a length, drew clear.

'Time, Mick,' Harry said.

Mickey appeared to hear the instruction, touched Vision with the whip, not a hit, just a wake-up call.

The response was immediate.

The big grey lengthened stride, put its head down, flattened, had pulled back the nearest horse within twenty metres, hunted down the leader in another thirty. Kicked past it, one length, two lengths, three, four, five, six, full of running.

Mickey straightened up, looked back at the horses behind him, began to rein in Vision. At the post, he was still three lengths ahead.

'Game old bugger,' said Harry thoughtfully.

Cam came up behind us, leaned on the fence next to Harry. 'Not short of kick,' he said, expressionless.

'Today,' said Harry. 'Today.'

I ate at Donelli's in Smith Street, Collingwood, whenever possible because I could write on the bill: *To be deducted from legal costs owing to the undersigned.* Then I signed and wrote in capitals, *JOHN IRISH, BARRISTER & SOLICITOR.*

The great man himself, Patrick Donelly, an Italian trapped in the body, the corpulent body, of an Irishman, brought the menus. His eyes lit up when he saw my guest.

'Good evenin to you, Mr Greer,' he said. 'Twice in a week, Irish. That outrageous bill of yours will be meltin away like the snows of Friuli in the springtime.'

'Oh, the snow's still thick and crisp and even in this frosty corner of Friuli, Donelly. Spring is some time away. What's the special?'

'In your fortunate position, Irish, I'd be havin the risotto moulds with tomato and red pepper sauce, followed by the lamb shanks, simmerin away since the early afternoon.'

'So be it. Two glasses of the Albrissi, please. And a compatible red of your choosing, maestro.'

When Patrick had swept off, Andrew Greer eased his long body down in the chair, said, 'Offhand, how much older would you expect Tony Ulasewicz to get?'

'Actuarial tables may not be a good guide here.'

'No. What makes the prick think it's better to owe Brendan a hundred and sixty grand than the Armits?'

'Armits weren't planning to kill him. Not soon, anyway.'

'I can follow that reasoning. How's Linda?'

I didn't say anything.

'That bad?' The long face didn't convey any sympathy.

A small explosion of happy sounds. Donelly had come out of the kitchen to greet a mixed group of six. He said things in Irish-Italian and put his big pink hands on some of them. The anointed shivered with delight, touched his arms, huge starched white linen sausages.

'Rosa says Linda's been seen to be kissed on the ear by Rod Pringle,' I said.

The glasses of white arrived. Drew took a tentative sip, screwed up his eyes, nodded approvingly. 'Surprised Donelly doesn't try to poison you,' he said. 'The ear. That's bad. The mouth is better than the ear. Your aunt can kiss you on the mouth.'

'Also she hasn't been back in six weeks. Urgent weekend work.'

'You could go up.'

'Urgent out-of-town work.'

Drew had another sip, sighed. 'Well, if I was a sheila, I'd cover your hand with mine and pull that sympathetic face.'

'Fuck off.'

Drew looked thoughtful. 'Bren O'Grady owes you,' he said. 'Bet he doesn't even watch Rod Pringle. Wouldn't mind if there was no Rod Pringle. See my drift?'

I drank half my glass. 'This is marvellously helpful, Andrew. You could advertise this advice service in the *Law Institute Journal*.'

'Just trying to cheer you up. I remember how you picked me up when Helen fucked off. Two handicap and a twelve-inch dick, I think you said the bastard had. Certainly wasn't the other way round.'

'Sometimes it helps to put a number on things,' I said. 'Listen, discussion of personal inadequacies aside for the moment, I'm trying to help an old bloke who worked with my dad.'

I told him the story.

'Why doesn't Des report Gary missing?'

'At present, he's not missing, he's just not home. The old bloke doesn't see him from year to year. Gary may do this kind of thing all the time.'

The first course arrived, followed shortly by a tall wine waiter with a swimmer's build. She pulled the cork expertly, put it in a silver bowl for inspection, poured half a glass for judgment. I passed the vessel under my nose and nodded. She filled us up. We ate.

'You wouldn't swap sex for this risotto,' Drew said, 'although it would be a close-run thing.' He wiped his mouth with a starched napkin. 'But you don't think Gary's popped down the corner for smokes.'

'No. Too many funny signs.' I listed them.

Drew took a mouthful, savoured it, studied the ceiling. 'For a lawyer,' he said, 'you've acquired some unusual powers of observation.'

'There's more.' I told him about Gary being followed by a man, Gary meeting Jellicoe, Jellicoe's murder.

'Jesus Christ,' he said. 'How do you manage to get involved in this kind of shit? What does Gary do for a quid? Apart from borrowing it?'

'According to his tax return, he's a security consultant.'

'His tax return. You've seen his tax return?'

'Yes.'

'At the flat?'

'No.'

He closed his eyes. 'Forget the question.'

'I've had someone look at his clients. Private companies

overseas, about a dozen of them. Companies owned by other companies. Registered in one place, owners registered somewhere else—Cook Islands, Cayman Islands, Luxembourg, British Virgin Islands. Andorra.'

I took out the two-page report from Simone Bendsten and passed it over. The waiter took our plates away.

'Nice names,' Drew said. 'Klostermann Gardier, Viscacha Ltd, Scazon, Proconsul No 1. Some kind of tax dodge?'

'Not by Gary. Declared an income of $345,000, paid tax on about $185,000. The tax people audited him, okayed all his deductions. Mostly business travel expenses, documented by American Express statements.'

'So?'

'Gary was a cop for five years. Drummed out, his ex-wife says. On the take. Then it's a job in security for TransQuik. Cop fallback position, generally not the beginning of a glittering career. Wrong. Last year, he declares three hundred and fifty grand as a global security adviser. And there's still a TransQuik connection. Worth $55,000.'

Drew read on, came to Simone's link-up of Aviation SF with Fincham Air and the director of TransQuik.

'Connection?' he said. 'The term tenuous was invented for describing connections like this.'

'I rang TransQuik. Four people say, sorry, never heard of Gary Connors. Then a man calls from Sydney, says all the company knows about Gary Connors is that he worked for them as a security officer and left of his own volition a long time ago.'

'Yes?'

'I took a chance. I asked how come an associated company was paying Gary large sums of money. Man said he didn't know what I was talking about. End of conversation.'

Drew was wearing his watchful courtroom expression.

'But not for long,' I said. 'An hour later, I get a call from a lawyer with Apsley Kerr Woodward in Sydney. She says she is instructed to tell me that TransQuik has no connection with Gary Connors or with Aviation SF.'

Drew raised his eyebrows.

'I never mentioned Aviation SF. Somebody at TransQuik knows Aviation SF paid Gary.'

'Ah,' said Drew. 'Well, maybe a little thicker than tenuous. But still. You want to walk carefully with TransQuik. Big end of town. All the towns. I take it you saw Linda tangling with Mr Steven Levesque the other night?'

Steven Levesque. The handsome man with the wayward hair and the genuine laugh. I nodded. 'What's he got to do with it?'

Drew sighed, shook his head. 'Levesque is TransQuik. Was, anyway. Levesque and the Killer Bees. Carson and Rupert and McColl. You should talk to my mate Tony Rinaldi. Remember Rinaldi? The fat bloke who used to sing?'

'Yes. Quit the DPP's office last year.'

'Well, you don't miss everything.'

'Only the important things. How is it that you miss nothing?'

'Nice little drop this,' Drew said, examining the label. 'Barone Ricasoli. A red baron. I miss nothing because I'm a citizen of the world, playing a full part in civic life. You, on the other hand, allow the affairs of the public sphere to pass you by while you master pigeonhole joints.'

'Dovetail. Tricky things.'

The main course arrived: dark meat falling off the bone, pool of glistening dark sauce, sweet potato with flecks of something, baby green beans, crunchy.

We didn't talk for a while. Finally, Drew said, 'Jesus, how can I get Donelly to owe me money, lots of money? Are these bits of apricot?'

'Stick around, make yourself known, your turn will come. Sooner or later, he'll be up for pinning a kitchenhand to the wall with a knife.'

The bottle was low. I signalled to the swimmer for another. 'So Tony Rinaldi knows about TransQuik?'

'Oh yes. More than he should, I reckon. I had a few glasses with Anthony one night, his wife went off with a librarian from Camberwell library. Female librarian. That hurt the boy. Bloody Eltham artist is one thing, big dick notwithstanding. At least he had a dick.'

We went back to savouring the shanks. The new bottle arrived. I waived the approval ritual, went directly to Go.

'A bitter man, Tony Rinaldi,' said Drew. 'First the wife's knee-trembling in the library stacks, then he gets shafted in the DPP's office. He reckons the DPP's a silent partner in this new place, The Dining Room. Top of Collins Street. Know it?'

I shook my head. I'd been too dazed by encountering Linda's perfume to notice much when I was last at the top of Collins Street.

'Like eating at the Melbourne Club, I gather. Only with decent food and Jewish members. Victorian grandeur, my client Simeon Haldane, Melbourne Grammar and Cambridge, tells me. That's Simon with an e stuck in. You went to Grammar, you'd probably know Simeon. About your vintage. Same dissolute appearance.'

'Charged with what?'

'Usual. Male minors, all orifices, possessing a range of educative pictorial stuff. Bit of light caning.'

'Sounds like an ordinary day at boarding school.'

'Simeon sat two tables away from the Premier at lunch at The Dining Room last week. The leader eats there all the time, takes the visiting money for dinner. Stuff themselves on prime Victorian meat. That's all Simeon wanted to do really.'

We breasted the tape together, put the implements down on plates naked save the bones.

'No,' I said. 'Simeon doesn't stand out in my mind. Could be any one of fifty people from school. Why did Rinaldi get the boot from the DPP?'

Drew was looking at his empty plate in sorrow. 'Not clear to me. Something to do with the Levesque gang. Tony was moving the flamethrower freely at that point, the wife, the librarian, the DPP, all blazing. Also, it was bottle three.'

I poured. 'Want to go to the footy on Saturday?'

'The footy? What, just pick a game? Any old footy?'

'Saints and Geelong.'

'Christ, what a pair. So, we'd be going for nobody, just like to see a game? Any old shitty game? That's it?'

'No. We're going for the Saints.'

Drew emptied his glass of Barone Ricasoli's 1986 Chianti Classico. 'We? You and the Prince?' Incredulous tone, loud. People looked at us.

'Well, not the Prince as a whole.'

Drew glanced around, a what-the-fuck-are-you-looking-at glance. 'The old buggers? You and the old buggers?' Even louder, more incredulous.

'Yes. Drew, steady, the other customers think we're about to have a fight.'

He sighed, looked around again, apportioned the rest of the Ricasoli. 'This is, well—you hear some strange things. I'll be fucked.'

I couldn't think of the right thing to say.

Drew sighed a few more times. 'Jesus, Jack, are you all off your fucking heads? The Brisbane bloody Lions at least represent a bit of the old Roys. So they train in Brisbane. What the fuck does that matter? Everybody plays all over the place. Footy in fucking Sydney, Brisbane, Perth, wall-to-wall cankerous Poms at every game. Where the hell did Fitzroy end up training? Not in Fitzroy. Some players never came near Fitzroy except to front up to the faithful to raise a few bucks. Footy players are just mercenaries, can't you grasp that? They're not like your old man, his old man, however fucking many bloody Irish played for the Roys. These are just contract players. And that's been going on a long time. Didn't stop the team being Fitzroy, did it? Did it?'

'So Saturday's pretty much taken up then?' I said.

'Hang on. All we have to do is pretend that the Roys aren't having many home games this season. When they play in Melbourne, they're home. In Brisbane and Sydney and Adelaide and fucking Perth, they're away. That's not hard is it? Fewer home games. Get a grip on that and we've still got the Roys.'

A large woman at the next table said loudly, 'Like bloody hell. Never heard such bullshit before.'

'Settle down,' said her companion. 'You shouldn't listen to other people's conversations.'

'Well, he's got a point,' said one of the four youngish men at the table on the other side.

'Point?' said another of the men. 'Are you out of your…'

'Drew, this may be an opportune moment to leave. I can't charge breakages incurred during an all-in brawl against Donelly's bill.'

We went to the pub down the street for the cleansing ale,

took taxis home. I was in bed trying to focus on the men and their fathers novel when the phone rang. It was Drew, serious.

'Listen,' he said, 'got home, poured a last little one, bit in a bottle going to waste, thought I'd give Tony Rinaldi a ring since he'd come to mind. Cheer him up, take his mind off librarians. Well, I remembered some of those company names, y'know? Your bloke.'

'Yes.'

'So I said to Tony, what's the name Klostermann Gardier mean to you? Know what he says?'

'No.'

'He says, he's had a few sherbets himself, he says, Where'd you hear that? That's a name gets people killed.'

I rang Drew from Taub's and caught him on his way out to court.

'Four bloody appearances today,' he said. 'In this condition, how can I get justice for the victims of a system designed to punish the poor?'

'Four of those?' I said. 'And not a single dead-set guilty and remorseless criminal arsehole? Tony Rinaldi. Will he talk to me about that stuff?'

Drew sighed. 'Ask him. I think I told him last night that I'd mentioned to you that he had an interest in the people in question.' Pause. 'I think I told him. Well, I must have.'

I said, 'Thank you. Go the Saints. Goodbye.'

Go the Saints. I'd said it. The first time. It felt like coming out.

Tony Rinaldi now had chambers in William Street. The secretary said he was in conference. I left my mobile number. Today we had to measure up for a library.

Charlie devoted the trip to Kooyong to explaining to me why no-one could be a joiner of any consequence without undergoing what sounded like a fifty-year apprenticeship starting at age four and supervised by the Marquis de Sade.

'So it's twenty-five years just sweeping up the shavings,' I said as we arrived at the address. 'I can imagine the feeling on the day they let you hand them a chisel.'

It was several million dollars worth of old neo-Georgian house behind a high wall. Through wrought-iron double gates, we could see a gravelled driveway that turned the corner of the house. Beside the gates, a wooden door was set in the wall. I tried the handle. It was open. We went up the path to a massive black front door under a portico. I pressed a polished brass button.

The door was opened by a tall, thin man in his thirties, designer cheekbones, black clothes, short fair hair. Alternate fingers of both hands wore rings, red stones on one, green on the other. He looked at us in turn, a look for each. Charlie was in his formal wear: white painter's overalls, clean, marked only by a faint oil stain here and there, and the jacket of a pinstriped suit he claimed to have got married in. It was not a claim anyone was going to dispute. I was in a dark suit and striped business shirt. With me carrying Charlie's sliding measuring sticks, we made a fetching couple.

The man tilted his head, brought his hands up and clasped them under his chin. Now the ring stones alternated, red, green, red, green.

'Stop and go,' I said. 'What about amber?'

He concentrated on me, unsmiling. 'You are who? Or what?'

I looked at Charlie. He was studying the garden.

'Here to take measurements,' I said.

'Oh. The carpenters.'

Charlie lost interest in the garden. 'Carpenters build a house for you,' he said. 'You need carpenters?'

'Yes,' said the man. 'To build some shelves. When you bring in the materials, please use the tradesmen's entrance off the lane.'

'Wrong house,' said Charlie. 'Let's go.' He turned and set off down the path.

'Say hello to Mrs Purbrick for us,' I said. 'Tell her Mr Taub is now booked up for the foreseeable future.'

'Ah,' said the man.

'And tell her Mr Taub is a cabinetmaker. A cabinetmaker is to a carpenter as a Rolex is to a sundial. Find that comparison illuminating?'

'Ah,' he said again. 'The library.' He put his hand to his mouth.

Charlie was almost at the gate.

'Mr Taub,' the man shouted, running after him. 'Please come back. Mr Taub. I've made a mistake, Mr Taub! Please!'

Charlie stopped, turned his head. His expression was unforgiving.

'Mr Taub, I'm so sorry about the misunderstanding. We are expecting carpenters. At some time. Shelves in the…in the pantry, I believe. I'm David, Mrs Purbrick's personal assistant.'

Charlie turned, examined David, then put out his right hand. David looked at it, hesitated, like a man offered a snake. Then he put forward four fingers held straight and tight, thumb up. Charlie's hand engulfed them. This hand could without effort turn David's slim and elegant digits into red slime.

It didn't. 'Pianist's hand,' said Charlie holding up David's hand for inspection.

I could see David's neck colour faintly, a drop of blood in a saucer of milk. 'Very bad pianist,' he said.

'Nonsense,' said Charlie. 'The hands. Got the hands. Practise every day. Where's the room?'

David led the way through the front door into a room the size of my sitting room, not so much a hall as a gallery, four-metre-high ceiling, polished floorboards, no cornices or skirtingboards, no furniture, half a dozen paintings. Big paintings, paintings the size of windows. The only one I recognised was a Michael Winters, a Greek landscape with an elusive brooding quality; a painting you would like to see a lot of.

We went through double doors into a corridor lit by skylights that led, eventually, to another set of doors. Halfway down, David indicated left. 'I'll get Mrs Purbrick,' he said and kept going.

It was an empty room of modest size, perhaps five metres square, two long, narrow windows, each framing a bare elm. Like the hall, it was devoid of ornament. Charlie paced out the measurements. I went to the lefthand window. The garden was formal, brick paving, old hedges and trees.

'Mr Taub. How punctual you are.'

A blonde woman of unknown age reduced to about forty by cutting, injecting and sanding was in the room, holding out a hand, palm down, to Charlie. Everything about her was short: hair, forehead, eyelids, nose, upper lip, chin, neck, torso, fingers, legs, feet, skirt. This led to a certain imbalance because her chest could not be called short. Many things it could be called. But not short.

Gingerly, Charlie took her fingers between thumb and forefinger. With his other hand, he pointed at me. 'My assistant,' he said, 'Jack Irish.'

Mrs Purbrick extended her left hand to me. I took it. For a second, the three of us stood there like a small ill-assorted Maypole dancing team without a pole. Then she dropped our hands and gestured dramatically at the room. 'Mr Taub, this is yours. Yours. All yours. Do with it what you will.'

She pirouetted, arms bent, fingers pointing outwards. 'I want to be surrounded by books. I love books. Books. I must have a room where I can breathe books. Floor to ceiling. I saw Sir Dennis's library. I knew only one made by you would be good enough.'

She smiled at us in turn, a little longer at me. There was a certain glitter in the eye.

'The deposit is fifteen thousand dollars,' I said.

'The books,' said Charlie. 'Big books, small books? Library, you make it to fit the books.'

Mrs Purbrick had moved over to stand close to me. I hadn't seen any movement but a hip was in contact with my left leg.

'Mr Irish,' she said, 'David will give you a cheque for the deposit. Mr Taub, build it and the books will come. To fit. David will arrange the right size books, don't you worry.' She looked at David, standing in the doorway. 'Size is David's concern.'

From the doorway, David said, 'Absolutely. Size is my department. Isn't it, Mrs Purbrick?'

She turned her head and smiled at him. You could see that extending her mouth sideways required effort and the lips could snap back like an old-fashioned purse. 'Bring the car around, will you, darling.'

His lips twitched and he disappeared. Her hip moved against my outer thigh, a contact and a rub, measured in millimetres. I found the experience disconcerting but not unpleasant.

Charlie took the measuring sticks from me. 'Write,' he said.

I got out my notebook. Mrs Purbrick made hip contact again, smiled and said, 'I'm in your incredibly talented hands, gentlemen. If you need anything at all, shout for David.'

At the door, she turned. Our eyes met. I thought the movement of her hairline indicated an attempt at a wink.

Charlie took about a hundred measurements and I said each one back to him before I wrote it down. Everything would be built in the workshop and brought here in sections to be installed over a few days. This meant that a mis-measurement of even a centimetre could be disastrous. When we'd finished, I found David and he let us out in a courteous and respectful manner.

I drove around to Gary Connors' apartment block and found a park right outside. 'What's this?' asked Charlie. 'Bunkers they need in Toorak now?'

'I'll be five minutes,' I said. At the front door, I pressed the button with Manager under it. A rich voice said, 'Can I help you?'

'I'd like to talk to you about Mr Connors in unit five.'

'In what connection?'

'His whereabouts.'

'May I ask who you are?'

'I'm a lawyer representing his father.'

'Do come in.'

The doorbolt clicked. I went into the lobby. The door on the left was opened by a man in his sixties, neat grey hair on a mound-shaped head, military moustache, reading glasses half-way down his nose. He was wearing grey flannels, a white shirt and a striped tie, a school tie. He put out his right hand.

'Clive Wendell,' he said. He didn't look the type to be caretaker of a postmodern bunker. A converted Edwardian mansion full of retired graziers would have suited.

I introduced myself. We went into his sitting room. It was

chintzy, silver-framed photographs on every surface, kelims on the floor, two regimental swords on a side wall.

'About ready for the pre-lunch gin,' he said. 'Join me?'

I declined. He went over to the drinks tray, poured a modest amount of gin into a glass, added tonic from an open bottle. Perhaps not the first G&T of the day.

'Police did mention Connors' family,' he said, sitting down. There was something wrong with his left leg or hip.

'When were they here?'

Wendell sipped, put his glass on a side table, leaned over and picked up a black ledger with red binding from the coffee table. 'The book,' he said. 'The good book. Thank God for the book. Relied on memory, I'd be buggered.' He pushed his glasses up, flicked pages, stopped. 'Fifth of April, morning.'

'What did they want?'

He looked puzzled, put the book in his lap, lowered his glasses. 'Well,' he said. 'Family reported Connors missing.'

I nodded. 'Of course. The police wanted to look around the flat.'

'Yes. Thorough too, I can tell you. No need to worry on that score. You can tell his father. No need for concern. Took the matter very seriously indeed.'

'He'll be pleased to hear that.'

'Sure he will. Worrying business. Still worry about my daughter. In Canada with three teenagers and I still worry.'

'We all do. Did they find anything of interest, do you know? They're being very non-committal with Mr Connors senior.'

He drank a teaspoon of G&T. 'Can't help. Wish I could. Had me let them in, shooed me off. Wouldn't let me through the door. Didn't want the waters muddied, I imagine. They were up there for a good forty-five minutes.'

'I suppose they identified themselves, left a card, that sort of thing,' I said.

More G&T. 'Absolutely. We don't let any old person in the front door here.' Wendell repositioned his glasses, raised the ledger and read. 'Detectives Carmody and Mildren, Australian Federal Police.'

'Federal Police. Not the local police?'

Puzzled again. 'Connors' father hasn't had dealings with them?'

'He reported his concerns to the local police. I suppose they handed the matter on.'

'Absolutely. Carmody, he was in charge, said missing people were a Federal responsibility. Cross state borders, that type of thing. Makes sense, doesn't it?'

'Impeccable sense. When did you last see Gary?'

'Oh, some time in March, middle of March. We arrived in the car park together, exchanged a few words.'

'The card the police left you. It's got a phone number on it, I take it. Can I get that?'

'Of course.' He adjusted his glasses and read out a number from the ledger. I wrote it in my notebook.

I stood up. 'Well, thanks for seeing me. Gary's father will be reassured.'

Wendell came out of his seat with difficulty. 'Pleasure. My good wishes to him. Worrying business. You read about these people murdered in Bangkok hotels. Still, experienced traveller. Seldom here, I can tell you. Off on business all the time. High-powered. Nice chap. Quiet.'

He saw me out.

Charlie was in a contemplative mood when I got back. We drove back in silence until, in Hoddle Street, stuck in the small-business traffic, in the rain, the exhaust-perfumed rain, the Stud's wipers making greasy smears, Charlie said one word.

'*Unwürdig.*' His face was turned from me, looking in the direction of a printery. He was thinking about Mrs Purbrick's library. The hands, the huge machines, were lying upturned on his thighs. It occurred to me that I couldn't recall seeing Charlie's hands in repose before.

I knew what he meant, although it contradicted things he had said to me. I didn't say anything until I turned up Gipps Street. Then I said, 'Utterly *Unwürdig*. Worse than *Unwürdig*. Since when did *Unwürdig* bother you? I thought you were making the stuff for the generations to come?'

Charlie didn't cheer up. 'Sometimes,' he said, 'I think the generations to come might be just as *Unwürdig*.'

I dropped him at the workshop's front entrance and drove around the corner to park in the alley. The mobile rang as I was getting out of the car.

'Jack Irish? Tony Rinaldi.' Brisk barrister's voice.

'Tony, you probably won't remember me…'

'Of course I remember you. On the town with that bloody Greer last night, I gather.'

'Can we have a little talk in confidence about the question Drew asked you?'

Pause. 'I'm sorry, Jack. I don't know what Drew read into my remark to him, but I think he's got it all wrong. In any event, it's all confidential stuff. I can't discuss it. You'll appreciate that, even if Greer doesn't.'

We said goodbye. Back in my office, I stared out of the window, listening to the industrial noises coming from across the road, thinking about Gary and the TransQuik connection. Did it exist? If it did, why would they go to such lengths to deny it? Who had reported Gary missing?

I got out my notebook, found the number on the card the Feds left with Clive Wendell, dialled it. It rang briefly, then blipped again.

'Offices on Collins,' a man said. 'The number you've dialled isn't presently in use.'

'What is Offices on Collins?'

'We provide full office facilities for limited or long-term rental.'

'Can you tell me who was renting that number on April 5 this year? I may have the wrong number.'

'Certainly, sir.' I heard computer keys clicking. 'The rental was for two days in the name of J. A. Ashton.'

'Do you have an address?'

'Sorry, sir, I don't have that information. It was a cash transaction.'

So much for agents Carmody and Mildren.

The phone rang as it touched the cradle.

'Jack, Tony Rinaldi. Forget the other call. What about today? Lunchtime?'

Tony Rinaldi came trundling down the riverside path towards me, the shortest member of a group of four trundlers. He was wearing a T-shirt saying *Even the Short Arm of the Law is Long* and he was a lot thinner than when I'd last seen him. Losing your wife to a librarian can have that effect.

I stood up. Tony saw me, panted something to his pack and slowed to a walk.

'Jack,' he gasped. He didn't shake hands, sank onto the bench next to me, short hairy legs stuck out. I sat down, let him recover, offered him the plastic bottle of mineral water he'd suggested I bring if I was going to interrupt him before he got to his watering hole.

He drank half the bottle, dribbled some onto his chest, panted for a while. Finally, he took a deep breath. 'Thanks, mate.' Ran his hand through dark thinning hair. 'Jesus, worst thing I ever did getting in with that mob. Bastards wait till you're so clapped out you can't breathe, then they pick up the pace, start asking you questions.'

He had another large draught of expensive water, took another deep breath. 'So, Klostermann Gardier. How's the name come your way?'

I told him. 'Gary calls himself a security adviser and one of his clients appears to be Klostermann Gardier. I'm clutching at straws here.'

'Gary connected with TransQuik?'

'He worked for them for about eight years. Left in '88. Security. He's an ex-cop.'

'Let's walk,' Tony said, pushing his way off the bench. 'Bit of a mystery man, weren't you? Didn't you marry one of the Ling girls?'

'Very briefly. Frances. She's married to a surgeon now. General surgeon. Cut off anything.'

He laughed, still short of breath. 'Frances and Stephanie Ling. I used to call them the Ling Erection Company.'

We headed for Princes Bridge, talking about student days. I wondered what the older generation of barristers thought of colleagues who walked around the streets in running shorts and sweat-soaked T-shirts with undignified slogans. Not a great deal, I would imagine.

On the bridge, Tony said, 'Drew tell you I quit the DPP's office?'

'I read about it.'

'Ten years I put in and here I am starting again at the bar. Like a twenty-two-year-old. Fat and balding twenty-two-year-old. Well, less fat than I was at twenty-two, actually. Plus my fucking wife's walked off and the bitch gets half of everything.'

We crossed Swanston Street, went down Flinders. The mild sunshine was gone, dark clouds gathering. In the shadow of the buildings, the day was cooling quickly.

I sidestepped a large couple holding hands and gazing in wonder at the bustle. Everything about them said down from Dereel for the day.

'Christ, it's freezing,' said Tony. 'I've got to go to Sydney in an hour, can't catch cold. Bugger this.'

He stepped into the street and waved.

Never mind that the cab was going the wrong way.

We got in. 'Corner William and Little Bourke,' said Tony.

'Have to go round,' said the driver. 'Can't turn.' He had

long blond hair in a ponytail, stylish dark glasses.

'Whatever,' said Tony, hugging himself. 'Go up Russell.'

'I can do this,' said the driver.

'Right. Not automatic that cab drivers know the way to anywhere.'

'Believe me,' said the driver. 'This is automatic.'

'Klostermann Gardier.' Tony looked at me, brown eyes, soft, intelligent eyes. He turned his head to the window. 'You're a friend of Greer's,' he said. 'He's a good bugger. My advice about these people is to walk away, Rene.'

He frowned. 'Christ, that was Russell. What are you doing?'

'Next one's quicker,' said the driver.

Tony leaned over, put his mouth behind the man's ear. 'How can the next one be quicker?'

'I'm a cab driver,' the man said. 'I know.'

Tony sat back. 'That logic,' he said, 'has become less and less compelling.'

The driver turned left into Bourke, into a jam. 'Oh Jesus,' Tony shouted, 'what the fuck are you doing, there's a fucking mall down there, go right next, right into Russell, can you grasp that, you idiot?'

'Excited,' said the driver, taking both hands off the wheel. 'No need. Shortcut. Believe me, I know what I'm doing.'

Tony didn't believe. He directed the driver every metre of the way until we were outside his chambers in William Street.

'So,' said the driver, not looking around. 'Was that so bad? Here we are, no problem. Ten bucks fifty. Coupla coffees and a focaccia.'

Tony looked at me. We got out the kerbside door. I found seven dollars. Tony opened the passenger door and put the money on the seat. 'No problem?' he said. 'Here's seven bucks, no problem. Be fucking grateful I pay you anything.'

'Have a good day,' said the driver. 'Cunt.'

I sat in a comfortable chair in Tony's panelled office and read an old issue of the *Australian Law Journal* while he showered. My ignorance of the law was disconcerting. Could I have forgotten that much? To forget, you must first know.

Tony came out, pink, combed, dark trousers, black shoes, knotting a spotted tie over a seagull-white shirt, carrying a towel.

'What happened to Stephanie? The younger sister, wasn't she?'

I nodded. I didn't like going back this far.

'She was a spunk,' Tony said. 'I remember she got in with that student paper crowd, superior little up-themselves arseholes.'

'She married an artist.'

'Who? I'd know him?'

'I doubt it. He killed himself.'

'Paintings be worth more then. Well, where do I start? I go back a good way with TransQuik. Before Levesque and Co. I did a bit of work for the company, they were buying up the odd collapsing trucking business. Manny Lousada, he was the owner then, bright bloke but perverse. He had a talent for the complex. Nothing was allowed to be simple. You arrive at a fairly simple, standard arrangement whereby you'd do a deal in two, maybe three stages. You show them your thing, they show you theirs. No. Not good enough. Manny wants six stages with fiddly bits at every stage and impossible delaying and opt-out clauses of all kinds, all for no discernible reason.'

He started rubbing his hair with the towel. 'One day, Manny rings me, he's had an approach, a terrific approach.

114

Foreign investor wants to buy forty per cent of the company. For five million bucks. That values TransQuik at twelve-and-a-half million, which is heading for twenty times earnings. Simply off with the fairies.'

Tony sat down behind the file-laden desk and took two red apples out of a drawer. 'Want one? I'm on the apple and chicken soup diet. Murder but it works.'

I declined.

He took a bite of apple and worked at it for a while. 'Assets were a lot of ageing trucks and a couple of ware-houses. Income about three-quarters of a million. Prospects not bad, but, Jesus, this is '84, transport not fucking information technology.'

The phone on the desk rang. 'Tell him I'm in conference,' said Tony. 'I know he wants to talk to me. He always wants to talk to me. I don't want to talk to him. Louise, I know the pressure you're under. Tell him to tell them everything is being taken care of. Nothing to worry about. I expect to hear today. I'll ring him tomorrow. Yes, I'll get there. Do me a favour, ring Wilkes, tell him I'll talk to him from the airport.'

He looked at his watch, looked at me and shook his head. 'You think having crims for clients is bad? You don't know bad until you have solicitors for clients.'

More apple. Most of apple. 'Well, speed this up. Excuse my mouth full. The deal offer comes through a solicitor in Sydney. His name is Rick Shelburne, two-person practice in Randwick. I rang around. Rather odd practice, they say. Nothing off the street. He pops up now and again for white-shoe boys in Queensland, developers, wheeler-dealers, suchlike. Said to have a talent for changing councillors' votes. He's also acted for a person in Darwin of major interest to the Feds. Been up there?'

I shook my head.

'I did my time,' Tony said. 'Thought lawyers could change things. Hah hah. The Territory's where you hear a little plane buzzing on a pitchblack night, you don't automatically think it's the Flying Doctor back from another mercy mission. Get me?'

'Roughly.'

'Well Shelburne was cause for concern. But we go to the next stage. This bloke flies in from Europe. Suite at the Windsor. He's called Carlos Siebold, a Paraguayan based in Hamburg, he says. Speaks English with a Spanish accent. But there's German in there, hard to explain. Smoothest thing I've ever met. Ruby ring on the right pinky.'

Tony rolled an invisible ring on the little finger of his right hand. It looked relaxing.

'Could be a cardinal, could be a fucking hitman,' he said. 'Anyway, Shelburne's there too, he doesn't say much. Siebold says he represents, this is the point, something called Klostermann Gardier of Luxembourg. A private bank. The price for the forty per cent turns out to be $4 million. That's still over the odds, but never mind. Siebold says, deal done, Klostermann will provide a facility of $20 million for expansion, principal repayable as share of after-tax profits over ten years.'

I said, 'Without having a Harvard MBA, that sounds like Christmas.'

'Many Christmases at once. And Klostermann is not the investor. It acts for the investor. Conduit. Siebold gives us the names of other freight companies the investor has money in. One in Manila, one in Hong Kong, one somewhere else, I can't remember. I took Lousada and his offsider, nodding twerp called Giddy, we went into the other room. I said to them, put simply, nobody offers deals like this. Let me check these people out. Well, Lousada's no fool, so we go back in and say we need a few days. Siebold says he's got other business, he'll be back in Melbourne on the Friday, wants an answer then.'

Tony examined the apple, gnawed around the core, threw the fruit's spine into the bin. 'I got in touch with the companies. Not wildly forthcoming but, yes, they said, Klostermann's kosher, the investor's passive, he's put business their way through other companies he's involved with. I still didn't like it. The Manila company had two directors. One was called Gerardo Vega. I rang a bloke I knew in Canberra in Foreign Affairs. You'd know him. Jeremy Powers? Did law around our time.'

'The name,' I said.

'Anyway, I gave him the Manila names and he faxed back a cutting from the *Economist* which said Gerardo Vega was a Marcos crony who had been in Europe offering to sell large quantities of gold on Marcos's behalf. So I ring the *Economist* and get hold of the writer. He says it's a team effort, the person I should talk to is based in Melbourne. How about that? Five minutes later, I'm talking to him.'

He got up and went over to a wall of doors, slid one, revealing a wardrobe full of clothes. The dark jacket for his dark trousers was hard to find because all garments in the closet were dark. But he appeared to know what he was looking for.

'Cagey bloke,' said Tony. 'Called Stuart Wardle. Says he can't tell me any more than's in the story. Then he asks me for some names so he can check me out. I gave him the president of the Bar Council and the Dean of Law at uni.'

Tony found his jacket. 'Ten minutes later,' he said,

'Wardle rings back. What exactly do I want to know? I tell him about the Klostermann offer. He says all he can do is give me a question to ask Siebold. He says, ask him to explain the relationship between Klostermann, Arcaro Transport—that's the Manila company—and two people: Major-General Gordon Ibell and someone called Charles deFoster Winter.'

'Can I write those down?'

'Sure, this is all history. Well, it wasn't much but it was all we had. We go back to the Windsor. Siebold's got Shelburne with him. Siebold is very charming. Came in the night before, off to America in a few hours. What's our decision? I ask him the question. He looks at me, twirling the ring, he says, "I can't answer that question, Mr Rinaldi, because I have absolutely no idea what you are talking about." And he says to Shelburne, "See these gentlemen to the door. I've wasted quite enough time on dealings with them." Goodbye, we're in the corridor. Five minutes, start to finish.'

'How'd TransQuik take it?'

'Well. The offsider, Giddy, he got all excited, wanted to go back to Shelburne and start again. Lousada says to me, "What's that question mean?" I said, "I don't know but Siebold didn't like it." Lousada thinks about this for a while, then he says, "Probably just as well. Only free lunch is at the Salvos."'

'Ever find out what the question meant?'

Tony shook his head.

'And TransQuik stayed a client?'

'For a while. Until Levesque took them over. Didn't matter much by then, I'd decided to go to the Bar.'

I searched my pockets and found the printout of Gary's other clients. 'These others mean anything to you?'

His eyes went down the list. 'No. What did Drew say about my reasons for leaving the DPP's office?'

'Something to do with Levesque. That's all he remembered.'

Tony nodded and picked up the telephone. 'Louise, ask Alan at the carpark to get the kid to bring the car around the front. Without denting it.'

He began putting files together. 'Jack,' he said, 'about eighteen months ago, a bloke called Novikov was shot dead in his garage in Doncaster, found by his wife. He'd been at the junior soccer club meeting. Not long after, the cops stop a car with a dud tail-light, hire car. Driver's clever with them so they get him to open the boot. In the toolkit, they find a silenced .22. The one cop, a farm boy, he sniffs the thing and he knows, silencer notwithstanding, it's been recently fired. To the station, make some inquiries, then the Novikov murder call comes through. They reckon they've got the culprit. Ballistics later find the .22 is the weapon that killed Novikov. Bryce, that's the man with the gun, he's tough for a long time, then he says he's just the driver, the bloke who did the job is a man he knows only as Eric. Met him twice. It takes a lot of hard work but the cops get lucky and eventually Bryce IDs a man by the name of Eric Koch. Koch calls himself a transport security consultant and among his clients is an outfit called Airbound Services. Freight airline.'

The phone rang. Looking at me, Tony said Yes three times, put it down. 'They pick up Koch, he makes a call, half an hour later, he's got guns from Apsley Kerr Woodward and a hotshot barrister from Sydney called Mitcham representing him.'

'Who owns Airbound Services?'

Tony smiled. 'Airbound is owned by another airline called Fincham Air.'

I said, 'Which is partly owned by CrossTrice Holdings. Which owns twenty-five per cent of TransQuik.'

He nodded. 'You've been doing your homework. Well, the cops managed to avoid this pair of lovelies getting bail and a cop called Jarman, Detective Shane Jarman, he's the one first talked to Bryce, he's now obsessed with Bryce and Koch. When it came to me in the DPP's office, I encouraged him, said to him, let's go for it, doesn't matter who pulled the trigger, these two conspired to kill Novikov. Novikov, he's a mystery. Looks like an ordinary travel agent. Could be mistaken identity. This prick Bryce could shoot but it didn't follow that he could read a Melbourne street directory.'

'Travel agent? For a travel agency?'

The phone rang again. Tony picked it up and said, 'On my way.' He closed his briefcase and went to the cupboard for a small black leather suitcase. 'Novikov, yes. Travel agency, yes. Called Jason's Travel. Walk down with me.'

The worried Louise saw us to the head of the stairs, giving Tony instructions all the way. I took his briefcase and we began the descent.

'Lifts are no more for me,' said Tony. 'Lifts are for wimps. Anyway, I'm pushing Shane Jarman to follow the trail, see where it goes. Everything says Bryce is telling the truth, that he was hired by Koch. The big question is obviously who hired Koch. Bryce is from Sydney, got early minor form, then he's clean. In fact, his putative source of income is as a cleaner. Almost certainly a hitman. Koch, he's American, ex-army, migrated in the eighties, first job with TransQuik in security, now he's some kind of Mr Fixit for Airbound and Fincham and others. He's even got international clients.'

Tony paused on a landing, looking at me. I waited.

'One's Klostermann Gardier.'

'Jesus.'

He nodded. 'Next development is Koch asks to see Shane Jarman. He wants to deal. He says he can make this Novikov business look like shoplifting ballpoint pens. Wants to go on witness protection straight away, out of the slammer, reckons he's in danger. Shane rings me, I tell the DPP. It's exciting stuff, Shane can smell something, I can smell something. We start the process. Make the calls. Do the paperwork. It's in train.'

Footsteps behind us. We both looked over our shoulders. A young woman in black, files clutched to her chest. We parted to allow her through.

'Two days later, the DPP calls me in,' said Tony. 'He says we won't be prosecuting anyone for Novikov, they've redone the ballistics and the two bullets didn't come from Bryce's gun.'

'How'd that happen?' I said.

Tony shrugged. 'Guess. I felt like I'd been shot between the eyes. I asked: who ordered the ballistics redone? The DPP doesn't look me in the eye, this is the man I regarded as a close friend, right? He fucking headhunted me from the Bar. No, the director looks out of the window and he says, "Don't be tiresome, Tony. Matter's closed. That'll be all." I thought about it, thought about going public, asked some quiet questions around the place, quit the next day. Same day, they find the murder weapon in Sydney. Tip-off.'

We crossed the lobby, reached the street. A red Alfa Romeo was double-parked opposite the front door. The driver was shifting into the passenger seat.

I said, 'I'm slow without lunch. Slow generally. You're saying this goes back to Levesque?'

Tony took his briefcase from me. 'Bryce and Koch are both dead. Bryce had an accident. Koch shot himself. Jarman's running a one-cop station in the Mallee. Day I got back to the Bar, Apsley Kerr Woodward offered me a brief worth maybe a hundred grand a year. What do you think I'm saying?'

'I wish I could be sure. And this Wardle, the journalist, that was the only contact you had?'

'That's it.'

'Thanks. Buy you a drink some time. Not mineral water.'

He nodded. 'Pleasure. Got your number.' I watched him go to the car, open a back door, put his bags on the seat. He looked back at me, said, 'Jack, I'm not getting it over to you. There's stuff I can't talk about. Klostermann Gardier don't give up. If your bloke's mixed up with them, walk away. That's the only reason I told you all this.'

I nodded. 'I tend towards the obtuse. Sounds like good advice.'

At the driver's door, he said, 'It was for me and it is for you. These people can Mortein anything. You might buzz around for a while but eventually you'll be dead. I'll call you. Get together with Greer. Have a meal. Nights are long these days.'

They were indeed.

I went to the office and found Simone Bendsten's card. The address was about six blocks away. I knew the place. It had been a tea-packing plant, red-brick building empty for years. Then part of it burnt down in the seventies, and it served as dero accommodation until two speculators bought the roofless shell in the early eighties. They turned it into four barnlike apartments with a shared courtyard in the middle. Probably the first lofts in Fitzroy, possibly even Melbourne. The building was a tombstone for a working-class suburb.

Entry was through the courtyard door, admission by buzzer. I stood in the damp and buzzed.

'Bendsten Research,' Simone said.

'Jack Irish. Simone, I've got a few jobs.'

She unlocked the door from on high. The courtyard had a glass roof and was full of greenery in huge pots. Her apartment was up iron stairs to the right. She was waiting in the doorway.

'Come in.'

She was in jeans and a big cotton shirt, socks, no shoes. Today, her dark hair was loose.

'Not dressed for business today,' she said.

Down a short passage into a room the size of two double garages, kitchen bench against the righthand wall, the rest of the space furnished for eating, lounging, working. In the middle, a fire burned low in an elegant black enamel woodheater. Simone's work table held a formidable battery of electronic equipment. Two monitors glowed blue in the low light.

We sat in Morris chairs with leather cushions. I told her about looking for Gary. 'I'm getting the feeling I should be careful on the phone. I've got some more names. People this time. One is Carlos Siebold. He's a Paraguayan lawyer based in Hamburg who acts for Klostermann Gardier. You looked them up.'

I spelled Siebold. 'Two others. Major-General Gordon Ibell. And Charles deFoster Winter.'

Simone said, 'I'll have to try a lot of databases, European, American. It'll cost a bit.'

'Stop when you get to three hundred bucks,' I said.

'Nothing like that. I'll call you tomorrow. At home?'

'Keep it cryptic. I'll come around.' I gave her the number.

I put in a few hours at Taub's, building the framework for the first of six mahogany mantelpieces Charlie was making to go into a mansion at Mount Macedon being rebuilt after a fire. Then I went home for a shower and a change of clothes and caught a tram into the city.

Only one Pom was on the cutting floor of UpperCut, a tall, elegant man with thick grey hair running back from his brow in waves. He was all in black.

'Chrissy, Chrissy Donato,' the man said. 'That's an awfully long time ago. I was just a boy then. She married the scrumptious Gary and went off to live happily ever after. Which in this case was about two years, I think. She popped in every now and again. Not for years now, though. What's she done?'

I was looking at the women in the chairs. The one nearest was leaning back, getting a hairwash and scalp massage. Her eyes were closed in what looked like sexual pleasure. 'Nothing,' I said. 'Her ex-father-in-law wants to get in touch.'

He gave me a look of total disbelief. 'She married again,' he said. 'The dears never learn, do they? Why they can't be happy just doing whatever it is they do with men, I'll never know.'

'Would you know her new name? If she took on a new name.'

'Of course she took on a new name. What's the point of taking on a new husband if you don't take the name? Might as well be married to the old one.'

He cocked his head, put a fingertip to the middle of his mouth. 'George might know. George knows everything. He actually *listens* to what people are saying. I gave that up years ago. No-one's told me anything remotely interesting since I was doing a certain Royal's hair in London. And that's a while ago, although you wouldn't think it to look at me, would you? Absolute bitch of course, but the gossip? She'd just given the man she married for his impressive equipment the heave-ho. Anyway, she couldn't bear being vertical for more than short periods. No-one was safe. I can tell you, I've felt that jewelled claw on my thigh. Rippling thigh.'

'George?'

He looked around and shouted, 'Linda, darling, get George to come out here, will you?' To me, he said, 'The old thing's in there fiddling the books.'

A man who could have been his slighter, shorter brother came out of a door at the back of the room. He was holding black-rimmed glasses at mouth level.

'What?' he said, not happy at being summoned.

'Chrissy Donato. She married Gary Connors. That didn't last. What then?'

125

'Married a man called Sargent. He owns all those ghastly wedding reception places. They bought the Mendels' mansion in Macedon.'

'Thank you, George. You may return to your culinary accounting chore.'

'Very fucking kind of you,' said George, pivoting.

On the tram, I thought about Gary. He might have more than one residence. People earning $350,000 a year could afford holiday houses. Perhaps the case of beer and the six bottles of wine were for his holiday house. Not a long holiday. The Mornington Peninsula perhaps? Somewhere along the Great Ocean Road? It wasn't a promising line of inquiry. Nothing about Gary said holiday house. And if he'd gone away for a holiday, he would be using his cards.

I rang Des from the office.

'Des, should have asked you. Gary have a holiday place? Somewhere he might go that you know of?'

Des sucked his teeth. 'Wouldn't know, Jack. The second wife might know.'

Chrissy Donato-Connors-Sargent had travelled some distance from a Housing Commission house in Broadmeadows. She now lived on the slopes of Mount Macedon, down a country lane behind high stone walls. I switched off and listened. Birdsong, the faraway buzz of a ride-on mower, the whop of a tennis ball being hit hard.

Chrissy received me in a conservatory full of jungle plants looking out onto a broad brick-paved terrace, beyond which was a thirty-metre pool, azure in a moment of sunshine. The tennis sound was coming from behind a creeper-covered fence.

'Mr Irish, Mrs Sargent,' said the large brown man in a dark suit who'd allowed me in.

She was sitting upright in a white metal-framed chair. There were at least ten other chairs in groups around two glass-topped tables.

I shook a long-fingered hand. Somewhere in her forties, Chrissy was taut-skinned, with short, shiny brown hair, strong cheekbones, big pale eyes. She was wearing grey flannels with turn-ups, brown brogues and a man's business shirt, striped.

'Sit down,' she said. 'Tea? Something else?'

I said neither, thank you.

The manservant nodded, departed.

'So Gary's missing,' she said, turned her mouth down. 'I can't find it in my heart to regard that as bad news.'

'That's a widespread attitude. But his father would like him found.'

Chrissy had a steady gaze. 'Even bastards have fathers, I suppose, but isn't it a bit late for him to be interested in Gary?'

'Why's that?'

'Well, they kicked him out when he was a little kid. Fostered him or something. He was sent to this chook farm in Tasmania. It was like a prison farm, he said. They took all the fosters they could get. He used to talk about how he had to get up in the dark, do four hours' work before school, four hours afterwards. I thought the experience had helped make him the shit he is.'

Fostered? On a chook farm in Tasmania? That didn't sound right to me. I'd have to ask Des about this. 'His father's major concern is the $60,000 he lent Gary.'

'Ah,' said Chrissy, 'now you're talking Gary.'

A gate beyond the pool opened and a man appeared, a tall man, no visible hair on his head, wearing only small, loose running shorts, white socks, tennis shoes. His thin, sinewy torso shone with sweat. He wasn't so much tanned as burnt the colour of a goldfish.

'Tennis machine's chucked in the towel,' Chrissy said.

The man walked to the pool's edge, bent down, untied his shoelaces, pulled off his shoes, ripped off his socks. Then he turned to face us, looked up, gave a hip-high wave, took off his shorts and underpants, kicked them away. He stood looking in our direction for a few moments, turned, bent his knees, did a flat racing dive. Jet aircraft with its undercarriage down. His arms were moving before he hit the water and he settled into an effortless killer crawl punctuated by racing turns.

'Be a bit cold in there, wouldn't it?' I asked.

'Alan's got a thing about fitness,' said Chrissy, wry expression. 'Helps him sleep. Asleep long before I get to bed.'

'I've really only got one question, Mrs Sargent. Sounds silly. Where would Gary go if he was scared, desperate, thought someone was trying to kill him?'

Chrissy didn't treat the question seriously. 'Someone like me, you mean? Have you got any idea how many people would like to kill Gary? It'd be like the Myer sale after Christmas. Push doors down to kill Gary. People killed in the crush.'

'No idea then?'

She watched Alan churning the water. 'Men are mad,' she said. 'In love for about sixty seconds, it's just the way you look, your tits. Can't love you for anything else.'

Alan did another duck-dive turn, emerged, ferocious head. Lean arms cleaved the water.

''Cept my dad,' she said. 'He wasn't like that. Loved mum. She was fat. He used to touch her ear, give it a little pull, always remember that. Walk with me to school, holding my hand. Remember that. Died when he was forty-eight.'

We sat in the huge fenestrated space, the house expensive beyond dreams, servants waiting somewhere, a beautiful woman, dresser of hair, a hardness to her mouth, fibro house in Broadmeadows floating out there in her past, sweet, sad memories of a patch of dying lawn, a father and a mother and a little girl. Arms around each other.

Below us, a rich man, thin, all body fat dissolved, was pushing himself: against water, against age, against the inability to sleep unless exhausted.

I tried again. 'Gary didn't have a holiday place that you know of? Anything like that? Somewhere he might go?'

Chrissy laughed. 'No. Not in my time. And not ever, I'd say. Gary wouldn't know how to take a holiday. Not a normal holiday. Sex tour, gambling junket, yes, holiday no.'

'There is one more thing. Personal thing.'

'Ask,' Chrissy said.

'When you broke up with Gary, was that for any particular reason?'

'Particular? Well…' She looked at me and smiled her wry smile. 'Gary couldn't leave women alone. It's a sort of insecurity thing. He couldn't stand to think that someone didn't care about him. He wanted women to fall in love with him. That was one problem. Then there was the violence. And the coke. He was just barely in control. The gambling, that was out of control. He was making big money at TransQuik in '85, '86, '87, and there'd be Sundays when all we had was loose change. And I had the bruises.'

'What was his job at TransQuik?'

'I never quite worked it out. He used to go to business meetings a lot. All over. Europe, Asia, America.'

'On his own?'

'Mostly. Brent Rupert, he was one of the bosses, he used to go to Manila and to America with Gary.'

She came to the front door with me. As we left the conservatory, I looked back. The thin man was emerging from another turn, water streaming from his head.

In the broad passage, Chrissy said, 'Something wrong about TransQuik. Always felt that from Gary's behaviour. Alan says someone told him there's funny money in the company. They had this American manager, Paul Scanga. He'd been in the American army. Dead eyes and these thick, short fingers. Creepy. Gary and I weren't sleeping together by then. Don't know why I was hanging on, beats me now. One night, Gary's off his face, he says Scanga wants to sleep with me, it's okay with him. I was packed and out of there in fifteen minutes. Less. He was lying on the sofa laughing at the television. Gave me a wave like this.'

She made a twirling gesture with her left hand. It spoke of profound indifference.

Beauty and manual dexterity do not of themselves bring happiness, I thought as I drove down the road towards the freeway. In the side mirror, I saw a car two behind me shift out for a better view. A green Jeep Cherokee. The driver was wearing dark glasses. He shifted the car back in.

Just another impatient driver on a busy road?

Down the freeway. The Lark liked freeways, a compact cat of a cop car bred to chase perps in sloppy oversprung V8s with big fins along Los Angeles freeways. Beyond the airport, an arrogant, paperweight Porsche came along, drew abreast, a hummingbird really. The driver, a bald man wearing thin dark glasses, back from a business trip to Sydney no doubt, heard the sound of the Stud's eight, the music of a serious piston ensemble, looked at the short, squat body, looked at me and decided to try it on. Generally, you let them go. That was sensible. And sometimes you didn't. And that was silly. But it was nice, silly but nice, simply to drop down a notch, get the growl, feel the torque bunched like a bicep. Then tread the button and, with one smooth kick of power, leave the other person behind. What more innocent pleasure has the century produced?

I let Mr Porsche go and thought about the dead security consultant Koch. Once employed by TransQuik. American. Ex-army. Scanga, TransQuik's manager when Gary worked there. American. Ex-army. Gary the security officer going to business meetings in Europe and Asia. Two dead travel agents, Novikov and Gary's friend Jellicoe. Rinaldi's allegation that Steven Levesque could derail a prosecution for murder.

I looked in the mirror for a green Jeep Cherokee.

Nothing.

'What's that noise?' asked Harry Strang.

We were sitting in a coffee shop in Ballarat, waiting for McCurdie. The sun was out and at the pavement tables the locals were exposing fishbelly skin. They looked stunned, like people from Irkutsk transported to Hawaii by aliens.

'Miles Davis,' said Cam. 'A John Denver for people who don't like words. And voices.' He was staring at the wiry man in black piloting the espresso machine. 'I know that bloke from somewhere.'

'Miles,' said Harry. 'Miles. Good name for a horse. Rode a bloke called Miles Ahead in the Irish St Leger. Bugger of an animal. Huge thing. Caught wide and ran fourth. Bloody miles behind.'

The man brought the coffees over. 'Two lattes, one short black,' he said.

Harry examined his coffee. 'That's black,' he said. 'I can tell you're a man knows black. Wear it. Make it.'

'Let me know if it's strong enough,' the man said. 'We can do it again.'

'Got you,' said Cam.

The man cocked his head.

'Demons,' Cam said. 'Played a few for the Demons. Right? Crackers Keenan's day.'

The man smiled, a self-effacing little smile, said, 'I wasn't much good.'

'You were good,' Cam said. 'Crook ankle, I remember.'

'Crook everything after some games.'

I saw McCurdie crossing the road. He was dressed for town: brown sportsjacket with bulging side pockets, grey flannels with turn-ups some distance above big brown shoes, checked Gloster shirt and a green tie wide enough to double as a table napkin. Even from a distance, I could see evidence that it had often served this secondary purpose.

McCurdie came right up to the window, peered into the cafe. Cam tapped on the glass, just below his nose. McCurdie recoiled like a startled horse, focused, recognised us. A smile of relief. He came in, had a good look around as he worked his way through the tables to get to us.

'Pretty smart place this,' he said, sitting down with care.

'Ensures we won't see anyone we know,' said Harry.

A waitress appeared.

'Cuppa tea, please,' said McCurdie.

'English Breakfast, Irish Breakfast, Earl Grey…'

McCurdie frowned at the table.

'Make it the Irish,' said Harry. He waited until the waitress had gone. 'Done the paperwork then?'

McCurdie looked uncomfortable, scratched himself under his jacket. 'Reckon.'

'Who's the new owner?'

'I. and J. Grogan. He's the wife's cousin. Had a few horses before.'

'Any luck?'

'One run third at Murtoa.'

'We'll put that down as No,' Cam said. 'He appreciate the finer points of this?'

McCurdie nodded.

'Explain the rules?'

'He knows what he gets he gets from me.'

'Settled in at Devine's?' asked Harry.

McCurdie nodded, more enthusiastically this time. 'Treatin us good, that Karen,' he said. 'Knows horses too. Spose you know what happened to the husband.'

'Some hoons rammed his horse float,' said Harry. 'Don't go near her on the track. She's the trainer now.'

'Who's the jock?'

'Tommy Wicks.'

'Mind if I have a word with the jock?'

'Yes,' said Harry. 'Don't go near him.'

The tea came in a pot with small jugs of milk and hot water. McCurdie eyed the makings with unease, big hands in his lap.

Harry poured the tea, as if that was his duty. 'Milk?'

McCurdie nodded.

Harry pushed the sugar towards him. 'Given the boy the drum,' he said. 'Field's a bit small. Wouldn't be too bad that. Problem is there's two dead-uns in it I can see.'

McCurdie drank his tea in two mouthfuls, poured a refill, added hot water, milk, sugar.

Harry nodded encouragingly at him, pleased by his pupil's progress.

McCurdie swilled tea, looked unhappy.

'Tell us, McCurdie,' Harry said. 'You look like the one didn't get picked.'

'Well,' McCurdie said, 'I reckon I feel out of it. Like it's nothin to do with me now.'

Harry leaned across the table. 'Believe me, son, the investment here, that's the feelin you want to have. But if there's doubts, now's the moment.'

Cam took a mobile phone the size of two matchboxes out of an inside pocket, flipped open the top, looked at McCurdie.

'Jesus,' said McCurdie, 'didn't mean it like that. I'm solid, I'm happy, I'm…'

'That'll do,' said Harry. 'Karen fill you in about today?'

McCurdie nodded.

'He pulls up all right today,' said Harry, 'you'll hear from me through her. Till it's over, don't call me. Want to talk, tell Karen, she'll tell me. Understood?'

McCurdie nodded again. Harry put out a hand and they shook. 'Full accountin when it's over,' said Harry. 'Things don't work the way we'd like em to, well, that's racin. Work, we'll find a place for a quiet drink. Off ya go.'

Cam and I shook hands with McCurdie and he left.

On our way out, the man in charge of the coffee machine said, 'Come again.'

'Make a point of it,' said Harry. 'Didn't know there was a decent black coffee out here in the tundra.'

On the way to Dowling Forest, Harry driving, I said, 'McCurdie feels left out of it. I, on the other hand, merely feel ignorant.'

'Sorry, Jack,' said Harry, 'shoulda kept ya informed. First thing to do is get some daylight between McCurdie and the horse. Bloke's got form. Turns up with another retread, no-one's goin to take a big note on him. Don't want him to be the owner, don't want him to be the trainer. So now Mr and Mrs Grogan own this ancient neddy and Karen Devine's the trainer. Done all the paperwork.'

'Could all be said to have happened a bit late in the piece,' I said.

We were approaching a roundabout, a Kenworth semi bound for Adelaide on our right, entering the circle, looming like a two-storey building. Harry slipped down a gear and accelerated. The truck's airbrakes moaned, the horns on the roof brayed.

'Frighten easy, these truckies,' said Harry. 'There's that. Can't get round it. Suggested to McCurdie he might make the sale a bit previous, that'll help. Any luck, the bastards won't be interested till it's too late.'

At the track, we parked under an oak, well away from the gate.

'Tell Jack what's happenin here, Cam,' said Harry.

'Best thing is Seminary Boy,' said Cam. 'Kell Morgan's horse. He's run twelve, third, third, four-year-old. Our mate's got a little eight-year start on him. After that, you'd say Bold Chino, run nineteen for four. Then maybe another old bugger, Killer Serial, he's eight, four from twenty-six, not seen in action very often.'

'The dead-uns,' said Harry.

'There's two to watch. Sharpish four-year-olds. Both fourth-up, done nothing. Hughie Hooray and Kukri Dawn. Both won twice at this distance. As I read it, both headin for town, got the times to break through. Kukri's won four under eighteen hundred, doesn't run places if he can help it. He can win this, so can Hughie. If that's what they want.'

'Well,' said Harry, 'the money will tell us what they want.'

I said, 'How come Tommy Wicks is on Vision? He's no loser.'

Both heads turned to look at me. I hadn't grasped something.

There was a pause.

'No,' said Harry. 'You wouldn't want to put a loser on the horse. You want the horse to win.' He held out an envelope. 'Do me a favour, Jack. Don't want it outside the family till the day. Spread it around, mix it, to begin. Ten, fifty. Take note smartly, you'll find, the bold fellas bring their bags out here. Keep goin till it's gone.'

We got out. I went first. No contact at the races.

Dowling Forest after a dry autumn, only the track green in the dun landscape. Sun shining today, faded lavender sky. I'd been here on autumn days so cold the jockeys came back with blue faces. Not a bad crowd, all the usual people, the hopeful and the hopeless punters, the stable workers, float drivers, friends and relations of the connections, got-nothing-better-to-do people, petty criminals. I found a spot on the mounting yard fence next to two women in their thirties, short legs in leggings, tired jumpers, smoking cigarettes between fingers the colour of mangoes.

'He's a bastard, Les's brother,' said the taller one. 'Wife and four kids, little Breanna's eight months, he's shovin this supermarket bitch, must be about sixteen.'

'Fucking men,' said the other. 'Don't even ask Glen where he's bin. Don't want to listen to the fucking lies.'

The horses for the fifth started coming round. Vision Splendid was in the hands of a tall young woman, jagged red hair, pale eyebrows, windburnt face. The horse was calm but alert, moving his head in an interested way. They'd gone easy on the grooming and he was a little off the condition I'd last seen him in.

In the mounting yard Karen Devine, looking sharp in a corduroy jacket, camel poloneck and pants over boots, exchanged a few words with tiny Tommy Wicks, gave him a hand up, held Vision's head and stroked his neck.

I looked around. Cam was further around the fence, smoking a cheroot, reading the racebook. In his impeccable country clothes, he looked like an Aboriginal-Scottish-Italian riverboat gambler who'd turned grazier.

I went into the concrete-floored betting barn, a deeply inhospitable place, people chewing hotdogs with the apprehensive look of submariners waiting for the depthcharge to buckle the plates, pop the rivets. The turf accountants were running a tight little book today. Vision was at land's end but a mere 20-1. Hughie Hooray and Kukri Dawn were both at 4-1, Seminary Boy was at 6-1, Bold Chino and Killer Serial were sevens. Then we went to a bunch on 12-1, a 14-1 and two sixteens. I opened the envelope: ten, twenty and fifty notes.

Caution set in quickly. I hadn't unloaded more than $400 when the price began to shrink. After $800, I was getting 15-1 and then the carrion crows came in for their peck. I finished on 10-1. Cam was right about the dead-uns. There wasn't any real money for Hughie Hooray and Kukri Dawn and they stayed at 4-1. Seminary Boy tightened to 4-1, then 3-1, then 5-2. The rest blew out a bit. That was it.

Out on the stand, you knew it was winter. The light wind carried rumours of cold, cold lands to the south-west. I took my usual seat, thinking not about horses but about Linda, the way she shed her clothes.

A man in a purple tracksuit, uncertain age, forty, sixty, Hawthorn yellow and brown beanie pulled low, came up the steps. He was wearing binoculars of the size normally mounted on concrete-seated steel pipe at observation points. A thousand places to sit, he chose to sit one bum away from me.

I considered moving, felt weak, extracted the new camera, the Lockheed Weapon Systems VE 3000, military special, not on general release, fresh from Abu Dhabi or wherever Cam bought Harry's gadgets. As instructed, cursorily, I applied my right eye, pointed, found the gates, nothing to shout about, probably ten times magnification. Then I obeyed the digital number pulsing at the left by twice pressing the button my right index finger was resting on. Vision-enhancing wasn't sales talk: in a blink, I could see the smear of lip balm on Tommy Wicks' snot furrow, the inside of Vision Splendid's left nostril, note the large ruby ring, turned outward, on the pinky of Kukri Dawn's jockey. The breadth of field claims weren't wrong either.

'Jeez,' said Beanieman. 'What's that show ya? Wanna swop? Gissa look.'

I reconsidered my original impulse and moved sideways about fifty metres. At the races, you can do these things without giving offence. Indeed, seeking privacy engenders respect.

They came out in a reasonable line, two or three stragglers. I held Tommy Wicks and Vision easily as they left gate five. Wicks made no attempt to go to the rail, kept the horse outside. A 16-1 no-hoper called Priory Park was in front. That was the way it stayed, no great pace on, the stragglers gaining some ground.

'Slow affair,' said the race caller. 'At the twelve hundred, on the rails it's Priory Park, length to Bold Chino, half-length to Pax Americana, on the rails Killer Serial, outside of him is Hughie Hooray, half-length back and further out is Seminary Boy and outside of him is the veteran Vision Splendid, backed in to tens from 20-1. Behind Seminary Boy, Kukri Dawn is on the rail. On the turn, Pax Americana putting on some pace, Bold Chino goes up to Priory Park, Priory Park making an effort, can't hold Bold Chino, who takes the lead.'

At the eight hundred, I saw Wicks give Vision Splendid

some leather. The horse responded, easing by Seminary Boy, going up on the outside of Hughie Hooray. Priory Park chose this moment to shift out from the rail, allowing Pax Americana to take its place in front of Killer Serial. I looked for Kukri Dawn. The jockey had taken it off the rails into position behind Vision.

'Traffic problems at the six hundred,' said the caller. 'Bold Chino in front, length back to Pax Americana on the rail, Priory Park on the outside hanging on. Half-length back to Vision Splendid on the outside and Hughie Hooray. Killer Serial's on the rail. Kukri Dawn gone out wide looking for a run. Half length to the rest of the field. Here comes Stretto on the outside, big run. Four hundred to go. Stretto goes past Vision Splendid, neck and neck with Priory Park, Wicks is looking for a way out. Now Kukri Dawn's making its run, gets up to Vision.'

At the two hundred, a gap appeared between Hughie Hooray and Pax America and Seminary Boy took it.

'Now it's Seminary Boy pulling in Bold Chino, goes for the line, too good for Chino, behind him a line, Stretto on the outside, half-length to Pax Americana, Priory Park, then Hughie Hooray, outside him is Vision Splendid, neck and neck with Kukri Dawn…'

Seminary Boy won by a length and a half from Pax Americana, with Bold Chino holding on for third.

Cam drove us home, whispering down the Western Highway. Harry didn't say anything about the race until he'd put away his second Big Mac and taken off the big linen napkin, one of a supply kept in the glove compartment.

'How's the camera, Jack?'

'Marvel of technology.'

Harry nodded. 'Should be. Coulda bought a decent yearling for the price in the old days.'

Cam said, 'Cheap stopwatch tell you all you need to know about that affair.'

'Tell you somethin,' said Harry. 'But there's more to know. Lots more.'

Senior Sergeant Barry Tregear's first dart went into the treble twenty, the second missed it by a hair, the third didn't.

'One sixty-one,' he said, took a big drink of his beer.

'On this fucken stakeout for two days. Milkbar. Jack, there's blokes in trees, in the roof, *on* the fucken roof, there's even a prick lying under the counter, Christ knows what he's going to do. We're waiting for Australia's Most Wanted. Red-hot tip-off.'

I threw a one, a treble twenty, a twenty.

'Two twenty,' Barry said. He sighted along his dart. 'The milkbar owner, he's made the ID, absolutely positive. A bloke called Krushka. Nice fella. Did time in Nam. Nerves shot to shit.'

I'd been in the army with Barry Tregear. I was nineteen years old, boy officer, last year of the war. Barry was a sergeant, the large, calm farm boy from Hay. Not so much a town, Hay, as some houses clustered together to escape the aching loneliness of the plains. One evening, Barry and I were lying next to each other, several dead people near us, day expiring in a sullen, smeared, tropical way, both hurting, bleeding steadily into the mud, praying: praying for an artillery barrage, praying it wouldn't land on us, praying the dark would hold off. Barry turned his head, mud all down the side of his face, and he said, not in a scared way, more like someone who'd had two picks, backed the wrong one, he said, 'Shit, wish I'd stayed in Hay.'

A very nice dart. Treble twenty.

'One-oh-one. Treble, one, double twenty. About ten minutes to closing, nine-fifty, it's raining, I'm having a leak against the back wheel, big relief, cunt sticks a shotgun in my back, right between the shoulder blades.'

Missed the treble. Twenty. Sip of beer.

'Bugger. Treble, one, double ten. He says, he says, "One move I blow you away. Hands on roof." They learn this shit from television.'

Treble.

'One, double ten. "You and your mate," he says, "Whatta fuck you want here?" I'm standing there, it's fucken freezing, rain's coming down my neck, can't stop the peeing, it's running down my leg, any second Australia's Most Wanted is showing up for the milk, and some cunt's got a shotgun in my back. I think, whatta fuck *do* I want here?'

I said, 'Shit, wish I'd stayed in Hay.' Threw. Got a treble.

Barry looked at me, laughed, body-shaking laugh. 'Wish I'd stayed in fucken Hay,' he said. 'You've never forgotten that, you bastard. One-sixty. Treble, treble, double.'

Zero. Twenty.

'Treble, treble, double ten. And then this Land Cruiser, comes down the street, I thought, it's him, oh fuck, did my quickest hip turn, that's not too flash I tell you, knock the barrel away with my arm. The prick pulls the trigger, big bang, into the ground, the Land Cruiser, he floors it.'

Barry drank some beer, sighted, threw, just a little explosion of fingers.

One.

'Double ten,' he said, didn't hesitate, plugged it.

'You might give a bloke a chance,' I said. 'So you lost Australia's Most Wanted?'

'Nah. While I'm jumping on this dork, my prick's still

hanging out, such as it is, frostbitten, the blokes at the end of the street get him. Turns out to be Australia's most harmless turd, happens to resemble the real thing. Also drives one of the same fucken tractors, same colour.'

'Upsetting.'

He nodded. 'Yeah. They offered me counselling but I already fucked her twice. Just went home.'

The barman put his head through the hatch, big head, broken nose, embattled remnants of hair, middle front tooth missing. 'Had B11 in here Friday,' he said. 'Called somethin else now, what is it?'

'I forget,' Barry said, showing no interest, looking at his glass. 'Could be Police Ethics Squad, could be Police Proctology Section. Pace of change's a bit rapid for me.'

He went over to the board, plucked the darts, went back and put them on the hatch counter. 'Do something about these fucken things, will you? Like throwing a dead chook at a wall.'

The barman did a bit of coughing. 'Asking about your mate Moroney.'

'Major part of their working day, I imagine,' Barry said. 'Asking what?'

'Drinks with. Stuff like that.'

'Tell em?'

'Fuck off.'

'Tell Moroney?'

'What d'ya think?'

'Done their job then. Mission accomplished.'

The barman frowned, withdrew.

Barry drained his beer, burped loudly, looked at his watch. 'Christ, got to go. Take a piss first. Hold my dick?'

In the gents, he stood at the stained and odorous urinal,

rocking back and forth, while I washed my hands.

'Any joy on that parking ticket in Prahran? I asked.

'On a hire,' he said. 'To a Dean Canetti, one n, two ts, ACT licence, paid with a personal credit card. My bloke ran a little query on him. You want to be careful here.'

'Why's that?'

'He used to be a Fed. Also with the NCA for a bit.'

He found a slip of paper in his shirt pocket. I took it. 'Point taken. Jellicoe?'

'Looks like a burg gone wrong. But there's worries. No signs of struggle and this Jellicoe's not small. Also, hit just once over the head, then strangled. These things, it's usually like six, seven, eight hundred blows. VCR's gone, CD player, but not the wallet. And there's no personal papers in the place. Not a fucking phone bill.'

I'd developed an uneasy feeling in the stomach, the feeling you get around midday when you've had no break-fast. 'What'd he do, this Jellicoe?'

Barry zipped up, came over to wash his hands. 'Worked for a travel agency. Had the name One World, something like that. Flinders Lane.'

'Connors?'

'A U-bolt. I gather the real problem was selfishness, holding on to stuff he should've been spreading around. It was resign or take a bullet in the line of duty. Up the arse. Known at the casino, big loser but the credit's good. Also, the books know him. Semi-mug. He put two hundred-odd grand into Laurie Masterton's piggy in the spring.'

On the way out, Barry asked for a packet of chips. He didn't offer to pay and the barman didn't ask. We stood at his car, a Falcon, at least half a dozen street drug users/ dealers in view.

Barry stoked a handful of chips into his mouth, offered me the packet. 'War on drugs,' he said, chewing loudly, head panning the length of the street. He licked his front teeth. 'Heard that arsehole in Canberra talking about it the other day. Winnable war. Familiar ring that.'

I said, 'Stay in Hay this time.'

More chewing noises, eyes flicking at the street life, turned to me. 'Jack, think about sticking in Hay yourself. The real thing here is this Connors.'

'Meaning?'

'He's TransQuik.'

'Tell me.'

'Don't ask. Leave it. They want snow in Darwin, these boys, it falls.'

'You could say a bit more.' I looked into his eyes.

He wasn't going to say anything more, crumpled his chip packet, tried to hit a parking metre, failed.

'Bastards move,' he said.

Stuart Wardle, the journalist who gave Tony Rinaldi a cryptic question to ask the man from Klostermann Gardier, wasn't in the phone book. I tried the Media, Arts and Entertainment Alliance and told a tiny fib, quite harmless.

'I shouldn't,' said the woman. 'He's not financial.' She gave me an address and a phone number. A woman answered on the tenth ring, no name, cautious tone.

'Stuart's been missing for about three years,' she said.

I told her my story.

The big two-storey terrace house was in Parkville, a few blocks from Harry Strang's immodest dwelling. The front door opened on a chain. I could see the right eye, nose and half the mouth of a tall woman with long hair.

I said, 'Jack Irish. On the phone?'

'Some kind of identification?'

I found my Law Institute Practising Member card. Lyall Cronin took it, looked at it, handed it back.

'I don't know if that reassures me,' she said, unhooking the door.

She was somewhere in her thirties, a plain woman, curved nose, hollow cheeks, a judgmental face, tall, square-shouldered, black hair pulled back, wearing a green army-surplus shirt and old denims. Barefoot. Pale ovals around her eyes said she'd been wearing dark glasses in a sunny place. That ruled out Melbourne.

I followed her down the long, broad passage, round the

staircase. 'I'm in the darkroom,' she said. 'Sorry to be paranoid. I've been somewhere illegally. They can buy muscle anywhere. And they do.'

The passage walls were covered in black-and-white photographs and dozens of framed photographs leant against the walls at floor level. Many of them seemed to be of women and children, sad, stoic women and wide-eyed, runny-nosed children.

'I don't usually fall under suspicion of being muscle,' I said.

Lyall glanced at me over her shoulder. 'You take up enough room,' she said.

The darkroom was off to the right in what had probably once been a large downstairs bedroom. There were two sinks and a long stainless-steel bench with an enlarger at one end. Deep trays were stacked in a rack above the sink. Next to it was a tall, narrow window, its black internal shutters open. Outside, a potato vine was threatening to make the shutters superfluous.

Lyall pointed at a stool. I sat down. She went behind the counter and resumed her task: guillotining the edges of a stack of eight by ten black-and-white prints. Line up an edge, adjust, slice, quarter-turn, adjust, slice.

'Got to get these off today,' she said. 'Well, what can I tell you about Stuart?'

Slice. She had strong hands, prominent veins, long blunt fingers, short nails.

'His disappearance to begin with.'

'I was in East Timor and Bradley Joffrin, who lived here then, was also away. He makes movies. Made *Disclaimer*. No?'

'No.'

149

'He's well known in some circles. Used to make anthro-pological documentaries. Anyway, Bradley was away somewhere, I forget where, PNG probably. He was in PNG a lot around then.'

She held a print to the light from the window. 'No,' she said and floated it into a big waste bin. I glimpsed a dark face, head tilted, smiling, a machine pistol.

'When was that?'

'July '95. I came back first, Stuart and Bradley weren't here. That wasn't unusual. Stuart never left messages, anything. Just came and went, never did any cleaning, never cooked, ate whatever was around and then he'd stuff money in the jar. Half the time it was less than his share, then it'd be four times as much. Anyway, we were his tenants.'

'Stuart owned the house?'

'His sister owns it. That didn't matter. Except that Stuart was supposed to manage the place and he didn't give a conti-nental. We got used to it, averaged it out, used the extra money to get a cleaner in when we were really pissed off. Anyway, this was a pretty weird household all round, every-one coming and going.'

She studied another print, cropped out bits with her hands, seemed to forget me. I waited.

'No,' she said, floated the print into the bin. Picked up another one, gave it the eye, put it down on the killing surface. Slice.

'Sorry,' she said. 'Sometimes you wonder who took the picture. Bradley came back a few days after me and then about, oh, I suppose a week later, Stuart's sister rang. Kate. She's a textile designer in Scotland. Their parents are dead, some awful story. She told me one night when she stayed here but I've blotted it out. Heard too many awful stories.

Well, blotted it out with help. We were smoking this Sumatran stuff Bradley used to get from his airline steward mate. It didn't mix with tequila, I can tell you.'

I said, 'Stuart's sister rang.'

She studied me. I looked back. On inspection, she appeared less plain. 'Bringing the witness back to the point, Mr Irish,' she said without rancour.

I hung my head in acknowledgment.

'Kate said Stuart always rang her on her birthday. Rang her or came to see her. So we got a bit uneasy, felt a bit bad about not having been a bit uneasy a bit earlier, looked in his rooms. Didn't know what to look for. Eventually we went to the cops. Bradley and I thought he'd walk in the door at any time. But Kate was so upset we had to do something.'

Lyall sliced the last edge off the last print. 'That's that,' she said. She looked at a man's watch on a woven leather strap on her left wrist, broad wrist. 'Let's have a beer.'

I followed her out of the darkroom and turned right, into a kitchen. It was a cheerful, neat and businesslike room: french doors to the right, bench along the back wall, mugs and crockery in a rack, a big chopping board, good knives on a magnetic strip, big bowl of apples, glossy green and red peppers.

'Water will be fine for me,' I said. I've been down the dark tunnel and starting early is a good way to take another trip.

She made no comment, poured a glass of water from a filter jug, took a stubby of Vic Bitter out of the fridge and twisted off the cap. We sat down at the pine table.

'I don't drink on the job, make up when I get back,' she said, looking at the stubby. She drank a third of it in a swig.

'Who do you work for?'

'No-one. Well, I suppose I work mainly for the agency. Populus. It's in Paris. And New York. It was a breakaway from Magnum. Know Magnum?'

'Robert Capa.'

'The one.'

'I thought photography was all electronic now? Digital. Whatever that means.'

She had a crooked, cynical smile. 'I'm a Luddite. My old man was a hot-metal printer, wouldn't make the shift to cold type. I'm the same about digital. I like seeing the picture emerging, coming at me out of the chemical swamp.'

Pause. 'Well, that's me. What's a lawyer doing looking for someone?'

'Favour for a friend.'

'And there's a connection between this missing person and Stuart?'

'Well,' I said, 'I know that there's a connection between the man I'm looking for and a private bank in Europe and that Stuart knew a lot about the bank. He helped out a friend of mine with information. In the mid-eighties. Long time ago, I suppose.'

She moved her head left, looked at me over her nose, drank some more beer. 'I suppose,' she said.

I tried to get going again. 'So Stuart never walked in the door?'

'No. The cops checked the airlines, customs, whatever, and they found he'd flown to Sydney on July 10. His car was here. In the garage. Did I say that?'

'No.'

'Wasn't unusual. He always took a cab to the airport. Anyway, he'd flown to Sydney on a redeye, 6.30 a.m. or something, and then he'd flown to New Zealand the same day. And that was that.'

'He didn't leave New Zealand?'

'No record of him leaving New Zealand.'

'No contact with anyone?'

'No-one we know ever heard from him again.'

'Never used credit cards, drew money?'

'No. Never.'

Lyall finished the beer and looked in the fridge for another one. Her hair slid forward and hid her face. 'Sure?' she said, straightening up, pushing back her hair, holding up a long-neck bottle of Miller's. 'I'm moving upmarket now.'

'I'm sure.' She wasn't plain at all. Strong cheekbones.

'Would Stuart have a reason for wanting to disappear?'

'They asked that. And Bradley and I both had to say that we didn't have the vaguest fucking idea. We'd shared the house with Stuart for three or four years and we knew exactly bugger-all about him. Liked him, enjoyed his company, knew nothing about him. Shocking. I knew more about his sister, and she'd only stayed here once.'

'He didn't talk about his work?'

'Well, no. He'd talk about stories he thought people should write. Lots of passion about that. Always on about the CIA. But if you asked him what he was working on, he'd say something like, "Oh, bits and pieces."'

'But he made a living as a freelance?'

A telephone began to ring somewhere in the house. Lyall put her beer down and left the kitchen. I went to the french doors. They led onto a narrow brick-paved courtyard surrounded by high creeper-covered walls. Plants in terra-cotta pots were dead or sickly. Leaves, yellow, brown, scarlet, lay in drifts everywhere.

'Disgraceful, isn't it?'

Lyall had come up behind me. I turned. She had her hands in her pockets, thumbs out, pelvis thrust. The beer had flushed her cheeks a little. She had a long neck, prominent collarbone. Where had plain come from? How does one form these judgments?

There was a moment of looking at each other.

'Where were we?' I asked.

She turned and went back inside to the table, sat down, picked up her beer. I followed, took my seat.

'They want me to go to China tomorrow,' she said, ran her left hand through her hair, drawing it back, showing strong roots. 'If I don't want it, fifteen other hopefuls do and are prepared to swim from Darwin if necessary. Cameras tied onto their heads.'

'Going?'

She drained the stubby and got up, went to the fridge. 'I said, "Let the Darwin to China Swimathon for Wannabees commence." I'm going to sleep, eat, walk around, drink, read, sleep, eat, walk around, read, drink, sleep. Keep at it till I get these things right.'

'Stuart made a living out of…'

The crooked smile. 'Back to business, Mr Irish. I don't think Stuart had to make a living. No sign of that. Kate gave the impression the parents left them heaps. Stuart went to high school in America, then to Columbia Journalism School. His parents were living in the States then. Both doctors. Stuart was big on the Philippines, working on a book on the subject. He had stuff published in *Mother Jones*.'

She read my eyes.

'It's American. Sort of public interest magazine. I haven't seen one in a while. Big on military-industrial-complex conspiracy stuff. But not loony. American lefty, very earnest, bit short on theory.'

'I'm a bit short on theory. Practice isn't that long either. Did Stuart work from here?'

'Had the room next to his bedroom as an office.' She drank some beer. 'Had? He still has. We never touched anything. Anyway, he's not officially dead. Kate won't apply to have him declared dead. She's absolutely convinced that he's walking around somewhere, that he's lost his memory and will get it back.'

'What do you think?'

Shrug. 'If he's alive, he's not in New Zealand. His picture's been on television, in all the papers, Kate spent a fortune getting posters put up everywhere. Someone would have seen him. The cities are like big country towns and the towns are like Hamilton in the 1950s.'

I said, 'I know this is a big ask, but could I have a look at his office?'

Lyall gave me a long look. 'Sure. I was going to suggest it. Help de-spookify it for me. Come.'

She went up the stairs first. It was no hardship walking behind her.

'It was okay while Bradley was here,' she said, 'but now every time I come home, I listen for sounds upstairs, listen for his music. He used to play this Afro–Caribbean stuff. I tried keeping his doors open, but one day I came back from Hong Kong and they were closed. I went absolutely rigid, didn't know what to do.'

Upstairs, there was a broad landing with three doors on either side.

'The cleaning lady had closed them,' Lyall said. 'I left them closed after that, told her never to leave them open.

Now every time I come back I expect to see them open.'

Stuart Wardle's office didn't look like the dabbling room of a dilettante journalist. Two walls had floor-to-ceiling bookshelves. A work table under the window held a computer monitor, keyboard and tower, a fax, telephone, answering machine. Stuart's chair was an expensive executive model, flanked by large wire wastepaper baskets. Twin two-drawer filing cabinets stood against the fourth wall, one bearing a compact copier, the other a compact stereo.

I opened the bottom drawer of the left-hand filing cabinet. Empty. Top. Empty. Next cabinet. Same.

'This phone used to be the line into the house,' Lyall said from the doorway. 'The one downstairs was an extension. Caused all kinds of shit when he left the answering machine on. You'd be downstairs, the phone would ring, stop before you got there, race upstairs, get in here, hear the last word of a message. That's one change we made.'

'Messages on this machine when you got back?'

'Lots. Always lots.'

'For Stuart?'

'Some. A friend from the States. She stayed here once. And the *Economist*. He'd done work for them. It's an English magazine.'

'I know.'

Pause, eyes locked.

A swig from the bottle, head tilted back. Long neck. The exposed neck is a sweet and vulnerable thing.

Lowered the bottle. 'More than your average suburban solicitor knows,' she said, 'Mr Irish.'

'Depends. Some are exceedingly well read, the others go into politics or crime.'

I found her smile attractive. And heartening.

'His sister had rung a few times,' she said. 'And there were three or four calls for Bradley. I wrote all the messages in the logbook.'

I looked around some more. 'The room was like this when you first came into it after your trip?'

'Yes. Nothing's been touched. It's been dusted, that's all.'

'Nothing on the desk? Wastepaper baskets empty? Filing cabinets empty?'

'Yes. He'd done a big clean-up. I don't know about the filing cabinets, never saw them open.'

'The clean-up, was that unusual?'

'I'll say. Two in two months was outstandingly unusual. Two a year was more like it. He used to buy those huge orange garden rubbish bags.'

'So he'd had a clean-up two months earlier?'

Lyall nodded. 'I helped him put the bags in his car. Five of them. Took them to be shredded somewhere. Paranoid about his waste paper.'

'Where would he keep his papers? Bank statements, credit-card statements, bills, receipts, that sort of thing? The tax stuff?'

'There were some in the filing cabinets. The missing persons guy took them.'

'Never gave them back?'

'Probably gave them to Kate. I don't know.'

'Can I see his bedroom?'

It was purely functional: double bed, one bedside table with lamp, chest of drawers. A built-in cupboard covered one wall.

'We tidied up in here,' Lyall said. 'Did his washing.'

'Any signs of packing? Clothes missing? Luggage?'

'Are you sure you're a solicitor?' she said. 'My feeling is

you've done this kind of thing before.'

'Instinct,' I said. 'I rely on instinct.'

She smiled, finished the beer. 'Hard to tell about clothes. Stuart wore jeans and T-shirts most of the time and he had plenty of both. His little aluminium suitcase isn't here. He only ever took that.'

On the way downstairs, I said, 'His car's here, you said.'

'It's still in the garage. There's nothing in it.'

'Check the boot?'

Pause. 'I don't know. Bradley might've. He had it put on these jack things, sort of mothballed.'

The garage was reached through a door in the courtyard wall. A newish Honda was parked behind an old BMW coupe on jacks. Five wheels were leaning against the back wall.

'You might like to wait outside,' I said. 'Just in case.'

Lyall took her lower lip between her teeth. A full lower lip, square white teeth. She handed over the keys, didn't move.

The ignition key unlocked the boot. The lid didn't come up automatically.

I got fingertips under the numberplate and lifted. It resisted. Came up suddenly. Empty. A strong smell of brake fluid leaked from a plastic container.

I looked around. Lyall had the fingers of her right hand to her mouth. But not alarmed. People who went into other countries illegally to take snaps would presumably not alarm easily.

'Nothing,' I said.

The glove compartment held a Melway map book for greater Melbourne and a VicRoads map book for country Victoria. Half-under the front seat was a crushed McDonald's packet.

I looked at the instruments. Only 56,657 km on the clock. Reconditioned engine, perhaps, clock turned back. Was that legal? The trip meter read 667 km.

Nothing here.

Back in the kitchen, I said, 'A final request.'

Lyall was getting another Miller's out of the fridge. 'I find it hard to refuse you,' she said. 'An uncomfortable feeling.'

We exchanged looks again. Plain. A very strange perception. 'Would you mind if someone gave Stuart's computer a lookover?'

She tilted her head. 'Is that all?'

'It's all I can think of at the moment.'

'Keep thinking,' she said. 'Something will come to you.'

It began to rain on the way back to the office, nondescript Melbourne rain that didn't even seem to fall. It seeped. The Stud's erratic wipers, hard-contact, soft-contact, no-contact, always added another pleasurable dimension to winter. Coming down the straight towards the Swanston Street roundabout, straining to see through the smear, my mind was on Lyall Cronin.

At the front door, a little tipsy, she'd said, 'My regards to Mrs Irish and all the little Irishes. Or should that be little Irish?'

I looked at her. She pushed her hair back with her left hand. She wasn't asking a question about the plural form and I did not have to answer the question she was asking. 'No Mrs Irish,' I said. 'One little Irish, living with a fishing boat skipper called Eric. Somewhere out there beyond Brisbane. I try not to think about it.'

'Well, then,' she said, 'my regards to the current stand-in for the previous Mrs Irish.'

That was the moment. The moment to say nothing, smile, offer a handshake, say thank you. The moment to be non-committal. To be non-committal and professional.

Bugger that. Linda was being kissed on the ear in public: 'Things are quiet on the stand-in front. I don't think I've given you my card.'

Many arrogant men in expensive leased cars are encountered at the Swanston Street roundabout. At any time of the day. I think they live in North Carlton. One of them hooted at me. I hit the brake, he came close to climbing the kerb. Nice moment. Immature, yes. There is a certain immaturity in taking pleasure at seeing terror in the eyes of a Mercedes driver. But parts of us are forever immature. I can name my bits.

No messages at the office but, better than messages, a cheque from Belvedere Investments, aka Cyril Wootton enterprises. I took my seat behind the tailor's table. Assumed the position. Tried to think. Stuart Wardle was possibly not a line of inquiry worth pursuing. So what if he knew something about Klostermann Gardier and Klostermann paid Gary large sums. That didn't link them in any useful way.

Stuart Wardle was probably a dead-end.

Still. The neatness of his office. Clean-ups.

I'll say. Two in two months was outstandingly unusual.

An untidy man who cleaned up before he disappeared. Suicides sometimes did that. Nothing in the wastepaper baskets.

Nothing in the filing cabinets. No personal papers.

No papers in Gary Connors' apartment. No papers in Jellicoe's house. Cleaned by professionals? Like the two men who called themselves Detectives Carmody and Mildren of the Australian Federal Police and spent forty-five minutes in Gary's apartment on April 5.

Gary. Gary was the point. On the last day that I knew anything about his movements, he was being watched by a man called Canetti, an ex-Fed with an ACT driver's licence.

This whole business was beginning to look complicated. Complicated and hazardous. Rinaldi thought Gary's link with Klostermann Gardier was a good enough reason to back off. Barry Tregear thought Gary's TransQuik connection was unhealthy for me.

Don't ask. Leave it. They want snow in Darwin, these boys, it falls.

I could tell Des that I'd made no progress, couldn't really do any more. It was the sensible thing to do. Rinaldi would approve, Barry would approve, Drew would approve.

Des's trim weatherboard, in a street full of helpful and strong young women, was going to be shot out from under him. An elderly man, no house, no capital, on the pension, where did that leave him? In some narrow partitioned-off space in a squalid firetrap of an accommodation house, possessions in a suitcase, lying on a stained mattress on a sagging bed, coughing phlegm, staring at the spotted ceiling, smelling the reek from the lavatory down the passage, hearing the body noises of the hopeless people on either side.

I took out the photograph. I'd looked at it every day since Des gave it to me. The three men in singlets on the scaffolding on the fateful day. A man turned away, unidentifiable. In the middle, a man laughing. The tendons in this man's neck stand out like balsawood struts under damp tissue paper. He has muscular stonemason's arms and a head too narrow for his short, slicked-down hairstyle. It is Des.

And next to him in the tiny picture is my father. He is big, big shoulders, arms, a full head taller than Des, dark hair combed back, wry mouth, amused, head turned to Des.

It was possible to see, in this small photograph, that my father is looking at Des with affection, enjoying his laughter. Des was a friend. That was the reason for finding Gary, for getting Des's money back. My father would have wanted me to help him.

My father would want me to help him.

The thought came to me unbidden and with it the cover of Linda's left-behind book, *The Mountain from Afar*.

Oh God, men and their fathers.

Music. Like the mountain, from afar.

I got up and went to the window. In the closing day, the street gleamed wetly, its heavily cambered surface like the black cracked back of some ancient serpent rising between the buildings. The music was coming from Kelvin McCoy's atelier. Classical music, Debussy, at a guess. The thought of McCoy finding inspiration for his greasetrap paintings in Debussy stopped me dead in my tracks.

I went across the street, stood at the door and listened, unashamed.

A woman's voice over the music. Then McCoy's ruined tones, saying loudly, 'Relax, darling. It's nothing to me. Absolutely nothing. I'm an artist, I work with naked women every day.'

Work? With naked women?

Indeed.

I stopped off at Taub's to collect Charlie, got him out the door in twenty minutes. At the Prince, Norm O'Neill was reading the *Herald Sun* sports section.

'Jack, Charlie,' he said, waving the tabloid, 'where'd ya reckon they get these footy writers? From the kinder? Bloody born yesterday. This clown here, knows nothin about the Sainters. All this dickhead knows, club coulda come down from Mars just last year.'

And to make an end is to make a beginning. Was that what T. S. Eliot said?

This thought in mind, I requested a round from the publican. Stan was looking a model of geniality, your plump old-fashioned landlord, dispenser of wisdom and good cheer. What drug could work the miracle of complete personality reversal?

'Doubled the offer,' he said, putting down my beer, leaning across the bar, not so much whispering as sniggering. 'They want the old photos pretty bad.'

And then he winked, leered, took on a turbo-charged plump model of geniality look. A-Mr-Pickwick-on-human-growth-hormones look.

I put my face close to his. 'Stanley, you're not listening. The photographs aren't just old photos. You're trying to sell sacred objects. They're worth more than your life. Much more. The people who'll kill you don't give a shit about life sentences. They could depart any second. You with me?'

Stan pulled back, still beaming like Mr Pickwick, Mr Pickwick turned compassionate outreach worker. 'Jack,' he said. The one word had an understanding and non-judgmental tone. 'Jack, excuse me, you're a nice bloke but you don't understand the dynamics of change. Don't mean to offend, you're gettin a bit like the old farts. Livin in the past.'

He examined me benignly. 'Not just the photos, Jack. The party don't just want the photos. Thought you'd grasped that.'

I took a big drink of beer. 'Tell me, Stan. Slowly.'

'Want the freehold. Melbourne HQ of the Brisbane Lions. New name. Listen to this. The Lions' Lair.'

'Inspired.' I drank more beer.

He gave me an encouraging look, the look Harry Strang had given McCurdie when the rustic trainer managed to pour his own tea.

'My suggestion that,' said Stan. 'Shoulda seen the bloke's face light up. Marketing magic. Total synergistic marketing.

These kids can't see the big picture. Takes years of interface with actual point-of-sale.'

'Actual point-of-sale? Is that the same as pulling beer? Beer that tastes of soap.'

He ignored the question. 'Me in charge, naturally. Pokies. Bistro. Big screen. Knock all the walls out down here. Arches. Then there's the upstairs. Guess.'

'Too hard. Haven't had enough years of interface.'

'Consider this. Two loft-style serviced apartments upstairs. How's that for out-of-the-square thinking?'

I gave him the cross-examination stare. 'Not so much out of the square, Stan,' I said, 'as out of your cotton-picking mind. Goodnight.'

I drained the glass, no heart for this discussion. Any discussion. Goodnight all. Went home.

Home felt a bit more homely when I'd cleaned out the grate and made a fire. I cheered up, put on music, Clementine Liprandi, voice like a faraway trumpet. In the freezer, four small Italian beef sausages from Smith Street's finest butcher were huddled in an ice cave, joined like Siamese quads. Into the microwave to defrost. Sausages and mash. Potatoes in the basket, still firm of body. I peeled, quartered, immersed, went out to the car to get the case of Heathcote shiraz from the boot. Rain hung in the air, was the air, dampened the honking, humming, wailing night sounds of the city.

Glass in hand, I pressed for the messages. Rosa. Drew, missed by minutes. No Linda.

No Linda.

That's the way it's gonna be, liddle darlin, I said to myself, put on the television for the news. A female reporter with a startled look took us through a small hostage drama in North Balwyn. Generally, the police, endowed with a strong sense of theatre, like to shoot someone to end a hostage drama. However, the protagonist wimped out and was led away, alive, unperforated. On to a bus crash in Queensland, very few dead, allegations of sexual misconduct against two army officers, calls for the resignation of a football administrator, a hostile reception for the Prime Minister at a welfare conference.

I missed the sport while I was mashing. When I got back, 'The 7.30 Report' was on and Dermott O'Sullivan was interrogating the Federal Treasurer, David Maclay. The subject was Money, Power and Politics.

O'Sullivan: *So Mr Maclay there's no unhappiness in the party about the influence of people who hold no elected office?*

Maclay: *Absolutely not. Dermott, we're a party of consultation and consensus. We listen to all our members and supporters. And we listen to all the voters of Australia. Always have, always will.*

O'Sullivan: *But some people get listened to more than others.*

Maclay, shaking his head in sad disbelief: *Dermott, seriously. Of course some opinions carry more weight than others! I don't ask people in the supermarket queue how to manage interest rates. Does the ABC choose the people on its opinion programs at random from the phone book?*

O'Sullivan, tilt of head, smile: *And I'm sure you're in the supermarket queue on a daily basis, Minister. But my point is that people in the party, elected people, have expressed concern that some unelected individuals seem to command huge power.*

Maclay: *Dermott, I'm really disappointed in you. Why don't you just come out with it? If you want to play Follow-My-Leader, at least try to be the leader. You owe the idea that a great Australian achiever, and I'm referring to Steven Levesque, has some undue influence on government to your ill-informed commercial media colleague Ms Linda Hillier. People expect more from the ABC, Dermott.*

Was there no escape from Steven Levesque? First Linda and now Dermott.

Maclay carried on: *In my twenty-odd years in politics, Dermott, I've never heard of or felt the influence of Steven Levesque. If you know something I don't know, please tell me.*

O'Sullivan smiled, his wry smile this time: *His companies are among the biggest donors to your party in all States, his former partner is the Attorney-General, the Premier of Victoria is said not to choose a tie without consulting him. And you know nothing of his influence, Mr Maclay?*

Maclay: *Dermott, whether you give the party five bob or fifty thousand dollars, you buy exactly the same amount of influence. Nil.*

O'Sullivan: *So the fact that Fincham Air last year won the coastal surveillance contracts for Northern Queensland and the Northern Territory owes nothing to Mr Levesque's relationship with your party?*

Maclay, frowning: *What are you getting at, Dermott?*

O'Sullivan: *Fincham Air is partly owned by a company called CrossTrice Holdings. And one of CrossTrice's directors is Lionel Carson, formerly a partner of Mr Levesque's in TransQuik Australia.*

Maclay: *So?*

O'Sullivan: *CrossTrice also owns a quarter of Consolidated Freight Holdings, TransQuik Australia's owner.*

Maclay: *You're being irresponsible, Dermott. And silly. My understanding is that Steven Levesque no longer has any active involvement with CFH or TransQuik Australia. But even if he did, what has he to do with Fincham Air winning a government contract?*

O'Sullivan assumed the look of a person holding four kings.

Are you aware, Minister, that a Brisbane newspaper will tomorrow publish a story saying that a former employee of Fincham says she saw photocopies of the other tenders for the contract before Fincham submitted its bid? And that she heard an executive of the company say, 'Steven says increase the flight frequency and go in a million under CattonAir.' She says she understood 'Steven' to refer to Steven Levesque.

Maclay's expression was bland, the look of a person who has dealt himself four aces.

I think you'll find, Dermott, that the newspaper will not be publishing that allegation tomorrow. I understand the person concerned now says she was misrepresented and the journalist involved has apologised to Fincham. But I don't want to be drawn into this sort of nonsense. And, Dermott, for your own legal wellbeing, I don't think you want to propagate defamatory material of this kind.

The ambush had failed: blanks in the magazine. O'Sullivan was unnerved by Maclay's display of superior knowledge and the interview fizzled out.

I found Barry's slip of paper, picked up the phone and dialled inquiries. 'Canberra,' I said. 'A Dean Canetti. I don't have a home address.'

A woman answered the phone, tired voice, young children in the background.

'Is that the home of Dean Canetti of MarketAsia Consultants?'

'Yes.'

'Is Mr Canetti available?'

Silence. In the background, a girl shrieked, 'Mum, she's pushing me again.'

'No,' said the woman.

'Go where?' said Shane DiSanto, former panelbeater, now operator of Veneto Travel.

'Canberra, Shane. The nation's capital. Heard of it?'

'Jack, no. Nothing there. Like a farm. No nightlife, nothing. Brown shoes with big rubber soles, that's what the men wear. The women all got their hair in buns. Listen, whaddabout a week in Bali? This package you won't believe, not a cent in it for anyone.'

'This is business, Shane. Today, this morning, coming back this evening. Is Denise around?'

'I dunno,' Shane said. 'Business, business. Nobody takes a holiday. Business? You want business class?'

'Economy. I'm paying.'

He dropped his voice. 'Listen, Jack. Fifty bucks cash I get you an upgrade from economy. Both ways.'

Shane had been a bit rough on Canberra, although his capsule description of the city's life and people was not without some basis in fact.

Canberra is a nice place to pass over on the way to Sydney. Even on the ground, the massive amounts spent on freeways enable taxpayers to pass through the capital at high speed. And massive spending on itself is what Canberra does best. This one city is the most expensive and longest running job-creation project in human history.

These thoughts came to me as I made my way to the top of the most recent employment-generator, the new

Parliament of Australia, formerly a rather nice hilltop. Following the design of American architects, an army of workers removed the hilltop and spent years replacing it with a neo-Aztec pyramid of sacrifice. A pyramid with its top lopped off and replaced by a triangular flagpole.

But I'd underestimated the appeal of the structure. The huge spaces were full of tourists. Coachloads of elderly people, eyes glazed, were being sheepdogged by hard-voiced tour guides when all they wanted to do was sit for a minute, rest the legs, think how nice it would be to be home with a book. Scrums of children moved around, girls bored, whispering to each other, boys yelping, pinching and punching. Japanese were eyeing the place uncertainly, like men who think they may be in the women's toilet.

It was a relief to get to the top, out into the weak sunshine, the biting little wind. I was tired, furry-mouthed. Opening the second bottle of Heathcote shiraz was now a matter for regret.

I went out on the flat top, on to the mountain meadow on concrete, looked down on the Disneyland lake. Off to the right, trophy buildings represented Art, Justice, Science. But the eye was drawn across the shining water, up another slope to a monumental building, the memorial to Australia's part in wars for Britain and America. The great place of the killing: honour the dead, believe in the glory, keep sending the children.

I felt for the pulse of patriotism. Two Irish were listed as dying for their country on the slate they were running in the war temple across the water. All I felt was a sense of waste. That and a recidivist desire for a cigarette.

Meryl Canetti was in her mid-thirties, jeans and a jacket, medium-height, thin, pale hair cut close to the head, memories of freckles around her nose. Smoking a cigarette, pressing it to her lips, hissing out smoke, looking around jerkily like a bird. When the cigarette came away from her mouth, her left hand went up to her eyes, nervous eyes, to her ears, to her hair, touching. She'd been a pretty teenager, attractive in her twenties, could be again if the feeling of panic ever went away.

She saw me coming, two quick puffs, dropped the cigarette, ground it, looked pointedly at the copy of the *Age* I was carrying.

'Mrs Canetti?'

Sharp nod, sniff.

'Let's find somewhere to sit.'

There was a cafeteria, not crowded. I fetched tea, watched her looking around, shifting in her seat like a child.

'I don't know a lot,' I said, sitting down. 'What's Market-Asia Consultants?'

'Import–export,' she said. Bitten-down nails. Thin lines, cracks, ran down from the corners of her mouth. 'I thought. Now I don't know. Believe that? Married for eight years. Two kids.'

'He went off to work every day?'

'Yes. Office in Manuka.'

'You don't know exactly what kind of work?'

She didn't answer the question.

'How can you just be missing?' she said.

The medication was only just keeping the lid on. She took a sip of tea, choked, coughed. Her eyelashes were short, almost invisible. I waited, drank some of mine.

'You said men came to tell you. When was that?'

'Eighteenth of April.'

'Did they tell you where your husband was when he went missing?'

'No. But I know where he was. Melbourne.'

'How do you know that?'

'The phone. Shows the caller's number.'

'He phoned you from Melbourne. When was that?'

'Charlotte's birthday. Third of April. She's the first. Mad about her, couldn't miss her birthday. Princess Charlotte he called her.'

She hung her head, shivered. 'Jesus, why can't you smoke in these places? Never been here. Watched the whole bloody thing go up. Waste of money.'

'How long had he been away?'

She bit at a nail on her right hand, checked herself, put both hands on the table. On the little finger, she wore a big ring, a greenish stone, oval, set in gold. 'When he phoned? About a week. Bit more. He went away a lot once, but not recently. Once it was five months, he came home five or six days in all that time. I used to go mad. After I had Lorna, she was, oh, a year old, he was gone for three months. Then we went to Noosa for six weeks. Unit on the beach, hire car, ate in restaurants all the time, three times a day some days. Everything. Lovely. You just forget. Till he goes away again.'

'But you don't know what he was doing when he went away?'

'Sometimes he said it was secret work. For the government. He speaks Thai and Vietnamese and Mandarin. That's a kind of Chinese. His mother was half-Thai. Never met her. Never met anyone in his family.'

I looked around. Secret work for the government.

Parliament House. This was an excellent spot to be discussing someone who did secret work for the government.

'Any idea what kind of secret work?'

Helpless look. Shake of the head.

'And he didn't tell you where he was going this time?'

Shake.

'Or how long he'd be away?'

Shake.

This was fishing without a hook.

'The men who came to tell you. Who were they? Police?'

'Didn't say. You don't ask, do you? Said Dean might have had an accident. That he was doing secret work…'

'For the government?'

She shrugged. 'Didn't say that. Can we go out? I need a smoke.'

We went out and found a smoking spot, in the wind, evidence vanishing as it left her mouth.

'They said I couldn't tell anyone about it.' Deep draw, expulsion, instant disintegration of smoke. 'They said we'd be taken care of. Mortgage paid out. All that. But I couldn't tell anyone.'

She had two more quick, shallow draws, threw the cigarette away, leaned towards me, took my left hand in both of hers, long fingers, squeezed. Eyes on mine, pale blue eyes. 'I thought, just forget Dean? That's what they want. Sorry, Dean's missing. End of story. Here's some money. Don't tell anyone. Sorry about the girls. I thought, fucking hell, do they think I can buy another Daddy for the girls? One day, they're grown up, and all they know is their Daddy went away and never came back.'

The end of the day was in the wind, a cold end. I looked out over the city. Designed by Americans, the city and its citadel. Built from scratch. Our Brasília.

'When Dean rang from Melbourne, did he give you any idea of what he was doing? Anything at all?'

She made a helpless shoulder movement, looked away. 'I shouted at him, started crying. I'd had it, it was all too bloody much. Birthday party, no-one to help me. Then Lorna, the little one, they're all rushing around, she fell and hit her head against one of Dean's bloody garden boulders, I never wanted the ugly things. He wanted these rocks, I couldn't see the point. Little girl lying there, not making a sound, blood pouring out of her head. I thought she was dead…'

She let go of my hand.

'Anyway, when he rang, it was after eleven that night, the girls were asleep, I wasn't going to wake them, just went ballistic, how can bloody work be so important that a father can't be at home for his little girl's birthday? Said that sort of thing. I mean, can you blame me?'

This was possibly therapeutic for Meryl but it wasn't helping me. The view was palling, too.

She fired up another cigarette. 'So, he said, Dean said, listen, pull yourself together, I'm not having a holiday here. He was cross. Really cross. Shouting. Never like that. Never.' Tossed her head.

Silence. I could feel her shivering.

'Christ, it gets cold. Then it's hot. Never felt well since the day I came here. Never. Hate the place.'

She shook her head, scratched her face. Chemical relief was needed. She turned to me, tears down her face, put out a hand, put it on my chest, on my heart, leaned her head. 'Love him so much,' she said. 'I just couldn't cope. Stupid, weak person.'

I put my right hand over hers, pressed it. 'No,' I said. 'You're a strong, brave person. What was he shouting?'

'He said, he'd been drinking, I can always tell, he said, "Two more days with this bastard Connors and I'm home and fucking Black Tide's over."'

'The name. Connors. You sure?'

'Yes.' Sniff. She sat back. 'Connors. That's what he said. This bastard Connors.'

'The other thing. Black Tide? Is that it?'

'Yes. Black Tide.'

'You knew what that was?'

'No.' Sniff. 'Well, knew the name, didn't know what.'

I waited.

Sniff. 'We went to a barbie at the Conroys'. Friends, well, Tony's a friend of Dean's. She says she can't talk to me any more.'

'Who?'

'Deirdre, Tony's wife. I rang her after they came to tell me.' She looked around, distracted.

Prompt: 'And at the barbie…'

'Tony said to Dean…They were doing the meat. I came out with beers and I heard Tony say, Black Tide's running again. So I asked Dean on the way home, what's Black Tide? A horse? And he said, forget you heard it. Don't ever mention it to anyone.'

She put a hand to her hair, stood up. 'Stuck in my mind. Black Tide. S'pose I shouldn't mention it to you. What the hell does it matter now? Got to go. Kids.'

I stood up. There was an intimacy between us. She came closer. 'He's everything,' she said. She touched her head to my chest. I put my lips to her pale hair, sweet-smelling, my hands on her shoulders. Total strangers on a former hilltop.

'Listen, Meryl,' I said. 'I'll try to find out about Dean. Don't sign anything, don't accept any offers these people make. I'll get a lawyer to ring you.'

She said, muffled, 'Aren't lawyers all crooks?'

I crossed my fingers. 'That's a myth,' I said.

Meryl gathered herself. She took something out of the top pocket of her jacket and offered it to me. It was a photograph of a man with a child on his shoulders.

'Dean,' she said. At the door, she looked back, raised a hand, feigned a smile. I raised a fist, felt stupid immediately. It was a symbol of strength, solidarity, hope. What did I know of strength, solidarity and hope?

I waited a while, went back inside, wandered around to the lifts. When one came, I politely allowed everyone in, decided to take the stairs. Caught another lift on the next floor. Getting into a cab, outside the front entrance, I looked back. The only person looking my way was a tall man in a grey suit, convict haircut, bony face. He was moving, bringing dark glasses up to his face. And then he found them uncomfortable, stopped to adjust the fit.

Could be nothing. Could be otherwise.

More than two hours to kill. I got dropped in the city centre, or that's what the man said it was, walked around, found a bookshop, bought a promising-sounding novel called *In the Emptiness of Time*, found a cafe, drank coffee, reasonable coffee. I saw many men in rubber-soled brown shoes, spotted a number of women with buns: insufficient evidence to back up Shane DiSanto's generalisation but certainly a worrying incidence. Enough to justify a large university research grant.

I didn't see the bony-faced man in the grey suit. But not for want of looking.

And still I was early for the plane. In the tawdry bar, I asked for a beer with half a shot of lime.

'Dynamite combination,' said the barman. He was young and pale, long nose, sleek fair hair, very likely a final-year student at the local university, cultural studies student perhaps, deconstructing our encounter.

'Beer cocktail. What kind of glass? Martini glass?' He had a look, a smart amused look.

Bartending was clearly a fun experience out here at Canberra airport. Low-level politicians. Public servants. Assorted jovial political parasites. Polite people. No hard-core drunks, no unpredictable people to take offence at your smile, throw a full ashtray at you, climb over the counter, get you in a headlock and try to drown you in the drip tray. Around here bartending was just a source of income and good party stories. About how you said all these smart things to this old fart who wanted a beer with lime.

Beer with fucking lime. I ask you.

These thoughts came to me while looking at the person. I was tired. I didn't say anything, just looked at him. He looked back, smiled another kind of smile, looked away. After a while, even the young and smart and playful recognise men at the edge of endurance.

'Coming up, sir,' he said.

Planes are good for thinking. Reading seems an unnaturally complacent activity when you are risking your life in a hissing aluminium tube that seeks to defy gravity. I studied the picture of Dean and his daughter. He wore rings on both little fingers, small rings with dark stones. He didn't look like someone who did secret government work, away for months at a time. He looked like a man who repaired things, washing machines, fridges, photocopiers perhaps. Went home at night, Holden in the drive at 6.30.

Two more days with this bastard Connors and I'm home and fucking Black Tide's over.

Dean Canetti was keeping an eye on Gary Connors on April 3. And he planned to spend two more days involved with him.

What did *with* Connors mean? Following him? Something else?

Two *more* days. Did that mean he'd been close to Gary for longer than the day of April 3? Gary had been overseas until April 2. He'd been away from home for more than a week when he telephoned on April 3. Had Canetti followed him overseas?

Canetti was from the government. But not the shopfront government. The hidden government. Gary was from somewhere else: corrupt policeman, then TransQuik, then a person consulted on security by impenetrable foreign companies, including Klostermann Gardier. But still a TransQuik person, according to Barry Tregear, a man not given to conjecture.

Canetti, the man from the government, and Gary Connors, the man from free enterprise, almost certainly bent free enterprise, came together. Presumably, the former was in pursuit of the latter. And then they vanished. On the same day.

Barry Tregear didn't move in the world of high finance. He moved in a low-finance world where making money generally involved taking it away from someone else. If Barry believed that TransQuik could make it snow in the tropics on a given day, it meant that smart cops knew not to mess with TransQuik.

Smart cops didn't mess with TransQuik. And the Director of Public Prosecutions didn't mess with TransQuik.

That was a status jump.

Did this mean that no-one messed with the assured and handsome Steven Levesque, multi-millionaire owner of a Sydney towerblock and of companies with exotic hideaways where Premiers relaxed? A man who was a major donor to a political party. And a man whose exalted name was invoked by a lowly female employee of a company that won a coastal surveillance contract. Invoked and smartly revoked.

Klostermann Gardier, acting for other interests, acting as a conduit, tried to buy part of TransQuik.

The bid failed because a journalist called Stuart Wardle gave Tony Rinaldi a question to ask. And Klostermann's agent, Carlos Siebold, found the question so offensive that he showed TransQuik's executives the door.

Steven Levesque bought TransQuik after Klostermann Gardier's bid for a big chunk was abandoned.

Tony Rinaldi said something.

Klostermann Gardier don't give up.

I, on the other hand, do. You can juggle bits of information for just so long. I asked a long-faced female steward for a whisky and soda. She smiled and went on her way.

At home, weary in the bone marrow, I got the whisky and soda, had two, went to bed. I fell asleep thinking about the $60,000 Gary had taken out of his father's bank account. It was a lot of cash to carry around. Was he paying someone off?

Dean Canetti?

The cast in my dream included my landlady, Charlie, Stan from the Prince, all in some rural setting. We were standing in a paddock, planning something, arguing. A rural setting with prolonged ringing. The ringing finally woke me.

'Early for you?'

Cam, a woman singing in the background, high voice, plaintive Mexican-sounding song. Recorded? The singer tried a phrase again, better this time. Haunting. Definitely not recorded.

'Anything that wakes me is too early for me,' I said.

'Two things. A bloke we should talk to on Sunday. That's late a.m. Free?' Cam didn't give away much on the phone. An example I had learned nothing from.

'Yes. I'll be at Taub's.'

'Pick you up 11.45. Second, my cousin's birthday party. You might like to come.'

'When's that?'

'June the second. Small affair. Don't get dressed up.'

'I'll put it in my diary.'

I showered, put on work clothes, set out for breakfast. At 7.10 a.m., the pavements of Brunswick Street were quiet. Everything else in the street had changed but 7.10 a.m. was still much the same. Only a few people on foot, even numbers of the purposeful and the Where-the-fuck-am-I.

The difference was that the latter seemed younger, paler and sicker these days, courtesy of waves of cheap smack. Cheap only a few times. Once-in-a-lifetime bargains.

I parked outside the newsagent, bought the *Age* and lugged it down the street to Meaker's. Sharon the actor came to take my order. She had the frozen-faced look of someone better suited to the three-to-ten shift.

'No conversation,' she said. 'Please.'

Grilled ham. Grilled tomato. Toast. Mustard. Long, strong black.

Enzio himself came out with my order. The cook: short, swarthy, balding, unhappy.

'This is an honour, maestro,' I said.

He put the plate down. 'Got a job in Daylesford. Gettin out of here.' He scratched his beard stubble.

Enzio began making announcements like this as soon as winter set in. Usually, he was off to warmer climes: Cairns, Broome, Vanuatu. I looked at the plate. He'd been generous, no portion control here.

'Back to the kitchen,' I said. 'We'll have a word later.'

He left. While I ate, I went through the paper looking for a mention of Steven Levesque. When I'd finished, I paid at the counter and stuck my head into the kitchen.

'Daylesford,' I said. 'Pretty. Gets cold, though. Sure this is a good move?'

'No respect here,' he said, stirring scrambled eggs with his left hand while using a delicate wristy action with his right to keep an omelette in motion. 'Bloody cook. Just a bloody cook.'

'Enzio, how can you talk about respect? Respect is for

ordinary chefs. You're beyond respect. Your customers won't let you go.'

A laugh-cough, a suspicious look out of narrowed blood-shot eyes. 'You hear this bullshit where?'

'Where? Everywhere. I meet a customer, that's what I hear. Enzio. That's what we talk about. Know something?'

Pink eyes shifted to me again, hands in ceaseless motion.

'People don't call this place Meaker's.'

Eyebrows up a fraction.

'The regulars, they call it Enzio's. Know that?'

He shrugged, took the pans off the heat. 'Hah. How come I only hear this when I'm leavin?'

I sighed. 'Enzio, people get used to brilliance. Take it for granted. I'm guilty. We're all guilty. From now on, I'm going to make sure you hear what the customers think.'

Enzio grunted. 'Think about it some more. Maybe.'

I patted him on the arm. It takes work to prevent the painstakingly woven fabric of your life from returning to its natural state of short bits of unconnected thread.

At Taub's, I started on the carcass of the western wall of Mrs Purbrick's library. Today, most cabinets are made of medium-density fibreboard, dressed up with veneers and the odd piece of solid timber. Charlie pretended not to know of the existence of MDF. A Taub cabinet began with a carcass of forty-year-old European ash. To that was attached a frame-and-panel exterior of timber chosen from The Bank. Taub panels floated in their frames: no glue. Joints, interior and exterior, were mortice and tenon or dovetail, all handcut.

Today, we had the ripping of the ash. Charlie had put out the wood, left me a list of dimensions on a strip torn from the edge of Tuesday's *Age*.

In ripping long lengths of bone-dry hardwood, there's an element of danger. The machine's purpose is to cut cleanly to precise dimensions. But to do that the timber must be forced into a sharp-toothed steel disc going at great speed the other way. The disc is unwelcoming, wants to reject anything coming at it. And, in the process of partition, one piece of timber must pass between the vicious blade and a machined-steel wall. The tolerance is minute. No guarantees of operator safety are available. Jamming is not uncommon. Pieces of wood have pierced throats, impaled people five metres away, men, usually men, pinned through the solar plexus like butterflies. Eternal vigilance is all: smooth feed, constant pressure against the fence, listen and feel for vibration and chatter.

Tiring work but relief from the ceaseless ramblings of the mind, the endless tongue-probing of tender places, of crevices harbouring decaying matter.

I was stacking the last three-metre length, helmet off, feeling the tension leaving my neck and back, when the doorbell rang. Charlie wasn't a great responder to the doorbell. The doorbell often triggered a need to explore the farther reaches of the enterprise. The more rings, the farther the reaches.

But Charlie wasn't here. This was bowls morning. Charlie was having breakfast at home, thinking about the humiliation he planned to inflict on certain junior members of the Brunswick Lawn Bowling Club.

I went to the door, sawdust on my face, in my hair, clinging to me like a garment. A tall woman in her late twenties, early thirties, short dark hair, masculine haircut from the fifties, tweedy jacket and flannels. The man was a little older, round glasses, jacket and tie.

183

'Mr Jack Irish?' The woman.

'Yes.'

'Sorry to bother you at work.' She had TV commercial teeth, black Smartie eyes. There was a tiny male cleft in her pale chin, impression of a fingernail in pastry.

Something told me not to smile back. These were not seekers after classic cabinetmaking. 'You haven't bothered me yet.'

They glanced.

'Come in?' asked the male, smiling. His eyes were tired, and fractionally too close together.

'Not open,' I said.

Their eyes met again. She said, 'Mr Irish, it's about Meryl Canetti. We're worried that you won't have the full context.'

I said, 'We. We are who?'

'We work for the Federal government.'

I said, 'Outside.' They backed off, onto the narrow pitted pavement, stood apart. Empty street, above us Melbourne's dirty-dishcloth sky. A grey car was blocking McCoy's exit.

'Let's see the ID.'

The man produced a flat leather wallet, flipped it open, handed it over. Photograph, seal of the Commonwealth of Australia. No name, just a line saying: *This serves to identify the holder as an employee of the Commonwealth of Australia.*

It gave a Canberra number to ring for verification.

'This is useful identification,' I said. 'What are you, clerks in the Department of Agriculture? Maybe you're in Weights and Measures. Work the scale, run the tape over things.' I handed the wallet back. 'And the phone number, that's useful too. Self-fulfilling prophecy.'

The man said, 'Can we go inside? Little public out here.'

They followed me in. I leant against a clamping bench.

'Anywhere to sit down?' said the man. His fair hair was combed sideways, little widow's peak, touch of grey at the temples. He could pass for a Uniting Church minister. Probably was on the side.

'This is a workshop,' I said. 'Generally, we work standing.'

He looked around, shrugged. 'Fine.' He seemed to be making an effort. 'I have to ask you not to repeat to anyone what I tell you or even that we have spoken to you. I'll be brief. Meryl Canetti isn't a well person.'

'How do you come to associate me with Meryl Canetti? Whoever she is.'

Smoothing of the hair, nod, understanding smile.

'Meryl's been under surveillance,' he said. 'For her own protection. You've been talking to her. We're trying to do the best for Meryl and her family.'

I didn't say anything.

'Mr Irish, Meryl's husband does important work, highly confidential work. Sometimes he has to be away for long periods. Meryl has difficulty coping with this, she's prone to fantasies, has depressions, mildly manic states.'

His expression asked me to show understanding, to nod. I didn't accede to the request.

'Another problem is that she won't stay on her medication for any length of time. After a lot of agonising...'

Pause.

'I'm sure you'll understand how difficult these things are. Her husband recently told Meryl that he couldn't continue with the marriage. This triggered something and she's taken to telling weird stories. Sometimes Dean's missing, sometimes he's dead. What is worrying to us is that some very strange people are encouraging her.' Pause. 'Follow so far?'

'Who do you usually tell stories to? Sheep?'

185

He looked down, gesture of contrition, flashed pink palms chest high. 'Sorry. Sorry. No insult intended. I'm concerned to avoid misunderstandings.'

'You're saying Mrs Canetti is deluded and that she was not told that her husband was missing. That right?'

The woman nodded. 'Right. Exactly.'

The man looked down, scratched his forehead above the left eye. 'Mr Irish, the reality is that Meryl Canetti may end up being institutionalised. We hope not. Another concern is that she and the people urging her on will make it impossible for Dean to carry on his work. Believe me, it's important work.'

'What is the work?'

'If I could tell you that, I would,' he said. 'And then I wouldn't have to do any more to convince you.'

After you've listened to hundreds of people buffing up their lies with bits of truth, you come to notice things: tension in the shoulders, quick blinks, taut tendons in the neck, a certain budgie-like movement of the head, tendency of the hands to comfort the mouth, the nose, the ears, even the teeth.

All I saw in this man was tiredness.

'This visit's got a point, has it?' I asked.

The man put his hands in his pockets. 'We wanted to make sure you knew what's been going on, that's all,' he said. 'You understand, this is a bad time for Dean. He should have sought help sooner but he's only human. May I ask you a question?'

I nodded.

'Would you mind telling us exactly what your interest is in Dean Canetti?'

'I don't have any interest in him. My interest is in finding Gary Connors. I take it Gary's known to you?'

He shook his head. 'No. I don't know the name. What's this person's connection with Dean Canetti?'

'He was following Gary on April 3.'

He frowned. 'Sure of that?'

'As I can be.'

He nodded, took out a wallet, extracted a card, offered it. 'The Federal Government values your co-operation,' he said.

Card with a telephone number, nothing else.

'We'd appreciate it if you'd talk to us first if you're concerned about anything to do with the Canettis. Tell the operator it's a Section Sixteen matter.'

'Section Sixteen?'

'That's right.' He held out his right hand, thumb up, tilted to the right. The open, honest, unaggressive way of inviting a handshake.

I shook it, a surprisingly hard hand, a hand that knew labour. The woman didn't put out a hand. She moved her mouth into the smile position. Man shakes, woman smiles. Would that be in the manual?

I followed them to the door. They were walking towards their car when the man looked over his shoulder, turned and came back.

'Jack,' he said, 'piece of no-bullshit advice. You don't want to be involved in anything to do with Dean Canetti. At the very least, it'll be a serious embarrassment. Could be much, much worse than that. I can't say more. Wish I could.'

I watched them go, woman driving.

Friday night. In the beginning, Linda flew back every Friday night. The anticipation started around Tuesday. One Friday night, at the front door, she stripped to her bra and pants, filmy black bra, tiny black pants, long legs, athlete's legs, ending in high heels. When I opened it, she said, 'Hi, I'm the flying fuck no-one gives. Except me.'

Not the time to dwell on the past. I poured a glass of Mill Hill chardonnay from Smeaton and rang Drew's office.

'Hanging around late?' I said. 'Cooling off from exertions in the mines of justice?'

'As we speak,' said Drew, 'deodorant is being applied to all hollows, cavities and deltas. To expunge the odours that adorn champions of the oppressed. Although I might add that some find them hugely stimulating.'

'Talking to one on the phone,' I said, 'I'm perfectly happy with an image of a solicitor behind a desk, finger marking the place in some legal tome. Resting on the vital precedent, perhaps.'

'Before the night's done,' said Drew, 'my sensitive fingers may well have tested a vital precedent or two. Although I hasten to add that I don't set out with ambitions of precedent-testing. Not at all. More an exchange of pleadings.'

'Close encounter of the fourth kind?'

'Indeed. With what I gather is called a babe.'

'The word is banned. Recent third encounter, would that be?'

'In Georges yesterday. Stunning creature in black. We fell

to talking about the coincidence of both ordering portions of smoked eel.'

'Goes beyond coincidence. Weird. Four first choices and you both go for the eel. I'd be frightened. Want to come to the footy tomorrow?'

He sighed. 'Going on with this madness, are you? How can I go to the footy when I don't give a shit who wins? I don't have that love-to-see-a-great-game, don't-care-who-wins mentality. That's all absolute bullshit.'

'Come.'

Pause. 'Christ, I don't know, I may not have got out of bed by then. Could be in a love knot. Where?'

'Waverley.'

'Settles the matter. Another time perhaps.'

'Sure?'

'Waverley? That's love. You go to Waverley because you love your team. Out there, in the wind and the rain, two sides you don't give a continental shit about? I give you an unequivocal sure, Your Honour.'

'So. Live a pointless life. Enjoy it. She's probably a hooker. Lots of hookers do lunch at Georges. Saw you coming. Is she tanned? Don't take her on a shopping trip.'

Instant of hesitation. 'You shit. Poison any well, wouldn't you? How's your personal life?'

'If a champion of justice changes his mind,' I said, 'the convoy leaves the Prince around 12.15.'

'Properly speaking,' said Drew, 'one old Studebaker Lark full of geriatrics isn't a convoy.'

'Fleet of memories.'

Comfort food, I needed comfort food. Eggs. I had eggs. Farm eggs, home-delivered in the heart of the inner city. The little old lady down the street sold me half a dozen a week, complete with authentic-looking substances stuck to the shells. She got them from her granddaughter, who was battling on a small farm on the way to the snow. That was the story. I liked it, paid six months in advance and she left them in my mailbox every Thursday.

An omelette, a simple cheese omelette, made with Parmesan melted in a little white wine. If I had any Parmesan left. Yes, rock hard and sweaty but otherwise in reasonable condition. Would that that could be said of me.

The phone rang. Simone Bendsten.

'Some progress,' she said.

'I might step around.'

Now she was dressed for business: cream high-necked blouse, black linen trousers. I sat in the same chair.

'Drink?' She pointed at an open bottle of red wine on the kitchen counter. I nodded, watched her go. Even in low heels, she had an unusual leg-torso ratio for a small person.

She came back with two long-stemmed glasses, gave me one, fetched a big wirebound notebook, sat down opposite me.

'Carlos Siebold,' she said.

'Yes.'

'Well, I turned up a Carlos. There's an outfit in Washington called the Richard Nixon Institute for Truth in Government.'

'Very droll.'

'Yes. Joke name but they're serious. Monitor the US Congress, the Washington bureaucracy. Huge database, most of it stuff on the public record, some definitely not. Some from really obscure sources. Carlos Siebold comes up in the hearings of the US Senate Foreign Relations

Subcommittee on the International Narcotics Trade in 1989. A witness says he was with a Filipino called Fidel Ricarte, he calls him a President Marcos crony, and he says, I quote: "Fidel said the money should go through Carlos Siebold in Luxembourg because the President trusts him." '

It crossed my mind, not for the first time, that the pursuit of Gary Connors was getting completely out of hand. 'What money is he talking about?' I said.

'Marcos's cut of profits from drugs being exported through Manila International Airport and Clark Air Base. The US air base.'

'Right.' Out of hand was putting it mildly.

'A Carlos Siebold also shows up in the London *Sunday Times* database,' she said. 'In a story on the arms trade written in 1990. The writers say a Tamil Tiger agent said under interrogation...'

'They were interrogating him?' I said. 'Tie him to the footrail in some Fleet Street pub. Flog him with sodden bar towels. Is that ethical for journos?'

She allowed me a smile. Somewhere between a polite smile and an amused smile. Self-contained person, Ms Bendsten. 'They don't say who was doing the dirty work. Only that the man said he negotiated with a Carlos Siebold in a hotel in Zurich to buy Russian-made weapons. The writers spoke to the office of a Carlos Siebold in Hamburg. An associate said Mr Siebold was a commercial lawyer with no links to arms dealings of any kind.'

'That's it?'

'For now. Plenty of other places to look. Then I did Major-General Ibell.' She looked at her notes. 'US Marine, active service in Vietnam, served on the staff of General Edwin F. Black, head of the US military in Thailand. Later on the staffs of the National Security Council and the Joint Chiefs of Staff. Military career seems to end in the mid-1970s. I found a Nixon Institute reference to him as president of a company called Secure International with offices in Washington, Hamburg, Hong Kong, Manila, Teheran and Sydney.'

'And the other bloke?'

'Winter, Charles deForest. One reference so far. Story on the CIA in the *Washington Post* in 1986. He's listed as one of about twelve high-ranking CIA officers purged in 1978 by the Carter government's new head of the CIA, Admiral Stansfield Turner. Winter's described as a covert operations specialist involved in CIA operations in the Philippines and Iran.'

None of this could possibly connect with Gary Connors.

'Want me to go on?' Simone said. 'It hasn't cost much so far.'

I didn't really but I couldn't bring myself to say so. 'Yes,' I said. 'See what you can do. And can you look for any reference to something called Black Tide. Australian reference.'

She wrote it down. We made some small talk, I said my thanks and went home down the dark streets, party sounds here and there, rain like mist around the streetlights, oilslick rainbows on the tarmac.

I made my omelette, ate it in front of the television, went to bed with my duelling book. As I drifted off, I was thinking that what I really wanted to do was write out a cheque for $60,000 payable to Des, bugger Gary and Dean and everyone else.

End of matter.

The youth club were looking more cheerful than I'd seen them at any time since the Fitzroy Football Club went tropical. After a small scuffle, Norm O'Neill won the front passenger seat. Argument about the day's racing at Caulfield resumed.

'Blind some people,' said Wilbur Ong from the back. 'Can't see the elephant till it farts. Clarrie Kendall is Croft's brother-in-law. This horse of Croft's turns up in three of the last four Kendall's got nags in. What's his job? His bloody job's to see Kendall's ponies get a run. And you keep backin the thing. Just a bloody donor, that's what you are.'

'Typical,' said Norm O'Neill, adjusting the fit of his flat cap. 'Always lookin in the wrong place for the answer. That's your problem, Wilbur, always has bin, always will be. Now take that horse Dunedin Star…'

'Christ,' said Eric Tanner. 'Bloody Dunedin Star. Bloody Dunedin Star again, I'm jumpin out of this vehicle.'

'Ten minutes to the TAB stop, men,' I said. 'I suggest you concentrate on your selections. And don't worry about the second.'

June the second. Birthday of Cam's cousin. The horse was running at Caulfield. On its record, there was no reason to believe the animal would earn its training bill today.

'Got somethin?' said Wilbur. 'Hot, is it?'

'Smouldering,' I said. Passing on tips is dangerous. On the other hand, I'd had three tips from Cam in four years. Record: 3–0.

Outside the TAB, I said. 'Fly Tonight, number six in the second. All care. No responsibility.'

Nodding vigorously, Norm led the charge.

Back on the road inside ten minutes. No-one had anything on the first race. We were closing in on the unhallowed ground when they came out of the gate for the second. Silence in the car. Eleven horses, twelve hundred metres.

Fly Tonight didn't put any strain on the pre-war hearts, led from start to finish, won by two-and-a-half lengths.

The exultation was deafening. When they'd finished patting me on the shoulders, Norm said, 'Know somethin, Jack, me boy. Had an eye on that horse meself.'

'Christ, no,' said Eric. 'Not another Dunedin Star.'

Waverley Park, gale blowing the rain horizontally towards the scoreboard end. It wasn't a day for pretty football. We found a spot on the edge of the big crowd of Saints supporters. Not quite with them, definitely not with the other lot. Geelong kicked two early goals against the wind. The Saints dawdled around a bit, then started kicking goals. The youth club made no comment until the sixth one without reply.

'Bloody handbags,' said Norm. He raised his voice slightly. 'Stick it up em, Sainters.'

'Go Saints,' said Wilbur, mildly.

'Much improved side,' said Eric in the measured manner of a judge.

The Lark conveyed home a wet but content foursome. The Saints three-goal winners. Spirits were further improved by a stop at a TAB to pick up the winnings.

'Jesus, Jack,' said Eric, 'they give you the money with a spade. What'd ya have on it?'

'The farm,' I said. 'Story of my life.'

We had a few beers at the Prince, talked about the game, no major disagreements. The loyalty transplant couldn't be declared a success until the youth club began making judgments about St Kilda players, tactics, the coach, the umpires, club management, the quality of the opposition, and which teams the Saints should hate most.

Stan came over, back to his normal state of grump, not the jovial Pickwickian publican this evening. 'Talked to my old bloke,' he said. 'Get no sense out of him. Won't sell. Gone out of his tree up there in the bloody sunshine.'

I said, 'Been out of that particular tree all the time I've known him.'

He put his elbows on the counter, leaned towards me. 'Jack, there'll never be a better offer for the bloody place. Talk to him, will you?'

I looked around at the patrons. Ten years would see off most of them. 'Let me think about it,' I said. 'Let me have a good long think.'

A ten-year think.

At home, sad, misty, loveless Saturday night, a chicken pie and two glasses of red took care of me.

One other table was occupied, by a fat man, about thirty or fifty, and a woman of the same size, possibly his daughter, possibly his wife. Or her mother. The man had made a wholehearted commitment to synthetics: styrofoam neck brace, polyester for shirt, jacket and trousers, brown nylon socks worn inside green plastic open-toed sandals. His companion was in a luminous purple tracksuit, huge white athletic shoes curling up at both ends, sweatbands on both wrists and a white headband on which one could just make out the puzzling words ILL TO WIN.

The pair looked hungry, hanging out for food, too hungry to converse, eyes flicking around, to us, to the duck-footed passers-by outside, to each other, disapproving, then back to the man frying flattened lumps of mince on the hotplate behind the counter. He had a thoughtful air, a sad-eyed middle-aged man who'd inherited his father's baldness and his wig, bought this dud Heavenly Hots franchise, six tables in the wrong part of a shopping palace in Doncaster, sellers probably now in a foreign country not legally obliged to return them. The man's faded wig, each hair once a lustrous strand in the scalp of a woman shorn like a sheep in some poverty-stricken Ukrainian village, had slipped back. It was now positioned several centimetres from the northern-most frown line, looking more like a jaunty hair hat than a hairpiece.

'Hoop's choice of venue,' said Cam, looking around with

interest. 'Paranoid. He lives in Hoppers Crossing, other side of the city. Fancy anything?'

'Tea might be safe,' I said. 'Just tea.'

Cam caught the proprietor's eye. 'What kind of tea you got?' he said.

'Tea?' said the man, looking happier. 'Tea? What kind of tea? Tea tea, that's what I've got. In little bags.'

'Two,' said Cam. 'Tea tea for two.'

Another customer came in, small man in a silky black tracksuit, neat dark hair, face of a dangerous schoolboy. Our jockey from the Kyneton race, Johnny Chernov. He went to the fridge, got a can of Coke, went to the counter, pointed at something sticky.

He sat down at the table next to us, adjusted his chair so that he was in right profile to Cam, took out a small mobile phone and put it on the table, popped his can.

'Been lookin at the video, Johnny,' said Cam. 'Don't like it at all.'

'What's it you don't like?' Chernov said. He took a swig of Coke.

'Don't like the way you got lost in the crowd at the turn.'

'So tell the stewards. Ride the fucking things yourself.'

The proprietor took the hamburgers over to the couple. 'Whaddabout the chips?' the woman said, licking her lips.

'Sauce,' said Synthetic Man. 'Need sauce.'

'Coming,' said the proprietor. 'Two hands, that's all I've got.'

Cam was studying Johnny Chernov's profile. 'Johnny,' he said, voice neutral, 'that's not a helpful attitude. I'm here on the owner's behalf givin you the opportunity to tell me why you lost a race. You can blame the horse, blame the track, blame anything.'

'Told the trainer,' said Chernov. 'I ride for trainers.'

'I heard what you told the trainer. That's why we're here.'

'Nothin to add,' said Chernov. He found a cigarette, lit it with a gold Dunhill lighter, blew smoke at the ceiling, took another swig at his can, put the cigarette in his mouth.

Cam looked at me, hint of a smile on his face. Then he put out a big hand, plucked the cigarette from Chernov's lips and inserted it into the can of Coke.

Hiss, puff of smoke out of the can.

'It's polite to ask, Johnny,' Cam said. 'Answer's yes, we do mind. Now I'm givin you another chance to tell us why you lost that race. Not what you told the trainer. Unhappy with your story, I'm comin out to the carpark with you, suspend you for a few races. Maybe fifty, maybe a hundred and fifty.'

Stony profile.

Cam put out his hand again, pinched the jockey's narrow chin between thumb and forefinger, brought his head around.

'People trusted you, Johnny. With their money. Tell us about why you deserve that trust.'

Chernov put his right hand on Cam's wrist, tried to break the grip on his chin, failed. 'Okay,' he said. 'Okay, okay.'

Cam took his hand away, leaving pale marks on Chernov's chin.

The proprietor arrived with a plastic plate holding a bun covered in what looked like pink candlewax. He put it down, went away and came back with two cups of watery tea.

When he'd gone, Chernov said, 'On the bend, the blokes in front, they slow the pace, these three come from behind, they sit on me, nowhere to go. The winner come over the top of us.'

Cam shook his head. 'No, Johnny, that's the same story. The vid shows different. The vid shows you had two chances to get out. That little Mundall, what'd he say to you, the bunch of you cruisin along there on the bend?'

Chernov said nothing, looked at his bun, made an impression in it with a long index finger, trimmed pink nail.

'We're done here,' Cam said. 'Don't think I'll risk this tea. Recycled teabags. What level you on, Johnny?'

'Could be dead tomorrow,' said Chernov. 'Jesus, dead tonight. Got a baby now.'

'That's medium- to long-term dead,' Cam said. 'I'm talkin short term.'

'Give you the money,' said Chernov. 'What you dropped. Cash.'

Cam said, leaning towards the man, 'Johnny, don't be silly. The money. We're not here about money.'

'You hear about Brent Chick?' said Chernov. 'Going for a run round that Aberfeldie Park in Essendon, near his place, got the kid with him. On his little bike. Car knocks Brent twenty metres, would've hit the boy too Brent hadn't pushed him. Miracle if he rides again. Right leg's broken, hip's broken, ribs cracked. Never catch the bloke. Car's stolen.'

'I read that,' Cam said.

'You read where Pat Moss's house burnt down? Middle of summer, no fires, no heatin on. Mystery fire. Lucky to get out, him and the wife. Just arm burns.'

'No,' said Cam, 'I never heard that.'

Chernov took out the cigarette packet, examined it, made to put it away.

'Smoke,' Cam said.

Chernov lit up, hissed smoke. 'There's others,' he said. 'Boys in the country, trainers, the battlers.'

Cam's eyes met mine.

I said to Chernov, 'You hear about Kevin Devine? Someone rammed his float?'

He nodded. 'He's one. There's others had trouble.'

'You want to give us a name?' said Cam.

Chernov looked down, shook his head. 'You gotta understand,' he said, looking up, straightening his shoulders. 'I'm on level three, you want to come up with me.'

Cam put out a hand and patted the small man on the arm. 'No call for that. We understand.'

'So what?' said Chernov. 'You want the dough?'

'No,' Cam said. 'What's gone's gone, Johnny. There'll be other times.'

Chernov stood up, sticky bun untouched. 'On my bike then,' he said and smiled an uncertain smile. 'Tea's on me.'

'Much obliged,' said Cam.

On the way back, on the Eastern Freeway in Cam's vehicle of the day, a gunmetal Brock Holden, he said, 'I'm runnin the data today. Spent a week polishin it. Sixteen hundred-odd country races, horses, form, jockeys, trainers, bloody hundreds of trainers, owners, even more owners, distance, weights, order of finish, sectional times, track rating, barriers, phases of the moon, anythin.'

'Looking for what?'

'Know when I find it. Like my cousin's party?'

'Very much. Best party for a while. Thanks for the invite.'

Cam put on a CD. A woman singing a Mexican-sounding song, the woman singing in the background when he'd given me the tip.

'Nice,' I said. 'Someone you know?'

He looked at me, ran his tongue over his excellent front teeth. 'Practises when she gets up in the morning,' he said. 'I may have to start runnin early.'

I could understand that.

Cam dropped me at the office. I had a lease to draw up for my client Laurence Baranek. Laurie was leasing a shop he owned in Sydney Road to his wife's cousin and he required a document that no tenant in his right mind would sign. In the course of drafting it, I fell to thinking about Simone's report on Major-General Gordon Ibell and Charles deFoster Winter. Senior US military man and senior US intelligence man.

Stuart Wardle suggested that Tony Rinaldi ask Siebold to explain the relationship between Klostermann, a Manila company called Arcaro Transport, and Ibell and deFoster Winter.

Stuart obviously knew the answer to the question. It might be inside his computer. I rang Eric, Wootton's computer geek. He was not a man to whom speech came easily. No doubt he babbled on all night as he surfed the chatrooms of the Net, but not otherwise. Yes, he had been to Lyall Cronin's house. Yes, he had taken away the computer. No, it had not yielded anything. Was there any chance that it would? Yes. Good chance? No.

'Well, keep me posted,' I said.

He didn't reply. Probably nodding.

I went home via St George's Road to pick up a Chinese take-away. The shop was empty. As always, Lester barked, 'How many?'

'One,' I said.

Today, he didn't just get on with the packing. He looked at me for a long time. Then he said, 'Jack? What happen to two?'

I sighed, 'Two went to Sydney. Didn't come back.'

He seemed to be relieved. 'Sydney,' he said, as if that provided a complete explanation. 'Yes. Be another two, Jack.'

'I might be at the end of my twos,' I said. 'You get just so many twos.'

Home. An A4 envelope in the letterbox from Bendsten Research. Linda on the answering machine. I switched off after her first word. Steel needed. Then I hit the button again, closed my eyes.

Jack, I should say this to you in person but I've got to say it now. I've been involved with someone else here. I didn't look for it, it just happened, a really stupid thing at work.

The ear-kissing.

It's over now. It was probably over before it began. Anyhow, listen, I had to tell you. I'm feeling a bit soiled. Soiled and stupid, so I'll keep away from you. Perhaps later…I don't know if you'll ever want to see me again. You could let me know about that. Whenever…whenever you like. Or not let me know.

Pause.

So. Well. That's it. My feelings…no, I'll just say goodbye. Goodbye.

I slumped in the chair. I'd known it was coming. Absolutely no doubt. You know. I'd been feeling sick about it for weeks. So why did I now feel even sicker? Love. Not a word for casual use. The life-scarred use the word with extreme caution. If you're lucky, you go through life held up by people loving you. But you don't know you're being held up. You think you're buoyant. You think the buoyancy came first, the love is a bonus you get for being buoyant. And that can go on for a long time. But then one day, the love isn't there any more and you're sinking, waving arms and sinking, all the old sources of love gone, the newer ones turn out to be fickle. They move on. No-one to hold you up, you're just a skinny boy, all ribs, knees and feet, out in the deep water, can't touch bottom.

Shake yourself. To carry on is all. Who said that? Rilke?

The phone rang. Drew.

'Put on your television. Seven.'

I found the remote, clicked.

The Audi came up in an undignified way, backwards, cable round the back axle, expensive German workmanship bouncing, grinding against the chalky cliffside, doors yawning, water spilling out. Bits of rubbery seaweed, greasy-looking, clung to the door pillars, dangled from the wheel housings. Halfway up, the front windscreen, shattered, opaque, big hole towards the passenger side, fell out, chose detachment rather than dishonour, committed itself to the ocean.

The newsreader said:

No bodies were found in the vehicle. Police believe the car's doors opened on impact and the driver and any passengers may have been dragged out by the powerful rip along the stretch of coast called The Teeth.

We saw the car close-up, being yanked over the crumbling lip of the land.

The voice-over said:

Police were called to the scene between Port Fairy and Portland early this afternoon when the pilot of a helicopter on its way to Portland saw the vehicle at the foot of the cliffs. Police rescue squad members abseiled down to attach a cable to the car.

The television helicopter went up, the view expanded: coastal downs, low vegetation, five or six vehicles beside a track, well back from collapsing cliffs. And the sea, dark blue, waves creaming against jetblack rocks. On the land, cattle, pale cattle, were grazing near the track. The cable was coming from a bulky, square vehicle, figures standing around it.

The vehicle is registered to a Melbourne company, Beconsecure International. Police have asked that anyone with information about the whereabouts of the company's director, Mr Gary Connors, of unit 5, 23 Montcalm Avenue, Toorak, contact the Police Helpline.

For a while, I sat in the comforting leather armchair, in the low light from the television, cold takeaway Chinese on my lap. I felt like going to bed, sleeping for a week. Instead, I dialled Des Connors. It rang for a long time.

'Hello.' He sounded far away and weak.

'Des, it's Jack Irish.'

A cough, clearing of the throat. 'Jack.' More clearing. 'Bit of a snooze. Front of the telly.'

'Des, have you heard from the police?'

'Police? No.'

'They found Gary's car today.'

'What?'

'Gary's car. They found it between Port Fairy and Portland. In the sea. Went over the cliff. No body found.'

Silence. More throat-clearing.

I said, 'You all right?'

'In the sea?'

'At the bottom of the cliff. Place called The Teeth. Track runs along the coast from there. On private land. A farm.'

'A farm, well,' Des said. 'Bit of a shock. Always thought he'd come to a sticky. Good thing his mum's not here to hear this.'

'We don't know that Gary was in the car, Des,' I said. 'Could have been stolen, dumped. Happens all the time.'

No-one stole a car in Melbourne and dumped it intact over a cliff near Portland.

Des sighed.

'The police will want to ask you some questions about

Gary. If you like, I'll talk to them in the morning, give them your number, get them to make an appointment to see you.'

'Yes,' he said. 'Yes. Thanks.'

'Goodnight, Des. I'll talk to you tomorrow.'

'Goodnight, Bill.'

I poured a glass of the open red, opened the envelope from Simone. A printout of a short item in the Capital City column of the *Australian Financial Review*, dated 27 July 1996.

It was headed: HANSARD LOST FOR WORDS.

Late on Wednesday, a somnambulant colleague found himself in the empty Press Gallery of the near-empty Senate chamber. The following exchange between conspiracy-fixated Independent Senator Martin Coffey and the Attorney-General, Senator Clive McColl, startled him from sleep:

Can the Honourable Senator confirm that recently a combined Federal Police and Victorian Police operation called Black Tide was closed down under pressure from the highest level of government?

Senator McColl: I take Senator Coffey's question on notice.

Could this have the makings of a story, our scribe wondered? The next day, to check his notes, he consulted Hansard's account of proceedings in the Senate for 24 July. That verbatim record heard Senator Coffey ask:

Can the Honourable Senator confirm that last year an important Federal Police operation was cancelled on financial grounds?

Late yesterday, Senator Coffey's office said that the Senator had no reason to dispute Hansard's record of

proceedings and that, after discussions with Senator
McColl, he considered the matter closed.

Simone had underlined the words *Black Tide*.

Telephone ringing.

'Jack, we talked on Wednesday. About your Canberra
trip.'

The tired man with the advice about Dean Canetti.

'Yes.'

'The person you were interested in. They found his car
today.'

'I saw that.'

'He was in it when it took the dive.'

'They didn't say they knew that.'

'No. Reasons for that. He was. They found the wallet.
You don't have to look for him anymore.'

'No.'

'Well, thought you'd want to know.'

'Yes. Thanks.'

'Goodnight.'

I spent a distracted evening: not reading, not thinking, not
watching television. Finally, I put out the lamps, went
upstairs, stood beside the side window and looked down on
the narrow street, streetlight gleaming on wet parked cars.
Nothing moved. I went to bed. In the strange way of these
things, I fell asleep instantly, slept like an exhausted child
until 7 a.m.

For breakfast, I had muesli. Ancient muesli. Recovered muesli. It tasted as I imagined food found beside a mummy in a pyramid would. Then I drove out to Des Connors' house in Northcote. Not much traffic, rain weeping out of a sky the colour of the best man's tie.

Des was up, saw me arrive and opened the front door before I got there. He was wearing a blue suit with wide lapels, a white shirt and a tie with red spots.

'Come in, Jack,' he said.

'Not this time. Lightning visit. You're looking pretty spruce.'

'Havin lunch with the girls down the street. They don't work Mondays. Vegetables only, she said. Dunno about that.'

'Very healthy,' I said. 'I'll be ringing the cops in about twenty minutes. When they come around, tell them you came to see me and we went around to Gary's place, had a look to see if he might be away on a trip. That way they won't get too excited if they decide to look for fingerprints and find ours.'

Des nodded. 'Just tell em what we did.'

'That's right. Those keys of Gary's. I might take them, have another look.'

He was back with them in thirty seconds.

We went out to the gate. 'Should be a grievin parent,' he said. 'Can't find it in me, Jack. All I can think is I done me dough. Goodbye house.'

I leaned over the gate, grasped his left arm. 'Even if the

dough's done, Des, you're staying in this house. Out feet first. In about fifty years.'

He blinked a few times. 'Sure, now?'

'Give you my word, good enough?'

He looked at me, some moisture in the eyes. 'Reckon,' he said. 'Bill Irish's boy.'

The things we bring upon ourselves.

I spent the day on the Purbrick library, cutting mortices. No hollow-chisel morticer in this workshop. A drill press, yes. Charlie wasn't averse to amateurs like me getting rid of most of the waste with the drill press but he could do the whole job much faster with a chisel, a piece of steel honed to the point where it could take shavings off a fingernail.

Early on, Charlie had shown me how to use the drill press to make it easier to get rid of waste in a mortice. But you sense things. It wasn't that he didn't want me to use the drill press. It was just that he didn't show any enthusiasm for it. Some machines he loved. He loved the tablesaws, loved the big industrial planer, gave it a pat like a man patting a bottom, an incorrect man patting a female rump, a lingering feel in the pat.

The message unspoken was that a person who took the occupation seriously would use a chisel to create a mortice. And when you'd felt dry, fine-grained timber succumb to the knife-edge, you agreed.

We had lunch in front of the stove. My soggy salad sandwich was from down the road. Charlie had corned beef, mustard, homemade sauerkraut, bread baked by the husband of one of his granddaughters, a stockbroker called Martin something who specialised in mining stocks. Charlie brought in half a loaf for me from time to time. It was sourdough rye, dense, intense, exactly what a rich Harvard MBA would produce in his kitchen for relaxation. On Sunday, get in touch with the earth. Monday, get back to screwing the planet.

'Six syringes outside today,' Charlie said. 'Coming to what, the world? Children. Shouldn't be smoking, they stick needles in their arms. Who's to blame? I ask you that.'

'The blame question,' I said. 'They ask that a lot on the radio. And in the papers. Very good question. It can also be a very stupid question.'

Charlie pondered this, staring at the last bite of sandwich in his huge hand. 'Men make their own history,' he said, 'but not in circumstances of their own choosing. Karl Marx.'

'Yes?'

'So some you can blame on the past, on other people, some you can't.'

'I like the sound of that,' I said, feeding my sandwich wrap to the fire. 'How do you work out which bit you can blame on which?'

'Think,' Charlie said. 'You think a lot.'

He stood up, rehearsed sending down a bowl, and went off, mind now turned to the prospect of inflicting further humiliation on the teen set at the bowls club.

It was darkening outside before I'd cut all the tenons, trial-fitted the pieces and was ready for the glue-up. Although Charlie had at least ten good reasons for not gluing-up near the end of the day, I loved to come into the workshop in the morning and take the clamps off a piece of furniture.

Glue-up tomorrow? No.

Cold hide glue for this job. You needed the slower drying time in case anything went wrong. I laid out the pieces on the low assembly table, used three brushes to apply the glue, worked at a steady pace. Then I fitted everything together, slid home the joints, applied the clamps, fifteen short and six long sash clamps, no metal touching wood. Next came fiddling with the clamp pressures, checking all corners with a square, measuring the diagonals with Charlie's measuring stick invention to ensure squareness.

Finally, I stood back and marvelled at my confidence, my cleanliness, at the fact that complicated glue-ups that had once terrified me more than my early court appearances ever did were now everyday matters.

Weary, fingers second-skinned with glue, pleased with myself, I went home. It was raining steadily, but the discovery of Gary's car had brightened my world. A dead Gary you didn't have to look for. If I could find some way of securing Des in his house, the whole matter was closed. Everything. Whatever business Dean Canetti had with Gary, it was over. And whatever Black Tide was, it wasn't any of my business.

In my domain, cleansed, restless, I toyed with the idea of ringing Lyall Cronin, handsome and world-weary photographer, suggesting a drink, perhaps a meal. Had she been mildly suggestive at the end of our encounter?

She'd been mildly pissed.

My confidence failed me. Not for the first time.

I was thinking about what to eat when the street gate buzzer sounded.

Simone Bendsten, fetching in short red weatherproof jacket, rain beaded on her hair. Behind her, a dark Honda was double-parked, engine running.

She held out an envelope. 'This was in my letterbox,

addressed to you. Mysterious. Got to run.'

I shouted my thanks after her. Outside the front door, I looked at the envelope. My name and address, care of Bendsten Research. Under that, in capitals: PLEASE DELIVER BEFORE 8 PM TODAY. PLEASE DO NOT MAKE TELEPHONE CONTACT WITH MR IRISH.

Inside, one sheet of A4 bearing a short message.

I sat in front with the driver. The taxi had picked me up on the corner of King William and Brunswick as the message said it would. Then the driver, a man in his sixties with the anxious look of a whippet, showed a talent for dawdling along, holding up traffic, then racing through traffic lights in the first second of red.

We drove all over the place: down Brunswick, left into Johnston, left into Nicholson, down to Victoria, right, right again into Lygon, left into Queensberry, right into Swanston. Twice he pulled to the kerb for a minute or two, twice he did illegal U-turns. After the second one, at the Faraday intersection, he drove half-way down the block and pulled up next to a man in a suit leaning against a parked car.

The man didn't hurry, opened the back door of the cab and got in. 'Evening, Jack,' he said. 'Left into Grattan, Dennis.'

He was big, a few kilos over correct weight, full head of greying hair cut short, shelf of moustache underpinning a delicate nose.

We crossed Rathdowne and went down Carlton Street beside the gardens.

'Left into Canning, right on the other side of the square,' the man said.

He had the cab stop at the back of the small square, next to a dark Ford. 'Give us twenty minutes, Dennis,' he said. 'Then pick up our guest on the corner. Let's get out, Jack.'

We got out.

A wet and windy Melbourne night, a small square of balding trees and scuffed grass, around it the terrace houses blank, defensive, leaves drifting through the streetlight like falling pieces of the sky.

He unlocked the driver's door of the Ford, motioned me to the passenger side. I got in. New car smell.

'Dave,' he said, holding out his right hand, moving his buttocks, getting comfortable. 'Smoke?'

'No. Dave's not enough. Not nearly enough.'

'Cloak and dagger. Always make you feel a bit of a prick.'

I said, 'Who are you?'

He found a wallet. I held it to the streetlight. He reached up and put on the interior light. Photograph. Commonwealth seal. Italic type saying the card served to identify the bearer as a member of the Commonwealth Office of Crime Intelligence.

Light off. I gave the card back. 'Don't know why I bother,' I said. 'You can probably get these made in a booth at Kmart. I'm in your car for one reason, Dave. To give you a message. Listening?'

He didn't look at me, studied the misty windshield, nodded.

'This is the message,' I said. 'Gary Connors, I don't give a shit. Dean Canetti, the same applies.'

He extracted a Camel filter from a packet next to the gear lever, wound his window down a paperback width, lit the cigarette with an old Ronson lighter, blew smoke sideways. It blew back.

I said, 'Thanks for the ride, Dave. I can manage the walk back from here. Goodnight. And goodbye.' I felt for the door handle.

He glanced at me. 'Pissed off? I'd be pissed off. Read that *Fin Review* clipping?'

'How do you know about that?'

He ignored the question. 'That's the only public mention ever of Black Tide,' he said.

'Black Tide? Blue Omo? What the hell is it?'

He didn't look at me, looked at the windscreen. 'There's only a few people know.'

I should have got out and walked home. 'Listen, Dave,' I said, 'there may be some mistaken identity here. You may be mistaking me for someone who knits beanies for a living.'

'The *Fin Review* piece,' he said. 'Senator Coffey changing his story. You get the point?'

'No.'

'Think the media would follow that up.' He smoked, a man born to smoke.

I waited. 'I'm listening. I shouldn't be, but I'm listening.'

Dave put his left hand on the wheel, curled the fingers around it. He didn't look at me. I looked at his hand, a boxer's hand, at his neat small nose. He'd got the punches in first, no-one had ever marked his face.

'The point here, Jack,' he said, 'the point's simple for an intelligent bloke like you. Change Hansard, shut up journos, that's kinder stuff for these people. It's nothing. Coffey, Senator Coffey, he got fed the question, didn't know what he was asking about. Anyway, he liked the sound of it, he went on the fishing trip. A wall fell on the cunt. Integrity went south, just its little arsehole winking in the dark, once, twice, gone.'

He still didn't look at me, examined his cigarette. 'For these people,' he said, 'getting their way is easy, it's trivial. It's just business. What's the price? What'll you take? Don't want money, what do you want? They shut down the local jacks everywhere that way. Long ago, just peanuts for them, peanuts for the monkeys. The money, you can't count it, there's nothing they can't buy. No-one. You're dealing with people, they can't buy you, they'll load you up, kill your friend, kill your wife, kill your child, kill you, it's all the same.'

I was feeling cold inside now, winter inside and out. 'I don't think you should be telling me this,' I said. 'I don't want to know it. I'm not involved anymore. I wanted to help Gary Connors' father by finding Gary. I'll find another way to help him.'

Dave wound down his window, wet air came in, cold city air, on it the faint sound of music, voices from somewhere. He tapped ash off the cigarette, had a last draw, sent the butt arching across the street to die in the gutter, wound up the window.

'I can appreciate the way you feel,' he said. 'Things we'd all like to step out of, shut the door.'

'I've stepped out,' I said. 'The door's shut.'

Dave turned his head and looked at me, the first real look. 'No, Jack,' he said. 'That's not possible now. They know you. Know your friends, your sister. Know you talked to Meryl. Help us see this thing through, find Gary, that's the best chance you've got.'

I was getting colder all the time. 'Who the fuck are you? Who the fuck are they? Who's tapping my phone? How do you know about the *Fin Review* clipping?'

'Only twelve people inside Black Tide,' he said, as if I hadn't spoken. 'Waterproof to fifty fathoms, we thought. One-way valve system, stuff comes in, nothing goes out. What happens with these operations usually, there's people upstairs want reports every second day, they pass them on, there's leaks like half-time at the football. That's why the other side's only about a day behind you. Not Black Tide. No reporting till we were finished, that was the deal. So when we got shut down in '96, we knew we had a dog inside. Dogs maybe. And we knew the pressure to squash us came from outside.'

He took out another cigarette, lit it, opened the window a crack.

'They,' I said. 'That part of the question. Who?'

'Don't worry about that part.'

'I don't even know why you want to find Gary. Why do you want Gary?'

'Gary's important to Black Tide. You don't need the detail. It's better that way.'

'Detail?' I said. 'You call knowing who *they* are fucking detail? I'm not going on any expedition with you. I'm not a concerned citizen. I'm just the bystander. More or less innocent. And I thought you said Black Tide was shut down?'

Dave sighed. 'Not appealing to your sense of civic duty here, Jack,' he said. 'Your instinct for survival. I'm relying on that. Your mark's on the slate, these people like a clean slate. Weeks, months maybe. Could be a year. But they'll wipe you, believe me.'

He turned his shoulders towards me, rested big fingers on my arm. 'Jack, this isn't some minor racket, rebirthing BMWs, that kind of thing. This is huge. The money's everywhere. Billions every year. Take you around this town, all the cities, take you around the bush, pick a town, show you buildings, businesses, whole law firms, real estate agents, travel agents, stockbrokers, hotels, resorts, greengrocers, restaurants. Name it, I'll show you. Drug money underneath, drug money in the cash flow.'

'Is that what Black Tide was about? Drug money?'

He paused. 'We were getting close, Jack. Going in the right direction, then we touched a nerve and a boot came out and kicked us up the arse. Big boot. Big kick. Now you've touched the same nerve. You can't untouch it.'

I didn't know what was going on but I was getting the idea. Not the point, perhaps, but the drift. Slowly. He was talking about TransQuik, about Steven Levesque.

'There's nothing I can do for you,' I said.

Dave smiled. It was a small smile, but it improved the hard face no end. 'You want Gary,' he said. 'We want Gary. In the beginning, we kissed him goodbye. Dead. Now we think he's alive. We think so because they think so. If he was dead, they'd know. Being the ones who made that arrangement.'

'They? I'm sick of they, Dave.'

'People who want Black Tide stopped. Powerful people outside, their friends inside.'

'What about Gary's car?'

'Gary drives off a cliff? Forget. It's a good sign.'

'I've been told Gary was definitely in the car when it went over the cliff.'

'Been told? Visitors the other day give you another call? I'd treat that information with caution.'

How did he know about my visitors? I said, 'Jellicoe, Gary's mate from the bottle shop. What about him?'

'Where'd you get that from?'

My turn to ignore questions. 'Koch and Bryce and Novikov. What's that mean?'

'You heard that where?' A hint of disquiet in the dry voice.

'Detail,' I said. 'You don't need the detail.'

Dave coughed, shook his head. 'Well, reinforces my confidence in you. The visitors the other day, what was the message?

'This is tiring. I repeat, I don't want to be in this.'

'Mention Gary?' he said.

'No. Just Canetti.'

'What about Canetti?'

'Said he was engaged in important government business and his wife was not taking pills, imagining things. Like being told he was missing, possibly dead. Probably.'

'What'd you tell them?'

'I told them my only interest in Canetti was that he was following Gary on April 3.'

Dave's mouth opened slightly under the thatch. I could see the tip of his tongue. 'Established that, have you?'

I nodded.

'Following him where?'

'At a bottle shop in Prahran.'

'What else do you know about them? Gary and Canetti?'

'Nothing after that. That's it.'

'Give you a number, your visitors?'

'Yes.'

'Call it. Tonight. Tell them that since Gary's dead, you have absolutely no further interest in Dean Canetti.'

'And then?'

'Then turn the mind to Gary.'

'You're taking it for granted that I trust you. Why is that?'

'Why wouldn't you trust me? We both want to find Gary. Your visitors want you as far from Gary as possible. It's not Canetti they're warning you off with that bullshit about Meryl. It's Gary.'

I thought about this. Then I said, 'Dave, I don't know

where to go on Gary. I've done the things that usually turn up traces. He's not using plastic, he's not buying tickets or hiring in his own name. I presume you know this. What's left to do, I don't know.'

'His old man. Talk to him.'

'He knows less than I do about Gary. Much less.'

'No. That's now, the recent past. Gary can't hide anywhere that's to do with the recent past. Nowhere's safe. If we find him, it'll be because he's somewhere he feels safe. That's going to come from way back. Talk to his father.'

I said, 'Is this the psychology of flight or what?'

'What it is,' he said, 'is the psychology of clutching at fucking straws.'

He put his right hand into his jacket and took out a small mobile phone. 'This thing's secure. Sounds a bit like I'm underwater, that's cause you're hearing me off a satellite talking through electronic condoms. Switch it on, press one-two for me. Keep it switched off except for five minutes around the hour. That's when I'll call you. Your cab's waiting. It's on me.'

I looked at him, heavy in the heart. 'That's a nice gesture,' I said. 'Thanks very much.'

'More where that came from,' he said. Another smile. The second one.

In the morning the rain had stopped, sunlight fell across the kitchen, fell into my lap where I sat at the table reading the form for Geelong, eating anchovy toast, drinking tea out of a bone-china cup. The cup and saucer were the survivors of twelve my wife Isabel and I had bought at an auction. Cup rising to the mouth, it occurred to me that this was the first time I'd used it since Linda became a feature in my life. After the bomb wrecked my floor of the old boot factory in North Fitzroy, I'd salvaged what I could, including the china cup and saucer, and moved to the stables. I'll go back when the place is rebuilt, I kept telling myself.

But when the time came, Linda found good reasons why I should postpone moving back.

One morning, while considering the limitations of my wardrobe, I said, 'It's my home. It's fixed. I want to go home.'

Linda was in the bathroom, brushing her teeth. I heard her rinse, swill the mouthwash. She came to the door, no makeup, handsome. 'For me, Jack,' she said, 'it's Isabel's home.'

I compromised. An agent found a tenant on a six-month lease.

Was that why I hadn't used the china cup? What did using it today signal?

Questions too deep. Questions too meaningless was more like it.

I thought about the big man in the car. Dave. The cocooning comfort of the car, the sounds of the city night around us, muted, the leaves blowing across the streetlight, falling onto the bonnet. Secret operations betrayed, all-powerful drug money, his knowingness. Convincing. This morning, sunlight in my lap ascomforting as a warm cat, it had an unreal quality. What made him think I could find Gary? What more could Des tell me?

The phone rang. A tremor of trepidation.

'Jack?'

Rosa. Relief.

'About time you answered your phone,' she said. 'I'm here to tell you, just when I thought it was all over for me, this hunk, this absolute babe, has come into my life.'

I cleared my throat. 'Bit early for this kind of conversation. How can a man be a babe?'

Long, languid sigh. 'Where are you, Jack? Marooned in the seventies. You should mix with younger people.'

'Tried that. Hasn't done me much good. How old is this babe?'

'Ah. The ear-kissing. I saw her on Rod Pringle's television show the other night. Radiant. Very striking.'

'How old is this babe?'

'Jack, what does it matter? Two people resonate, that's all that counts.'

'Resonate? The point about resonance is lack of contact. How old?'

'Hmm. Thirtyish. Going on.'

'Little more precision, please. How old?'

'God, you're a bore. Twenty-four. Thereabouts. Very mature.'

'At least one mature person in a relationship is a good idea. What does he do?'

'He's a sommelier. At Maquis in South Yarra. He's so

knowledgable about wine, he's a wine authority, he…'

'A wine waiter. Three-week TAFE course. You're having it off with a wine waiter and you're giving him about sixteen years claim. How do you manage to get these things so absolutely right?'

'Fourteen. No soul. Not an ounce of poetry in your body. Many, many relationships of this kind are wildly successful.' Pause. 'Wildly. Wildly.'

'Wildly? Who said that? Elizabeth Taylor? Zsa Zsa Gabor? Catherine the Great?'

'Jack, why would Lucy feel guilty about Dad's death?'

Changes of subject by Rosa were standard but this one caught me flatfooted.

'What? How do you know she felt guilty?'

'She says so. In her diary. I've got all her diaries and letters in a big box and sometimes when I'm in a good mood I read bits. I've just been reading the new diary she started after I was born.'

'Diaries?' I looked at the digital clock on the microwave. 'Eight-twenty a.m. I thought you didn't wake up before noon? Medication problem, is it? You can tell me.'

Light laugh. 'Up for hours, walking on the beach, reading. Listen, I've got it here, she says, "Sunny afternoon. Dad drove me to the cemetery. I was quite composed while I was at Bill's grave, but on the way back it was suddenly too much for me. Dad pretended not to notice the tears. What haunts me night and day is that I could have saved my darling. I will carry that to my grave."'

'Just emotional,' I said. 'People get like that. Blame themselves for anything. He was in a fight.'

'A fight? I thought he was attacked. She always talked as if he was attacked.'

'He was in a fight outside a pub. Grandpa told me that. Many times.'

Sitting alone, sun on my legs, teacup in my hand, my father lost, unknown to me, no memory of a touch, my mother always keeping me at a distance, my first wife just packing up and leaving, my second wife murdered by one of my clients, none of that obscured the memory of my grandfather's quiet voice, grating voice, each word a rake of gravel. I could see his eyes moving over my face, an examination, a search for evidence of something, brief rest on my hair, my forehead, a look into my eyes, examination of my nose, my mouth. Sitting in a captain's chair in the sun, all the years gone, I could see that mouth, my grandfather's mouth, mean, bloodless, disapproving mouth.

And I could hear him. He never called me Jack.

Irresponsibility. It can be in the blood, John. Your father's blood. In you. You always need to guard against it. Bar fighter your father, labourer and bar fighter. That's how he died. Fighting outside a hotel.

Rosa said, 'Why would she blame herself…?'

I didn't want to talk about it. 'No idea. Lovely chat, apres wine appreciation, apres brief sleep, beach walk, diary reading, whatever. Unfortunately you find me at the beginning of a working day. I'll have to say goodbye.'

Silence. 'You resent happiness in others, don't you, Jack?' said Rosa. 'Well, that's perfectly understandable.'

I felt a coldness in my heart and I said, flippant voice, 'It's always nice to have one's frailties understood and forgiven.'

She felt the coldness, it passed to her across the wire.

'Jack, I didn't mean that, Jack, listen, I meant…'

I said, 'I've got to go. Miles to go. Promises to keep.

Woods lovely dark and deep. Don't accept any *en primeur* offers.'

'*En* what?'

'You pay now and get the wine later.'

'I'm not sure brothers are worth the trouble,' she said, a tremble in her voice. They don't seem to have any utility value.'

'Except to tell you that they love you,' I said.

I had never said that to her before. It had never crossed my mind to say it. Any more than it had occurred to me to be the one to offer the kiss on meeting or parting.

A long silence. 'Is that so?' she said, stronger voice now. 'Well, perhaps they have some limited use.'

Taub's. I had to let myself in. Not unusual. Charlie often failed to take the door off the latch.

Cold. That was unusual.

In winter, which was most of the year in Melbourne, Charlie's first act was to light the big potbelly. The building took at least an hour to warm up.

No Charlie. I felt a pulse of anxiety in my throat, phoned.

It rang. Rang. Rang.

'Ja, Taub,' he said. It sounded like a command.

I breathed out. 'So,' I said. 'The work. Who needs the work? How many lives you got? The work, the work can wait. Lie in bed, think about how the pishers gave you a good thrashing.'

Charlie laughed, the full laugh, leading to wheezing and sniffing. You didn't hear the full laugh too often. The Charlie minimalist smile was enough to make you think you'd said something acute.

'On my foot,' he said. 'The toes. Can't walk. Like a cripple.'

'On your foot what?'

'What? What you think? The ball. The bowl.'

I said, 'Oh. Sorry to hear that. Didn't realise it was a contact sport. I'll just struggle on here on my own then.'

Charlie said, 'Ten to eleven in the morning. Two hours before you see I'm not there?'

'I thought you were at the back, being very quiet.'

The snort. 'Tomorrow, I make up the time.'

I said goodbye, put down the phone. Boss of Taub's today.

I went over to my glue-up of the evening before, admired my efforts, set to work taking off the clamps, all a little less tight now. A very pleasant task, spiced with anxiety about the perfection of the joints, the squareness of the frame.

Boss of Taub's. A person could come in wanting something made. From time to time, a person did. Hi, they said. This is really old-fashioned. Terrific. Like Europe. More machines though. We stayed in this villa in Italy. In Umbria? Yes? Part of Italy. And there was this table. Really unusual. Long, I don't know, from here to that wall. And narrow, that's the difference. I've looked everywhere, they're all too wide. But amazing, it had three sets of legs? Six legs? The outside ones sort of go outwards. I'll draw it for you. Dark wood. Think you can make that? In pine. I'll stain it myself. Not too many knots. I'll need a price. I have to tell you, I've been ripped off by some so-called carpenters.

Listen politely. Show the person the door.

A person didn't come in.

I passed the day in solitude, absorbed by the effort of bringing into being something people would admire and which would outlive them. I pushed away thoughts about Gary Connors, about the morass into which I had ventured so blithely.

A good day.

Charlie once said, elevation of chin, narrowing of eyes revealing that he was about to deliver a message, 'Jack, make something, you look at it, you're happy. The work it took, that's not work.'

At home, cleansed by the day's honest efforts, I was struck by the disgusting condition of the place. A frenzy came over me. As I vacuumed and scrubbed and dusted, my mind turned over the questions I should have asked Dave. The first one was why on earth I should believe him. I was on the downstairs de-cobwebbing when the phone rang.

'Jack, Lyall Cronin.' Voice deeper than I remembered.

'You find me with a featherduster in my hand.'

Measured interval.

'If I'm interrupting something…'

'Between me and this featherduster you can come,' I said. 'A welcome interposition.'

She laughed. 'Interposition. Good word. Bandied about a lot in suburban legal practices, I imagine.'

'Endlessly bandied.'

'Jack, I remembered something, I don't know if it's of any use.' Pause. 'You might want to drop by some time?'

'I want to. When's a good time?'

Pause.

'Well, when's a good time? Thursday? Friday? Actually, now's a good time. No, God, Tuesday night, it wouldn't be a good time for you…'

Sight, identify, fire. Not a millisecond of hesitation. 'Tuesday night's a very acceptable time. I could holster the featherduster, shower, be around shortly.'

'Good. Yes. Well. You know how to find it.'

'Yes. Well, see you.'

I stood for a moment, thought about my motives, decided not to think about them, went upstairs to shower, get the glue off my fingertips. Then I considered driving, phoning for a cab, instead walked down to Brunswick Street, fended off two pushers, got a cab, Ukrainian driver. I was in safe hands. He was a qualified surgeon and an Olympic skier, shockingly unappreciated in his adopted land and seriously thinking about going back.

Lyall Cronin's hair was damp, black, back from her forehead. Cotton sweater, jeans. Barefoot. Taller than I recalled. Even barefoot.

'Mr Irish.' The crooked smile. 'That was quick.'

'Like to see the ID?' I asked.

'I think I remember you. Come in.'

She led the way down the passage into the room on the right, a room I hadn't seen, a comfortable sitting room, long and narrow, assortment of armchairs, two big sofas facing each other, paintings and photographs on the walls, books and newspapers on the coffee table. On the CD player, something classical, piano. A near-full bottle of red wine and a glass stood on the ornate wooden mantelpiece above a badly made and dying fire.

We stood.

'More wood,' she said. 'We need wood. Not much left. Bradley did the wood. There was always a huge pile in the garage. I have no idea how to buy wood.' She turned, shrugged. 'First winter alone in this house. It's much too big for one person but I can't bear the idea of sharing with strangers. That part of life is over. If I didn't love it so much, I'd find something smaller.'

'Let's see what's left.'

She put on shoes. I followed her down the passage, through the kitchen, across the courtyard into the garage. Half a dozen logs were in the corner just in front of Stuart Wardle's BMW. I squeezed in, just managed to get them all into my arms.

On the way back, Lyall said, 'Bringing in the firewood. Essentially a male preserve.'

I said, 'And we want to hang onto it. Not a lot of preserves left.'

'I want you to hang onto it,' Lyall said. 'I want you to feel ownership of the firewood preserve.'

'Empathy. Essentially a female preserve.'

She had a good deep chuckling laugh.

In the sitting room, I said, 'Would you be offended if I reconstructed this fire?'

Our eyes met. Lyall tilted her head, looked thoughtful. 'No,' she said, 'I think that falls into the firewood preserve. What kind of idiot objects when someone else volunteers to get dirty and burnt?'

'They're out there, I'm told,' I said, picking up the tongs to start the messy work of unpacking the heap of charred wood. 'A dangerous strain of idiot.'

'None around here,' she said. 'When you've got it inflamed, would you like some red? White? There's beer. I'm over beer now, may never drink beer again. The red's a bit special.'

I said, 'Once inflamed, red would be nice.'

She went away while I had a go at resuscitating the fire. When I came back from washing my hands in the downstairs bathroom, she handed me a glass. 'It's called Hill of Grace.'

'I know the bounteous hill. From the time when I was a responsible social drinker. And non-millionaires could afford it.'

'This is the bounteous 1988. Courtesy of Bradley Joffrin. Two unopened cases in the pantry. It was the day you were here. I was looking for dried food. Bit unsteady. The room's so big, bodies could be in there. Shelves about a metre deep. They were in the corner under all sorts of things. I sent Bradley an e-mail in Los Angeles. "Two cases expensive, unobtainable wine found in pantry. Await instructions." He sent an e-mail back. "Listen, bitch, you pass this way but once. Drink."'

'You'd like a person for that.'

The crooked smile. 'Like him, love him. Love him's fine. In love with him's the problem. I was in love with him for years. Never mentioned it. No point. He's gay. Huge loss to womankind.' She raised her glass. 'Straight womankind. Cheers.'

The Hill of Grace was like drinking a liquidised alcoholic plum tart. We sat down on sofas opposite each other in front of the fire, now in aggressive form.

'Talent for reconstructing fires, Mr Irish,' she said, looking at the blaze through her glass. 'To be honest, I've got to confess to vaguely false pretences. I don't think that what I remembered will be of much use to you. Thought it would be nice to see you again.'

I said, 'Well. That's cheeky. Think you can get away with wasting a high-powered suburban solicitor's time. Make nuisance calls.'

She turned her head, half-profile. I remembered thinking that she had a judgmental face. 'I rather hoped so.'

'If it's show and tell,' I said, 'I considered phoning you the other night. Imagined getting the busy-this-year-feel-free-to-call-thereafter.'

We looked at each other.

'So,' she said, the smile. 'Shown you mine, got a glimpse of yours.'

We both looked into the fire, uncertainty about the next step in the air.

'I didn't think about eating,' she said. 'You forget that other people don't have lunch at 4 p.m. Are you before or after eating?'

'Possibly beyond,' I said. 'I had a pie mid-afternoon. The local pie tends to steer the mind away from food for a while. Days. Weeks sometimes.'

'I'll get the other half then,' she said. 'Needs to breathe a bit. That's what they say.'

'No arguing with they,' I said. 'They know everything.'

I watched her leave the room, admired her lean buttocks. At the door, she turned her head, caught me looking. The smile. I got up and stood beside the fireplace.

She came back with a large plate, wedges of cheese and a packet of water biscuits. Under her arm, another Hill of Grace. She put the plate on the coffee table, found a waiter's friend on the mantelpiece and removed the cork like a professional.

Then she walked around the sofas, came right up to me. We looked at each other. She wasn't wearing lipstick. I swallowed. 'Very professional with a corkscrew,' I said, hearing the awkwardness in my voice.

'Very handy with a poker,' she replied. She put up a hand, ran it over my shoulder quickly, a ghost touch, a phantom touch, felt down my body, in the groin.

I put fingertips to her mouth, brushed her full lower lip. There was a flush on her cheekbones.

Her hand went behind my head, long, strong fingers, pulled me down, kissed me on the lips, a full kiss, mouth slightly open, hard, then soft.

I put my hands on her hips, pronounced hipbones, pulled

her to me, felt her pubic bone against my erection, frisson of pleasure down the spine into the pelvis. When my hands went under her cotton sweater, touched the skin of her waist, she shuddered.

'My learned friend,' she said, breath against my face, voice even deeper than usual. 'Let's just do it.'

We came back downstairs in time to save the fire.

'Try the uncompromising goatsmilk something,' she said. 'The one with the ash on it. A cheese bore at that place in Richmond sold it to me.' She cut off a wedge, chewed reflectively. 'I've never understood the ash,' she said. 'Must be religious.'

'Ash Wednesday. Penitent cheeses. Sprinkling ash on foreheads. You could be right.' I tried a crumbly portion with a sip of the Hill. The combination of tastes forced me to close my eyes. 'In this case, the religious connection is clear,' I said. 'I think I've been forgiven.'

She sliced cheese, pushed the plate across. 'This other stuff's not bad either. Made by a woman in Tasmania.'

We ate cheese, drank wine, talked, all strangeness gone. She didn't know anything about football but seemed to know an alarming amount about many other things, laughed a lot.

I got up to put some more wood on the fire. The wind had risen, hollow sound in the chimney. I leant against the mantelpiece.

Lyall had her back against the sofa arm, legs on the seat, firelight on her face, handsome features, once thought plain. She held up her glass. 'Sexy evening,' she said. 'Much nicer than getting pissed alone and making phone calls that wake up people in other time zones.'

'Clear improvement on house cleaning, too.'

'I inquired about you,' Lyall said, eyes on mine. 'You're described as a person of dubious reputation who escaped prosecution for shooting and killing two ex-policemen.'

I said, 'Well, there's a perfectly simple explanation.'

'Tell me when I'm lying down in case I faint at the gruesome detail.'

In the morning, I woke early, sat upright, no idea where I was. Lyall put a hand on my arm, drew me down.

Later, at the front door, I said, 'Good drop that Hill of Grace.'

She came up close, turned her palms outward, put them on my thighs, high up, little fingers in my groin. She offered her mouth. I kissed it, a lingering, delicious contact, unwillingly terminated.

'Beard rash is the danger,' I said, short of breath.

She stood back, put two fingers on my chin, rubbed. 'Beard rash. Taking on plague proportions says the World Health Organization.'

Looking.

'Phone,' she said. 'Phone or I'll stalk you. Clear?'

I rubbed my chin stubble. 'Stalking's a criminal offence in Victoria.'

A nod. 'So press charges. See where it gets you.'

I said, 'Press something. Several things.'

A walk home early on a winter day, cold city coming to life, elm, oak and plane leaves in damp and dirty drifts, pungent exhaust fumes, some rich people getting into expensive cars, clean, pink people, wrestling wide-eyed children dressed like lumberjacks into babyseats. At the Grattan Street traffic lights, the woman passenger in a grey four-wheel-drive, blonde, thin-lipped with anger, eyes burning, was speaking to the driver. He was dark-haired, pale, in a suit, looking straight ahead. His window slid down and he threw a half-smoked cigarette into the street, didn't look where it went. A shaving cut under his sideburn had left a tear of dried blood. As the window hissed up, the woman screamed, 'In our bed you fucking bastard.'

I exchanged a glance with the elderly woman waiting with me. 'It's the children I worry about,' she said.

Home, under the shower, nozzle turned to Punish. Feelings of wellbeing and elation tinged with vague feelings of guilt. I was getting dressed, thinking about Lyall, when I saw Gary's keys on the chest of drawers given to us by Isabel's brother.

One sock on, I picked up the keys. There were six: building front door, unit front door, back door, alarm system, mailbox. And a long key.

Post box key. Why hadn't I noticed this before?

That was why his mailbox was empty. He had a post box somewhere. Where?

Toorak post office, probably, Toorak Road. His unit was only a few blocks away.

No number on the key. I couldn't try every post box at the Toorak post office without getting arrested.

I went downstairs, ate muesli. Thinking. Gary's post office box number wasn't a secret. I finished the bowl of Tutankhamen's after-life travel rations, found the telephone book, found the number. I was dialling when my stupidity dawned on me. This couldn't be done on my phone. For all I knew, my phone was connected to the public address system of a shopping centre.

At the office, I checked the answering machine. Mrs Davenport. Cyril Wootton would have to wait.

I went across the road and knocked on McCoy's front door. Knocked. And knocked.

At length, a sound like a barrel rolling down stairs. Then

animal sounds, piglike grunts, grunts becoming words. Vile, enraged words. The door shuddered, shuddered again, was wrenched open with enough force to bounce it off the inside wall.

McCoy filled the entire doorframe. Unclothed from the waist up, a sarong-like garment below. On inspection, I could see that it was a canvas painter's drop cloth, splattered and smeared with paint and other things too awful to contemplate, big enough to protect the floor of a small warehouse. The upper portion of McCoy was massive, hirsute, covered with what looked like coconut fibre, the stovepipe throat merging imperceptibly with the shell head, a head now dense with stubble thinning out only around the eyes. And then reluctantly.

And the eyes, the eyes: small black buttons pressed into grey plasticine. Vicious buttons, merciless buttons, killer buttons.

'My phone's not working,' I said. 'Use yours?'

'Certainly,' said McCoy. 'What time is it?'

'Nine o'clock. That's a.m. In the morning.'

He scratched his head. 'Wouldn't know the day of the week offhand, would you?'

His downstairs phone was in the vast creative area. I tried to keep my eyes averted from the works in progress but couldn't help noticing that McCoy was branching out, extending his artistic horizons. That explained the noises—not inner-city noises—heard recently. A chainsaw was propped against a big section of tree trunk which it had been mauling to no apparent purpose.

I looked away, dialled the power company, went through six stages, pressing numbers, the hash key. Then I got the *All our wonderfully helpful staff are not quite ready yet to face a day of dealing with you whingeing shits* message five times. Ghastly wailing soulful Irish-type music was played in the intervals. Finally, a human came on, zipping himself up, presumably.

'I'm worried about my bills,' I said. 'I'm not getting them.'

'Name and address, sir.'

I gave him Gary Connors' name and address.

'The bills have been sent, sir. In fact, there's a fairly large amount owing. Disconnection is the next step.'

'Sent where? What address?'

She gave me a Toorak post office box number.

'There must be some sorting mistake being made,' I said. 'I'll pay the bill today.'

I rang Wootton's courier, an obese and melancholy retired postman called Cripps who purred around the city in a yellow 1976 Holden fetching and delivering on a strictly cash basis. The fee seemed to be fifteen dollars no matter where or what. I had no doubt that Cripps would take a body to the Northcote tip for fifteen dollars. I told him where and what and to pick up the key from the cook at Meaker's.

'Twenty dollars,' he said, flat voice.

A terrible thing, inflation.

'In the envelope with the key,' I said. 'Deliver to the same person.'

Cripps did the entire deed in ninety minutes.

In Meaker's, drinking a long black, I read Gary's mail. Lots of it. I flipped through for envelopes without windows. Very few. I opened the few. Offers from people who'd undoubtedly found him on mailing lists. No personal correspondence. I opened some of the windows. Bills, ordinary bills, two credit-card statements, these worthy of later examination, some threats of disconnection, a plea to renew membership of the Pegasus Total Fitness Centre, a notification from the body corporate of his building of a five per cent rise in fees.

Nothing. Twenty dollars down the drain. I fanned out the window letters. One caught my eye. Shire of Moyne, an address in Port Fairy. Port Fairy. Gary's car was found between Port Fairy and Portland. Why would the Shire of Moyne send Gary a bill? Did they think he'd pay them for retrieving his car?

A bill for rates. $260.00. Under property description, it said: Sligo Lane RSD 234.

I rang Des, found him home, drove out to his place. He was pottering around in the front garden, waiting for me. I leant on the front gate.

'Quick question, Des. Why would the Shire of Moyne send Gary a bill for rates?'

'Shire of Moyne? Never heard of it.'

'Shire's office is in Port Fairy.'

'Port Fairy, ah.' He nodded. 'Port Fairy. Didn't know he'd hung on to that. Told me he had it on the market. That's donkey's ago.'

'Had what on the market?'

'His Aunty Kath's old place, little farm. She left it to Gary. No-one else to give it to. No kids the two of em. He went first, Colin. Nice bloke. Col Dixon. Had cows, them black and white ones.'

'This is where?'

'Warrnambool way, out the backblocks there.'

'Got a photograph of Gary, Des?'

'Only when he was little. Well, there's one with his mum when they give him his handcuffs. In uniform.'

'What does he look like?' How had I got to this point

without knowing what Gary looked like? Because appearance doesn't matter when you're looking for someone's plastic trail.

Des considered the question. 'Smaller than you,' he said. 'Bit thinner. Goin bald, dunno where that comes from, mother's side probably. That's about it.'

'Anything you'd notice about him?'

Des frowned, sniffed, brightened. 'Oh yeah, gold tooth here.' He pointed to his right canine. 'And he's got a big ring, gold ring, on the little finger.' He held up the large pinky of his left hand. 'They haven't found a body, have they?'

'No. Just curious.'

The day was raw, heavy cloud churning in off the ocean, spits of rain driven near-horizontal by a wind that was headbutting the weary windbreaks that defended almost every farmhouse. We drove around the backroads for almost half an hour but failed to find anywhere from which we could get a sight of Gary's inheritance.

'He'd be alone you'd expect?' asked Cam. We were parked at the side of the road. I'd told him the whole story on the way down, cruising lawlessly at one-fifty in the muscular Brock Holden.

'As I understand it.' Which was imperfectly to say the least.

Cam lit a Gitane, studied the herd of Friesian cows eyeing us, looked around at the wet landscape. 'Well,' he said, 'he's there, you sit tight, I'll have a yarn with him, give him my real estate agent card.'

He reached over for a laptop computer on the back seat, opened it, then fiddled with the sides, took off the keyboard. An automatic pistol and about twenty rounds of ammunition lay snug in grey foam. He extracted the weapon, handed it to me.

'What happened to the Ruger in the little aluminium briefcase?' I asked.

'Today it's all computers,' he said. 'Just pull the slide back and aim. See if you can miss me.'

'Shouldn't I be doing the talking?'

Cam glanced at me. 'You sold any real estate?'

I shook my head.

'There you are,' he said, started the engine, a muted, powerful growl. We went to the intersection, turned left into Sligo Lane. About three kilometres on, we turned left and went through an open gate onto Gary's late aunty's farm, onto a rutted track.

Just below the brow of a small hill, the track turned left. We went over the top and a collection of battered farm buildings in a hollow came into view.

Cam said, 'Make a fire on a day like this.'

'No vehicle.'

'Round the back, in a shed. Might take a drive around there, do that, your rep, don't bother the missus, know where the man on the land's to be found. Out in the shed, worryin about cockchafer, ryegrass.'

The track turned into a trident, the middle prong running to the house, the outer paths going around it to outbuildings. Only its chimney was giving the small tilted weatherboard the strength to deny complete victory to time and the prevailing wind. The roof was rosy with rust. Side weatherboards had fallen off the house, revealing rough timber studs, dark with age, and laths oozing plaster. Two verandah posts dangled uselessly, bases succumbed to wet rot.

Cam took the left fork. We went around the house. Sheds, sheds large and small, some weatherboard, some corrugated iron, all sagging, senile, close to shot.

'Quiet here,' Cam said.

We completed the circuit, Cam did a U-turn, stopped passenger side on to the front gate. He reached into the back for his sportscoat. 'Seriously in hiding this would be,' he said. 'Any shit at that front door, I'm goin right rapidly. Small edge on goin left, they say.'

I swallowed, full of fear. 'Who says that?'

He looked at me, the sallow, impassive face, Australian minestrone of genes, dark and dangerous broth. 'The livin, they'd know. Put a few into the doorway. Anywhere. Make a noise.'

He got out, put on his nubby sportscoat, adjusted his collar, took his time, gave an exaggerated shiver, went through the open gate and onto the concrete path bisecting an abandoned garden once loved by someone.

I pressed the button. The window slid away. Astringent polar air came in, wet, stung my lips, my eyes. I had the automatic in my hand, deadly and comforting extension of the arm, pointing at the floor between my knees, unsteady knees, the weapon perfectly balanced, silky smooth and sexual to the hand, to the web between thumb and forefinger.

Cam was at the front door. He knocked.

I turned my body, brought the automatic up to just under the windowsill. Why should Cam do things like this? What made me think it was acceptable to drag him into my sordid affairs? How was it that I could accept his offer to go to the door with only a whimper of protest?

Waiting. I'd forgotten to pull the slide back, Jesus Christ. I pulled it, precise slippery sound of oiled metal parts machined to impossibly small tolerances.

Cam knocked again.

Waiting. Cold. A tractor far away, sound borne on the winter wind.

Cam scratched the back of his neck and knocked again.

Waiting.

He turned his head, put up his right hand and beckoned me with the index finger.

Relief.

I got out, walked up the path, pistol behind my back. Cam was putting on thin black gloves. At the front door, I handed the weapon over.

Cam held the killing wand at the end of a slack arm. 'Don't think there's a party on here,' he said. 'Want to go in?'

I nodded.

Cam tried the doorknob. The door opened, unhappy on its hinges.

Passage, dark, narrow, faded peeling wallpaper, doors right and left. The smell was of damp, of decay, of the secret earth beneath the house deprived of sun for a hundred years, of the smoke from trees beyond number reduced to ash, of meat roasted, boiled, fried.

We went from room to frayed room. Everything of value had either been sold or pilfered. Deep impressions on the carpets showed where a double bed, wardrobes, chests of drawers or dressing-tables, armchairs had stood. There was no fridge, two mantelpieces and cast-iron fireplaces had been ripped out, even the bath in the lean-to bathroom was gone. All over the house, cigarettes had been ground into the carpets, empty Vic Bitter stubbies lay in corners, broken in the fireplaces.

I went over to the kitchen window over the sink and looked out. Rain, wind lifting the corrugated iron sheets on the roof of a shed. On the highest point behind the out-buildings, a grey fibreglass tank stood in a space cut into the hillside. Presumably to stop it being blown over when empty. Rainwater would be pumped up to the tank, flow back by gravity. I turned on the sink tap. A rusty trickle came out.

Out the back door, a relief to get into the light, the wind.

In the open space behind the house, water lay in pools reflecting the moving sky. We inspected the big shed first. It was the milking barn, concrete floor, milking stalls, wide gutters. The back door had blown off and the wind was threatening to lift the roof.

Next door had old oil stains on the packed-earth floor, probably the machinery shed, empty now except for unidentifiable bits of metal lying around.

Two smaller sheds, one too dangerous to enter, had no obvious purpose. The large feed barn was holding up reasonably well. Inside, two stacks of hay bales down the sides had toppled inwards, obliterating the central aisle.

I looked around for tyre tracks. Hopeless. It had been raining here for weeks. No track would last more than a few hours.

'Well,' I said, 'it had to be done. Let's go.'

We walked around the house, through a grove of dying fruit trees, packed the pistol away and left Gary's aunty's farm.

Twenty minutes later, on the highway, Cam said, 'Locals picked the place pretty clean.'

'Probably the neighbours,' I said. 'Surprised they didn't take the fibreglass water tank. Newest thing on the property.'

'Good stuff fibreglass,' Cam said. 'Doesn't rust. Poisons you but it doesn't rust.'

'Turn round, let's get back there,' I said.

Cam didn't blink, braked gently, changed down. Inside twenty seconds, we were heading back to Gary's aunty's farm.

'Don't tell me,' Cam said. 'I like surprises.'

As we went down the track to the farmhouse, I said, 'Around the back. Got a torch?'

Cam pointed at the glovebox. I opened it and found a slim black flashlight. We got out.

'Up there,' I said. Cam's eyes followed mine to the water tank.

We climbed the small hill, buffeted by the wind, getting wet. A path led up the side of the cutting, taking us to a position above the tank, looking down at its slippery top, at the manhole cover.

'Why?' Cam said.

'Rusty water coming out of the kitchen tap,' I said.

'Could be coming from somewhere else.'

We looked down on the farmhouse. There were two corrugated-iron rainwater tanks, one on either side of the house.

'No gravity down there,' I said, stepping gingerly onto the tank, taking careful steps to the cover.

I put the flashlight in my mouth, knelt on the wet surface. The cover had a moulded handle. I pulled at it and it came off easily, almost causing me to slip sideways.

I put my hands on the tank, leant forward, looked into the opening.

Pitch dark. Smell of decay.

I took the flashlight out of my mouth, found the button, switched it on, pointed into the tank.

'Christ.'

He was looking at me, lying on his back in a few centimetres of dark water. His mouth was open. Part of his lower jaw was missing, a congealed mess with pieces of white bone showing. His shirt was dark, the colour of the water he was lying in.

He'd been standing in the tank when he was shot. Shot several times from above. By someone who had walked him up to the tank at gunpoint, made him climb into it, leaned over the hole and shot him.

Gary Connors?

No. I could see his top teeth, good set of top teeth, no gold canine.

'Nasty?' asked Cam.

I nodded, got to my feet, took the steps back to land.

I had the photograph in my wallet. I got it out, handed it to Cam with the flashlight. He stepped over to the manhole, casual, confident steps, knelt, shone the torch into the tank.

He coughed, looked over his shoulder at me, non-committal look, examined the photograph, looked into the tank again.

'Him, I'd say,' he said. 'Rings on the little fingers.' He put the cover back, found a handkerchief, did a careful wipe. 'Your bloke?'

'No.' Dean Canetti.

We went back to the car. 'Kitchen tap,' Cam said, offering his handkerchief. 'And anything else.'

I went inside, uneasy, wiped the kitchen tap, the back door doorknob.

Outside, Cam was leaning against the car, smoking, looking at the outbuildings. There was an air of menace about the place now: a man had been murdered here. Executed.

'Bloke shot in a tank,' he said. 'Changes the way you see a place.'

We looked at each other. Without saying anything, we walked over to the feed barn, skirting the pools.

The big door came open under protest.

Walls of hay bales fallen, come apart. A mound where a broad aisle had been.

Cam went over to the pile, took a broken bale, pulled it off the heap, another, another.

I joined him, pulling hay away, getting hay all over my clothes.

Cam stopped.

I stopped.

Cam took his right foot back and kicked the hay.

Something solid.

Another grab of hay.

The tail-lights of a car, a dark-grey car.

In seconds, Cam had uncovered the back door, tried it, locked.

The front doorhandle, more scrabbling, Cam pulled it open.

The body came out sideways, falling into the hay, bringing with it a powerful smell of putrefaction.

For a moment, I thought I was going to be sick, swallowed, stood back.

Cam looked into the vehicle.

'Another one in there,' he said. 'Head shot.'

'Going bald?'

'No.'

I kicked away some more hay from the back of the car, stood back, found a pen and wrote the registration on the palm of my left hand.

'Let's get out of here.'

'Put the hay back first,' said Cam.

Heavy rain, sheets of water, began to fall as we turned into Sligo Lane. 'Nice rain,' Cam said. 'Hate to have to change these tyres. Japanese tyres.'

I sat in silence, trying to think calm thoughts, until I felt my heartbeat return to normal. Then I took out the tiny mobile, looked for the On button, found it, paused.

No.

I put the phone away.

'Think of anythin else,' Cam said, 'don't tell me. Goin home now.'

The trip home was sedate, just under the speed limit all the way. I got Cam to drop me two blocks from Taub's.

'Thanks for the company,' I said. 'Not the best sort of outing.'

'Could have been worse,' said Cam. 'Last outing like this I went on with you, a bloke hit me with a shotgun. Often. Kicked me too.'

'There's that,' I said.

'Anyway, I never went on this trip.'

'Unless you went alone,' I said.

Charlie was back, hobbling around. I did an hour's work on the Purbrick construction, then stepped out of sight, switched on the tiny mobile and punched one–two.

It rang three or four times.

'Yes.'

'Dave?'

'Yes.'

'Recognise the voice?'

'Yes.'

'Use names on this thing?'

'Yes.'

'I found Canetti. Dead. Shot in a water tank on a property belonging to Gary near Warrnambool.'

'Oh shit,' said Dave.

'Two others dead there too, two blokes in a grey Camry.'

'Jesus. Not Gary?'

'No.'

'Look for ID?'

'I'm averse to sticking my hand into the jackets of people who've been dead for a fair while. What about you?'

'Point taken. Get the registration?'

I read it off my palm.

'Possibly hired talent,' he said. 'From far away. Didn't think Gary had it in him.'

'Gary? All of them?'

'With help maybe. Don't know who. You shouldn't have gone without someone watching your tail. Very risky.

Keep an eye out?'

'What do you think?'

'Dealing with pros here, Jack. You haven't been putting the mobile on.'

'Busy.'

'Had something to tell you. Dean hired a car on April 3. Firm in South Melbourne. Phoned for it. It never came back. Turned up yesterday. April 5, some bloke had it parked for him at the Hyatt. Same day it got nicked from the carpark. Yesterday, the cops find the shell, stripped, in a shed out in Brooklyn.'

Pause.

'Anyway, the bloke who parked it never came back. I showed the car parkers some faces yesterday. Probably our friend. There's also the trip mileage. Bit more than the round-trip down to where he parked in the sea.'

Canetti had hired the car. Two days later, Gary had dumped it in Melbourne.

'This is getting urgent,' said Dave. 'The worry is the other side gets nervous about you now, decides to do something.'

'What about the casualties out there in the sticks?'

'Don't expect to see it on the news. Gary. Work on Gary. And put the mobile on.'

I put the phone away. But not quickly enough.

Charlie came around from behind the pillar, wiping his hands on several metres of paper-thin, fragrant plane shavings.

'So,' he said. 'Mr Important Lawyer, got a new walkie-talkie. Smaller even. Should be getting on with a simple piece of work, three days late. No. He hides behind the pillar for a talk on the little phone.'

'Legal business,' I said. 'An important client.'

He looked at me sadly. 'Hah,' he said. 'Horse business, that's what I think.' Muttering, he limped off.

I wished it was horse business.

She came to the door in a towelling dressing-gown, knee-length, long, lean legs showing, hair damp again.

We stood in the hallway, both awkward.

'This is better than ringing,' Lyall said. 'I was just thinking about setting off on a stalk.'

'No need to approach me with stealth,' I said. 'I respond well to the full-frontal approach.'

She smiled the crooked smile, took my jacket lapels in her hands. 'I'm not terribly full in the frontal,' she said. 'A source of humiliation to me as a teenager.'

She loosened my tie, pulled it off, hung it over a peg on the hatrack.

I slid my right hand into the front of her gown, felt ribs, moved upwards to the lower curve of a breast. 'Beautifully adequate in the frontal,' I said. I was having difficulty speaking.

Lyall looked me in the eyes, unblinking, unbuttoned my shirt, got to the waist. Her right hand kept going south, slowly, deliciously south, stopped, began to explore.

I loosened the belt of her gown. It fell open, flushed chest. I bent to kiss her breasts.

One hand in my hair. 'Why do you always find me with wet hair?'

I disengaged my lips. 'Just lucky,' I said. 'I like your hair wet.'

'Feeling damp all over,' she said. 'For some reason. Let's talk upstairs.'

'I'm not clean,' I said.

She took my hand. 'I could stand another shower.'

'Standing is what it may come to,' I said.

It was after 9 p.m. before we got around to eating at the table in the warm kitchen: scrambled eggs made with cream and Roquefort cheese and tarragon, dash of Worcestershire sauce.

'You have many talents,' I said, drinking some of the riesling I'd fetched from the car. 'Culinary, amorous, photographic. I've never quite understood photography. It chooses you, does it?'

Lyall combed her hair with her fingers. She was wearing a big grey cotton sweatshirt and trackpants, hair pulled back, no makeup.

'You mean I can scramble eggs and I'm randy? Photography just happened to me. My mother was a painter, quite good, I think. She stopped when she got married, had my brother. Women did that then. Still do, probably. Just stop, turn it in. As if it were nothing, something you'd outgrown. You got down to the real work, the husband, the kids. Anyway, she pushed me to paint. It didn't take much pushing. I ended up besotted by art, the whole thing, painting and painters, went to art school in Sydney, won a scholarship to go to the Slade in London.'

She forked up some scrambled egg, chewed, drank some wine. 'Nice wine. I was very intense. Art is all. I blush to think about it now.'

'Blushing becomes you. The chest blush is particularly attractive.'

She hooked her ankles behind my right calf, squeezed. 'Anyway, the intensity didn't help me eat. I was on the

254

breadline when I got a part-time job with a portrait photographer. A man called Rufus Buchanan.'

'An explorer's name,' I said. 'First man up the South-West Passage.'

She laughed, moved her head from side to side. 'That's right. I don't know about the south-west. But show Bucky a passage, he'd attempt to explore it. I was the darkroom assistant. All the customers were people making a big quid out of London real estate. Did you ever see those Snowdon pictures of the Royals? Misty, airbrushed to buggery.'

'I have them in a scrapbook,' I said.

'That's what Bucky's customers wanted. Misty pictures, all imperfections gone. The women used to ask: "Can you make my neck look longer?" or, "I say, any chance of getting more space between Julian's eyes?", that sort of thing. Bucky was good at it. Randy little snake, real name Colin Biggs. From Liverpool. You had to beat him off with a stick two or three times a day. It was very tiring, but I'd worked in Aussie pubs, I could handle that. The good part was that he hated the darkroom, except for groping, so he wanted me to do that, taught me the trade. And he knew his stuff, he'd had a real arse-kicking apprenticeship.'

She added some wine to the glasses. 'That's the long answer to a short question,' she said. 'Less about me. Tell me about why you shoot ex-policemen.'

'No. More about you.'

'Well, the awful thing about my career,' she said, 'is that it begins in a dramatic way. I could process film, so I started taking pictures. Then I went on holiday with a boyfriend. We were in a little place in Belgium near the German border. Pretty fountain, people around it. I was taking pictures when a car pulled up on the other side, outside the bank. Then two men came out of the bank and two men got out of the car with machine pistols and shot them both. I got, oh, seven or eight pictures. Full sequence. IRA revenge killing. British Army officers, the dead men. The guy I was with, he was an operator. On the phone to a photo agency in London, they ran a quick auction of my pictures. After commissions and giving the guy his cut, I ended up with what looked like an enormous sum then. Still looks pretty big, actually.'

'And you had a new career?'

'I hadn't even been paid for the IRA pictures when the agency rang, did I want to go to Beirut? Well, yes. I was so astoundingly green and naive. They didn't tell me that my predecessor had been kidnapped and murdered and no-one else would go near the place.'

She ate and drank. 'Anyway, I survived Beirut, utterly terrified at times. You get used to it. Get used to anything. Took some not bad pictures. And it went on from there. For a long time I kept saying: just one more job, then it's back to painting.'

'Not any more?'

'No. I think the painting's gone. Makes me feel sad sometimes.' She looked at me. 'But not for the past twenty-four hours, my learned friend. I've been feeling pretty chipper. Post-orgasmically chipper.'

I finished my scrambled egg. 'What happened to post-orgasmic tristesse?'

'Only the French,' she said. 'The French can't enjoy anything without it making them sad. They cry over food.'

'On the subject of crying, married ever?'

Lyall sat back, put her feet in my lap. 'Very definitely. For five years. To a photographer, a French photographer. That's how I know about the crying. He's dead. Shot in the back in Bosnia three years ago.'

'I'm sorry.' I took her hand.

She nodded. 'We'd been divorced a long time. I hadn't thought about him in years, to tell the truth. We broke up in a very loud and messy way. Then I find out I'm still down as his next-of-kin and he's left everything to me. In a will he made after the break-up.' She turned her head away. 'Only a Frenchman would do that.'

A moment of silence. Then Lyall said, 'And that is more than enough of me. Tell me about the Irish women.'

I released her hand. 'My first wife left me for a man who performed minor surgery on her. Irresistibly attracted to the scalpel. Took our daughter with her. We'd only been married about eighteen months. I got over that. A former client of mine murdered my second wife. In a carpark.'

'Oh,' she said and bit her lower lip. 'My turn for sorry.'

More silence. We sat for a moment, not looking at each other. The survivors. We who are left behind. Then I picked up her hand and kissed her long fingers. 'That's enough sorries. I need to ask you some more things about Stuart.'

'Shit,' Lyall said. 'I meant to tell you last night. Before the passion swept me away. I found the phone logbook we recorded messages in. I haven't needed it since Bradley left. I'd forgotten but I went away first, East Timor for the London *Sunday Times* colour supp. Bradley and Stuart both took messages for me and each other from the thirtieth of June. Then Bradley must have left because Stuart took messages for both of us from the fourth of July. Here's the last one he put in the book.'

She handed it to me. 'Seventh of July,' she said.

A neat hand had written the date and the message: *Brad: Ring James Margo (Margaux?). You know number.*

'He flew to Sydney on the morning of the tenth?' I said.

'Yes.'

I looked at the entries before the seventh. The house had a busy phone. On the sixth of July, Stuart had made six entries: four calls for Bradley, two for Lyall. On the fifth, he'd recorded seven; on the fourth, five calls for Lyall and four for Bradley.

I went further back. I couldn't see a day when fewer than five messages were noted.

'Part-time job just taking messages,' I said.

She nodded. 'That's nothing. Blissfully quiet time. Bradley could get twenty calls a day. Easily. Drive you mad if he wasn't here. Making movies. What a business. Please give Brad an urgent message, please get him to ring back. Five or six projects on the go, dozens of people involved, all on the phone, everything's urgent.'

Lyall finished her glass. 'Of course, it's only urgent today, tomorrow there's a new dream. Hardly anything ever gets made but they don't give up hope. Nothing is ever dead.'

'The two days,' I said, 'eight and nine July. No calls recorded. Why would that be?'

Lyall shrugged. 'Don't know.'

'So when you came back, you found calls dating back to when?'

'Tenth of July.'

'Date's certain?'

'The answering machine puts a day and a time on messages. When I got back, its awful voice said Thursday for the first message. Thursday was the tenth.'

'So Stuart must have wiped Tuesday and Wednesday without recording the calls.'

'Be a first for Stuart. Punctilious recorder of calls. Listen,

I just thought of something else. It all seems so long ago, it went right out of my mind. Stuart's new video camera was also gone. Tripod's here.'

'What did he use it for?'

'Interviewing someone. He bought it before I went to East Timor, at least a week before. I think. He had me sit in a chair in the sitting room, camera on the tripod. Wanted to make sure he had the focus right, the sound level, that sort of thing.'

'Interviewing who? Do you know?'

'No. Stuart wouldn't tell you that. But he was pleased with himself. I remember he went away for a couple of days, took the camera. Came back and he was behind the computer for days, headphones on.'

'Headphones?'

'He had a dictaphone, tape recorder thing. It's up there. No tape in it.'

She got up and came around the table, stood behind me, leaned over me. I felt her breasts against my head. 'I'm feeling wonderfully tired,' she said. 'Must be the squash. Might have a little lie down. Interested?'

'Only if you promise to keep your hands off me.'

Lyall laughed. 'Riding no-hands? I can do that. Come.'

We sat in Harry's wood-panelled projection room, in the armchair seats.

'Show Jack the stuff, Cam,' said Harry. He was in a dark suit, face glowing from the second shave of the day. He looked at his watch. 'Need to get a move on, goin out to dinner.'

Cam had his laptop open, plugged into the big monitor. 'Had so much data, couldn't run the program this bloke wrote for me on this thing,' he said. 'We went to this place in town and ran it on a brute computer, tower like a fridge. Didn't work too good, he rewrote the program on the spot. Twice.'

He hit some keys. The names of fifteen horses appeared on the big screen, all linked by arrows to names.

'Had no luck till we concentrated on owners of winning horses. This lot are all owned by syndicates. We did their histories, they're all top bloodlines, bought at auctions by the names you see there. These people are not known to anyone in the business. Just people who kept stickin their hands up, signed cheques.'

He tapped keys. The horses now had syndicates of owners.

'The syndicates have owned other horses. But we stuck with the fifteen recent winners they own. Ran the syndicate names through every database you can buy or steal.'

In each syndicate, one name went bold.

'These people. They've got something in common. All

listed as bad credit risks and all been involved in some kind of litigation with a finance company called Capitelli. Big biscuits involved. All lost.'

Cam tapped a key. The other people in the syndicates were highlighted.

'The rest,' he said, 'they're all connected to the Capitelli losers. Family, mostly. But mostly people with different names.'

He tapped again. A diagram appeared. Horses, syndicates, the bold person in each now linked with Capitelli.

Another keystroke.

Capitelli linked with two names: G. L. Giffard, H. A. Giffard.

Cam said, 'Directors of Capitelli. G. L.'s in his sixties. Lives in a unit in Bondi. H. A., that's his sister. She's in an old-age in Queensland.'

I'd put in a long day at Taub's, catching up on the Purbrick library. Bits of my body, lower back, base of neck, harboured dull pains. 'This is a bit late in the day for me,' I said. 'You've got fifteen winning horses in the bush owned by syndicates of people who are all connected to one member. That would be the norm. That's how syndicates get formed. The difference you say is that all the key members once owed money to a finance company called Capitelli. Am I seeing this clearly? Or at all?'

Harry said, 'Cotton on quick, Jack. That's why you're my lawyer.'

Cam shook a Gitane from the packet, lodged it in the corner of his mouth. 'Sounds simple,' he said. 'Just pulverise and sieve a mountain of rock.'

'The effort's clear,' I said. 'What's it mean?'

'Capitelli owns the horses,' said Harry.

'Giffards.'

'No.'

Tap. Capitelli joined to another name: Kirsch Realty.

'That's who really owns Capitelli,' Cam said. 'Queensland company. Giffard fronts Capitelli. Went through four steps to find that out. And we're still guessin then.'

'I like this presentation but I'm getting lost,' I said.

'Ronnie Kirsch,' said Cam. 'Owns the horses.'

'Somebody's got to own them. They win by themselves. More or less.'

Harry laughed, his hoarse big-man's laugh, carefully tapped a centimetre of Havana cigar ash into the ashtray set into the arm of his chair.

'These fifteen winners we concentrated on,' Cam said, 'the Kirsch horses, they're with these trainers, bush trainers.'

Six names.

'Now there's a funny thing about this lot. All these trainers have been in financial shit.'

'Funny? I thought training *was* financial shit.'

'Financial shit involving loans from one company.'

'Capitelli?'

'Not directly. Company called Krua Finance. Belongs to Ronnie Kirsch's brother-in law. Anyways, for this bunch of trainers, financial shit ended when the syndicates come along.'

'The prize money,' I said.

Cam shook his head. Tapped.

New diagram. Set of horses, with jockeys and trainers.

Tap. Another set.

It went on.

It stopped.

'Point of the slipper, Jack,' said Harry. 'This lot ride in

lots of combinations, many combinations, sometimes just the two. But put these buggers on the track, the Kirsch horses win. Our races, Kyneton, Ballarat, both Kirsch winners.'

'Merit,' I said.

'Merit? Well, merit wins some of em.'

Harry pulled in a mouthful of Cuban smoke, savoured it, sent it drifting over to me, a cloud of Cuban fallout to die for. For and from. Many losses ached in me, but at certain times the Cuban loss was a sudden stiletto in the heart.

'Tell me, Harry,' I said, 'I've got a few things on my mind.'

'The fifteen,' said Cam, 'it's just in the time we've looked at, they come over like good horses. Good but unreliable. Don't stay with the same trainer, no loyalty. Bugger doesn't win for a while, he's off somewhere else. Then he gets a win. Like the footy. Sack the coach, team wins the next game. But he always goes to one of the six.'

'Well, I see it. But how much can you make setting up something like this?' I said.

They both looked at me. Harry drew on the cigar, looking at Cam. He took the tight brown truncheon away from his lips, oozed aromatic smoke. 'A bit,' he said. 'Enough.'

'We had the TAB figures in,' Cam said. 'Looked at eighty Kirsch wins. There's money for them all over the country. Queensland stands out.'

'It's millions, Jack,' said Harry.

'The bloke runnin it here for Kirsch is called Dingell. Jeff Dingell. Moved from Queensland. He's got a big place other-side Macedon. His own lake, tennis courts, huge heated pool, four-car garage, another house on the property. There's three Queensland goons live there.'

'Sure it's the right person?' I asked.

Cam nodded. 'Had another talk to Johnny Chernov. Very brief talk. I parked next to him at a McDonald's near the bridge, said to him through the window, look away, I'm going to say a name. It's the right name, look at me. Just look.'

'And?'

'He looked.'

'What now?'

'Can't have this kind of thing goin on, Jack,' Harry said. 'Offerin the hoops a quid's one thing, usually doin your dough anyway. Bloke takes a quid from you, he's probably takin a quid from four others in the same race. Tryin to kill em, that's something else. Can't blame the trainers, can't blame the hoops. Bad for business. Bloke's got to go back to Queensland. Got to know people want him to go home.'

I looked at Cam, who was looking at me impassively. Harry was also looking at me.

'I don't know why you're looking at me.' I sighed. 'Why are you looking at me?'

Harry coughed politely. 'Mentioned the matter, vaguely you understand, to Cyril Wootton,' he said. 'He reckons there's a certain person, kind of person would be helpful here, this person would give you a kidney if you were short.'

I looked from one to the other. 'Jesus,' I said. 'I'm going to kill Wootton.' I thought about the message on my answering machine.

Jack. No chance to say you're the bloke got the fucken result. Bargain result, K-Mart price for that result. Listen, I'm grateful, you understand? That's serious, mate. Anything. Ring me, I'll fix it. I'm solid, right? Cheers.

I sighed again, took out my notebook and wrote Brendan

O'Grady's name and number on a page. I tore it out and gave it to Cam.

'When you talk to him,' I said, 'this is all you're allowed to say about me: Jack says thanks for the message. Nothing else. Clear on that?'

'Got it,' said Cam.

Harry smiled at me. 'Teamwork,' he said. 'That's what wins races.'

To my office, full of dead air, not opened for days. The office of a barrister and solicitor said the dirty plate outside. It was badly in need of cleaning. The practice of the law. I couldn't remember when I'd done anything that resembled the practice of the law. I could: Laurie Baranek's outrageous lease. It resembled the practice of law. Vaguely.

I was becoming more and more like Barry Tregear and the men in the long-gone Consorting and Major Crimes squads. You needed a team list to tell them from the people on the other side.

A suburban solicitor without the law. Lesser breeds without the law. Who said that? Kipling? He could have been referring to dogs. Dogs know no law. Obedience, perhaps. Law, no. Many lesser breeds of dog. The smaller ones, packed with venom and cringe.

The answering machine: Mrs Davenport. Four times.

Then Linda. Breath-stopping no more. Perhaps just a small breath stopped. Linda, with drink taken.

Jack Irish. Speaking to the machine of. Linda. How often do you say your own name? Remember Linda? I have difficulty remembering Linda. Never saw myself as a Linda, anyway. I told you that. Between the sheets.

Pause.

Anyway. Hard to catch you. Well, the catch was reasonably easy. Sorry. It wasn't a catch. It was, I suppose. I came to your place....No, that's you catching me. Listen, you won't care, why should you? I'm giving this job the shove. Or it me. It me is probably right. What did that journo on the Mirror *say? Never pee in your own handbag. That always puzzled me. A male journo. Dead.*

Pause.

Yes. Handbags. I suppose it's a version of the doorstep. Why couldn't I see that before? I feel like a handbag. Shove any old thing into it. Open the catch, shove it in. It's there, it's available. Whichever, I'm out of here. Shover, shovee, it's shove. Just the money to be sorted out. The man wants me off the premises. He's moved on, finds it awkward having me around.

Pause.

Sorry. I'm a bit pissed. I'll try again.

Pause.

Or you could try. No. I'll…Goodnight. Jack. Goodnight, Jack Irish. Goodnight.

What did I feel? Sadness, that's all. Sadness on top of weariness. What night was that message recorded? The machine didn't have a time stamp. I sat back in the chair, swung my legs onto the tailor's table, stared at nothing, thought about finding the man in the water tank, Dean Canetti, father of Princess Charlotte, a man executed from above, his shattered face now dissolving. And the men in the car, the smell.

In what order had they died? Killed by one person? With help maybe, Dave said. The outside enemies of Black Tide? Did that mean Levesque?

Tired, nodding off.

Knock at the door.

I sat up, startled. 'Who's there?'

'Simone Bendsten.'

She was dressed for going out, high-collar coat, open, underneath a black velvety-looking number, low in the north, high in the south. It suggested, possibly by optical illusion, that Ms Bendsten was two-thirds leg. Was that a peculiarly Scandinavian configuration? In the genes? Only empirical research could answer that question.

'I was going to put it under the door,' she said, holding up a yellow A4 envelope.

Very svelte in velvet. Svelvety. I was tired.

Simone came over and put the envelope on the desk.

'I followed up the Secure International reference in the European databases. That's Major-General Gordon Ibell. And I found a mention in this Swedish source of a company called Eagle Exprexxo they say was involved in transporting arms to Angola. The American side in Angola. To Unita. Jonas Savimbi.'

Jonas Savimbi. Where was he now? Tired. Long days and athletic sex. A balanced life, that was what was required. Short days and unathletic sex. 'You followed up Secure International. And you got to Eagle?'

'Twice, actually. There's also a mention in the *International Herald Tribune* about a case still before the French courts. About missiles, small missiles, I don't quite understand missiles. They were found in a semi after a freeway accident. The semi owner says he was hired by a company called Redan. Redan says it got the job from an agency, a freight agency. The agency says it understood the hirer to be Eagle Exprexxo but has nothing on paper.'

'That's good work,' I said. I hadn't registered much.

'More,' she said. 'I found a piece in an American magazine.'

'An American magazine.'

She had a concerned look, concerned about me, not a look I wanted to encourage in women.

'You're tired, Jack. If this is useful, we can follow it up.'

I blinked a few times. 'Good idea,' I said. 'I'll read the report, give it some thought.'

'A good night's sleep,' she said. 'Does wonders.'

I saw her to the door. Across the street, the McCoy studio was dark but within a piano was tinkling. The hirsute charlatan was presumably doing something to music, something that did not require illumination.

I closed the front door, put Simone's envelope into my safe, the hinged false bottom I'd added to the tailor's table, headed for home. A call to Lyall, soup, then bed.

An old Volkswagen blocked my driveway, the student from across the road. I cursed him, turned left at the corner, parked in my landlady's driveway. She was in Queensland, taking the sun with all the other Melbourne landlords and landladies. I took the short cut up her drive and across her dark backyard to the wall.

Hand on the high wooden gate leading to my stable, I paused, scalp tightening, some atavistic instinct awakened.

I put my eye to the widest gap between the boards.

Looking to the left, I could make out my front doorway, a darker shape in the gloomy bluestone facade, see the window to the left of the doorway, to the right, the open-fronted wood shelter with its sentry-box roof.

Nothing to be seen. I relaxed, took my eye from the crack, grasped the gate handle.

A light came on upstairs in the double-storeyed house next door.

I looked up. Opaque glass: a bathroom.

Something made me put my eye to the crack again.

I saw him instantly, leaning against the wall beside the wood shelter, faint light from the upstairs window now falling on his face.

His head was cocked. Listening?

A bony face. Bony head. Short hair.

The man in the grey suit outside Parliament in Canberra. The man bringing dark glasses up to his face. And then finding them uncomfortable, stopping to adjust the fit, looking down.

He was waiting for me, dressed in black. Perhaps someone else nearby.

Waiting to kill me?

Dave's voice in my head.

The worry is the other side gets nervous about you now, decides to do something.

I backed away slowly from the gate, turned and walked carefully across the dark courtyard, down the driveway.

Find Gary. The only way to save my life, according to Dave at our meeting on the windy night.

Talk to Des.

Talk to Des about what?

If we find him, it'll be because he's somewhere he feels safe. That's going to come from way back.

I drove to Northcote, not taking my usual route, going up St George's Road, watching the rear-view mirror, eyeing the cars at intersections. I crossed the railway line, parked in High Street, waited, watched, did a U-turn, parked on the other side. Saw nothing out of the ordinary.

Des showed no surprise at seeing me.

'Come in,' he said. 'Watchin this nonsense on telly, eatin a bit of chocolate. The girls give it to me. Never buy chocolate. Seen the price of chocolate?'

We sat down on the brown cut-velvet armchairs with wooden arms in the dim room, photographs on the mantel-piece, wedding pictures, pictures of two couples, two women, each with a baby, two men next to a car, a couple and a fair-haired boy.

'Have some.' He offered the bar of chocolate.

'No thanks.'

'What about a beer? I could use a beer.'

'Beer would be nice.'

He came back with two open stubbies of Vic Bitter and glasses. We poured.

Des wiped his lips. 'Goes down a treat, don't it. Can't

drink on me own, never got in the habit. Wish I had, too late now.'

'Des, I've got to ask you about Gary,' I said. 'They may sound like silly questions but I've got to ask.'

'Ask,' he said, waving a big hand. 'Ask.'

'If Gary changed his name, what would he change it to?'

Des looked away, gave me a sidelong glance. 'Changed his name? Why would he do that?'

'If he wanted to hide, he might change his name to make it hard to find him.'

'Oh, right. Get ya. The whole name. I was thinkin somethin different like him callin himself Bruce Connors or Wally Connors.'

'He might use a family name,' I said. 'People often do that. Like his mother's maiden name.'

'Keegan?'

'Perhaps. What about the aunt who left him the place near Warrnambool? What was her surname?'

'Dixon.'

He had a small sip of beer, chewed it thoughtfully. 'Funny boy, Gary. Reader he was, great reader, read anythin. Sit here on the floor in front of me, me readin the paper, he'd be readin the front and the back page. Just a little bloke. Ask me questions. Like, what's nude mean, Dad? Bit embarrassin, I'd say, ask yer mother.'

His eyes were on the mantelpiece, on the photographs.

'Used to tell other kids we wasn't really his mum and dad. Any new kid around here, Gary'd tell him he wasn't really Gary Connors.'

Something was nagging at me. 'If he wasn't Gary Connors, who was he?'

'Had a whole story, name and all. Got it out of a book,

272

probly. How his parents were these rich people in England and people wanted to kidnap him and get all the family's money, so his mum and dad sent him to live with us. Told em he'd be goin back to England soon as the danger was over. Funny boy, Gary. Could've come from bein an only, I don't know.'

He took another sip of beer, admired the glass, nodded at it. 'Good drop this, Bill. Don't drink by myself, never got…'

A vehicle stopping. Close by. Further along the street.

I went to the window and looked out through the crack at the side of the heavy curtain. Two women getting out of a small white car.

I came back to my seat. 'The name, what was it?'

'The name?'

'His story about not being Gary Connors. What did he call himself, Des?'

He looked at me for a second, far away, hadn't noticed me getting up. 'The name. What was the name now? Three names. No. No use in sittin here tryin to think of it.'

'Try, Des. It's important.'

'No,' he said, 'don't have to try. Just go down the passage to the boy's room. All his books there. Mum wouldn't hear a gettin rid of em. Every last one of em there. He used to write the name in his books.'

He left the room. I sipped beer, listened to cars going by, only two cars. A quiet street. I could bring down a terrible visitation on this street. Men with guns who would shoot anyone. Young and old.

…kill your friend, kill your wife, kill your child, kill you, it's all the same.

Tramping down the passage. Des, with a book.

'Here we are,' he said. '*Boy's Book of Adventure*. Might have a read of this myself. Bloody paper's got nothin but sorrow in it.'

He sat down, opened the book, showed me the flyleaf.

A slanting, childish handwriting, large capitals, upsweeps on the terminal letters of each word.

Christopher Anthony Armstrong (Kit).

I read it out.

Des shook his head. 'Never could work out why he'd tell that story. Strange. Still, can't all be the boy's fault.'

He looked at his half-empty glass of beer. Losing the taste for it. He was tired.

'Wasn't much of a dad. Not like me dad was for me. I dunno, never had me heart in it after the first lad. Set in the ways. Never kicked a footy with Gary. Could be that.'

'I doubt it. Kicking the footy is what kids do for their dads, not the other way round,' I said. 'This is a good start, Des. Very good. Now this is important. If Gary was thinking about a safe place to go to, what would he think of?'

Des straightened his shoulders, had a sip of beer. 'Safe place? Got me there.'

'From long ago, Des. From when he was a boy.'

He thought, shook his head. 'Around here, you mean?'

'Anywhere. Anywhere he went when he was little.'

As I said that, Chrissy Donato-Connors-Sargent's voice came to me. Something about Gary being kicked out when he was a little kid. Fostered? On a chook farm?

'Des, I talked to Gary's second wife. She says he told her he was kicked out by his parents, fostered by these people on a chicken farm. Like a prison farm, I think she said. Mean anything?'

274

Des put his head down like a vulture. 'Gary? Fostered? Gary? Well, always one for the tall story but that's a shocker. His mum'll be spinnin. That's his mum's cousins' place he's talkin about. Tassie. Went there three, four times. That's all the Tassie he knows. Loved to go there, always pesterin to go.'

'The prison farm in Tasmania?'

Des snorted. 'Prison farm, my foot. Little chook farm. Never went there meself. The wife did. Not keen on them ferries goin across Bass Strait. Don't mind a decent passenger ship. On em in the war. Didn't mind em at all. Feel the bugger's built to take it.'

'Little chook farm. Still there?'

Des finished his glass, moved his teeth, tasting. Stopped doing that. Nodded a few times.

I said, 'Des, the chook farm. Still there?'

He straightened his back. 'Chook farm? Dunno. Lost touch there. Not my side. Gary had a thing for the girl, the daughter. Used to get letters from her. Bit like him, I gathered. Come along late in the piece, fat lady pretty much sung. Then she got in the family way, one of the local pointies, the wife said. Had a few of em with me in the army. Good blokes but you wouldn't breed from em. No. Pretty much a dead-end. Out there. Island.'

His eyes were closing.

'Where's the chook farm, Des?'

'Tassie somewhere. Near Hobart.'

'The people's name, Des? The name?'

'Painter. That's the name. Painter, the wife's cousins.'

I got up. Des jerked awake. I picked up his hand, clasped it gently.

'Off, are you? Give you another beer.'

'Not tonight, Des,' I said. 'Other times. Let myself out.'

'Bill,' he said. 'Mate, good to see ya. Just sit here, watch a bit of telly. Terrible nonsense…'

I put the remote control device under his hand. Touched his forehead, brushed my hand over his hair, ruffled it, couldn't help myself.

In the Stud. No home to go to. Bring down misery on anyone I touched.

Christopher Anthony Armstrong. The Painter family. Chicken farmers. A girl.

I took out the tiny mobile phone, punched the buttons. Instant response.

'Yes.'

'I've got names to run from April 5.'

'Yes.'

'Keegan. Dixon. Painter. Christopher Anthony Armstrong or Kit Armstrong. Someone was waiting for me at home tonight. Out of sight. A man I saw in Canberra the day I talked to Meryl.'

'What's he look like?'

'Tall. Short hair. Bony head.'

Dave whistled. 'So you're not at home, then?'

'No.'

'Stay away. I'll see what I can arrange.'

'I've got something else. A long shot, exceedingly long. Somewhere he might be. In Tasmania.'

Pause. 'You've been busy. Listen, drive to Tullamarine now. Park in the short-term parking area. Go to the international terminal. Find somewhere you can watch the Qantas check-in and keep a lookout for me. I'll run these names, be there inside an hour. And Jack…'

'Yes.'

'Don't contact anyone, don't tell anyone anything. Got me?'

I drove around the streets of Northcote for a while, then I took the direct route. Along Brunswick Road to the Tullamarine Freeway. At the airport, I got the old raincoat out of the boot. Dry-mouthed, empty feeling in the stomach, I headed for International.

The wait was brief. I saw him from a long way away and he jerked his head towards the exit.

On the way to his car, Dave said, 'Good name that, Christopher Armstrong. Person of that name flew to Hobart on the day the hire car was dropped at the Hyatt. What's the place you've got?'

I told him about Gary and his connection with Painter's chook farm. He unlocked the car as we approached, got in, unlocked the passenger door. When I was seated, he got out again, walked to the front of the vehicle. I could see him take out his mobile, dial with his right thumb, speak, listen, speak, put the phone away.

'Go tonight,' he said, easing his big body onto the seat. 'Fly from Essendon, just down the road.'

There didn't seem to be any reason to object.

Two passengers in an eight-seater aircraft. Dave sat across the aisle, dark suit, hands in his lap, eyes closed, closed since before take-off. Outside, flashing lights on the wingtips.

Flying across Bass Strait at night in a twin-engined aircraft, crew of two. A small car had picked us up at the Essendon terminal, driven us across the tarmac to a far reach.

No baseball caps worn backwards here. Short-haired men in blue shirts, ties, unhurried, looking at glowing instruments, seldom at each other, sitting back in their seats. Men at work.

'Tell me about Black Tide,' I said.

Dave opened his eyes, found his packet of Camels, lit up with the old Ronson.

Silence for a while.

'Money laundering,' he said. 'Looking for the laundrymen. Victorian Police operation, fraud people, not drugs. Six Vics and six of us from Canberra. Small, very tight. We reckoned it was leakproof. That was the mistake.'

One of the men up front was talking quietly into his throat mike. An atmosphere of peace and calm, of competence and confidence.

'Started with these South Africans,' Dave said. 'Two of them. Business migrants. Know what that is?'

'They have to bring in a certain amount of money.'

'Invest it, create jobs, that was the idea,' he said. 'These blokes, they're cousins, they've got the money all right. But the money doesn't come from South Africa. It comes from Hong Kong. The cousins go into the travel business. Not how they made their money in the old country, they're making a fresh start. Buy a little travel agency in Carlton. Then one in Camberwell. It goes on. All over Melbourne. But also Sydney, Brisbane, Perth. Darwin. All over. About thirty of them. They borrow money from Hong Kong to finance the deals.'

He looked at me, drew, blew a thin stream of smoke upwards. 'Now the first interesting part is this. These are all small businesses, two three people. After they get bought, it's just weeks before the old staff's gone. New people. People without experience in the travel business. And the cousins don't link these businesses, form a chain, use the clout of a chain with the airlines. No. They stay small independent businesses.'

Hissing through the night, pleasantly warm in the cabin.

'Well,' said Dave, 'they turn into pretty good businesses. Turnover goes up nicely, not spectacular but up. And everything gets declared for tax.'

'Good business migrants,' I said. 'Success story.'

'Excellent migrants. Excellent managers. The cousins do a lot of managing. And they create jobs. For the relatives mainly. We work out after two years, there's nearly twenty relatives in the businesses. Fly around. The family's in every agency at least twice a week. In Melbourne, once a day. Hands-on management. This success story only comes to the attention of anyone when a young woman comes in to the cops in Melbourne with a strange story. She works for one of the cousins' agencies, ends up talking to the frauds. She doesn't know much but it smells strongly. Then there's a problem. She vanishes. Gone.'

Dave put out his cigarette. 'That was a mistake for the cousins. They could have bluffed their way out of her story. But gone, that's different.'

Silence. 'That's how Black Tide got started. It's slow work but the picture comes out after a while. It's not only the businesses doing well. They are and they're paying the interest on the loans to Hong Kong. Big interest. The customers are also doing well. When we run the sums, we find the average amount in travellers' cheques bought by the cousins' customers is about twice what you'd expect on the national figures. And something else. We find lots of the customers put cash in their credit card accounts before they go overseas. For months before they go travelling, they regularly stick small amounts into their credit cards, always in cash, turn them into debit cards.'

I was beginning to see light. Gary's friend Jellicoe of WorldWind Travel, efficiently bludgeoned to death in his sitting room. Novikov, the travel agent shot dead in his suburban garage.

'And these customers,' said Dave, 'they're not high-income people. Some of them come off the dole or the pension just a month or two before they open a bank account with a modest sum, put more in regularly, apply for a credit card. Modest credit limit. And because they're not on benefits and they're not avoiding tax, the sweep doesn't pick them up.'

'The sweep.'

'Social Security runs a sweep through all the government databases every six weeks or so. Matches the data. About ten million matches tried every time. See what comes up.'

'That's legal is it?'

Dave shrugged, lit another cigarette. 'There's worse goes

on, much fucking worse,' he said. 'Back to Black Tide, what we found, these customers all pass through Hong Kong or Manila or Bangkok, usually on the way home, and they cash most of their travellers' cheques there, take out most of the money in their credit card accounts. Then it's gone. Average expenditure's around ten grand. Lots of repeat business for the cousins' agencies too. This one waitress, she goes six times in two years.'

'Out of the tips,' I said.

Dave nodded. 'That's the domestic side of the business. The foreign side is even better. Say you're a young Italian, German, whatever, you're coming to Australia. Backpacker. You're a German, you go to the travel agency your friend knows about, you give them, say, 5000 Deutschmarks. They give you an *Untergrundbahn* ticket, torn in half, something like that.'

'Public transport's not cheap in Germany,' I said. I knew what he was talking about.

He acknowledged the joke with a lip movement. 'You get to Sydney, Melbourne, somewhere they tell you to go, you meet someone, give him your half ticket, he matches it with his half ticket, gives you an envelope full of dollars, cash, thirty per cent over the exchange rate. Maybe more. Cheapest holiday you'll ever have. Who needs travellers' cheques?'

'The money, what's involved?'

Shrug of the big shoulders. 'Impossible to say. Many, many millions, they're moving a fair bit. Not as much as they'd like but this is just part of washing the street cash, other cash.'

Adrift in fatigue, mind wandering. 'Gary,' I said. 'How does this involve Gary?'

'Gary's a frequent flier, he came to the drug people's attention long ago. But he declared a lot of income, paid his taxes, didn't spend more than he declared, didn't appear to have any offshore money stashes. Not a target, not an interesting person. Then one day, this is late in the life of Black Tide, the glue on Jellicoe reports him talking to Gary. Now Jellicoe was a matter of serious interest to Black Tide. His agency, WorldWind Travel, it wasn't owned by the cousins. But people, young, they turn up at a cousins' agency, other places, then they turn up at WorldWind. And the reverse. Sometimes five, six a day. Some sort of cut-out going on. We knew, don't touch any of the kids. Touch a customer, everything goes on hold. In Sydney, we had a good thing going until this prick of ours, he has a little word with a customer in the belief that an elegant short-circuit is available.'

I wasn't following well.

'Lost that, two million manhours, personfuckinghours. Anyway, that's one side of Jellicoe. The other, lots of tourists pop in. He's a half-ticket man. We checked his car in a parking garage one night, two hundred and ten grand in the boot, tens, twenties, fifties. There's two more like Jellicoe we know of in Melbourne. One in St Kilda, one in Fitzroy.'

'What about Gary?'

'Like I said, Gary came up late in the day. What do you know about Gary?'

I was taken off-guard. 'He's TransQuik. He's Levesque.'

Pause. 'That's right. We didn't know whose money the cousins were washing until we made Gary with Jellicoe. Then we knew. Then all Gary's flying around, Hong Kong, Manila, Bangkok, Europe, the States, all his talking to people in places you can't get any kind of audio, suddenly that all made sense.'

'Not to me,' I said.

'We could have taken the cousins out. Easy. We had more than enough. But where does that get us? Basically, the cousins are like a bank. They move money around for a fee. Whose money are they moving? That's the question.'

'What's the answer?'

'We were getting there. Gary's the key. He's the link. The current passes through him. So it had to be Gary. And that's where we touched the TransQuik nerve.'

'What happened?'

'They shut Black Tide down. Orders from above. Over. Finished. All the files taken, computers swept, cleaned. Nothing left. It was like someone died. Like your mother shot your dog. Eleven months of nothing but Black Tide. It wrecked three bloody marriages because people never went home. The boss looked at the wall for the whole day, drinking coffee. Then he went up in the lift, into the big man's office, there's two other people in there. The big man says to our boss, just pull your head in, this is Cabinet-level stuff and you're a fucking Detective Inspector. The boss grabs him by the tie, pulls him out of the chair, punches his lights out. Jaw broken, teeth on the one side, they're sticking out his cheek. Hadn't been pulled off, he'd have killed the bastard.'

'That was a way of saying goodbye, was it?' I said in spite of myself.

He made a sound, not a laugh, not a cough. 'Bought a lawn-mowing round up in Queensland. Mackay. Taking the mower off the trailer one day, a bloke in a Falcon stops, blows his head off with a shotgun. Unsolved.'

He looked at his watch. 'Got to make some arrangements,' he said. He loosened his safety belt and went up the aisle to the cockpit, blocked the whole entrance with his frame.

I put my head back, closed my eyes, not thinking of sleep, not considering sleep possible, fell asleep.

I woke up in the last seconds of the descent. Touchdown was two small bumps, a minor whining noise, a consciousness of the safety belt. Out the door, stairs folding out, stiff-legged into an icy Tasmanian night, polar wind blowing, feeling old.

A man was waiting for us, standing next to a Toyota four-wheel-drive on the tarmac. A fortyish man in a suit, thin, tired-looking in the grey artificial glare of the floodlights, wind rearranging his sparse hair. Dave talked to him, hands in pockets, half-a-dozen sentences exchanged, both expressionless, pat on the arm. The man walked away, towards the terminal building, wind lifting the flap of his jacket, toying with his hair.

I thought, planes at your disposal, vehicles. Dave had influence in the right places.

Parked at the top of the hill, last-quarter moon and high scudding cloud, we could see the chook farm Gary loved. Painter's little chook farm, place of memory, girl of memory.

Not so little. Not a farm either. A battery operation: huge barn that would house the living egg machines, another barn about a third the size, a small building, probably the office. About two hundred metres from the chicken barn, up a track, a small house sat on a level patch of hillside.

We had driven past it, gone a long way, beyond earshot, waited, come back, driven beyond hearing again, turned, crept back, barely twenty kilometres an hour.

'A SWAT team is the way you'd do this,' said Dave, ducking his head to light a cigarette, left and down below the dashboard.

He came up, cigarette shielded in his palms like a sixties schoolboy. 'Intelligent SWAT team. But since that's a contradiction in terms, you'd end up with a dead Gary. You always do. They might as well write you a guarantee the bloke'd be dead.'

He was matter-of-fact. We could have been studying the pictures on the illuminated menu in a McDonald's drive-through for all the excitement he was showing.

I returned to the point where I'd fallen asleep. 'What was the reason given for shutting Black Tide down?'

Dave looked at me, blinked, as if he'd forgotten all about the subject. 'Oh. Jeopardising success of a major national operation in progress. Endangering lives of undercover operatives. Bullshit. Major national operation no-one knows anything about. The ghost ship of criminal operations. The phantom. All bullshit.'

'That's some nerve you touched.'

'Very powerful reflex action.' He sighed. 'Right from the top. Cabinet-level reflex.'

'Levesque?'

'Gary'll tell us that. That's why we went after Gary.'

Another sigh. 'Anyhow, the shut-down, that's why we knew it was Gary, our interest in him. And we really knew bugger all about him.'

'But you didn't give up. Is that what you're saying?'

'That's right,' Dave said. 'We just waited. When the chance came, we fired up Black Tide again, a different kind of Black Tide this time, not official, but not without friends. And we went for Gary. The first time, we were playing it by the book, we'd probably never have got to him. This time, dog and goanna rules. Rolled the prick, rolled and boned him. In Thailand, loaded him with half a kilo of smack, he's looking down the barrel at twenty years, thirty bodies in a four-man cell, rats crawling up his arse. Canetti did the job, did a great job. He's got the lingo, spent time in Thailand, knows the locals. Then he had two illuminating hours with Gary, a scared Gary, videoing his memoirs. Couldn't take more time. Gary was just there on a stopover. But Canetti got plenty to start with. The rest, that's a few days' work, going over the details. But first we wanted Gary back in the country, everything as usual, no suspicions aroused that we'd rolled him.'

'What did Gary tell Canetti in Bangkok?'

Dave ducked his head below the dashboard, took a deep drag, came up, expelled smoke. 'That's the fucking problem.

We don't know. Canetti rang from Bangkok, he's highly excited, he says, wait till you see this, you'll cream your jeans, it'll hang Mr S. That's all he said.'

'Mr S?'

'Levesque. Mr Smartarse.'

'How did Gary get back here?'

'Everything had to be normal. Gary flew on to Melbourne, direct. He was coming from Europe. Because Canetti's got his testimony on video, Gary's with us now. Doesn't behave, he's on "Australia's Funniest Home Videos". And he can't go to his bosses, say: "Sorry, I told people about you cause I didn't want to go to jail in Bangkok for twenty years." They'd kill him on the spot.'

I was starting to understand.

'There was a risk,' said Dave. 'What if he gets straight off the plane, onto another one, he's gone, out of the country, vanished? But we knew he didn't have a cash stash anywhere, not enough put away to hide out in Ethiopia, Bangladesh. Anyway, nothing like that happens. He gets the Audi, drives home. We pulled our bloke off him then, too risky otherwise. A third party spots her, it's over, Gary's dead, we've got a video of a dead man telling stories. Maybe we shouldn't even have tailed him home, who the fuck knows. Looking back, why the hell did we? Either Canetti had him by the balls or he didn't.'

He glanced at me, ducked his head, drew on the Camel. 'Anyway, that's the last we saw of him.'

'And Canetti?'

'We didn't want him to fly with Gary. Too risky also. He came back on the next flight. We know he was on the plane, know he got off. That's all we know. That's when the looking for them both started.'

'He wasn't met?'

Dave looked at me, scratched the dense moustache with the index finger of his left hand. 'Meet him? Canetti was the only cleanskin we had. You didn't go near Canetti. Nobody knew Canetti except three of us. We waited for Canetti to finish the Gary interrogation and call us.'

He picked up his cigarettes, weighed the packet, looked at me again.

'Well,' he said, 'that was Black Tide. Started with twelve. And tonight Black Tide's more or less me and you, Jack.'

'I don't recall being asked to join,' I said.

He smiled. 'No. Me neither.'

We sat in silence for a while.

'What we'll do,' said Dave, 'we'll just freewheel down there, lights out, pray some pointy in a truck doesn't come along. Stop around the corner, walk back, up round the side to the house.'

'Dogs,' I said. 'Looks like a place with dogs.' In an instant, the adrenaline was running again, I wasn't feeling tired and old, wasn't feeling scared. It occurred to me that this was probably a bad thing.

'Dogs we can handle. A few dogs.' He opened the glove-box and took out a flat foil-wrapped package, the size of a large bar of chocolate.

'What I'm going to do here,' Dave said, 'is try to bluff the boy out. Had a bit of success with this. Which means fuckall. Still, avoids some prick shooting him, shooting other people, possibly innocent people. Doesn't work, we've got a problem. But. Same problem if there's two of you or fifty-two testosterone-crazed arseheads with guns. Important thing is Gary alive.'

I said, 'What do I do?'

He touched my arm, the big fingers. 'Jack, only thing is Gary alive. Gary dead is everything gone. Black Tide one and two finished, total waste of time, bent bastards win. Again.'

'I do what?'

'Put the light on him, get the cuffs on. You're the cuffman. Apart from that, nothing. You know his old man. It might help. The bluff fails, we creep away, try something else. What, I can't think at the moment. Might come to me.'

He coughed. 'Also might not.'

'The bluff?'

'Just a bluff. Pray the phone's on. Pray the fucking mobile network's got this part of pointyland covered. They say it has.'

He was looking into the valley, at the dark buildings. 'Dean Canetti,' he said. 'Ordinary bloke, not big, more guts than John Wayne. If John Wayne was real.'

I didn't owe anything to this man, didn't even know his surname. Far from it. It was courtesy of him that I had gone so far up the sewage creek in an unsuitable vessel. He had managed to get me into the canoe and then to convince me that disembarkation was not an option.

He deserved nothing. But he was a man doing the right thing, a brave man. I felt a warmth towards him.

Dave raised his elbows, flexed his shoulders. 'Well, let's see how it goes.'

'Shouldn't I be armed? He's killed three people if I read this thing right.'

He released the handbrake. We began to move. 'One man with a gun's plenty,' he said. 'You might get excited.'

We rolled to a stop off the road. Dave found the handcuffs, flat high-tech things, not metal, light.

'Just get it on the wrist, press closed. A spring locks it.'

He opened the boot, took out two bulky bulletproof vests, dull black nylon windcheaters, a long matt-black flashlight. We took off our coats, put on the gear. The vest was surprisingly light. There was something in my right windcheater pocket. A handkerchief, a folded handkerchief. From the last operation, presumably. Ironed and folded by someone. A loving spouse?

We walked back half a kilometre, climbed a fence at the strainer post. Not easily, in my case, carrying the flashlight.

On Painter's soil, Painter's buildings to the right. Damp soil, spongy. We walked to the left of the big buildings, Dave in front, uphill, going becoming heavy.

'Fuck this,' Dave said quietly. 'Go down, take the road.'

We went downhill, walked between the big tin sheds. Chicken factory no more. Some rust, things lying around, general air of disuse. We turned left, walking just off the track, uphill, protected by a row of young evergreen trees.

The dark house. Low brick dwelling, old. On the site long before the egg factory. Fence, straggly hedge, vehicle gate off to the right. At the front gate, an old truck was parked, Dodge or Ford.

Ten metres from the truck, Dave stopped, knelt. I knelt close to him, feeling my heartbeat now.

'I'm making the call.' Soft, steady voice. 'If I get him, I'm heading straight for the front door. You get behind the truck, watch my left arm. Goes up, put the light on the front door. When I've got the gun on him, get up there, don't hurry, don't spook him. Cuff him. Okay?'

I nodded, heart thumping now.

Dave took out his tiny mobile, pressed a button. The numbers glowed. He punched in a combination, put the phone to his ear.

I could hear the telephone ringing in the house.

Ringing.

Ringing.

Our eyes were locked. Dave looked faintly amused. With his right hand, he unholstered an automatic pistol from under his left armpit.

Ringing.

'Hello.' A tentative woman's voice. Fear in it.

Dave smiled, a rueful smile.

'Gary Connors, please,' he said.

Silence.

Dave held up the phone for me to hear.

The receiver being put down on a hard surface.

Silence.

Noises.

I looked at the dark house. What was happening in there?

A voice said, 'Gary Connors.'

A tired voice but not sleepy.

'Gary. Detective Inspector David Gwynne of the Australian Federal Police. Hello. I'm outside. Your house is surrounded by police officers. What I'd like you to do is come to the front door, open it, come out with your hands in the air. That's the easy way. The trained killers around the house have other ideas. Destroy the whole place, everyone in it. With me?'

Dave stood up and started walking towards the house, phone at his left ear, pistol in his right hand, down. When he got to the truck, I scuttled after him, got to the left front wheel of the truck, peered around the bumper.

'No-one will harm you, Gary,' Dave's quiet voice was saying. 'Give you my word. I want you alive, very much alive. And you'll stay alive. Cover you with my own body at the door, these trigger-happy bastards aren't going to risk shooting me.'

He went straight up the path, onto the verandah, stood to the left of the front door, facing the wall, back to me.

He was still talking but I couldn't hear what he was saying.

He stopped talking. Closed the phone. Put it in his windcheater pocket.

His left arm went up.

I stood up, arms on the truck bonnet, aimed the flashlight.

Brilliant, intense beam of white light on the front door, old six-panel door, paint peeling. Above it, a fanlight, dusty etched glass.

Waiting. No light in the house.

Dave facing the wall, up against it, close enough to touch the doorknob, right arm bent, pistol barrel at his nose.

Waiting.

Light on somewhere in the house, glow behind the fanlight.

Waiting.

He wasn't coming out. He'd spotted the bluff.

Waiting. Sweating in the cold, under the bulletproof vest. Heartbeat felt in the throat now.

Waiting. Dave would have to do something soon.

Do what? There was no fallback position.

Waiting.

Doorknob turning.

The door was being opened, swinging inward. Slowly.

I was holding my breath.

Someone. A man.

Hesitating.

Then he stepped forward, came out. Arms in the air, blinking against the flashlight beam.

Long hair, balding. Beard. Jeans and a sweater, barefoot. My size, roughly.

Dave was pulling the door closed behind him. He said, 'Keep going. Stop. Now I want you to kneel down slowly, Gary. Keep your arms up.'

I came around the front of the truck, holding the light on the man, walking as normally as I could, getting the handcuffs out.

Gary knelt down, looking down.

I got to the verandah, behind him.

'Bring your arms down slowly,' Dave said. 'Out wide, behind your back.'

It took a second to get the handcuffs on. Dave looked at me, not a look of interest.

'Lie down, Gary.'

Gary lay down, on his stomach, head turned to one side.

'Who's in the house?' Dave asked.

'Just a woman,' Gary said. 'She's scared. Don't frighten her. She's not involved.'

'What's her name?'

'Glenda.'

Dave knocked on the door. 'Glenda,' he said loudly. 'Don't be afraid. We're policemen. Nothing to be afraid about.'

A passage light came on. The door opened. A woman in her forties, fair hair, worn face, pretty face, nightgown clutched at the neck.

She saw Gary, moved to go to him.

Dave put up a hand, stopped her. 'No, Glenda,' he said. 'Gary's fine. Not being hurt. He won't be hurt. Taking him away for questioning. You'll be told where he is, given a chance to speak to him. Understand?'

She didn't take her eyes off Gary. Said nothing.

'Good,' Dave said. 'Now can I ask you to pack Gary's things? Shoes, socks, underwear, so on.'

She turned and went inside, still silent.

'Get the vehicle,' Dave said to me, holding out the keys.

I went down the track at a brisk pace, back inside five minutes, parked beside the truck, went up the path.

Dave was leaning against the wall, nylon sportsbag next to him, gunhand casually at his side.

'Time to go, Gary,' he said.

Gary got to his feet with difficulty. 'Shoes,' he said.

'Later,' Dave said. 'Hold the cuffs, Jack.'

I got a grip on the handcuffs and we walked down the path. Behind us I heard the door open.

'Love you,' the woman said, voice breaking. 'Love you always.'

'Love you too,' said Gary. 'Always love you.'

At the vehicle, Gary said, 'Surrounded. Just the two of you. What a prick, what a prick.'

'I wouldn't argue with that,' Dave said. 'A murderous prick.'

'Didn't kill Dean. They did, the two men. I shot them.'

Dave nodded. 'Talk about it,' he said. 'Might swallow that. Depends on how helpful you are.'

'I'll help.'

Dave had the back door open. 'You'd better. What happened to Canetti's tape?'

'Burned it.'

'What about your father's money?' I said. 'Where's that?' I hadn't thought about the money for days.

Gary looked at me, quizzical. 'How do you know about that?'

I said, 'I'm his lawyer and I'm here to get his money back.'

'Not even two cops,' said Gary. 'One cop and a lawyer. Jesus Christ.' He thought for a moment. 'There's fifty grand or so in the shed. I'll show you.'

'Got to get that,' I said to Dave. 'It's the reason I got involved in all this shit.'

Dave looked at his watch. 'They'll be here soon.'

'Who?'

'Two other people. Flying from Canberra. I couldn't wait for them. Okay, let's drive down there.'

To Gary, he said, 'On the floor. On your face.' To me, 'Other kind of cuffs in the glovebox.'

I found them. 'Put them on his ankles.'

'Jesus,' said Gary.

'Let's get these bloody vests off.'

We took off the windcheaters and the ballistic vests, put the jackets on again.

'Drive, Jack.'

We drove down to the barns, Dave holding the pistol against Gary's spine. When we'd stopped, Dave said, 'Okay, where's the stuff?'

'Hard to explain,' Gary said. 'I'll have to show you.'

'Bullshit,' said Dave. 'Where?'

'Got to move boards. Take me in, I'll show you where, you can do it.'

Dave looked at me. 'We can come back,' he said, 'take this place apart at our leisure.'

I shook my head. 'No. The woman may know where the money is, nothing here when we come back. I want the money tonight.'

Dave sighed. 'Okay.'

He got out, pulled Gary out of the back seat. I lit the way with the flashlight, went around three steel drums on the concrete driveway, long time since a vehicle went in here, opened a small door in one of a big pair, went in first.

I shone the flashlight around. It was a huge concrete-floored space, once the storehouse for the battery operation. To my left, three sets of heavy-duty industrial shelves rose to the roof, wide aisles between them. They were still full of supplies, neat stacks of 100-kilo bags of what could be chickenfeed pellets, big cardboard cartons, rows of fifty-litre plastic containers of liquid, some greenish, some water-coloured. Giant rolls of something. One shelf held several dozen cartons of canned dogfood.

I was right. It was a place that had dogs. Lots of dogs. Once.

'In the office,' Gary said behind me. 'Over to the right.'

In the righthand corner, an office had been created by enclosing the space and giving it a door, a window and a roof, presumably to enable it to be heated.

We walked across, me in front, Gary shuffling awkwardly barefoot behind me, Dave at the back. At the office, Dave said, 'Okay, that's it. Where?'

'Open the door,' Gary said.

I opened it, shone the flashlight around: formica-topped

metal desk, three plastic chairs, a filing cabinet with a kettle and a toaster on top of it, big old-fashioned bar heater. The walls were panelled in dark-brown imitation wood.

'Push the filing cabinet away,' Gary said. 'The panel right behind it comes away. There's a sportsbag in there.'

'Stand against the window where I can see you, Gary,' Dave said. 'Any shit happens, I'm going to shoot you in the groin. Several times. Get the stuff, Jack. Take care. Booby-trap's not unknown.'

I went in, put the flashlight on the desk, pointing at the window. The filing cabinet moved easily. Empty. Behind it, I could see that the plastic sealing strip between the panels was loose.

I got a nail behind it and it came away. I put three finger-tips into the gap between panels and pulled the corner one away from the wall, put my hand in.

A bag, flattened to fit into the space. I pulled it out, with difficulty. A cheap nylon sportsbag, zipped, heavy. On the table, I unzipped it, shone the torch into it.

Notes in neat bundles held by thick rubberbands. Hundreds and fifties, easily fifty thousand dollars.

I zipped the bag, came out. 'Everything's here,' I said.

'That's my man,' said Dave. 'Let's get out of here, wait for them at the gate.'

But we didn't have to wait. As I shone the light on it, the small door creaked open and a head came in. A sleek dark head and a pistol.

'Dave? You?'

'Tony,' Dave said. 'Come and meet Gary, man who's going to make it all worthwhile for us.'

The man came through the door, followed by another man, also in a dark suit, bigger, fleshy face.

297

'G'day, Dave,' said the second man. 'Couldn't bloody wait, could you?'

'How many people does it take to apprehend one fugitive?' said Dave, a lightness in his voice. 'This is Jack Irish, to whom we owe everything.'

They walked towards us, two businessmen, dark suits, white shirts, one carrying a pistol at his side, the other lighting a cigarette with a plastic lighter.

When they were a few paces away, Dave said, 'Well, boys, the end's in sight.'

He raised his pistol and shot the man called Tony twice, in the head, in the chest under the collarbone.

Then he turned and shot Gary, twice, three times, all in the upper chest, swung the weapon in my direction.

I switched off the flashlight, jumped sideways.

Pitch dark.

Dave fired.

Black. Just the memory of the muzzle flash fading on my retinas.

In the darkness, I crawled for the huge shelves, crawled carrying a bag and a torch. Not thinking, instinctively trying to get something between me and the gun.

The guns. The other man would have a gun.

He did. The muzzle flash lit the blackness for an instant, the bullet passed well over my head, hit the corrugated-iron wall with a bang.

I kept going, found the shelf by crawling into an upright head first. Pain, lights in my eyes. I crawled to the right, met no resistance, went left, felt the corner of the shelving with an outstretched hand.

Got around the corner. Stood up, chest heaving, trying to breathe soundlessly, leaning against the shelf.

Blackness. Silence.

'Get the doors open, Ray, get the vehicle in here.'

Dave.

I put the bag down, found a space for it on the bottom shelf. No use to me dead. Stuck the torch down the front of my shirt. The bulletproof vests. Oh shit.

Get as far away from the doors as possible. A vehicle was going to come through the doors, light up the whole space.

Walking carefully, left hand out to feel the shelves, down the space between the shelves and the back wall. How many rows of shelves? Three? Four? Could there be an exit in the back wall? In the short wall?

Move right to touch the back wall. Walk slowly, feel for a door. Not much time, the other man out the small door by now.

Noise from the doorway. Bumping, tin being kicked, grunting.

'Fucking bolts won't come up. Give me a hand here.' Ray, the fleshy man, wrestling with the big doors. Big doors unwilling to open.

Moving slowly, feeling the wall.

Silence.

Bumped into something, something toppling.

Glass broke, loud in the silence.

Two bangs. One bullet low, screaming off the concrete near my feet. One into the wall behind me, flat, tinny smack.

Silence. More noises. Swearing. Something said. Dave's voice.

Outside an engine coming to life with a roar. The small doorway was a light patch in the blackness.

He was going to ram the recalcitrant doors, push them open.

Strong smell of something. Paraffin. The glass breaking. I felt ahead in the dark, felt a shelf against the wall. A bottle, big glass bottle, old-fashioned quart bottle. Felt beyond. A row of bottles.

I took it off the shelf. Screw top. Sniffed. Paraffin.

'Get the drums out of the way.' The fleshy man's voice.

The three steel drums outside the entrance. They had to move them before they could ram the door.

I took the bottle, went back the way I had come. Faster than I had come. Nothing to bump into, I knew that. Left hand on the wall, back to the corner, to the office.

I felt for the office wall.

Turn right. End of office.

My right foot went into something slippery.

Tony. His blood. Suddenly a strong smell of blood.

I knelt, felt, found his head, recoiled. Put my hand back.

He made a gurgling noise. He was breathing.

On. Where did he keep it? Jacket pocket, right jacket pocket.

The suit jacket was open. I felt down his side, wet, down. Pocket, got my hand into it, scrabbling, found it in the outside pocket.

The plastic lighter.

I felt around for his pistol. It was in his hand, right hand, when he stuck his head into the doorway. Then he was walking towards us, lighting a cigarette. Where had he put the weapon?

Bugger this, use the flashlight, they were both outside.

I groped myself, struggling to get it out.

Engine revving. Huge bang.

I stood up and ran, ran into the dark, not caring, managed to run blind to near the shelf against the wall, clutching the bottle, clutching the lighter.

Felt my way to the shelf. Get the screwtop off. No nonsense about squeezing and turning when they bottled this liquid.

The left-hand door flew open violently, swung right open, bounced off the inside wall, headlights lighting up the barn.

Wick? Oh shit, collar, tear it off. No. A neatly folded handkerchief, in my windcheater pocket. I tore a strip off with my teeth.

I couldn't get it to go into the neck of the bottle. Big scared fingers couldn't stuff the cloth in.

Something, something thin.

He was reversing, getting ready to smash open the other door.

In the dim light from the headlights, I saw a nail, a rusty six-inch nail, on the shelf. Grabbed it, clumsy fingers, pushed at the strip of cloth.

Going in, going in. In. Bit sticking out. Shake bottle, wet bit sticking out.

Calm came down on me. Detachment. Too much adrenaline, too much sex, too little sleep.

Perfect calm. Perfect love driveth out fear. Ditto for sensory exhaustion.

Did this stuff work? I read about it in *The Bridge at Spandau*. Worked in the Hungarian uprising. That was 1956, however. About as old as this paraffin.

The vehicle hit the door so hard it came off its hinges, slid across the concrete, sparks, noise, the four-wheel-drive in the barn, the suddenly lit-up barn.

Coming into the doorway behind it. Dave, arm outstretched, pistol looking for me.

Dave. The man I'd believed, admired, felt a warmth towards.

You're dealing with people, they can't buy you, they'll load you up, kill your friend, kill your wife, kill your child, kill you, it's all the same.

Dave knew the people he was talking about. He was one of them.

'Hey, Jack,' he said, not a shout. 'I've made a mistake. We'll work something out.'

Lighters never work when you want them to. I'd been a smoker once, I knew that.

I clicked. How could I doubt? Who needs a Dunhill?

I touched the blue flame to the wick, ran to the end of the aisle and threw the bottle. Bowled it, like a grenade.

In the air. Wick burning.

Dave in front of the vehicle now, pointing the pistol to the left, to the short wall of the barn.

Ray, the fleshy man, half-out of the four-wheel-drive, no weapon visible.

Dave seeing me, seeing the flying bottle, arm coming back, no two-handed marksman Dave. Wrong, two-handed marksman, left hand coming up to steady the right hand.

To kill me.

Paraffin bomb falling short. No matter, falling at Dave's feet, big splash of liquid, no shot, Dave stepping back, off balance.

Nothing.

Breaking glass, no bang, no fire, just spreading liquid, could be water.

Nothing. Oh God.

Total failure.

Perhaps you need petrol. Yes, that was it. They used petrol. Molotov cocktails rely on petrol.

Too bad.

Dave regained his balance, still the two-handed grip, steady, now for the target practice.

'Oh, Jack,' he said, 'you silly prick.'

A voice from the door, a female voice.

'Where's Gary?'

Dave turned his head.

Fleshy-face turned.

Glenda, in the doorway. Hands at her chest, hand showing, hand in her nightgown.

Across the space, I saw her eyes move to the bodies. They lay in a huge dark pool. Tony, sprawled, crucified. Gary, barefoot, on his side, a man sleeping.

'Bastards,' she said. 'Bastards.'

She took her hand away from her throat, her hand from her chest, shot the fleshy man somewhere, he fell over, she fired at Dave, three or four times before she hit him, in the middle of his body, walked over to him, he was upright, half-turned, doubled up, pointed the weapon at him at close range, at his neck. Bang, he jumped back a metre, fell over.

'Bastards,' she said.

She looked up and saw me and I was terrified.

'I'm Gary's father's lawyer,' I said. Loudly. 'Came to make sure Gary wasn't harmed.'

Pathetic.

Glenda threw the gun away. Contempt for the gun. It skidded across the concrete, spinning, came to rest.

'Great work,' she said, sinking onto her haunches on the cold concrete, hands to her face, rolling over like a puppy. 'Fucking great work.'

I went outside, walked past Gary, dead, Tony, dead or dying, sleek dark Tony, Dean Canetti's friend, Dave's trusted associate, walked past Glenda, alive, sobbing, past the fleshy man, he might live. Live, die, I didn't care. Walked past Dave, certainly dead. Didn't mind that either. Past the four-wheel-drive, out the door, into the cold Tasmanian night.

The sky had cleared. Sky impossibly clear and clean and deep. Dense with stars, like city lights seen from a high place.

Last man standing. The Molotov cocktail man.

I took deep breaths, good, clean Tasmanian air, first lungs to use this air. Numb.

Who do you call? These dead and dying people were mostly from the government. Or were they? Did it matter? Two of them had tried to kill me.

'Don't know what to do.'

Glenda. Behind me. Shoulders down. Killer. Dream love of Gary Connors. The person of last resort. The one you call.

I pulled myself together. Jesus, Tony might live. Do something.

I turned, went to Glenda, put an arm around her cold shoulders. She came into my armpit, became small, shaking, uncontrollable shakes.

I said, 'Go to the house, love. Ring the emergency police number. Tell them to send a helicopter, tell them where. Then start a fire down here, love, big fire. Something the helicopter can see.'

'Right,' she said. Sniff. 'Right.' She set off at a run up the slope.

I steeled myself. Went back into the barn, looked straight ahead, collected the sports bag with the money, walked out, got into the four-wheel-drive, drove away.

Survival of the innocents.

The drone came to my ears seconds before I saw the source. I was looking north but the aircraft came out of the west, just a dirtspeck against the dirty grey beginning of the day. It came down without hesitation, bumped and lurched on the sheep-paddock strip, slowed, slewed around, taxied to within five metres of where I stood beside the vehicle and turned side-on.

The door opened and Cam appeared, black poloneck sweater, leather jacket.

'G'day. Wiped that motor?'

I nodded, picked up the sports bag with the money.

He looked around, impassively studied the falling-down shed, the rutted road, the bleak and wet landscape. 'Well,' he said, 'seen the attractions of Tassie now. We might go home, have breakfast.'

Inside the Cessna, the pilot was fiddling with something on the instrument panel. His peaked cap was facing backwards. *Crapdusters Australia*, it said across the front.

'Can't find Triple J,' he said. 'Got to have that station.'

I groaned.

On the way back, high over the cruel grey strait, Cam said to the pilot, 'That strip, that's an abalone strip, right?'

The crapduster looked at Cam, frowned, pushed back his cap, scratched his number one haircut. 'Y'know,' he said, 'go so many places, I forget.'

Cam nodded. He seemed pleased with the answer.

I drowsed. I wanted to go home, to take off my clothes, have a shower, go to bed and sleep. A deep, dreamless sleep.

The landing was silky. So silky that I did not register my return to earth.

In the Brock Holden, running the freeway, I said to Cam, 'Four people dead. Nothing to do with me.'

'Before you got there?'

'No. While I was there.'

He looked at me. 'While?'

It was too early in the day, whatever day it was, to tell the story. 'I misjudged this bloke,' I said. 'I think his friends might want to have a word with me.'

Cam punched a button on the console. Muddy Waters from every direction, drowning in the Waters.

I woke up in a big bed, white sheets, white blanket, white room, clean-smelling sheets, light of day from huge uncurtained windows.

What day? Where?

I sat up, alarmed, swept the bed linen away, naked, heart pumping. Then I remembered. I went to the window and looked out on a wide arc of the city. Below me lay Albert Park lake and beyond that Middle Park and the bay. Off to the right, I could see the Westgate Bridge and Williamstown.

Time? I found my watch beside the bed. Just after noon. I'd only slept for five hours.

Only? How many hours did I have?

I wandered around the apartment. Little had registered earlier in the day. It was the penthouse, minimally furnished, no pictures, huge windows taking in the whole city, polished boards underfoot, a kitchen like a high-style operating theatre, a gym and a sauna and a Japanese bath and two showers in the football team-sized bathroom.

'Belongs to a bloke I know, never there,' Cam had said. How did he know people who owned places like this?

On the coffee table in the sitting room, I found two new shirts, new underpants, my jacket and pants in a drycleaner's bag, a mobile phone, a ring with three keys, and a plastic card with a magnetic strip and a barcode. A note from Cam said:

> Food on the ground floor. The mobile's clean. Car
> in bay 12 in basement 1. The card gets you through
> the doors.

In a shower, water boring into me from all directions, I tried to work out what to do. No Gary to look for now. No videotape of the Bangkok interrogation.

Gary was TransQuik. And Dave was TransQuik, TransQuik inside the government. Possibly a late recruit to the TransQuik cause, recruited after Gary's disappearance, perhaps even later. I'd been looking for Gary on behalf of TransQuik, a late recruit myself.

What had Gary told Dean Canetti in Bangkok? Something explosive. Dean said:

…wait till you see this, you'll cream your jeans, it'll hang Mr S.

Mr Smartarse. Steven Levesque.

Dried, dressed, I got out my notebook, looked for Chrissy Donato-Connors-Sargent. She was home.

'Chrissy, you said something about someone telling Alan there was funny money in TransQuik…'

A warder with a look that said a mass breakout could be imminent showed me into the interview room.

Miles Crewe-Dixon, formerly accountant to Alan Sargent, was waiting for me, smoking a cigarette. He was in his fifties, a round-faced man, not grown slim on prison food, neat hair, straight, grey, short. He had the air of someone you could trust. I'd appeared for a childcare centre owner with a similar look. The convictions in New Zealand were under another name.

We shook hands. 'Thanks for seeing me,' I said.

'My pleasure. Breaks the monotony of a model prisoner's life.' The right side of his face scrunched up. He had a facial tic.

I sat down. 'Alan Sargent sends his regards.'

'Give him mine. Chips down, only client prepared to be a character witness. I can do something for you? Ask.'

'TransQuik,' I said. 'Alan says you thought the potato wasn't entirely clean.'

Miles smiled, sardonic smile. 'Where the legend begins,' he said. 'Steven Levesque. Little company is seed of empire. Like Rupert Murdoch.'

I prompted him. 'Levesque bought TransQuik from Manny Lousada.'

His facial tic. 'I did that acquisition for them. Before that they were only in the household move market, undercutting everyone, all the other small companies, pushed some of them to the wall, then bought them for bugger-all. The

Killer Bees they called them, Levesque and Brent Rupert and McColl and Carson, his partners.'

'Where'd the money come from?'

'Asking the important question. Rupert's family owned Pert Clothing. Big company once. Lots of money. Levesque had bugger all, just brains. His old man was a tram conductor, migrant, Lebanese–French. A West Heidelberg boy, now that's a hard school. Grew up in an Olympic Village house. They built those places in about three days in '56. Not too many of the local kids went on to Melbourne Uni and Harvard.'

'Ones I know mostly went on to juvenile detention and Pentridge. How'd you get involved with Levesque?'

He lit a new cigarette from the old one, offered the packet. I shook my head.

'I knew Brent's older brother. I did some work on their early acquisitions. Looked over these little transport companies. Pretend to be representing some Queensland outfit. Happens all the time. Then I didn't hear from them for a while. Came back to me in '84. I was doing pretty well by then, had a bit of a reputation. Not them though. Their wheels were coming off. The whole enterprise sailing south under all canvas. Brent had milked the Ruperts dry. Pert Clothing was up for sale.'

'Why was that?'

'Well, between professional colleagues, they'd got themselves into serious shit, helped by the banks, who thought lending money to a Rupert was a zero-risk proposition. And Brent relied on Levesque. Steven claimed he only needed two minutes with a business's balance sheet to know everything about the company. On the basis of this talent, they bought crap you would not believe. Harvard MBA. He's got one, y'know, Steven. Now I laugh when I hear the magic words "Harvard MBA". Master of Bugger-All.'

'So they needed accounting advice?'

Miles laughed until his tic stopped him. 'Accounting, business advice. Lots of it. My opinion was that the three wonderboys were looking down the barrel at doing some time. Rich, don't you think? Now one's the bloody federal A-G, the other one bankrolls the Libs, and I'm doing time for some piddling malfeasance.'

'Very rich,' I said. 'What could you do for them?'

'Well, they were trying to unwind some deals, handle some very menacing inquiries from the Tax Department. The big thing was, they'd gone in for a share play, no names, not big by market standards, but much too big for them. A person who must remain nameless because he has people killed, this person convinced them to buy a large number of shares in company X for him. Bought in small parcels over about a year in the names of all these little companies they owned but were registered in Levesque's mother's name, his father's, Rupert's hippy cousins stoned witless in Nimbin, all kinds of names. But not bought with the nameless person's money. No, oh no. With the Killer Bees' own money, borrowed.'

New cigarette. Through the slit windows, I could see a Lombardy poplar in silhouette against the dying light.

'The deal was,' said Miles, 'that when the person makes a takeover bid for the company, Levesque, Rupert and company sell him their holdings off-market. At a discount to the market price but a nice profit over what they paid.'

'What would that amount to?'

'They expected to make six or seven million clear.'

'And didn't?'

Miles scratched his upper lip. Tic. 'One morning the shares went into freefall. By the close, the twelve million they'd spent was worth about two. The person, their trusted associate, was unavailable. No longer in the country. Finally, he rings Levesque from somewhere, Egypt I think it was, and says, sorry it didn't pan out, that's business. And he offers them two million for their holding.'

'One could almost feel for them.'

'Yes. Well, I talked to the banks for them, got a bit of relief, unwound a few of the loonier deals, but basically they were a basket case. Then Levesque gets me over to HQ in East Melbourne, very pleased with himself.' He paused. Tic.

'They've found a buyer for fifty-one per cent of TransQuik. An American freight outfit called Eagle Exprexxo, based in Tampa, Florida. That's E-X-P-R-E-X-X-O. For fifty-one per cent, Eagle offers $20-odd million, I can't remember the exact figure. I remember I started laughing. That valued TransQuik at around $40 million— a company that had never made a profit. And this is 1984, mind you. Serious offer, says Levesque. They see our potential, springboard into the region, etcetera. All that bullshit. I said, let's see it on paper.'

'What did Levesque want from you if he was such a hotshot business analyst?'

'Nothing. He didn't want me at all. Brent Rupert wanted me. To look at the deal. It was dawning on him through the coke haze that Levesque was dangerous. Could take a long time for things to dawn on Brent in those days, I can tell you. The short of it is that the next week we have a meeting with two lawyers. One is Rick Shelburne from Sydney. Well, I'd been at the sharp end of a few things by then and the sight of Shelburne made my scrotum shrink. Heard of him?'

I nodded. 'Someone said he had a talent for winning over councillors.'

Miles smiled. Tic. 'He used to be a spook, my Sydney friend tells me. ASIS. Worked for the Americans in the Philippines. He's mixed up with very strange things.'

Tic.

He looked out of the embrasure at the coming night, moved his lips soundlessly. Faintly glazed look. 'Hate the nights,' he said. Tic. Tic. 'I'm a prison librarian and Rick Shelburne's presumably on the beach at Noosa. Says a lot about the criminal justice system.'

Tic.

'And the second lawyer?' I said.

He shook himself, looked at his cigarette, extracted a fresh one from the packet. 'Person you wouldn't cross either, Carlos something. German-sounding name. I forget.'

'Siebold. Carlos Siebold.'

'Siebold. That's right. He's representing the Americans. Well, not directly. There's a bank in Luxembourg involved, forget that name too.'

'Klostermann Gardier.'

'Correct. Absolutely. The finance will come through them, he says. He wants a new company set up to own TransQuik, a Hong Kong-registered company. The Killer Bees to own forty-nine per cent of that. Another company will own the fifty-one per cent. Not the American company.'

'Not Eagle Exprexxo?'

'No. A company that owns Eagle.'

'Complicated.'

More laughter and tics. 'And this Carlos whoever, he says the bank, on behalf of whoever, they'll lend TransQuik

$40 million for acquisitions. Through the Hong Kong holding company. Terms to be discussed.'

'To my untutored ear, an attractive offer.'

Miles smiled. He had a nice smile, a smile a child would like. 'Untutored ear. I like that. I've been trying to learn to appreciate classical music. Funny how you spend your life. All I ever did was chase money. Never read a book.'

The glazed look was coming on again, more glazed.

'So,' I said, 'what did you recommend?'

He blinked, once, twice, focused on me. 'Yes. Yes. Well. I'm not saying I was a stranger to complicated propositions. Not at all. No. Put up a few of my own by then. Propositions aren't necessarily bad because they're complicated. No. The problem is they're often complicated because they're bad.'

Miles smiled, reflected on the wisdom of this statement, looked at the window, eyes narrowed, cigarette burning in his fingers, forgotten, ash fell off, onto the formica.

We were running out of time: they eat early in the slammers, even the genteel white-collar slammers.

'What advice did you give them, TransQuik?'

Alert again.

'Sorry, tend to drop off at the end of the day. Early start. I took Levesque and Rupert and McColl into the next room. I said to them, nobody offers deals like this. This is like the fax from Nigeria offering you free money. Rupert was nodding, he agreed. McColl was watching Levesque like a puppydog, watched Levesque like that all the time. Levesque smiles, McColl smiles. He'd fart in front of the Queen if Levesque went first. Well, Levesque gives me a hard look. He didn't like my opinion at all. "We've checked these people out," he said. "We're happy."'

The warder came in, still worried that his collection

of lawyers and accountants and pyramid salesmen and shirt-lifting priests were going to storm the walls. 'Five minutes maximum, Mr Irish.'

Miles said, 'I told Levesque the offer was outside my experience. He says, he's looking at me like a hungry animal, he says, "What, you want to consult an accountant? Our accountant needs his own accountant?" I said, "No, I'm suggesting some caution." You know what he said?'

'What?'

'Levesque looked at me, he's got a smile where he opens his lips slowly, you see more and more teeth. Then he said: "Fuck off, Dixon, whatever your name is. Double-barrelled bullshit artist. You're small-time. You'll always be small-time. You're not required. Piss off. Get out."'

We didn't have much time left. 'Did they take the offer?' I asked.

He nodded. 'They paid off all debts, squared the Tax Department, unloaded the shares. Then, about nine, ten months later, the buying spree started—Leeton Stevedoring, Pacargo Air, that's a freight airline in Papua New Guinea. Travel agencies. Truck stops. Got a new CEO, too. An American, he'd be the new owner's man.'

'How would you rate your judgment now? Good deal for Levesque and his partners?'

Miles was tired. Tic. A still facial moment. Tic.

'I hate the bastard, concede that,' he said. 'My judgment was to take care. I'm not saying I wouldn't have said go for it when we knew more. But as it stood it wasn't a deal. It was an offer of money. Question is, what kind of money is it? You need to know.'

'What kind did you think it was?'

'I'm a bit of a stickybeak. I tried to run down Eagle

Exprexxo. Had a bit of experience with Cook Islands, Caymans, places like that. In the end all I got was that Eagle had a link with a Manila company, the name's gone…'

What was the name Stuart Wardle had given Tony Rinaldi to put to Siebold? It came to me.

'Arcaro Transport?'

'Absolutely. Arcaro. And both of them, they both had links with another company part-owned by a company owned by these two trusts. It's complicated stuff. You need to draw it on paper. Anyhow, I got nowhere. Then I asked a mate of mine in Sydney, knows everything this fellow, gave him the names. He got back, he says, "This is The Connection. Walk back, walk back very, very carefully."'

'The Connection.'

Rapid nods, smile, no tics, another puffing cigarette combustion transfer. 'The Connection. I'd never heard of it. My friend says, doesn't mince his words, "Don't fuck with these people, Miles," he says, "it's the good old boys from Manila."'

Behind me, silent entry like a butler, the warder coughed. 'I'm afraid that's it, Mr Irish.'

Impeccable screw behaviour in this place. Not like screws at all. Perhaps there were front-of-house screws, with the real screws inside.

Miles put out his hand. His lethargy was gone, replaced by a feverishness. 'I didn't ask any more questions. Listen, come back, I've got other interesting stories. Tell Alan, tell him, tell him I don't forget. I'll show him that when I get out of here. Good man, excellent person. Alan. Yes.'

I came out of the neat jail, a jail designed to look like a motel, a compulsory-stop motel, and aimed the Lotus down the highway. A long day entering its twilight, a day following a night rich with unpleasant surprises. I felt invigorated, mind fresh. Perhaps the adrenaline pump wouldn't shut down? Was I to be permanently primed for fight or flight until I simply fell over?

Sticking on the speed limit in the red Lotus from Basement 1, I thought about Miles Crewe-Dixon and his facial tic. Miles and Steven Levesque. TransQuik and Eagle Exprexxo of Tampa, Florida. Stuart Wardle and Arcaro Transport and Major-General Ibell and Charles deFoster Winter. Gary Connors and Klostermann Gardier. Steven Levesque and Klostermann Gardier and The Connection. Good old boys from Manila.

The Connection. Good old boys from Manila.

Brent Rupert, he was one of the bosses, he used to go to Manila and to America with Gary.

That was what Chrissy Donato-Connors-Sargent had said.

What had Lyall said about Stuart Wardle?

He was big on the Philippines, working on a book on the subject.

Good old boys from Manila.

I tried to remember what Simone Bendsten had told me, couldn't recall a word. It seemed like a month had passed. I'd been too tired to register anything.

Ring her. No.

Then I remembered: her unread report was in the secret compartment of my desk.

In and out quickly. They wouldn't be expecting me to come back to my office, not at night and alone.

I found an illegal park a hundred metres down the street and was in the office inside a minute, didn't put on the light, had the envelope in my hands in thirty seconds. Out the front door, turned the key in the deadlock.

Rain like mist, tarmac shining. Light on across the way in McCoy's studio, some artistic atrocity being committed. On the pavement, a steel rubbish skip. How did McCoy decide which of his efforts to throw away? Toss a coin?

I looked down the street towards the Lotus. Half a block beyond it, I could see the dark bulk of a four-wheel-drive parked outside the back doors of the old chutney factory.

Mr Pigtail the warehouse developer having a late inspection, gloating over the profits to come.

I was ten metres from the car, walking in the street, when two blocks down a car turned the corner, came towards me, turned right into St David Street.

Two men in the four-wheel-drive, slumped in the front seats, just the tops of their heads caught for an instant in the headlights of the car behind them.

Warehouse converters?

No. I knew who they were.

I stopped, froze.

Run for the Lotus?

A movement in the driver's seat of the big vehicle. The driver sitting upright.

Get to the Lotus, unlock the door, get in, get it started.

It was an unfamiliar car. It would take me seconds to find the ignition.

No. Too late.

Run for it. Run back. Run for Carrigan's Lane and Smith Street.

The four-wheel-drive started up, headlights came on.

Run.

I hadn't gone five paces when I knew I'd never get to Carrigan's Lane, never get to Smith Street.

Look back. The big vehicle pulling out from the kerb, squeal of fat tyres.

Run. Run for what? Never get my office door open in time, two locks to open.

Running, hearing the vehicle behind me, look back, headlights fifty–sixty metres away.

Running. Run for McCoy's door, could be open.

Look back. Never get to McCoy's door.

Head, shoulder and arm leaning out of the vehicle, out of the window behind the driver. Something in the hand.

Oh Jesus, I'm dead.

McCoy's rubbish skip. Get behind the skip.

Flat sound, not loud, whine of lead off the tarmac in front of me.

Oh Christ.

The skip. Nearly there.

I could hear the engine roaring. Close.

I dived for the steel box, bounced on the cobblestones, landed on my elbow, my right hip, pain shooting through my whole body.

Huge bang next to my head. Bullet hit the skip.

Crawl, crawl behind the skip.

Behind it.

The sound of McCoy at work on his tree trunk. He wouldn't hear anything above his own din.

The four-wheel-drive went into reverse. Back ten metres. Brake. See the brakelights red as blood.

Trying to get a clear shot at me. Legs not good enough.

Forward. Savage left turn. Brake. Reverse lights.

As the vehicle backed onto the pavement, I crawled around to the other side of the bin, the narrow side. Breathless, little involuntary fear noises in my throat.

Scream of the engine, right turn, forward, looking for me.

I tried to crawl back. My right leg seemed to be paralysed.

Crawl. Drag yourself.

Too late. Too late.

I looked up into the face of a man in the back seat of the four-wheel-drive. A fat face, bald head, mouth open. He looked like a white seal. A happy white seal with a pistol, silencer on the end.

He steadied both forearms on the windowsill, sighted down the barrel, not in a hurry. On my chest. Getting it right.

I felt nothing. Fear gone. Not even despair. Just a thought about my daughter. I didn't write often enough. Didn't tell her I loved her often enough.

To die in the rain, in the gutter, next to a rubbish skip. Not right.

Here it comes. I closed my eyes.

McCoy's front door crashed open, bucket of light thrown over me. Roaring chainsaw noise.

McCoy. In the doorway. Plastic face shield pushed back

on the huge head. Chainsaw in his right hand, running, roaring chainsaw, blade pointed at the ground.

The gunman raised his pistol instinctively, fired at McCoy without aiming. A chunk of wood came away from the doorpost centimetres from McCoy's head.

'FUUUCK!!!'

Bellow of McCoy outrage. All in one fluid movement, he brought his left arm over, picked up the roaring chainsaw in both hands, weightless. Raised it to head height.

Threw the running chainsaw.

Threw it like a dart.

Threw it at the man who had fired at him.

Across the space. The heavy cutting machine, carbide-steel cutting teeth on a chain, flying across the space.

Into the man's face.

The man falling back. Going back with the running chainsaw.

The scream. One terrible piercing blood-red expulsion of sound.

The vehicle shot forward, tyres howling, swung into Carrigan's Lane, went over the kerb, right front fender hit the brick wall, back came around, grinding along the wall, fountain of red and white sparks. Down the lane, engine screaming in first gear.

Alive.

In the rain, in the gutter, next to a rubbish skip.

Alive.

McCoy and I looked at each other.

'Shit,' he said, rubbing his beard stubble. 'Fucking Stihl chainsaw. Next to new. Four hundred bucks.'

I swallowed. Strange taste in the mouth. Like iodine. Who knows what iodine tastes like?

'Maybe he'll bring it back,' I said and I looked at my right hand. It was twitching, little jerks. It was like looking at someone else's hand. I got up, grasped my right hand with my left.

McCoy eyed me. 'One of your old clients,' he said. 'Passing by, thought he'd say hello.'

I was limping away, feeling my arm. Over my shoulder, I said, 'Some bloke bought one of your paintings. Seriously disturbed to do that, looking at it makes him much worse.'

In the Lotus, slick with sweat on a winter's night, I took the long and illogical way back to Cam's friend's apartment. I was in Richmond, breathing almost normal, pulse slowing, when Eric the Geek, Wootton's tall, stooped, unsocialised computer genius, came into my mind. He lived in Richmond, off Lennox Street. I'd given him a lift once, not a word out of him for the whole trip.

I parked beside the Richmond Oval and found his number in my notebook. He answered on the third ring. I didn't identify myself.

'That hard disk, find anything?'

Silence.

'You there?'

'Yup.'

'Find anything?'

'Yup.'

'Much?'

'Nope. Wiped. But.'

'But?'

'Didn't clean it properly. Trawled a few bits and pieces.'

'Got a transcript?'

'Yup.'

I told him where to bring it. He arrived in five minutes, a man in an anorak, collar up, beanie topping a long head, driving an ancient Renault. Why do all old Renaults have one door a different colour?

Eric didn't say anything, kept his long head slightly

averted, pushed an envelope at me, retreated.

To his back heading for the car, I said, 'Thank you, Eric, send me the bill.'

In the white penthouse, sitting in a Barcelona chair, the city lights lying at my feet, I drank my host's Glenfiddich and read Simone's report.

> Jack, I followed up the reference to Secure International (that's Major-General Gordon Ibell) in the European databases. I found a mention in a Swedish source of a company called Eagle Exprexxo they say is linked with Secure and was involved in transporting arms to Unita, the American-supported side in Angola led by Jonas Savimbi.
>
> I tried Eagle Exprexxo and found a mention in the *International Herald Tribune* of a case still before the French courts involving hand-held missiles found in a semi after a freeway accident. The semi owner said he was hired by a company called Redan. Redan said it got the job from a freight agency. The agency said it understood the hirer to be Eagle Exprexxo of Tampa, Florida, but had nothing on paper.
>
> In 1983, an American magazine also mentions Secure International and in rather vague terms talks about a secret organisation of ex-CIA and American military people called The Connection.

The Connection.

Miles Crewe-Dixon's friend in Sydney knew about The Connection. It was tied up with Arcaro Transport and Eagle Exprexxo. He told Miles to walk back very, very carefully. 'Don't fuck with these people,' he said. 'It's the good old boys from Manila.'

Something was beginning to dawn, a thread of light, on the faraway horizon. I read on.

It says the group has been involved in arms-for-drugs deals and money-laundering and has strong links with the CIA and other intelligence services and with the Shah of Iran and President Marcos and Pakistani and Hong Kong druglords and money movers.

That's it for the moment. There are some leads to follow from these mentions. I await your instructions.

I took a chance. Too late not to take chances. I punched Simone's number on Cam's mobile. A clean mobile. What did that mean?

Her voice.

'Simone, Jack, the American magazine in your report. What's it called?'

'*Mother Jones*. Strange name.'

'Who wrote the piece? Remember?'

'Hold on.'

She was gone for a long time it seemed.

'There? Someone called Stuart Wardle.'

She spelled the name.

'Thanks,' I said. 'I'll be in touch.'

Stuart Wardle.

I sipped some Glenfiddich, swilled it around the cavities, looked at the lights, the electric world seen from above, thousands of pinpricks of light, minute smears of colour. Thoughts came unbidden. Dave shooting the man called Tony, my torch on Tony, making it easy, a man with smooth hair and a nice smile. Dave turning the gun on Gary and shooting him. Three times, loud noises, nothing much to see, a man stumbling backwards and sagging at the knees, his mouth opening.

Sitting in the Barcelona chair, high above the twinkling world.

A doomed person. People lay in wait for me. I wanted to keep Des Connors out of the poorhouse. Des Connors, stonemason, workmate of my father, father of Gary.

I saw the fat white seal face, mouth open, the small hotspot of flame in the muzzle as a gunman fired at McCoy.

Preposterous.

How could a backstreet Fitzroy no-practice solicitor become entangled with international dealers in arms and drugs? The viperous Brendan O'Grady seemed as nothing now, no more than the kindergarten bully.

Miss, Brendan's hitting me.

Stuart Wardle. The man who had the question for Carlos Siebold. The man who vanished.

I opened the envelope from Eric the Geek. Two pages of fragments found on Stuart Wardle's hard disk, most of them no more than a line or two, one longer. I went straight to the long one.

Someone saying:

…flying Marcos gold from Clark Air Base to Pine Gap. Eagle Ex was adding a heroin sweetener. All we had to do was collect the stuff, deliver the gold to one place, the smack to another. Some of the smack was in transit for the States. That's what Leeton was for. That's why we bought Leeton. Eagle wanted a complete loop. Today the business is really complicated. Not just a carrier. It's a buyer and carrier and bulk distributor and money-launderer. It's driven most of the little shits out of business, killed them if necessary.

Of course, he's got the firewalls up now. Moved on. But he's been in blood up to his navel, the bastard.

Leeton? What was Leeton? I'd heard the name recently. Miles Crewe-Dixon talking about TransQuik. The TransQuik buying spree after Klostermann Gardier bought half the company. Leeton Stevedoring, that was it.

I looked at the other fragments. None of them made any sense. Except one. It read: Connection. I didn't know we were in bed with these Yank bastards until it

Who was the person speaking?

Someone being interviewed by Stuart.

Stuart had bought a video camera and a tripod.

Suddenly, the adrenaline let-down, the burst of cortisol dissipating. I felt drained of all strength, tired, hungry, a headache coming. The premises ran to one can of consomme, one can of tuna and six packets of wafer biscuits. I constructed a meal from these ingredients, ate it, showered, and went to bed, out with the light.

In the morning, waking with a start again, I caught a tram into the city and paid $880 for a dark suit and a silk tie at Henry Buck's. It felt like a suit day, not a ballistic vest and black windcheater day. I drank coffee in McKillop Street while they hemmed the trousers. Then I caught a tram back to the apartment block and got the Lotus out of the basement.

As I turned into St Kilda Road, it occurred to me: had the men seen me arrive at my office the night before? I was sure there was no four-wheel-drive in the street when I parked.

How could they have been waiting for me, then?

Unless they were following me. Unless they'd somehow got onto my trail, perhaps followed me on my trip to see Miles Crewe-Dixon, followed me back to the office.

Eyes flicking to the rear-view mirror, I drove back through the city, up Swanston Street and, at the last second and without indicating, turned into the Tin Alley entrance to Melbourne University.

No vehicle followed me. The Lotus fitted neatly into an illegal parking spot. I waited for five minutes, watching Tin Alley: young people, the odd older person, no-one who looked remotely like someone sent to kill me. I got out and did a walking tour of the campus, passed through the old stone law school, thought about my father meeting my mother somewhere here, Drew and me as students, loitered often to look for someone behind me. Then I went back to Tin Alley, left the campus and crossed Royal Parade, went up to Degraves Street and worked my way around to the lane behind Lyall's house, the lane that led to the garage.

A large bin was in the lane, waiting to be wheeled into the street. I looked at my new suit. What a terrible idea. Where do ideas like this come from?

I pushed the bin against the wall, got onto it with great difficulty, swung a leg over the wall.

Lyall was in the kitchen, looking at me through the window. Her head went to one side in a birdlike movement of inquiry. I completed the ascent, dropped awkwardly and painfully to the other side. She opened the back door, a barefooted person in jeans and a white school shirt, sleeves rolled up. She leaned against the jamb, arms folded.

'An unorthodox method of entry,' she said, the hint of a

smile in the eyes not the mouth. 'Not unwelcome but puzzling.'

I was trying to brush the marks off my pants, said, 'Variety. They say it's important in a relationship. Variety and surprise. I read that. Also I'm trying not to be seen by certain parties.'

She came across the courtyard, came up to me, close, I could smell her, took me by the $880 lapels.

'Dark suit, spotted tie, every inch the lawyer,' she said, lips a handspan away, closing in. 'And I know my inches. Not home for two nights. The stalker is out there.'

'I was abroad,' I said, hoarsely. 'Learning how not to make a Molotov cocktail.'

'Useful negative knowledge.'

I wanted to make love to her without a second's delay.

The instinct for survival intervened. Dave had called upon that instinct, the night I sat in his car, in the wind-blown square, on the plump seat, the last leaves losing their hold on the trees.

'Listen,' I said, 'Stuart's car. I need to look for something.'

She didn't release my lapels immediately, kissed me on the lips. 'Feel free,' she said.

'That comes later.'

I opened the driver's door, put a hand under the front seat. The crumpled McDonald's packet. I opened it. Wrapping of a McFeast, smears of something now fossilised. Plastic cup. A cash register slip.

A cash register slip with a date.

Stuart Wardle bought this wholesome meal at a McDonald's in Morwell in Gippsland on July 8, 1995.

I closed the car door gently, fearful of disturbing the vehicle on its axle stands.

Not time for caution now. I rang Simone on the mobile.

'One last request,' I said. 'Brent Rupert. Can you see if you can find out what happened to him? Any mention on the local newspaper databases.'

'Give me fifteen minutes,' she said.

I went inside. Lyall was in the kitchen, at the stove, looking good from the back.

'Hungry?' she said. 'I'm having an early lunch. Pasta with a tomato and anchovy sauce.'

Food. I was famished, instantly salivating.

'Yes, please,' I said.

We ate lunch, drank a glass of red wine, talked and joked, weak sunlight on the floorboards. A feeling of unreality came over me. Was I the person at Painter's bloody egg farm? Was I the person waiting to die beside the rubbish skip outside McCoy's?'

While Lyall was making coffee, I rang Simone again from the sitting room.

'Easy,' she said. 'The last story about Brent Rupert is his death in an explosion. It says he was a near-recluse believed to be suffering from a serious illness.'

Muscles in the back knew something. The musculature knew more than the addled brain.

'When was this?'

'Early hours of July 9, 1995. Gas cylinders under his house appear to have exploded.'

Stuart Wardle was eating a McFeast in Gippsland on July 8, 1995.

'Where did he live?'

'On the Gippsland lakes. Near Metung.'

I thanks her and went back to Stuart's car to look at the mileage on the tripmeter: 667 km.

In the glove compartment was a VicRoads guide to country Victoria. Where would half of 667 km get you if you were travelling from Melbourne, passing through Morwell? I followed the Princes Highway with my finger, adding up distances.

Smart muscles. Intuitive muscles.

The mileage on Stuart's tripmeter, the mileage for his last trip in the car, that mileage would take him to Metung and back.

Stuart had bought the video camera to interview Brent Rupert.

Seriously ill Brent Rupert.

Brent Rupert, partner of Steven Levesque and the Attorney-General, Mr McColl.

Of course, he's got the firewalls up now. Moved on. But he's been in blood up to his naval, the bastard.

That was Brent Rupert speaking on the transcript trawled from Stuart's computer hard disk.

Brent Rupert gave his dying testament to Stuart Wardle, expert on the Philippines. Was the deal that Stuart would wait until after Brent's death to publish?

Not a long wait. A matter of hours.

And soon after that Stuart went to New Zealand and never came home again.

Stuart Wardle never went to New Zealand.

Stuart Wardle's passport went to New Zealand.

Stuart Wardle probably died in this house.

Stuart Wardle could save my life.

I went back to the kitchen. 'Where's that phone log?'

'There. On the counter. I was looking at it again yesterday. Brings things back to you. And mystifies you.'

'What's mystifying?'

Lyall came to the counter, flipped through the book. 'July 3,' she said. 'Message reads, Bradley for Stuart, "Martin says you can use the box. He'll tell them and leave the key with Alice." Mystifying.'

'Know the names? Martin and Alice?'

'No. Stuart's phone index thing's here somewhere. The pop-up thing.'

She found it and came back, put it on the table, ran the pointer up to A, pressed the catch.

'Alice, Alice. Here, Alice. No surname.'

I pulled the index across, took out the phone and tapped the numbers. Ringing. Deep breath, offered the phone to Lyall.

'Ask her about Martin and the box.'

She put the phone to her ear. 'Hello. I'm trying to get hold of Alice. Ah, hello Alice. I'm a friend of Stuart Wardle's, Alice. Yes. Actually, he's been missing for quite a long time. Yes. We don't know. Alice, do you know someone called Martin? Yes, that's probably him. He left a message here in July '95 saying Stuart could use the box and collect the key from you. Can you remember that? Ah. Right. I see.' Long listening pause. 'Well, that clears that up. Yes. Thank you very much, Alice. Bye.'

Lyall gave me back the phone.

'So?' I said. 'Don't make me wait.'

'Safe-deposit box at a place in Collins Street.'

I breathed out loudly.

'Martin is Martin Seeberg, one of Stuart's American friends. Used to live in Melbourne. I think I vaguely recall him now, might have come here once or twice. She says Martin still gets bills for the box. She sends them on to him in the States. He hasn't been back for years, she says.'

'The key. Where would the key be?'

'Probably took it with him.'

Was this the time to say it? Yes.

'I don't think Stuart went to New Zealand,' I said. 'I think Stuart was murdered. Possibly on the road between here and the Gippsland lakes. Possibly somewhere else.'

She didn't blink. 'It had to be something like that, didn't it?' she said. 'At the back of my mind, I always knew it would be something like that.'

'Put on something warm,' I said. 'I think we're going to find out why Stuart died. I'm going to bluff them into opening Martin Seeberg's safe-deposit box. I'm going out the back gate. Pick me up opposite the movie house in Faraday Street.'

I went out the back gate, down the lane, studied the street. Nothing.

333

'Allison,' said the manager, 'please come down with us. I'll need a witness when I open the client's box for Mr Irish.'

We went downstairs, manager, secretary, me, Lyall at the rear, down to the repository of secrets, to the rows of safe-deposit boxes.

Martin Seeberg's box was one of the bigger ones.

At the last moment, the manager got cold feet. 'We should wait for Mr Seeberg's permission in writing,' he said. 'I'm not happy about this.'

I said, 'I'll say it again. The last person to use this box, my client Stuart Wardle, has been missing for three years and is thought to have been murdered. I'll get a court order but it'll take a day. You have a witness. I don't seek to take anything away or to open anything. All I want to know is what the box contains.'

He nodded, unhappy. 'Yes, all right.'

The lock opened with a snap.

Grey steel slide-out box with a hinged lid. He slid it out, carried it over to a carrel.

We crowded around him.

With a flourish, he opened the lid.

Empty.

We set off back to Parkville in silence.

'Stuart was murdered because of an interview,' Lyall said. 'Is that what you think?'

I nodded. 'Bits of a transcript are on his computer hard disk.'

Lyall said nothing, looking out of the window. We were at the Victoria Street intersection, when she said, 'He asked me about video copying. How you did it.'

I came close to sideswiping an old Datsun. 'When?'

'When he bought the video equipment. The day he was learning to use it.'

'What did you tell him?'

'I told him to go to Imagebank. They do all sorts of photographic work, video, make certified copies, do vision enhancing, manipulation, that sort of thing. They seal and store stuff for you. Very efficient.'

'Where are they?'

'In South Melbourne. Fawkner Street.'

No-one has done the trip between Victoria Street and South Melbourne faster. We left in our trail many frightened people, people on foot, people in all forms of motorised transport.

I parked in a loading zone. How did contravening a municipal ordinance rate against the laws I'd seen broken in the past twenty-four hours?

'July 1995?' the bearded man said. 'That's not a problem. What's the name?'

I told him. He went to a computer terminal.

Lyall and I looked at each other. She was wearing a soft leather jacket, brown, hair loose. I put my hip against hers, pushed. She put her hand down and ran her nails up my thigh.

'Large men in suits make me randy,' she said. 'It's a power thing.'

'This is not the time or place,' I said.

The man looked up. 'Yes, Stuart Wardle, paid with a MasterCard. We copied two videotapes.'

Another moment to hold the breath.

'Store them?' I said.

He tapped the keys.

I closed my eyes.

'No.'

We went back to Lyall's house by reversing the way we'd left it. I followed the same route from Faraday Street, walking across the university campus in the darkening late afternoon. A wet wind was pulling at people's hair and clothes and they had their chins down, holding books and files and bags to their chests.

This time I didn't have to climb Lyall's back wall. She was waiting to let me in the gate. Inside, I sat at the kitchen table and stared at the wall, mild panic rising. After a while, I said, 'I should have said this earlier. People are trying to kill me.'

Lyall was at the fridge, getting out coffee. She didn't look around. 'An everyday predicament for your suburban solicitor, would you say?'

'I would not, no. I'd better go. I shouldn't have come back. Without Stuart's tape, I'm feeling a bit vulnerable. Plus I don't want to bring anything down on you.'

She came over and ran fingers through my hair. 'What about the police?'

I shook my head. 'Some of these people *are* the police.'

Lyall sat down opposite me. 'You think Stuart came back here from his interview, transcribed it from the videotape, had the videos copied?'

'Yes. Not necessarily in that order.'

'And was murdered where?'

'Well, I didn't want to say it, but here most likely. Then the place was searched. That's why his workroom got the second big clean-out in months.'

'So they probably found the tapes.'

'Probably. The safe deposit was the real hope.'

'But if he had copies made, he wouldn't keep the originals and the copies together. Not if he was worried about them. One set might be here somewhere.'

We sat in silence for a long time, Lyall with her elbows on the table, chin in her palms. The day was fading into night, no lights on in the house, gloom gathering in the kitchen.

She got up, put on lights, went to the window. 'I'm trying to think about the days after Stuart's sister rang and said she was worried, what sort of things Bradley and I noticed. All I can think of is Bradley saying "Stuart's been driving around without his spare. That's a really stupid thing to do."'

'His spare?'

'Spare wheel.'

In the garage, on my first inspection of Stuart's car, I'd seen the wheels leaning against the back wall.

Five wheels.

'So Bradley didn't take the spare out when he put the car on blocks?'

'A man came and did it. But that's what Bradley said. Stuart had been driving around without his spare. He must have seen it out.'

I could feel a tightness in my stomach.

'Might have a look,' I said.

Lyall found the car keys.

I went out to the garage. It was fully dark now, wind and rain muting the traffic noise from Royal Parade. No light. I found my way to Stuart's car by feel, running my hand along the rough unplastered brick wall, finding the BMW's right tail-lights, the boot lock.

The ignition key unlocked the boot. I remembered that the lid didn't come up automatically, you had to get your fingertips under the numberplate and lift.

As before, it resisted, then came up suddenly.

The strong smell of leaked brake fluid.

I ran my hands over the bottom of the boot, a heavy-duty plastic lining.

A depression in the middle.

The spare wheel housing.

Something in the depression.

I pressed. It didn't yield.

I felt the edges of the boot lining. Locking clips on each side. Six locking clips. I twisted them to vertical, grasped the lining with a hand on each side.

It came up.

I put my right hand under it, into the large sump in the middle, found the object.

Found a handle. Pulled it out.

Too dark to see anything. I left the boot as it was, bumped my way outside.

The kitchen lights sent a broad white carpet across the courtyard.

I was carrying a small aluminium suitcase, a worn suitcase with battered corners.

I couldn't wait. Standing in the rain and wind, I pushed the catches sideways, opened the case.

Lyall in the kitchen doorway. 'What?' she said.

One thing in the case. A grey A4 document box, the kind with a spring clip inside.

I couldn't hold the suitcase and open the box. Lyall came across in three strides, took the box out of the case, opened it.

I expelled breath, said, 'Jesus, finally the Irish have some luck.'

Fiery wink at the edge of my vision, a blow to my chest, shoulder, not painful, a push, a powerful push, felt myself going backwards, turning, came right around, saw a man at the corner of the house, a man in black, arms outstretched, dull grey pipe in his hands pointing at me. Bark, bark of an old dog, a grey-muzzled dog, token bark, wink of flame with it, another bark and wink.

I was falling, staggering. No, I didn't want to fall, I wouldn't fall, steadied myself, didn't fall, came back upright, suitcase in my left hand, put out my right hand. Get Lyall out of the line of fire, push her, push her away. My hand reached her, shoved, I saw her stumble backwards, away from me.

Looking at the man in black.

In the light from the kitchen now.

I knew him. The tired man from the Federal government who called on me at Taub's with the woman with the gleaming tight-set teeth. Fair hair combed sideways, little widow's peak, grey at the temples. A Uniting Church minister on the side.

Jack, piece of no-bullshit advice. You don't want to be involved in anything to do with Dean Canetti. At the very least, it'll be a serious embarrassment. Could be much, much worse than that.

He was right. It was much, much worse than that.

The bastard. One of the murderous bastards…*kill your friend, kill your wife, kill your child, kill you, it's all the same*…A cold rage was in me now, no fear. He wasn't going to kill anyone here, not here, the bastard, not here, I can't afford to lose another person, not a single person, lost too many people, not one more, not a single…

He was pointing the pipe at me, smiling, not a Uniting Church smile, not an understanding and empathetic smile, more the smile of someone who has caught you out in a logical error, takes pleasure in your discomfort.

Bastard. Not taking anyone from me, not taking me from anyone, not here, not tonight…

My left arm came around, no thought to it, threw the aluminium case at him, saw it in the air, lid open, saw him take his left hand off the pipe, put it up to block the case. I went for him, lunged across the space between us, got to him just after the case, got both hands on the pistol, felt the heat of the silencer. Loud bark in my face, burning air against my cheek. I tried to break the weapon from his hand, failed, took a hand off it, tried to hit him, swiped at his face, missed, tried again, felt the contact, saw the gun butt coming…

A burst of light in my eyes, pain in my head, falling sideways, trying to hold onto him, his face back in focus, smooth clerical face, grey eyes…

One grey eye gone, hole where an eye was, dark hole, warm liquid on my lips, the man falling away from me.

I got up, surprised at my ability to get up. Standing.

Last man standing. Again.

No.

Another man standing. In the shadow of the house, not far away, weapon in hand, weapon that had taken away the man's grey eye, weapon still pointing at him.

Lyall was on the ground, getting up. I walked over, not a sure walk, put out a hand to her, pulled her up, very little strength available. She rose, came to me, put her head on my chest, a person unharmed, and I was grateful beyond measure.

The man came out of the shadows.

A man in black. Short hair, lips parted.

Lipstick on the lips. Dark red. Gleaming teeth.

Not another man standing.

A woman standing. The clergyman's partner at Taub's, the woman with the TV commercial teeth and the black Smartie eyes, the tiny male cleft in her pale chin, the finger-nail pressed into dough.

She walked over to us, putting the weapon into her armpit, looked me over, calm eyes, cold eyes, looked at Lyall, patted her on the shoulder like a coach, looked at me.

'All right?' she said.

I couldn't speak, didn't want to speak.

'You'll live,' she said. 'You're on your feet, you'll live.' To Lyall she said, 'Take him to St Vincent's casualty. Thing's probably out the other side, touched nothing. Luck. Like the movies.'

She took a wallet out of a hip pocket, held it to the light, found a card, gave it to Lyall. 'Give them this. Anyone. Tell them to phone the number. Then book into the Hyatt, stay as long as you like, bill's not your problem. We'll clean up here. You stay away for a while.'

At me. 'It's not over, Jack.'

I looked at the man lying near the corner of the house, the man who tried to kill me, the big black pool spreading around his head, looked down at my shoulder, pulled myself together. 'It's over for this suit,' I said. 'Can't find ányone to invisibly mend bullet holes anymore.'

She said, no change of tone, around the mouth a small inclination to smile, 'We can't mend. All we can do is pay.'

I looked into her eyes and I saw nothing. She stooped and picked up the document box, still open, the tapes pinned by the spring clip.

'Take this with you,' she said. 'Less for the cleaners to do.'

Looking at each other. Pain in the side building up now, quickly.

'Tasmania,' I said. 'Know about that?'

Black eyes. Giving away nothing.

'Come this far, Jack,' she said, 'do what you have to do.'

The woman doctor who cleaned the wound looked like Ava Gardner in *Bhowani Junction*. She wasn't impressed with the injury.

'Call this a gunshot wound?' she said. 'I've seen worse from knitting accidents.' She pointed at my old scar. 'Now that's a gunshot wound. Are you a dangerous person?'

'This is called blaming the victim,' I said. 'The people who shoot *me* are dangerous.'

'I'll give you some painkillers. Come back and have the dressing changed tomorrow. Always the chance of foreign matter in there, dirty cloth fragments.'

'Steady on,' I said. 'These are Henry Buck's fragments. I paid top dollar for them. And the shirt's one hundred per cent Australian cotton, nothing foreign about it.'

We didn't go to the Hyatt. We went to the penthouse apartment, not talking, coming down. In the study, I slotted one of Stuart's videos into the player, pressed the button.

On the big screen, a man appeared, out of focus at first, then sharp, a man with cropped hair, just stubble, a handsome, ravaged face. He was sitting in an armchair, long-fingered hands lying on the arms.

Lips hardly moving, he said in a soft, cultured voice:

Of course, Stuart, this isn't some little smack operation, bunch of clever chaps, few kilos in statues of the blessed virgin, in the coconut milk tins, in some mule's bowels. This is an international business run by Americans. Ex-CIA, ex-army, well connected. That's why they called themselves The Connection, I presume. And we ended up, because of our greed, unforgivable greed, we ended up as the Australian arm of it.

A voice off-screen, faint American accent:

Just for the sake of the record, Brent, when you say we, you mean…

Lyall said, 'That's Stuart.'

The ravaged man said:

I mean me and Steven Levesque and McColl and Carson, of course. Led by Steven but willingly led, not an innocent among us.

I looked at Lyall. She raised her eyebrows. 'I don't understand,' she said.

'This is the grail,' I said. 'Stuart's news story from heaven. It killed him. Now the trick is for us to stay alive.'

'The media,' Lyall said. 'Go to the media.'

I could hear Dave at our first meeting, sitting in the car in the little square, watching the leaves blowing in the cold, wet wind.

The point here, Jack, the point's simple for an intelligent bloke like you. Change Hansard, shut up journos, that's kinder stuff for these people.

He was these people. He knew.

'No,' I said. 'We'll have to be the media ourselves.'

I rang Eric the Geek, told him what I wanted to do. He arrived twenty minutes later with a laptop and a suitcase of electronic gear.

'Streaming video,' he said, a gleam in his eye. 'Always wanted to do this.'

It took the rest of the night and the first hours of the day. At 8.30 a.m., Eric, exhausted but happy, went home. Lyall was asleep in the big white bedroom, head beneath a pillow. At 9 a.m., I rang the newspaper.

'Editor, please,' I said. The secretary came on. 'Jack Irish to speak to Malcolm Glasser. He knows who I am. Tell him it's his son's lawyer.'

345

He came on. 'Jack,' he said. 'I wish you wouldn't identify yourself that way.'

I said, 'Malcolm, I'm going to give you a website. Ring me back inside half an hour. If not, I give it to everyone. You've got a tiny edge on the rest of the world here. Tiny.' I gave him my number.

Glasser was back in ten minutes.

'Utterly unbelievable,' he said. 'Jesus, story of the decade. Bigger than that, much bigger. How the hell do you fit in here?'

'I don't. You running it?'

'Fuck, yes, fuck the risk.'

'There's no risk, Malcolm.'

At 11 a.m., I began to ring television stations, radio stations, other newspapers, giving them the website.

My fleshwound was aching, but I didn't mind. I ache, therefore I am. Alive.

Could be much, much worse than that.

By the end of the day, the whole world was reading the story of Steven Levesque and TransQuik, watching the haggard and dying Brent Rupert telling his electrifying stories about a transport empire founded on drug money, money provided by Klostermann Gardier of Luxembourg. Klostermann Gardier, banker to The Connection, an invisible organisation run by people with high-level American military and intelligence connections.

The audiences learned about massive drug importations, about bribery and murder, about Steven Levesque's ability to stop prosecutions, derail police investigations, and control politicians and bureaucrats at the highest levels.

They learned about how TransQuik, through the cousins' travel agencies, even laundered the cash that flowed into the

346

hands of the people to whom they sold drugs in bulk.

A full-service company.

And Brent Rupert, often visibly weary, sipping something colourless from a small glass, had total recall. He named the names, put dates and places to everything. Names high and names low. Including Gary's name, as the go-between, the carrier of messages, the arranger, TransQuik's Mercury.

It was dark outside, raining, the city a smear of lights, when Lyall woke up, came to the door of the study and stood with her hands in her hair, pushing it back.

'I didn't know where I was,' she said.

On the television screen, the 6 p.m. news was ending with shaky footage of Steven Levesque shot from outside a moving car. He was seated between two large men, averting his head.

She came over and stood behind me, put her hands on my shoulders. 'What's the time?' she asked.

'Bollinger time,' I said.

On a cold, clear Wednesday, high and pale winter sky, whiplash wind, we went to Moonee Valley racecourse.

Wootton was leaning on the mounting yard rail, looking like an advertisement for what upper-middle-class men should wear to the mid-week races. Not far away from him, I recognised Cynthia, his head commissioner. She'd had her hair cut short since I'd last seen her and she was looking inconspicuous in an off-white trenchcoat and a drab scarf.

Lyall and I watched the horses being walked. Vision Splendid came along, accompanied by Karen Devine's jagged-haired strapper. The big grey look good, unfussed by the crowd, tight as a proper bullboar sausage, but with bandages on all legs.

'The grey,' I said. 'Vision Splendid. That's the one we're here to see.'

'What's wrong with its legs?'

'Nothing. That's why they're bandaged.'

She gave me a look. 'Can I ask you again? What exactly *do* you do for a living?'

I looked back, looked her over, took my time. She was worthy of study: colour in her face from the cold, hair tied back loosely, big tweed jacket, man's white cotton shirt, corduroy pants. 'Suburban solicitor, with all the breadth of cultural and other interests that the term conveys,' I said.

'And we are talking broad.' She took the *Age* out of my hand. It was open at the form.

Cam came down the rail, dark-grey suit and black polo-neck, elegant and insolent-eyed as ever. He joined Wootton for long enough to say a few words, light a cigarette with a match from a paper matchbook, blow smoke over the man's head and tuck the matchbook behind the triangle of red handkerchief in his top pocket. Marching orders delivered. Harry never handed them over until the last minute.

Wootton closed his race book and glanced around, a worried expression, the look of someone trying to decide whether to go to the toilet now or chance it. He fished the matchbook out of his pocket and stared at it. Cynthia appeared at his side. I couldn't see him pass it over, but she didn't linger any longer than Cam had.

'It says here,' said Lyall, 'that Vision Splendid is an unremarkable veteran who failed miserably at a comeback attempt in Ballarat.'

'Who says that?' I took the paper and looked. 'Bart Grantley. Shrewd judge of equine performance. Got any money?'

'I am carrying a sum of money, yes.'

I told her what to do.

She said, without expression, 'Do I understand you to be disputing Mr Grantley's expert opinion?'

'No. He's right. Spring in there and do it.'

By the time we got out on the stand, the caller was saying, '…load of money for the ultra-veteran Vision Splendid, number six, Tommy Wicks up, trainer, K. Devine. Not exactly an unknown quantity this horse, form goes back to when some of the jockey's riding in this race were getting their second lot of teeth.'

'He's being sarcastic about my fifty bucks,' Lyall said.

'They're like that. Lots of cruel people in racing.'

We found a good spot. Looking down, I could see the McCurdie family. They'd formed a defensive circle, warily eyeing the city folk around them, alert for pickpockets, handbag-snatchers and perverts.

The caller went on: 'Sizeable plunge, the bookmakers have hauled it in from 40-1 to tens very smartly. No, it's down to eights, there's money for it interstate, some money, fair bit for this time of the year. World's full of optimists. Either that or they're clever people, visionaries. Well, ladies and gentlemen, Tommy Wicks carries the hopes of the Viagra generation here today. They shall fall to rise again. At the barrier for the fourth, sixteen hundred metres, field of eleven, well-mannered lot, I think they're letting the elderly horse go in first. Seriously, they're going in nicely, five or six to come…'

I could feel Lyall looking at me. I was taking the menacing post-Gulf War camera out of its case.

'Suburban solicitor,' she said in a musing and mildly questioning tone. 'I wonder what big city solicitors are like? I'd like to know one. They'd be involved in serious stuff, wouldn't they? Wars and famines, bribing presidents and kings, laying waste to whole fucking continents, that sort of thing?'

I put the technology to my eye, wandered around, found the gate, obeyed the digital instruction. Then I could dwell on Tommy Wicks's nose and look at one of Vision's liquid and stoic eyes. 'No,' I said. 'They only do the boring stuff.'

On my thigh, long fingers fell, casually as a leaf dropping, no purpose, no intent, simply an open hand come to rest.

'Away in a clean line,' said the caller. 'Melanie's Child the best, leads The Gallery, January One on the inside, Vision

Splendid's handy on the outside, dropping back quickly, replaced by Honey Dew, then comes Fatbat, Kilberry Lad, Shebeen, out wide is Drumlanrig improving quickly and bringing up the rear Count Waldersee and Pericard.'

With twelve hundred to go, the field had divided into two. Vision Splendid was the backmarker in the bunched front group of five, a length clear of the sixth horse.

'Not a lot of pace on here,' said the caller. 'Might be out of respect for the senior citizen now lying fifth behind Drumlanrig, Shebeen, January One and in front The Gallery looking strong. At the thousand metres, Drumlanrig hanging out. Shebeen's gone up to January One and Vision Splendid's almost level pegging with Drumlanrig. In the back group…'

'What's happening?' Lyall asked.

'Looking good,' I said. I had clear sight of Tommy Wicks as they came down the straight towards North Hill. He was riding a patient race, tucked in behind the three leaders, waiting for his chance to take the gap between Drumlanrig and Shebeen.

At the five hundred, beginning the turn into the run for home, I could see Tommy beginning to ease Vision forward. 'Now,' I said. 'Go for it, Thomas.'

The caller said, 'At the five hundred, the pace is on now, the veteran Vision Splendid's staying with them, he's going forward, oh dear, January One's shifted out, he's bumped Shebeen, nasty knock, Drumlanrig's checked, lurched sideways, that's knocked Vision almost onto the rail, stewards won't like this one bit…'

In the confusion, I lost sight of Tommy for a second, found him, saw the snarl on his face, could almost hear the foul words he was shouting at Drumlanrig's teenage jockey.

Swearing wasn't going to help.

I looked down. McCurdie was pulling his hat down, trying to get it over his eyes, shut out the awful day.

'Three-fifty to go,' said the caller, 'The Gallery's in the clear, going for the doctor, confusion sorted out behind but too late for the plunge horse and the rest…'

I found Tommy Wicks again.

Tommy didn't believe it was too late.

He put Vision Splendid into a space the width of its head between January One and the rail, appeared to make contact with the jockey. January shifted out again, this time bumped The Gallery.

In the straight, two hundred to go, Vision and The Gallery.

'Here's a turn,' the caller shouted, 'plunge horse's through on the rails, unbelievable finish this, Wicks has shouldered his way through, gone up to The Gallery, the veteran's moving like a three-year-old, they're well clear of the rest, stride for stride, fifty to go, The Gallery's holding on…'

I could feel Lyall's fingertips digging into me, getting close to my thighbone.

The horses were both at full stretch, low to the ground, necks extended, jockeys riding hands and heels, willing the creatures to make one final desperate effort.

'Going to the line together, can't separate them,' shouted the caller. 'The Gallery may have held on by a hair in a nostril. What a race. They're calling for the picture to separate them, my feelings is The Gallery…'

I put the glasses down, felt my shoulders slump, Lyall's grip on my thigh loosen. Down below, the McCurdies were in shock, looking around in a dazed way, like people surprised to have survived an accident.

We waited.

'Is it digital?' Lyall asked.

I looked at her. 'What?'

'The camera. Is it digital?'

I didn't say anything.

Waited.

'Number six gets it,' said the caller. 'Vision Splendid by the narrowest of margins over The Gallery, third is Shebeen.'

Jock McCurdie, his wife, daughter and the two nephews were in a laughing, hugging, crying circle, like a depleted all-age, all-gender football team winning its first grand final for forty years.

'Well, the bookies have been monstered here, ladies and gentlemen,' said the caller. 'Here and elsewhere. Turns out the visionaries were right. They'll be pulling the ancients out of the retirement paddocks as we speak. K. Devine the trainer, trains at Lancefield, must be something in the air out there…oh, oh, there's been a protest. Second against first. I think it relates to Tommy Wicks forcing himself through on the rail. So. The excitement isn't over yet.'

'What's this mean?' Lyall asked.

I ran my fingers through my hair. 'Second-placed horse's jockey says he'd have won if our bloke hadn't nudged him coming into the straight. If the stewards agree with him, we come second.'

'How do they decide?'

'Look at the video, interrogate the jockeys, consult the taro cards, disembowel chickens.'

We waited.

The McCurdies had gone back into shock. Jock had

his arm around Mrs McCurdie's ample shoulders, talking into an ear. I knew what he was saying: There'll be other times, love.

We waited.

Down below, I saw Cam leaning against the fence, a study in indifference, smoking a cigarette, reading the race book.

There'll be other times, love. Probably not.

The speakers crackled. The caller had been silent for a moment, now he said, 'Protest dismissed. Result stands. Vision Splendid is the winner of the fourth.'

The McCurdies went mad again. There won't have to be other times, love.

'Jesus,' said Lyall, 'I don't know if I could stand this kind of tension regularly. How much have I won?'

I said, 'Four grand and your money back.'

'Wow. I'll give you half.'

'No,' I said. 'I had a bit on myself.'

On our way out, Cam came up behind me. 'Some pictures to show you,' he said. 'Usual spot.'

I left Lyall at the Stud and found Harry's BMW, got into the back. Cam passed three large colour prints over his shoulder.

The first was of a house, a huge new timber house. It was in a lake. You could see the gouges made by the house as it slid down the hillside, coming to rest tilted sideways, half underwater.

The second picture showed a collapsed jetty and in the water in front of it, the prow of a sunken motor cruiser. Beside the cruiser, the tops of three vehicles could be seen, two four-wheel-drives and a Mercedes Benz, its bonnet star proudly visible.